Hello there!

Thank you from the bottom of my heart for choosing to read *The Paper Mill Girl*.

As with all of my other novels, there's a wonderful feisty young woman at the heart of this story. In *The Paper Mill Girl*, our heroine is Ruth Hardy, and as regular readers will know, I tend to throw a lot at my heroines for them to overcome! All of the action and drama revolves around Ruth and her family. She's another fictional young woman I am proud to have brought to life.

I've set *The Paper Mill Girl* once more around the village of Ryhope, where I was born and bred. It's a small village on the north-east coast with a beach fringed by high cliffs.

The paper mill in the book is located just outside Ryhope, a half-hour walk along the clifftop overlooking the North Sea. The location of the mill in the book is where Hendon Paper Mill once stood, although the paper mill in the book – Grange Paper Works – is fictional. It's been a lot of fun researching paper mills from over a hundred years ago, and I'm grateful to everyone who has helped.

I really hope you enjoy reading *The Paper Mill Girl*. It holds a special place in my heart.

Glenda Young

Praise for Glenda Young:

'Real sagas with female characters right at the heart'
Jane Garvey, *Woman's Hour*

'The feel of the story is totally authentic . . . Her heroine
in the grand Cookson tradition . . . Inspirationally delightful'
Peterborough Evening Telegraph

'In the world of historical saga writers, there's a brand new
voice – welcome, Glenda Young, who brings a freshness
to the genre' *My Weekly*

'Will resonate with saga readers everywhere . . .
a wonderful, uplifting story' Nancy Revell

'I really enjoyed . . . It's well researched and well written and
I found myself caring about her characters' Rosie Goodwin

'Glenda has an exceptionally keen eye for domestic detail
which brings this local community to vivid, colourful life and
Meg is a likeable, loving heroine for whom the reader roots
from start to finish' Jenny Holmes

'I found it difficult to believe that this was a debut novel, as
"brilliant" was the word in my mind when I reached the end.
I enjoyed it enormously, being totally absorbed from the first
page. I found it extremely well written, and having always loved
sagas, one of the best I've read' Margaret Kaine

'All the ingredients for a perfect saga' Emma Hornby

'Her descriptions of both character and setting are
wonderful . . . there is a warmth and humour in bucket loads'
Frost Magazine

'A gripping saga' *People's Friend*

By Glenda Young

Belle of the Back Streets
The Tuppenny Child
Pearl of Pit Lane
The Girl with the Scarlet Ribbon
The Paper Mill Girl

GLENDA YOUNG

The Paper Mill Girl

HEADLINE

First published in 2020 by
HEADLINE PUBLISHING GROUP

First published in paperback in 2021 by
HEADLINE PUBLISHING GROUP

5

Cataloguing in Publication Data is available from the British Library

ISBN 978 1 4722 6856 3

Typeset in Stempel Garamond by Avon DataSet Ltd,
Arden Court, Alcester, Warwickshire

Printed and bound in Great Britain by Clays Ltd, Elcograf S.p.A.

MIX
Paper from
responsible sources
FSC® C104740

Headline's policy is to use papers that are natural, renewable and
recyclable products and made from wood grown in well-managed
forests and other controlled sources. The logging and manufacturing
processes are expected to conform to the environmental
regulations of the country of origin.

HEADLINE PUBLISHING GROUP
An Hachette UK Company
Carmelite House
50 Victoria Embankment
London EC4Y 0DZ

www.headline.co.uk
www.hachette.co.uk

Grace Emily Foster

Acknowledgements

My thanks go to Jean Stirk, author of *The Lost Mills: A History of Papermaking in County Durham*; Sarah Stoner, Meg Hartford and Jackie Caffrey from Sunderland History Groups Online; Ryhope Heritage Society, especially Brian Ibinson and Peter Hedley; Rév. David Chadwick of St Paul's Church, Ryhope; Dr Rob Shepherd; Sunderland Antiquarian Society, especially Norman Kirtlan, Phil Curtis, Linda King, Ron Lawson, Denise Lovell and Chris Sharp; Keith and Julie Dewart of the Guide Post Inn, Ryhope; Sharon Vincent for her knowledge of women's social history in Sunderland; Steven and Pauline McBride of the Hendon Grange pub, Grangetown; Paddy Cronin, chief executive at Edward Thompson of Sunderland, and his superb assistant Caroline Porterfield; Sue Woolnough and Michael Stanyon of Frogmore Paper Mill, Apsley, Hertfordshire; Fourstones Paper Mill, Hexham; Julian Harrop and the team of volunteers at Beamish Museum; Durham County Records Office; Tyne and Wear Archives; Allison Hicks and Angela Wilkinson of Fulwell Community Centre; Steven Murphy; Jay Sykes; Bryan Irving; Izzy McDonald-Booth of National Glass Centre, Sunderland; Louise

Hardy at North East Business and Innovation Centre; Laura Brewis of Sunderland Culture; Katy Wheeler of the *Sunderland Echo*; Lisa Shaw and the team at BBC Newcastle; Simon and Laura from SUN FM; Corinne Kilvington; Claire Pickersgill at Sunderland Empire Theatre; Mary Groody and Sadie Willoughby of Ryhope for sharing memories of working at Hendon Paper Mill; Neil Sinclair, author of *Sunderland's Railways*.

Huge thanks also to my editor Kate Byrne at Headline and to my agent Caroline Sheldon, two inspirational women from whom I continue to learn a lot. And to Barry, for the love, support and endless cups of tea when I lock myself away to write.

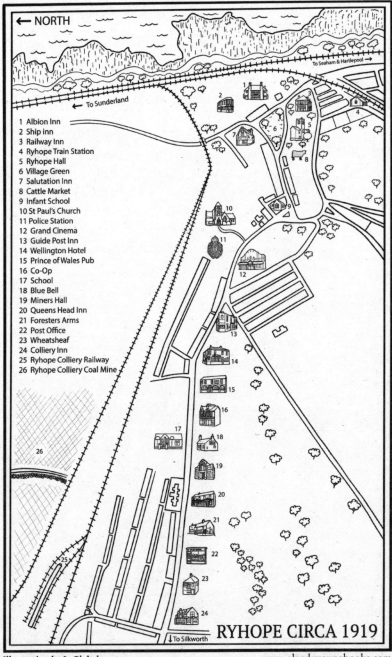

← NORTH

To Seaham & Hartlepool →

← To Sunderland

1 Albion Inn
2 Ship inn
3 Railway Inn
4 Ryhope Train Station
5 Ryhope Hall
6 Village Green
7 Salutation Inn
8 Cattle Market
9 Infant School
10 St Paul's Church
11 Police Station
12 Grand Cinema
13 Guide Post Inn
14 Wellington Hotel
15 Prince of Wales Pub
16 Co-Op
17 School
18 Blue Bell
19 Miners Hall
20 Queens Head Inn
21 Foresters Arms
22 Post Office
23 Wheatsheaf
24 Colliery Inn
25 Ryhope Colliery Railway
26 Ryhope Colliery Coal Mine

↓ To Silkworth

RYHOPE CIRCA 1919

Illustration by Jo Blakeley

www.glendayoungbooks.com

Chapter One

September 1919

Ruth Hardy walked into the yard at Grange Paper Works, and the cold air nipped her face. Women streamed past her, some linking arms and chatting, all of them heading to the black iron gates that led from the mill to the road. Some of the women would return to husbands and children, to homes with coal fires in cosy, warm rooms. Some would return to a cooked meal. None of these would be waiting for Ruth.

There was a spit of rain in the air that brought a sea-salt taste to Ruth's lips. Behind her the ocean roared. She took her hat from her pocket and pulled it over her long brown hair, then scanned the gates where Bea always waited. She spotted her sister holding on to the gate, anchored in case she was cut adrift and floated out on the tide of women. Bea worked in the machine room, where her job was to keep the floor clear. It was a safe place to work and Ruth was grateful she didn't need to worry about her little sister. Well, not at work anyway.

She made her way through the crowd, raising her hand to wave. Bea was a year younger than Ruth's seventeen years, smaller too, and she looked lost in the throng of women streaming from the yard. She had Ruth's features – there was no denying they were sisters – but there was a fragility to Bea. Ruth had a more determined, no-nonsense look about her. It was there in the set of her mouth and the glint of steel that flashed in her eyes.

Ruth reached Bea and kissed her on her cheek. It was how they always greeted each other at the end of their working day. She noticed that her sister looked as drawn and tired as she felt herself.

'You all right?' she asked.

Bea nodded. 'You?'

'I'm tired,' Ruth said. 'You look it too.'

'I've told you, I'm fine,' Bea said quietly.

Ruth grabbed Bea's hand and the girls threaded their way through the crowd. Once they reached the road, they upped their pace. They were determined to get home quickly, for it was a long walk through muddy fields along clifftops overlooking bays of coal-blackened sand. In the fields, they lifted their skirts to stop them trailing along the wet soil. They walked in silence. Suddenly Bea stopped in her tracks.

'Did you hear the news today?' she said.

Ruth didn't break her stride. 'Come on, we can't stop. Mam and Dad will be waiting.'

Bea ran to catch up.

'What news?' Ruth asked when her sister was back at her side.

'I heard the men talking. There's to be a new owner. Someone's bought the mill from the Blackwells.'

This was news Ruth didn't know, and it came as a shock. Old Mr Blackwell had passed away months ago. Ruth had heard that his wife had neither the experience nor the desire to run the mill on her own. Many said it was no job for a woman, but Ruth's friend Edie said she'd heard of women running paper mills elsewhere.

'Did the men say who the new owner will be?' she asked.

Bea shook her head. 'No names were mentioned. But I heard he's a stickler for discipline. There's talk of changes being made when he takes over. All our shifts might be changed. And they say jobs will go too.'

Bea's words hit Ruth hard and a chill ran through her. 'They really said that?'

'That's what the men were talking about today. They were huddled in groups around the room, so I took my brush and swept around them, listening. They ignore me, don't even see me. I'm as quiet as a mouse.'

Ruth felt unsettled. It was another problem to deal with, and she could do without it. 'Well, little mouse,' she said. 'If you hear any more, you must tell me.'

Bea nudged her. 'Did you see your boyfriend today?'

Ruth glanced at her sister. 'He is *not* my boyfriend,' she laughed.

'You like him, though, I can tell.'

'Rubbish,' Ruth replied.

She walked on with her head down so that Bea couldn't see the smile on her lips or the flush in her cheeks. This rush of emotion happened every time she thought of Mick Carson. He worked on the railway that brought raw materials from the docks to the mill, such as esparto, a coarse grass that grew as far away as Africa. Ruth had met him a few times. The first time, they'd smiled shyly at each other when their paths crossed in the yard. The second time she caught sight of him, she'd waved and smiled a friendly good morning, and to her delight, Mick had waved back with a cheery hello. She'd found out his name from Edie, who knew a lot of the men at the mill. Since then, the two of them had talked often if they met in the yard. Oh, it was nothing serious, always light-hearted and fun, but she enjoyed chatting to him and passing the time of day. And Mick seemed to enjoy her company too. She had told Bea about him and Bea had teased her ever since.

Ruth and Bea continued to walk, leaving the paper mill behind, its chimneys belching smoke. The mill was a long, low building on a clifftop overlooking the sea. Work never stopped, not even at Christmas. When one shift ended, another began. The machines worked constantly, clattering and banging, turning raw materials into paper. At one end of the mill, the railway delivered raw materials of rags, grass and wood pulp. And from the other end, paper of all sizes and qualities was loaded up to be taken away.

Over four hundred men, boys, women and girls worked long hours in shifts. They were allowed one day off each week. Ruth and Bea earned a fair wage, although it was far from a fortune. From what they learned from the girls they knew working in domestic service, their jobs were a damn sight better than being at the beck and call of a housekeeper. There was structure at the mill. Everyone knew what was expected. The hours were long, but Ruth and Bea enjoyed working there for the most part. However, what Ruth had just heard from Bea about a new owner coming in and jobs being lost was bad news. She really could do without having work problems on her mind along with everything else. She needed to talk to her friends Edie and Jane the next day to find out if they'd heard anything. Jane's boyfriend Davey Winter, a brute of a man who never cracked a smile, worked in the machine room. She wondered if he might know something.

Bea started lagging behind as they walked along Ryhope Road.

'Come on, Bea, hurry up,' Ruth urged. She spun around and waited for her sister to catch up. She couldn't help noticing again how pale Bea was. 'Are you sure you're feeling all right? You're looking peaky.'

Bea's hand flew to her face. 'I'm fine,' she said quickly.

'You need to stay in tonight. Look after yourself.'

She raised her chin. 'Can't. I'm going out.'

'With Jimmy again?'

Bea nodded and Ruth's heart sank. She didn't like or trust Jimmy Tate. She knew him from school. He was lazy back then, copying other people's work, even passing it off as his own. And he was still lazy now. Some people never changed. Jimmy was a shirker, a lazy good-for-nothing who drank too much. Try as she might – and she'd tried very hard for her sister's sake after she found out Bea and Jimmy were courting – she couldn't find one redeeming feature.

'You don't want to be going out gallivanting, or whatever it is you do with that boy,' she said.

'Jimmy's not a boy; you make him sound soppy. He's a grown man. He's got a job now.'

Ruth couldn't fail to notice Bea's defensive tone. 'Yeah? And how long's that going to last?' She tried to keep her voice calm, but she felt an anger building the way it always did when Jimmy was mentioned. She knew that Bea could do much better than the wayward lad. 'He doesn't stay five minutes anywhere he works. He turns up late and falls asleep when he gets there.'

'That wasn't his fault; he told me what happened,' Bea said.

'Oh Bea. Open your eyes and see him for what he really is.'

Ruth let the subject drop. Whenever Jimmy's name was mentioned, a darkness settled between the sisters that often took hours to lift. She didn't want to upset Bea or fall out with her. It would take more than a lowlife like Jimmy to come between them. But she wished to high heaven that he had never come into her sister's life. He was a bad 'un and no mistake. Everyone in Ryhope knew it. Everyone, that was, except Bea.

As the girls walked on, ahead of them a welcome sight came into view. It was the spire of St Paul's Church, a signal they were almost home. The night was drawing in as they turned on to Cliff Road. They walked past the Uplands, a grand house in its own grounds. Ruth usually enjoyed peering in through the windows to see the splendour of its furnishings. But this time, she didn't stop.

Suddenly she slapped her hand against her forehead. 'Damn it!' she cried. 'I've forgotten the eggs. I promised Mam I'd pick them up from High Farm.'

'I'll go,' Bea offered.

'No,' Ruth said firmly. 'You get yourself home. Make sure Mam and Dad are all right. Get the lamp burning for them, stoke the fire up if it's needed and put the kettle on.

I'll walk to the farm. Tell Mam I'll cook tea as soon as I get in.'

Bea scurried on while Ruth retraced her steps. High Farm was on the edge of the village green and sold milk and eggs from the farmhouse. Ruth's business was conducted briskly with the farmer, Ralphie Heddon, a big fella with a thatch of straw-coloured hair and rough hands as big as shovels. He was well built and muscled with a ruddy face from years spent working outdoors.

'Six white, six brown,' he said as he placed the eggs into a box. 'Just as your mam likes them. How's she doing these days?'

'She's just the same,' Ruth said. It was her standard reply. It was easier and quicker than giving everyone who asked the painful details of the illness that was slowly taking her mam's life.

'You still looking after her yourself, then?' Ralphie asked.

'Me and my sister do all we can,' Ruth replied. 'My dad's not great himself these days. We've got him with his gammy leg and Mam with her bad chest.'

'You take too much on yourself, lass. You should get someone in from the village to help look after your mam when you and your sister are at work.'

'And how are we supposed to afford that?' Ruth bristled. It wasn't a question she expected an answer to.

Ralphie smiled kindly. 'You've got a heart of gold, lass,' he said.

It was a phrase Ruth had heard many times. She loved her family deeply; it was only right that she did what she could. She delved into her purse. 'Here,' she said, handing money over.

Ralphie pocketed the coins, then placed two extra eggs into the box. He winked at Ruth. 'I always used to have a soft spot for your mam when she was a girl, you know. Take these with my compliments. Tell her I'm asking after her.'

'I'll tell Dad about your soft spot, shall I?' Ruth laughed.

'Well, he's hardly going to come down here and give me a kicking, is he, not with his bad leg. Mind you, back in the day, he would've sorted me out. Oh! The temper he had on him in those days!'

Ruth kept quiet about her dad's moods, which affected him still. 'See you, Ralphie,' she said, and walked away with the box in her arms.

Ruth's exhaustion continued making itself felt in her neck and shoulders. How she ached after her day at the mill. Her work there was relentless, slicing cuffs and collars from clothes brought into the rag room. Long, low benches ran the length of the room, fitted with sharp knives that the twelve girls had to sit astride. With their nimble fingers they took the rags from wicker baskets, then ripped open the thick seams, tore off buttons and cut the rags into pieces. Hours and hours they spent ripping and tearing, slicing and cutting.

The only pleasure to Ruth's day was working with her best friends Edie and Jane. The three had been friends since their first day at the mill. They'd worked their way up to the rag room from sweeping the machine room, a job that Bea held now. Dark-haired Edie, with her ready smile and forthright comments, sat on Ruth's right. On her left sat Jane, the eldest of the three. Jane was engaged to Davey, who Ruth wasn't keen on. He seemed a little too forward for her liking. She'd felt uncomfortable under his lecherous gaze when Jane had introduced him to her. He was a big man, well built, with thick arms. He wore a heavy moustache that made him look older than his years. Ruth didn't think she had ever seen him smile.

Sitting on the bench cutting rags played havoc with Ruth's back, and it ached. But at least she didn't have far to walk now. Heading past the village school, she took one last lingering look at the Uplands on Cliff Road, and that was when she spotted Jimmy Tate beside a stone wall. It was definitely him. She recognised his dark curly hair, his shapeless black jacket, along with his scuffed boots and his grubby trousers with a hole in one knee. The scarf at his neck was one Bea had spent many nights knitting. But the girl who was with him tonight, the one he had his arms around, was one Ruth didn't know. She gasped. The nerve of the lad! She was furious.

'Oi!' she yelled.

She wanted Jimmy to know she'd seen him and that she knew what he was up to behind her sister's back. She waited for him to look up to see who was shouting, but he was wrapped around the girl, lost in his own world. Ruth marched towards them. She had always thought Jimmy lazy and a coward. She'd never had him down as a two-timing love rat as well. But she wasn't in the least surprised. She wondered if there was anything Jimmy could do that *would* surprise her. Well, perhaps he could turn up at their door in a suit and tie, with a pocketful of wages and a bouquet, professing undying love for Bea and respect for their mam and dad. That would certainly be a surprise. But here he was, canoodling with a girl on

Cliff Road. Bea must have just missed him. Ruth was glad. The sight would have broken her sister's heart.

'Oi! You two!' she called again.

This time Jimmy looked up. Ruth saw the startled look on his face. He'd been caught. He stepped smartly away from the girl, and she spun around.

'Hey, who do you think you are?' she yelled.

Ruth glanced at her. She was a bonny girl, with dark hair and green eyes. 'I need a word with Jimmy,' she said sternly. 'Alone.'

'Jimmy?' the girl implored.

'Go,' he said.

The girl looked from Jimmy to Ruth and back again. 'But . . . Jimmy?'

He shook his head. 'Go,' he repeated. 'I'll come and find you later.'

Once the girl was out of earshot, Ruth glared long and hard at Jimmy. She saw him fidget. He ran a hand through his thick hair, rubbed his chin.

'What do you want?' he said at last. He kept his eyes fixed firmly on the ground.

'You're disgusting, you know that?' Ruth spat. 'My sister thinks the world of you. You're supposed to be courting her and you go and do something like this?'

Jimmy opened his mouth to reply, but Ruth wasn't finished with him.

'How many girls have you got on the go in Ryhope?'

'It's not like that,' he said sullenly. 'I was just cheering her up. She'd had some bad news.'

'Cheering her up?' Ruth hissed. 'Is that why you had your tongue down her throat and your hands on her backside?' She held tight to the box of eggs with one hand, and with the other poked Jimmy in the chest. 'Now listen, you. I don't like you one little bit. I never have. I don't trust you an inch. I know you, remember? We were in the same class at school and you were a thief and a liar back then. You're no better now.'

Jimmy shuffled awkwardly.

'But for some strange reason that I'll never understand, my sister likes you.'

He pulled himself up to his full height and squared his shoulders. 'Are you going to tell her?' he asked.

Ruth sighed heavily. She wanted nothing more than to tell Bea what a lowlife, cheating scumbag her boyfriend was. But she knew it would break her heart. She knew how much Jimmy meant to Bea. Her sister talked of little else. Ruth had seen the light dance in Bea's eyes after she'd come home from spending time with him. He was the only thing, the only person, who could put a smile on her face. Heaven knew there was little enough for Ruth and Bea to smile about at home, looking after their poorly mam and coping with their dad's mood swings. Ruth didn't want to steal any of Bea's joy from her with the truth about Jimmy. But neither would she let her sister be taken for a fool. If she told Bea what she'd seen, she'd have to choose her words carefully and pick the right time.

'Get out of my sight,' she hissed.

Without another word, Jimmy turned and walked sharply away.

Ruth hurried on, her heart heavy after the encounter. She wanted to protect Bea – she had to. There was no one else looking after her sister; they only had each other. Their mam was too poorly to speak some days. Their dad, since he'd been confined to the room in the pub where the family now lived, had become irascible. His moods changed quickly, his anger directed towards his daughters, though Ruth was the one who bore the brunt of his bitter words. She was his firstborn, he told her; she should do her duty and look after her parents.

She tried her best. She cared for her mam, propped her up on pillows, washed her and brushed her hair. She sat at her bedside and talked for hours, a one-way conversation that left her drained. As for her dad, she provided support for him to lean on when he needed to walk from his chair to his bed. She brought him the evening paper, and he devoured every word on each page, for he hated to miss any news. She cooked all the family's meals, making hasty pudding for breakfast, warm oats and milk baked on their coal fire, before she and Bea set off for the mill each morning. And when she returned exhausted from a hard day's work, when all she wanted was to sit down and put her feet up, close her eyes and rest, she had to prepare a hot meal for the four of them, for her mam was incapable and her dad didn't know how. He'd never had to cook or clean in his life. Jean had done everything before she fell ill. Now Harry expected his daughters to take on her domestic role.

Bea helped, of course, but the bulk of the responsibility fell on Ruth's shoulders. She took it all in her stride. This was her life, looking after and caring for her family. She kept their room clean and made sure the rent was paid each week to their landlady, Mrs Pike. The rent came from the money Ruth and Bea earned. What was left bought their food. There was nothing for treats, nothing to save. Every penny went into looking after their parents, each other and the room where they lived at the back of the Guide Post Inn, one of Ryhope's oldest pubs.

The Guide Post Inn sat on the corner of Burdon Lane and Ryhope Street South. It faced Ryhope's Grand Electric Cinema and was a favourite with those treating themselves to a night at the pictures. It also faced the police station, and for that, Ruth was grateful, it added an extra air of safety she welcomed. Not that the pub's landlady, Mrs Pike, ever needed to call the police. Mrs Pike was a hard-working woman who ran a tight ship. She kept her pub spotless and its reputation intact. She was short and dumpy, with a large bosom. She wore black ankle boots with a fur trim, even in summer. Her greying hair was piled high on her head in a bun fastened with pins, not a strand out of place. Her face was set stern, always watching, on the lookout for anything in her pub that needed attention. She might have been in her late forties, even her fifties, it was difficult to tell and Ruth never dared ask. If she had done so, she would have been given short shrift.

Nothing and no one slipped past Mrs Pike's beady eyes. She was often to be found standing at the open door to her pub, passing the time of day with those walking by. It was her way of finding out what was going on. She especially liked to chat with the mothers who came past pushing bairns in prams. She loved making a fuss of the bairns. She kept a packet of boiled sweets in her pocket ready to hand out to any youngster who might like one.

The Guide Post was still referred to as an inn, but Mrs Pike had long ago stopped taking in lodgers. It used to cater to weary travellers who stayed overnight before continuing on their journey south to Stockton, or north to Newcastle. Now the rooms were used by the landlady as her home. All except the one at the back, which she rented to the Hardys.

There were windows in the room, but no view to speak of; just the yard with its barrels and boxes and the gate that led to the cobbled lane. Inside, it was light, with warmth coming from a coal fire. Ruth and Bea shared a bed that was old and creaky, and it groaned each time one of them turned over. At the other end of the room, underneath one of the windows, was a bigger bed for Harry and Jean. It was Jean's sickbed now. Two armchairs and a small sofa sat in front of the fire. Behind this was a wooden table and four chairs. A sideboard ran under another window and held a water jug and bowl. The netty was outside in the yard, shared with Mrs Pike and her customers.

The once vivacious Jean Hardy was now little more than a shell of a woman. She spent her days propped up in bed with a pillow at her back and a sadness etched on her face. Some days her chest wheezed heavily. But in her watery eyes there was a tiny reminder of the same steely glint Ruth had inherited.

Life hadn't always been so tough for the Hardys. The family had once had their own home, a miners' cottage in a pit lane. That was in the days when Harry had been working, before the accident that had laid him off. With no job at the mine, the family had lost their pit house and their free coal supply. Ruth knew how much this had hurt her dad's pride. Not only had he been thrown out of his home, but he couldn't find work elsewhere in Ryhope, not with his damaged leg. Now his world was confined to the four walls of the room at the back of the pub, and this darkened his mood further. Mrs Pike popped in when she could, did a bit of shopping if needed while Ruth and Bea were at work, and Ruth was grateful for her help.

There were three public rooms in the Guide Post Inn: snug, billiard room and lounge. The snug had upturned beer barrels to sit on instead of chairs and stools. It was a poky little room, a place where women weren't allowed. Next to it, the billiard room was thick with tobacco smoke. The lounge was the largest room, with seats and tables and a makeshift stage. The pub piano stood there, played by Mrs Pike herself, who could turn her hand from a sombre hymn to the frivolity of a music-hall song that would have everyone up on their feet. All the rooms had coal fires, and on a cold night with three fires roaring, it was cosy indeed.

On Saturday nights, at eight p.m. sharp, Mrs Pike employed a singer in the lounge for an hour. The songs could be heard all the way in the back room, and the Hardy family would sing along. It was a highlight of their week. There was a different singer each week. Ruth liked the male singers best; their voices carried further. On Saturday nights Bea was often out with Jimmy. Ruth could have gone out too. Edie was always asking her to go with her to the pictures. Jane too had asked her to join them. This was in the days before she met Davey; since then, Ruth noticed that Jane was even quieter than she used to be. But Ruth had no money to spare to enjoy the pictures or a fish supper on a Saturday night with her friends. Instead she stayed in to look after her parents.

When she arrived home with the box of eggs from High Farm, she pushed Jimmy to the back of her mind. She cooked the eggs with ham for tea, then she and Bea made a start on washing plates and pans. Ruth could hardly keep her eyes open. The weight of the day lay heavy on her shoulders and a headache was building. She wanted nothing more than to slip into bed. But first she had buckets of coal and water to fetch from the yard. Then there was her mam to settle and her dad to help. And all the while, her stomach churned. She knew that Bea was planning to head out to meet Jimmy. She glanced up from the dirty dishes at her sister's face. She really was looking tired and pale.

'You sure you're feeling all right?' Ruth asked her.

Bea shrugged. 'Why wouldn't I be?' She concentrated on cleaning the plates and looked away from Ruth's gaze.

'Don't stay out too long with Jimmy,' Ruth said. She had battled with her conscience since she'd seen Jimmy with the girl on Cliff Road. She knew she should tell Bea about it. But she also knew how headstrong Bea was. There was a chance that the more Ruth bad-mouthed Jimmy, the more attractive he'd become in her sister's eyes. Bea had always been stubborn, contrary, doing what she wanted and paying no heed to the consequences. Ruth was the exact opposite, holding back when in doubt where Bea would rush in without a care. And that was why Bea taking up with someone like Jimmy made Ruth feel nervous. For who knew what mischief a lad like that could get up to and drag her sister into?

'Watch what you're doing tonight,' she said quietly. She didn't want their parents to hear.

Bea bristled at her sister's words. 'Just because you don't like Jimmy, it doesn't mean he doesn't make me happy.'

'I know. Just promise me you'll be careful. He's got a bad reputation in the village.'

16

Bea didn't answer. Ruth watched as she ran a brush through her hair, threw on her jacket and gave her mam a kiss on the cheek.

'Are you seeing your young man again, love?' Jean asked.

'Yes, Mam,' Bea replied sweetly.

'Bring him home for tea one day. It's about time we met this lad of yours,' Harry said sternly.

Bea gave Harry a peck on the cheek and walked quickly out of the room.

After she'd gone, Ruth finished her chores. She brought in a bucket of coal from the yard, then one of water. Back and forth she went, lugging the heavy buckets. Her arms, neck and back screamed and ached. Her head throbbed with pain. All done, she settled her mam and kissed her on the forehead.

'Night, love,' Jean said.

Ruth helped her dad walk from his armchair to the bed, then retired to her own bed at the other end of the room. The sisters' bed was angled away from their parents', but even so, they all had scant privacy. She sank on to the bed and untied the laces in her worn boots, then slipped the boots off and pushed them under the bed. She wondered where Bea was, where she and Jimmy spent their time. She doubted they would be welcomed at Jimmy's house. Ruth had heard tales of Jimmy's mam being too fond of beer. She was sometimes found drunk in the street. Once more she wondered if she should tell Bea the truth about what she'd seen on the way home from High Farm. It would torment her if she kept it to herself, but would it be worse for Bea to know?

She undressed quickly, slipped her nightdress over her

head and slid under the eiderdown. In the darkness of the room, she ran through her thoughts from the day.

If it was true a new owner was taking over the mill, what might it mean for her? Might she and Bea lose their jobs? Without money coming in, how would they live? Mrs Pike was friendly enough when the rent was being paid, but Ruth couldn't see that friendship extending to letting the Hardys live rent-free. And then there was her mam and dad; neither was in good health, but they couldn't afford the doctor. Ruth was doing her best, but was it good enough? Her dad's dark moods were taking their toll. She was trying to be extra chipper around him, to give him no cause for concern. But she was feeling the pressure and it was becoming too much to bear, bringing her own mood down.

And then, of course, there was Bea. Ruth sighed and pressed her eyes shut. Bea. Her little sister. She hadn't looked well today, and despite her saying she felt fine, Ruth knew she was out of sorts. Ruth didn't want much for herself; everything she wanted was for others. She wanted her mam to be well again, for her dad's mood to lift, and for Bea, little Bea, to be happy. She wanted the Saturday-night singer to be a man this weekend, a man with a deep voice singing jolly songs to put a smile on her dad's face. She wanted Mrs Pike to be understanding if the rent was late. So many worries whirled in her mind.

She shook her head as if to dismiss the dark thoughts, and allowed herself to dream, a game of 'what if' to chase away the blues. What if she had someone to look after *her*? Someone to bring her a cup of tea in bed on a morning. Someone to cook her a meal, or fill the tin bath with warm water and hand her a cake of soap. And oh, it wouldn't be the carbolic soap that she was used to, but one scented with roses. What if there was someone else to carry buckets of water and warm them on the fire? What if . . . she shivered with delight . . . what if the someone was a man with dark hair and strong arms who would kiss her and tell her he loved her? It wouldn't be a man like Jane's boyfriend Davey Winter, or a man like Jimmy Tate. But then who would it be? A man like Mick who worked on the mill railway? What if Mick wrapped his arms around her and whispered in her ear? Ruth fell asleep with a smile on her face.

It was much later when Bea returned and clambered into bed. The bed creaked and groaned. Ruth stirred.

'Ruth? Are you awake?'

She turned over in bed to face her sister. 'What is it?' she said sleepily.

Bea reached for her hand in the dark. 'I've got something to tell you.'

Ruth tried to bring her sleepy thoughts to focus on what Bea was saying. She hoped she was about to tell her that she'd learned the truth about Jimmy, that she'd seen the light and dumped him. But what her sister had to say was far worse than anything Ruth could have guessed.

'I'm pregnant.'

Chapter Two

Ruth's emotions were in turmoil; like nothing she'd experienced before. She was angry at Bea for getting caught out. She was furious with Jimmy for taking advantage of her sister, although Bea told a romantic tale of how much she loved him. And then her anger gave way to a horrible sadness in the pit of her stomach.

Under the bedcovers, the sisters talked long into the night. They turned over the dates, trying to work out how far gone Bea was. Ruth wondered whether it wasn't too late to do something about the situation. But who did she know to ask about such things? She told Bea that keeping the baby wasn't an option unless Jimmy proposed, which she felt unlikely. How on earth could they afford to feed a baby? Bea laid her hands protectively across her stomach and repeated to Ruth that she loved Jimmy. They whispered for hours and neither of them got any sleep.

The next morning as they prepared for work, they tried their best not to give their mam and dad cause for concern. Ruth cooked oats and milk on the fire, then washed and dressed. She brought in a bucket of coal and another of water while Bea made sandwiches to take to work, and for their parents to eat during the day. Ruth helped her mam wash as best she could and soothed her dad with calm words when he complained about the emptiness of the day ahead. But neither girl gave a hint as to what had been said. They both knew too well the shame that a baby born out of wedlock would bring to the Hardy family. If word got out, Bea might even be sent to Sunderland Lunatic Asylum, which lay at the southern edge of Ryhope village, at its border with Seaham. It was a large, forbidding building with spires and turrets and long lines of tall windows, a hospital for those suffering from diseases of the mind. Unwed mothers were taken there too, their shameful secrets hidden from sight. Many of the women would never return from asylum life. Whatever happened, Ruth would never let her sister go there.

Ruth took Bea's hand as they set out for the mill. As they walked, she wondered out loud if there was a woman they knew who could get rid of the baby. Bea was defiant. She insisted that it was just a matter of time before Jimmy would propose. Ruth had to bite her tongue. What she knew about Jimmy Tate would upset Bea no end. She decided to forget Jimmy, forget he existed. All that mattered was Bea's welfare, and Ruth would do all she could to protect her sister and her family from shame.

They crossed the muddy fields to the path that ran along the clifftop to the mill. Ahead of them the mill's chimneys punctured the sky, and a familiar unpleasant smell floated above. Ruth pulled her woollen jacket around her as the wind picked up. The clifftop path took the girls to the railway yard at the back of the mill. They crossed it quickly, but Ruth kept her eyes peeled just in case she saw Mick. She felt foolish, for what was she hoping for? That a handsome train driver might be interested in someone as plain as her? And yet she was surprised at how disappointed she felt when there was no sign of him.

Ahead of them was the mill itself, made up of many outbuildings. There were esparto warehouses, and beating houses where pulp for the paper was made. Engine rooms stood alongside a bleaching room where strong acids were used. Ruth had heard this was one of the most dangerous rooms at the mill, although danger was present almost everywhere. She had been told of a reckless young lad having both legs wrenched off when he'd climbed on to a papermaking machine. The dangers of the mill were impressed on all of the workers; it was their duty to put safety first.

Ruth and Bea walked quickly past these buildings as men and boys streamed inside. Some of them knew Ruth or recognised Bea, and hearty good mornings were called. Finally, ahead of the girls was the machine room where Bea worked. Ruth hugged her sister tight.

'We'll talk more tonight,' she said.

Bea froze. 'We won't. I'm going out to see Jimmy.'

Ruth laid her hands on Bea's shoulders and looked her straight in the eye. 'No, Bea. We need to talk.'

Bea pulled away. 'You can't keep treating me like a child!' she cried. 'I'll do what I want!'

'It's doing what you want that's got you into the predicament you're in now,' Ruth said.

Bea turned from her sister and ran into the machine room.

'Bea!' Ruth called, but Bea didn't turn and her call was lost on the wind.

She walked on, past the offices where the wages were counted and the mill's paperwork was done. It was also where the owner had his office. She thought again of the news Bea had given her about the new owner and wondered once more who it was.

Inside the rag room that morning, it was Ruth's turn on duty at the sorting machine. She loaded the rags into the huge metal drum, then pulled down on the heavy metal handle, and the machine came alive, driven by the mill's generator. The drum shook violently, shaking and agitating the cloths to clean them before the girls cut them into rags. Ruth watched as dirt fell to the floor through a wire mesh. Human hair was tangled there too. Sometimes, if the girls were lucky, a coin might fall from a pocket that had gone unchecked by those bringing the rags in. Perhaps a widow had missed a penny tucked away in her dead husband's trousers when she'd given them to the rag and bone man. Or it might have been the rag and bone man himself who hadn't checked thoroughly. Today there were no coins, just dirt and hair and the familiar stench of sweat – and worse.

As the machine vibrated furiously, Ruth knew she had to concentrate on her work. But her thoughts were with Bea and her baby bombshell that had exploded the night before. Lost in her reverie, she felt a warm touch on her arm.

'Morning, Ruth. You all right, love?'

She turned to see Edie at her side. Her friend was always so cheerful and lively. Even though she was dressed in her dreary grey and brown work clothes, there

23

was a radiance about her. Her sparkling blue eyes shone, her face was bonny and bright.

'Waggy's left the room to go to the netty. Thought I'd nip over for a chat while she's out.'

Waggy was the girls' nickname for their supervisor, Miss Wagstaff. They only ever used it when she was out of earshot, as they were too scared of her sharp tongue. The woman must have been a beauty in her time, all the girls thought that. It was still there in her translucent skin, but there was a stern and bitter look to her features now. Her black hair was scraped back from her face and held tight with pins. Ruth glanced at the seat where she usually sat. Sure enough, it was empty, which meant it was safe to talk. However, the noise from the sorting machine meant the girls had to shout to be heard. Ruth was desperate to speak to Edie, but what she wanted to talk about would have to wait until they had privacy.

'You're looking a bit down in the mouth,' Edie shouted.

'Can we talk at dinner time?' Ruth yelled.

Edie gave her arm a squeeze. 'Course we can.' She scuttled back to her seat.

The morning passed slowly. Ruth struggled to keep her eyes open as lack of sleep caught up with her. The news about a new owner at the mill, which had seemed so important the day before, now paled into insignificance. She gave it little thought, focused as she was on Bea. At midday Miss Wagstaff rang her hand-held brass bell, the signal for a half-hour dinner break. On cold or wet days, the girls ate their dinner in the rag room, hardly moving from their seats on the bench. The air in the room was always thick with dust, and Ruth didn't enjoy eating indoors.

'It's windy out, but let's get some fresh air,' she said to Edie.

Edie looked over to where their friend was sitting alone. 'Should I ask Jane to come?' she said.

Ruth's heart dropped. She hated leaving Jane out of their dinner-time chat, but the weight of what she had to say was such that she couldn't bear to tell anyone but her best friend. 'Not today,' she said. 'I need to speak to you alone.'

The two girls left the rag room and stepped into the cold autumn day. Edie threaded her arm through Ruth's and they walked together down the slope from the mill towards the sea. There was a bay there, a small stretch of coal-black sand surrounded by rocks. Ruth and Edie picked their way over stones and settled in the shelter of the rocks. Ruth took her sandwich from her pocket. Edie dipped into her handbag and brought out her own dinner.

'Ham?' Ruth peered at Edie's lunch.

'Ham,' Edie sighed. 'I don't even like it. But Mam reckons it's good for me. I've got something else too.' She opened her handbag again and brought out two pock-marked green apples. 'From the tree in our garden,' she said. 'There's one for you.'

Ruth took her sandwich from the page of newspaper that Bea had wrapped it in that morning.

'I've got beef paste, if you want to do a swap?' she offered.

'Go on then, saves me having to eat this bloody ham.'

'Have you spoken to Jane much today?' Ruth asked as they ate.

Edie shook her head.

'She's been quiet lately,' Ruth remarked.

'You mean since she met Davey?'

Ruth nodded. 'She's different somehow.'

'Timid,' Edie agreed. 'She was never like that before.'

'Do you think we should have a word with her, find out if anything's wrong?'

'I've been wondering about that myself. She looks sad all the time too.'

Ruth looked out to sea as she chewed. The tide was frothy, churning and angry but still far enough away to pose no threat. She kept her gaze on the waves.

'Edie?' she said quietly.

'What, love?'

'Do you know anyone . . .' she began hesitantly. 'I mean, do you know someone who could help a girl if she was in trouble?'

'Is it Mick Carson's?' Edie said without missing a beat.

Ruth glared at her friend. 'Mick Carson? What's this got to do with him?'

Edie stared at Ruth's stomach. 'Well, I'm assuming if you're asking a question like that, it's because you've got yourself in a state. And the only fella I've ever known you be keen on is Mick who works in the rail yard. You need to get out more, Ruth. There's a world outside that poky back room at the Guide Post Inn, you know.'

'No!' Ruth was horrified that her friend could think that of her. How little Edie knew her, she thought. She'd never even had a boyfriend before. She shook her head. 'It's not me who needs help.'

'Then who?' Edie said, puzzled.

Ruth gave a long sigh. She closed her eyes and blinked back tears. 'It's our Bea.'

Edie put her arm around Ruth's shoulders and was about to speak when they heard someone shouting behind them.

'Ruth! Ruth!'

They turned to see a young lad, no more than twelve years old, running down the slope to the beach. Ruth recognised him. He was one of the boys who worked in the machine room.

'Ruth! You've got to come. Your Bea's taken poorly at the mill!'

Chapter Three

Ruth scrambled to her feet. 'Where is she? What's happened?'

'She's up there,' the boy said. He pointed to the long brick building housing the machine room. 'She fainted dead away. I think she hurt her head when she fell. She asked for you as soon as she opened her eyes. I ran to the rag room to fetch you, and a girl in there told me to look here.'

Ruth ran to the machine room with Edie following. Although she had once worked there sweeping the floor, it had been a long time since she had been inside the room. Around her the machines clattered and banged. At one end of each machine was what the men called the wet end, where water flowed with beaten pulp of rags, grass and wood, sliding into the machine on great iron-mesh pans. From the other end of the machine, at the far end of the room, came out folds of paper. It was a process that Ruth would never fully understand, as women weren't allowed to work the machines. Their work at the mill was confined to the rag room, sweeping and cleaning the machine rooms or sorting paper in the counting room.

Two men wearing flat caps and shirts covered by waistcoats walked over to her.

'You the sister?' one of them asked.

'Yes, where is she?' Ruth said urgently.

The taller of the men pointed along the length of one of the machines. 'She's behind the Penshaw machine,' he said.

Ruth knew exactly where that was from her time working in the room. She knew she shouldn't run. She'd been told many times to tread carefully wherever she went at the mill. Safety was drummed into every woman and girl, every man and boy from the first day they turned up for work. But she couldn't help it. She had to get to Bea. Breathless, she flew to where her sister was sitting on the cold floor and dropped down beside her, kissing Bea's face and hugging her tight. Edie stood nearby with her hands on her hips, watching.

'I'll be fine,' Bea insisted. 'Go back to work, both of you. I don't want you getting into trouble because of me.'

'Bea's right, Ruth. Waggy'll be on the warpath if we're not back in the rag room on time.'

'You go, give her some excuse about me,' Ruth said.

Edie shook her head. 'I'm not leaving you.'

'What happened, Bea?' Ruth said.

'One minute I was sweeping, and the next thing I knew, one of the lads was picking me up off the floor. I must have passed out.'

'You're not hurt, are you? You're not bleeding anywhere? Any stomach pain?' Ruth asked.

Bea knew immediately what she meant. 'No, no blood,' she said.

'Can you stand?' Ruth asked.

'I'll try.'

'Edie, come and take Bea's arm and I'll get this side.'

Together, Ruth and Edie helped Bea up on to her feet.

'Have you eaten since breakfast?' Ruth asked.

Bea shook her head.

Ruth delved into her pocket and brought out her half-eaten sandwich. 'Here, have this.'

Edie handed over the remains of her own bread. 'You're going to need all the nourishment you can get in your state,' she said.

Bea glared at her, then turned to Ruth with a face full of thunder. 'You've told her?'

'I had to tell someone, Bea,' Ruth said firmly.

'I know someone that can get rid of it for you,' Edie began hesitantly. 'There's a woman in Ryhope, down on Scotland Street, she'll do it. Course, you'll have to pay her, but she's kind and it won't hurt much, not really. The pain goes after a few days.'

Ruth wondered how she knew so much about it. Had she been through the same thing herself, caught out with a baby from one of the fellas she knew? Edie was more experienced in the ways of the world than she was.

Bea's hands flew to her stomach. 'No! It's my baby, mine and Jimmy's. You're not our mam, you can't tell me what to do.'

Ruth laid her hand firmly on Bea's shoulder. 'We'll talk about it tonight at home.'

'Ruth, we've got to get back to work,' Edie said, worried now.

Ruth stared long and hard at her sister. 'You sure you're going to be all right, young 'un?'

Bea nodded.

'Right then. Eat your dinner, get yourself outside for some fresh air and take it easy this afternoon.'

Ruth and Edie walked away, leaving Bea by the Penshaw machine. Ruth turned to wave, but her sister was too busy eating.

'I hate leaving her,' she said.

'She'll be fine,' Edie said. 'If she's old enough to get herself into the scrape she's in now, she's old enough to look after herself.'

'I'm not sure, Edie. She's just a kid, only sixteen.'

'And you're not much older. There's little more than a year between the two of you. If anyone called you "just a kid", you'd not be too pleased.'

'She's my little sister. Surely you of all people, with all your brothers and sisters, can understand why I feel so protective?'

'And she'll always be your little sister, no matter how old you both get. But she's a young woman with a mind of her own. Give her some space.'

'But—'

'No buts, Ruth. I heard you say you were going to talk to her tonight. When you do, let her speak, and listen to her. She might be just a kid to you, but she's got a baby inside her, and that changes everything.'

Ruth wondered again if Edie was speaking from experience.

'And when she talks to you about this lad . . .'

'His name's Jimmy,' Ruth said. 'Jimmy Tate.'

Edie shot her a look. 'Not Jimmy Tate from Railway Street?'

Ruth nodded. 'Do you know him?'

'I know his mam,' Edie said. 'Or at least I know *of* her. She's got a few problems, likes the beer too much. My mam's had a few stand-up rows in the street with Connie Tate.'

'She sounds a rough 'un.'

'She is,' Edie said.

Edie linked arms with Ruth and they headed back into the dusty air of the rag room. They were the last two girls to return from dinner break. When they entered the room, Miss Wagstaff took her pencil and marked a black cross against their names in her book. Ruth noticed this immediately and walked up to Miss Wagstaff.

'My sister took unwell in the machine room. I had to go to her,' she said.

Miss Wagstaff raised an eyebrow in her heavily powdered face and looked from Ruth to Edie. 'And it took both of you to attend to her? Back to work, girls, this instant.'

'Yes, Miss Wagstaff,' Edie said as she took her seat on the bench.

Ruth remained where she was.

'What is it now, girl?' Miss Wagstaff sighed.

'I don't think I should be black-marked for caring about my sister,' Ruth said firmly.

She felt the eyes of the other girls on her. No one had ever dared confront Miss Wagstaff before. She stared hard at the supervisor and saw a twitch at the corner of the woman's mouth.

'The black mark will stay. Now sit,' Miss Wagstaff said sternly.

Ruth didn't move.

'Sit! Now! Back to work!' Miss Wagstaff yelled.

Ruth turned her back and began to walk to her seat on the bench between Edie and Jane.

'Is Bea all right?' Jane asked.

Ruth nodded in reply. She settled into her afternoon's work with a heavy heart. Her stomach rumbled with hunger, and she remembered she still had the apple in her pocket that Edie had given her. Her mouth watered at the thought of biting into the crisp, juicy fruit. Then she felt guilty thinking about eating it; she should have handed it to Bea earlier. Well, it would have to wait until they were walking home; she would give it to Bea then.

The afternoon passed slowly. All Ruth wanted to do was make sure Bea was all right and get home to her mam and dad. When the signal for the end of the shift finally came in the form of Miss Wagstaff's brass bell, she didn't hide her relief.

'What number Scotland Street does this woman live at?' she asked Edie.

Edie told her the house number, then put her hand on Ruth's arm. 'Tell Bea not to be frightened; Mrs Jones will be kind.'

Ruth bade farewell to Edie and Jane. She tugged off her work cap and shook her long hair loose. Then she pulled her woollen hat over her head and headed out to the yard. Women streamed past her to the gates and she scanned the crowd for her sister. She saw several young girls wearing black coats just like Bea's, but none of them was Bea. Her heart leapt in her chest. Where was she? Had she fainted again? Was she lying on the floor by the paper machine, unnoticed amidst the machines' bang and clatter? In the three years since Bea had worked at the mill, there hadn't been a single day when she wasn't waiting by the gates at the end of the day. Ruth didn't know whether to turn and run back to check. She stood stock still as the throng of women surged past her. She was jostled and bumped by women desperate to get home. Where was Bea? Ruth spun on her heel and decided to head to the machine room to look for her sister.

She had to push past the women coming towards her. 'Watch where you're going, love!' one shouted.

'You're keen! Going back for another shift, are you?' another one laughed in her face.

Ruth fought her way through the women, intent on finding Bea. As the machine room came into view, she spotted Bea leaning against a brick wall, gulping in air. But as she began to run towards her, she realised her sister wasn't alone. There was a man with her, a man with his back turned towards Ruth so that she couldn't see who he was. When she reached Bea, the man politely stepped aside and raised his flat cap. Ruth was stunned to come face to face with Mick Carson.

Chapter Four

The shock Ruth felt at seeing the railway worker was overcome by her desire to attend to Bea. She wrapped her arms around her sister and hugged her.

'What happened?' she asked.

'I'm all right, Ruth, don't worry,' Bea said softly.

Mick stepped forward. 'I found her just now looking the worse for wear. Are you her friend?'

Ruth turned to look at the man who had helped Bea. She saw his dark eyes, dark hair and trim black moustache. His flat cap sat at an angle and he wore no jacket, just a striped shirt with sleeves rolled up and buttons up to his neck. Over the shirt he wore braces to keep his trousers up. Ruth couldn't help notice his bare forearms, how muscled and strong they were. But it was his face she would remember, and the way his eyes sparkled when he smiled.

'I'm her sister,' she said quickly, then turned her attention back to Bea. 'Did you faint again?'

'No, I was just a little dizzy,' Bea said. 'I'll be fine. I want to go home.'

'We'll take it easy,' Ruth said. She linked arms with her

sister, ready to head away. But before they set off, she turned to Mick. 'Thank you for looking after her,' she said.

'My pleasure,' he replied. 'And it's nice to meet you again, Ruth, although I'm sorry it's because of your sister being ill. Do you think she'll be all right? I don't mind staying with you both until she recovers.'

'She'll be fine, we'll walk slowly,' Ruth replied. 'But thank you for such a kind offer.'

'Well, I'd best get back to work. The gaffer won't be happy if I'm away too long. I was taking paperwork to the mill office, said I'd only be gone five minutes. The new owner is changing the system for the railwaymen; we're being asked to hand in all kinds of paperwork we never did before. He's a real stickler for discipline, this new fella, so I've heard. Posh, of course. But then if I owned a mill, I might allow myself airs and graces.'

'The new owner's taken over already?' Ruth asked, surprised.

'Haven't you heard?' Mick asked.

She shook her head. Bea had been in her thoughts all day; she'd paid little attention to any gossip in the rag room.

Mick tipped his cap at her. 'I'll be seeing you, Ruth Hardy.'

Ruth and Bea walked away arm in arm. Just before they reached the mill gates, Ruth turned her head. Mick was waiting where she'd left him, watching her. She waved, he returned the gesture, and Ruth felt a warm glow inside.

When the girls finally arrived home at the Guide Post Inn, Harry was in a foul mood. He complained long and loud about them being late and about how his dinner should have been on the table an hour ago. Jean was asleep, her long silver-grey hair spread on the pillow. Ruth set to work the minute she walked through the door. She put coal on the fire and water on to boil; she lit the oil lamps and made the room cosy. By the time their tea of sliced cold beef with potatoes was ready, Harry's mood had improved, and Jean was awake and pleased to have her girls home. Ruth, Bea and Harry sat at the small table while Jean ate from a tray in her bed.

When the meal had been eaten and the dishes washed up, Ruth saw Bea slip her arms into her jacket.

'Oh no you don't,' she said.

'I'm going out to see Jimmy. You can't stop me,' Bea replied.

'You've not been well all day. You need to rest. You're not going anywhere tonight.'

Harry laid his newspaper on his lap. 'What are you two being so secretive about? It's bad manners to whisper!'

'Nothing, Dad,' Ruth replied quickly, and turned back to Bea. 'You're staying in.'

'I'm not!' Bea walked from the room and slammed the door behind her.

'Bea?' Jean called.

'Where's she off to?' Harry said.

Ruth knew she couldn't tell her mam and dad what was going on. The shame of having an unwed pregnant daughter was something they wouldn't be able to live with. She had to keep quiet, for now, at least. She'd tried to talk to Bea about the woman Edie had recommended, the one on Scotland Street, but Bea had simply shaken her head. The best Ruth could hope for was to have a word with her when she came home that night. They could talk in bed, close together under the bedcovers, without their parents overhearing.

'She's out with a friend,' she told her dad.

'Is it that lad again?' he said.

Ruth noticed the angry tone of his voice. She nodded.

'And who is he, do you know?' Harry demanded. 'I've told her umpteen times to bring him home so I can take a look at him, and not once has she said that she will.'

Ruth saw her parents exchange a look.

'She's not said a word to me about who he is,' Jean said. 'Has she told you, Ruth?'

'He's called Jimmy,' Ruth said. She felt she could say that much at least. It wasn't exactly betraying Bea's confidence. 'Jimmy Tate.'

Her mother rolled her eyes. 'Not Connie Tate's son?' Ruth remembered Edie's words about Connie. 'She's got the devil in her, that one,' Jean said.

'She likes a drink, that's true,' Harry said.

'Likes a drink?' Jean cried. 'She'd sell her own son if it meant she could get her hands on a barrel of ale.'

'Is she really that bad, Mam?' Ruth asked.

'She is, love. Or at least she always used to be. I hope Jimmy hasn't turned out the same, although they say the apple never falls far from the tree. Weren't you at school with him, Ruth?'

'He was a useless lump back then and I daresay he's not changed much,' Ruth said.

'Then what on earth's our Bea doing with him?'

Ruth sighed. 'That's what I'd like to know.'

'You'll have a word with her, love, won't you?' Jean

asked. 'She'll listen to you. We wouldn't want her getting serious with the lad.'

Ruth's heart sank. 'Yes, Mam. I'll look after her.'

'You always do, love. You're a good lass. I don't know what we'd do without you.'

The next morning was crisp and fresh. Ruth had been fast asleep by the time Bea had returned home the night before, and they'd had no chance to talk. Now, as they walked to the mill, she tried to bring up the subject of Mrs Jones again, but her sister closed her down.

'I won't do it, Ruth, I won't. Jimmy loves me, he says so.'

'If he loves you, then he'll marry you,' Ruth said firmly. 'Has he asked you yet?'

Bea was silent. The question hung between them.

Before they parted in the mill yard, Ruth made sure that Bea had her sandwich in her pocket.

'Be sure to eat it in little bites, when you can, during the morning. You've got to keep your strength up.'

Bea turned her eyes to Ruth. 'To look after the baby?'

Ruth shook her head. 'To look after you.'

The sisters hugged and Ruth headed to the rag room. As she drew close to the door, she saw someone waiting. She recognised Mick Carson straight away. She stopped in her tracks and took in the sight of him.

'Morning, Ruth Hardy!'

He was carrying what looked like a roll of newspaper in his arms which he offered to Ruth. Ruth saw green leaves poking from the top. It could only be a bouquet of flowers. Her heart jumped. She'd never been given flowers before!

'Thought you could use these, what with your sister being poorly and all,' Mick said.

Ruth took the parcel from him. It was a lot heavier than she thought a bunch of flowers would be, and there was a strange smell too. But what did a bouquet have to do with Bea not being well? Were the flowers for Bea and not her? Oh, how foolish she felt.

'Leeks from Dad's garden,' Mick said proudly. 'He's got that many he won't miss a few. They'll cook up into a smashing pudding or soup. I could ask Mam for her recipe if you'd like. I can bring more if you need them, and we've got potatoes too. I mean, only if you want them. I don't want to give you things you don't need, but I could . . .'

'Leeks?' Ruth interrupted. She peeked into the newspaper cone and couldn't help but laugh. She should have known better. She wasn't the sort of girl men gave flowers to. It was bonny girls like Edie, with her quick wit and ready smile, who received flowers. But still, there was a kindness in Mick's practical gift that she appreciated.

'. . . I could bring more.' Mick whipped off his cap. 'I'm sorry, Ruth. I talk too much when I get nervous.'

'I hope I don't make you nervous. That's the last thing I'd want,' she said.

From inside the rag room came a sound that made her stomach churn. It was Miss Wagstaff's bell, signalling the shift was starting. And here she was, still not at work, and she knew she'd be marked down with her second black mark in as many days.

'I've got to go,' she said. Without waiting for Mick's reply, she ran into the rag room carrying the bundle of leeks. The other girls looked up from their work, and a hush descended on the room.

'Late again?' Miss Wagstaff barked. There was a menace in her voice that sent a shiver down Ruth's spine. 'Leave your parcel. You know the rules.'

Ruth placed the leeks wrapped in newspaper by the door and went to take her seat between Edie and Jane, but Miss Wagstaff wasn't finished with her yet.

'Not so fast, Miss Hardy. Your presence has been requested elsewhere.'

Ruth heard Edie gasp, and from the corner of her eye she saw Jane staring at her. She could feel the eyes of all the girls burning into her. She would have given anything to be sitting with them rather than standing in front of the supervisor. She felt her face burn.

Miss Wagstaff looked up from the sheets of paper in front of her. 'You're to report to the mill office immediately.'

Ruth was confused and scared. Was she to be disciplined for her black marks? 'Me, Miss Wagstaff?'

Miss Wagstaff knew she had an audience of the girls in the room. Cruelly, she played up to them, taking vicious enjoyment in making Ruth squirm. She shielded her eyes with one hand and made a show of pretending to look around, searching for someone.

'I don't see another Miss Hardy in this room, do you? Of course it's you, girl. Now go, and don't keep him waiting.'

Ruth heard some of the girls giggling from the back of the room. She swallowed hard. 'Who shall I report to in the mill office?' she said.

'You're to ask for Mr Hewson,' Miss Wagstaff instructed.

Ruth noticed the emphasis she placed on the name. 'Mr Hewson? Who is he? Have I done something wrong?' she asked.

'Take your head out of the clouds, girl,' Miss Wagstaff said. 'Don't you know anything about what goes on at the mill? Mr Hewson is the new owner. Now go – and don't keep him waiting!'

Chapter Five

Ruth walked quickly to the mill office. She was confused and afraid. What could the new owner possibly want to see her about? She was just a girl who worked in the rag room. Was she to be disciplined for having two black marks against her? But she'd been given her second black mark just moments ago. She couldn't possibly be disciplined for one mark, could she? And anyway, surely the mill owner wouldn't take it on himself to chastise her after four years' good service? Had Waggy reported her? Might she get the sack?

There were tears in her eyes and a lump in her throat as she made her way across the yard. It wasn't as if she'd been late, not really. Waggy must have seen her standing outside the door, and yet she'd still rung her bell, not bothering to call her in to start work. She thought of Mick and his gift of leeks. If only she hadn't stopped to talk to him at the door, she wouldn't be in such trouble now. Despite herself, though, she couldn't help smiling. Fancy thinking he'd brought her flowers!

As she neared the office building, she felt her heart skip. She'd been into the mill office many times; all the girls had. It was where they collected their wages each Friday afternoon. But she'd never had cause to go further than the wages office on the ground floor. She'd heard tell that the mill owner's office was at the top, so that he could keep watch over the mill.

She took a deep breath and knocked once, twice on the main door. No answer. She knocked again and a voice yelled, 'Are you deaf? I said come in!'

She pushed the door open and was met by a stern-faced woman she recognised as Dorothy Smith, one of the clerks at the mill. Dorothy was even older than Mrs Pike, who was the oldest person Ruth knew.

'I've been sent to see Mr Hewson,' Ruth said. She barely recognised her own voice. She was shaking, and yet her voice sounded confident, strong and calm.

Dorothy raised an eyebrow. 'And you are?'

'Ruth Hardy.'

'He's expecting you. Fourth floor.' She indicated with her hand. 'The stairs are through that door. Take them one at a time and don't run.'

Ruth headed to the stairwell and began to climb. At each landing was a wooden board showing the number of the floor she was on. On the fourth landing, she paused and swallowed hard, still nervous, then set out along the dark corridor. At the end was a white-painted door with a sign reading: *Mr Hewson, Grange Paper Works*. This was it.

She glanced back along the corridor, but there was no one to be seen. Her anger towards Waggy had given way to a strange curiosity about what and who she would find behind the door. But she was still scared, afraid she was about to be given her marching orders. She took a moment to help calm her racing heart, then knocked hard on the door. This time she leaned close, listening. There was silence. She was about to move closer when the door swung open and she almost fell inside.

In front of her was a tall, thin man with white hair. He was the smartest-dressed man she'd ever seen. He wore a grey jacket and matching waistcoat over a white shirt and black tie. And in the lapel of his jacket was a delicate pink rose.

'Ah, Miss Hardy, I've been expecting you.' He extended his hand. 'I'm Oswald Hewson, pleased to meet you. I've heard a lot about you.'

Ruth's heart skipped. Pleased to meet you? A handshake? Did this mean she wasn't to be given the sack?

She took Mr Hewson's hand and shook it. His skin was smooth and cold.

'Please, take a seat.' He indicated a chair positioned in front of a large, solid table. On the table were piles of papers and books.

Ruth watched as Mr Hewson took his own seat, then forced herself forward to the empty chair. She didn't take in any of her surroundings. She was so terrified, she could only focus on the man in front of her. She sat, and as they faced each other across the big desk, her gaze was drawn to the rose in his jacket. She'd never seen a man wearing a flower before. Even the women in Ryhope only wore them for special occasions such as weddings and funerals. But Ryhope men? Never!

She realised Mr Hewson had caught her looking, and she quickly looked away.

'Ah! My daughter gives me a fresh rose each morning for my jacket,' he said brightly.

Ruth saw the way the lines at the corners of his eyes creased when he smiled. His eyes were blue and clear, and set against his white hair, the whole effect gave him a kindly look. It helped calmed her racing mind. She wasn't as afraid as she'd felt moments before, and her breathing began to return to normal. She glanced again at the pink rose, then sat up in her chair and focused on Mr Hewson's face. She hoped that whatever he had to tell her, even if it was to give her the sack, he'd do it quickly, get it over with. Her mind ran on. She'd have to go back to Ryhope, tell her mam and dad what had happened and start asking around the pubs for work. She could start with the Guide Post Inn, ask Mrs Pike if she needed any new staff, and then—

'Miss Wagstaff has given me a good report of you, Miss Hardy,' Mr Hewson said.

Ruth snapped her attention back to the man across the desk. 'Sorry, sir?'

'You're a good worker, she tells me, the best in the rag room. Hard-working, conscientious, and you care about the welfare of others.'

Ruth was dumbstruck. She opened her mouth to speak, but nothing came out. Whatever she'd expected Mr Hewson to say, it certainly hadn't been this.

'She tells me you're something of a spokesman for the girls,' he continued. He allowed himself a chuckle. 'Or should I say a spokes*woman*?'

'I believe in doing what's right for all the girls who work in the rag room, sir.' She wondered if this was why she'd been summoned to see the mill owner. Had she gone too far in standing up for the other girls when Waggy's sharp tongue had upset her workmates and friends?

'I think you could be just the girl I'm looking for,' Mr Hewson said. A smile played around his mouth.

'Sir?' she said, confused.

He pushed himself back in his chair and glanced out of the window. Ruth wondered what was going on. What was he thinking? It was impossible to tell. She watched as he stood and began to pace back and forth with his hands behind his back.

'Have you heard of the River Wear Commissioners Office, Miss Hardy?' he asked as he walked.

Ruth doubted there was anyone in Sunderland who hadn't heard of this most important committee. The Commissioners were integral to the trade of the Wear, the river that ran through the centre of town. Sunderland's shipbuilding and trading prosperity depended on good management of the Wear.

'Yes, sir,' she replied.

'Good,' he said, still pacing. 'A friend of mine, a family friend, is one of the Commissioners.'

Ruth wondered what this had to do with her, but she kept quiet, waiting for him to get to the point. Above all, she felt relieved that she hadn't been sacked. But the whole situation was confusing, and she wouldn't allow herself to believe she was off the hook yet.

'He has a son who was injured in the war, in France,' Mr Hewson continued in his matter-of-fact way. 'Unfortunately, the young man has been unable to work since he returned from the front. However, I'm told he's made good progress, and his doctor says he can now carry out light duties without too many problems.'

Ruth couldn't stand the suspense any longer. She had to speak. 'How does this involve me, sir?' she said. Her words came out of her with more force than she'd intended.

Mr Hewson looked at her. 'That's the spirit, Miss Hardy!'

She wished she was back in the rag room with Edie and Jane and the others. She'd give anything for her day to return to normal.

'It involves you because I need a hard-working girl I can trust,' he continued.

'Me, sir?'

'You, Miss Hardy. Miss Wagstaff tells me there's a black mark against you in the attendance book. I will make it disappear if you do what I'm about to ask.'

Ruth kept quiet about the second black mark. If Mr Hewson didn't know about it, then she wasn't going to tell him.

'The name of my friend's son is John Hepple. He's been left badly injured, has to walk with a stick. I've offered him a job at the mill, and I want you, Miss Hardy, to take him under your wing when he starts in the coming weeks. He'll be working in . . .' Mr Hewson faltered a little before carrying on. 'He'll be working in the rag room.'

Ruth gasped. No men ever worked in the rag room. Everyone knew it was women's work. Had she heard correctly? 'In the rag room?'

Mr Hewson nodded sharply. 'It's just about all he can manage. He'll be seated all day, which will be beneficial for him. I need you, Miss Hardy, to show him what to do.'

'Of course, sir,' Ruth said.

'Look after him. Make sure the girls don't spread

gossip about his injuries, or about anything else for that matter.'

'Yes, sir,' she said.

'Thank you, Miss Hardy. You may go back to work now.'

Ruth stood and was about to leave the room when a thought struck her. Mr Hewson had spoken to her kindly and had picked her from all of the girls to be trusted to look after his friend's injured son. She had a burning question on her mind and if she didn't ask it now, then when could she? She might never be in a position to speak so candidly again.

'Sir?'

Mr Hewson looked at her.

'Is it true that jobs will go now you've taken over? There have been rumours . . .'

He appeared affronted at the question, and Ruth wondered if she'd gone too far. 'Where did you hear this?' he said sharply.

Ruth gazed out of the window to the mill yard. 'It's on everyone's lips,' she said.

Mr Hewson tapped his fingers on his desk. 'I can assure you, Miss Hardy – and the girls in the rag room, the men in the machine room, the warehouses, the railway, the bleaching rooms, beating rooms, boiler rooms, all of the rooms at the mill – no jobs will be lost.'

Ruth's heart leapt as he carried on.

'In fact, just the opposite. Grange Paper Works is the largest paper mill in the north of England, and that's exactly how I want it to stay. We may even expand in the coming years, take on more workers. If gossip is suggesting otherwise, I'll have each supervisor send word to their staff with immediate effect. I can't have my workers concerned about their future; that would never do. And I am grateful to you for alerting me.'

Ruth walked out of the room with a smile on her face. She was overjoyed to hear that no jobs would be lost. Her mind was drawn to the pretty pink rose in Mr Hewson's lapel. How odd it had been. Everyone knew roses bloomed in summer, not the cold days of autumn. Nothing seemed real. Her world had been knocked out of kilter. To be called into the mill owner's office and asked to look after a new worker would have been unusual enough. But for that worker to be a man doing a woman's job? Why, it was unheard of! She wondered why she and not Waggy had been asked to look after John Hepple. Because she could handle anything that was chucked at her? How many times had she heard that? *Good old Ruth*, that was what folk said about her. *You can depend on Ruth*. Or *Ask Ruth, she'll help!*

She walked slowly back to the rag room with much on her mind. A man coming to work with them? It was unthinkable! She couldn't wait to tell Edie and Jane.

Chapter Six

'Where'd you get those leeks?' Bea asked as the two girls walked home that evening.

Ruth peered at the green leaves poking from the top of the newspaper. 'They're a gift from the train driver.'

'Mick Carson? See, I knew he was your boyfriend,' Bea teased.

'Do you want to know a secret?' Ruth linked arms with her sister and pulled her close. 'I really wouldn't mind if he was.'

'How was your day?' Bea asked.

Ruth told her about being called into Mr Hewson's office and his strange request. Bea let her words sink in and then warned her sister about the extra burden of working alongside an injured ex-soldier.

'Some of them aren't right in the head any more after what they saw in the war,' she said. 'You've already got Dad with his bad leg. Now you'll have another injured fella to look after at work. Did Mr Hewson offer more money for this favour he's asked?'

'It's not a favour, it's promotion,' Ruth said defensively. 'Well, sort of. Next to old Waggy, I'm the one he trusts most in the rag room.' She didn't know why she was defending the mill owner. But there'd been something in his face, in the way his eyes sparkled when he smiled, that made her think of him warmly.

'Well, did he?' Bea persisted. 'Did he mention paying you more money for this promotion you think he's given you?'

Ruth couldn't fail to notice the sarcastic tone in her sister's words. She knew Bea was looking out for her best interests, in the same way Ruth would always look out for Bea. She chose not to respond, because Bea was right, no extra money had been mentioned.

'What was Mr Hewson like?' Bea asked. 'Was he posh?'

'He wore a rose in his jacket,' Ruth said.

'A rose? At this time of year?'

'Maybe he's got a greenhouse. He can probably afford one. I bet he's got a gardener. Says his daughter gives him a fresh rose every day to wear in his lapel.'

'His daughter? I wonder how old she is – did he say?'

Ruth shook her head. 'He didn't say much at all, just asked me to make sure the soldier doesn't get gossiped about at the mill.'

From the corner of her eye she saw her sister put her hand to her mouth to stifle a laugh.

'Good luck with that,' Bea said.

When the girls arrived at the Guide Post Inn, they entered via the back lane, as they always did. Mrs Pike didn't like them using the pub's front door. She was strict about such things; said it set a bad example to see young girls on their own walking in and out of any pub, never mind her own. Ruth respected her wishes. The last thing they needed was to get on the wrong side of their landlady.

As they let themselves in through the wooden gate to the yard, Ruth laid her hand on Bea's shoulder.

'How are you feeling? Are you up to helping me cook tea tonight for Mam and Dad?'

'Course I'll help you. I'm not an invalid, just pregnant.'

'You're going to have to tell them, you know,' Ruth said.

'Not yet.'

'Then soon, right?'

'What'll they do, Ruth? Will they disown me, throw me out?' Bea asked. In that instant, Ruth saw how nervous her sister was. She looked young and fragile and small.

'They'll do their best, love. Won't Jimmy take you in at his house? If he loves you like he says he does, he should have offered and you know it. A girl in your condition can't be expected to continue courting a fella if he's not going to do the right thing.'

Bea was about to reply when they heard a noise behind them. Ruth spun round. Bea gasped. Mrs Pike was standing there, a sweeping brush in her hand. Ruth put her arm around Bea and pulled her close.

'Mrs Pike!' She tried to keep her voice calm. She was nervous about how much the landlady had overheard. 'We didn't know you were there.'

Mrs Pike eyed the two girls carefully and took her time with her reply.

'By, lass, I've heard some things in my time running this pub,' she said at last.

Ruth's heart dropped. This was bad news indeed. Mrs Pike missed nothing that went on in the Guide Post Inn.

It had been too much to hope that Bea's words had gone unheard.

'How far gone are you, lass?' Mrs Pike was looking at Bea's stomach.

Ruth stepped forward, shielding her sister with her body. 'We've just found out,' she said defensively. 'We haven't decided what to do about it yet.'

'Well, she's not staying here in her condition, I'll tell you that now.'

'Mrs Pike, please!' Ruth pleaded.

But the woman would not be moved. 'A young girl like her having a baby? She's got no husband, no morals, no—'

'Mrs Pike!' Ruth snapped.

The landlady laid her sweeping brush against the brick wall in the yard and stood with her arms crossed at her stout waist. 'Come on then, let's hear your sob story. But if you think I'm daft enough to fall for it, you've got another think coming.'

'She's engaged, if you must know. The wedding's coming up.' Ruth bit her tongue. Where had her lie sprung from so easily, so unexpectedly? Wishful thinking, perhaps? But she would tell any lie in the world to protect Bea and her family.

'Engaged, eh?' Mrs Pike said. 'Well, that puts a different slant on things. A ring on your finger will make all the difference.'

'So you'll let her stay, then?' Ruth asked.

'Don't see why not,' Mrs Pike said. 'As long as there's no gossip gets out about this around Ryhope. You know what the place is like for spreading rumours. Course, if her husband moves in, there'll be more rent to pay.'

'What? You can't put the rent up! We wouldn't be taking up any more space than we already do!' The thought of Jimmy moving into their room was abhorrent to Ruth.

Mrs Pike reached for her sweeping brush again. 'We'll talk about it at a later date, once the wedding's over,' she said. And with that, she bustled away inside the pub.

'Come on, Bea,' Ruth said with a resigned air. 'We're going to have to tell Mam and Dad now before they hear it from Mrs Pike.'

Jean and Harry were sitting on the bed and Ruth was happy to see they were playing cards. She was happier still to see a rare smile on her dad's face.

'Who's winning?'

'As if you need ask,' Jean replied. 'Me as usual.'

Ruth laid the leeks on the table.

'Ruth's been given leeks by her boyfriend,' Bea said.

'Thought we could have them cooked up in soup for our tea,' Ruth suggested.

'Good idea,' Jean said. 'I didn't know you had a boyfriend, Ruth. Is he a lad from the mill?'

'He's no one, not really,' Ruth said as she removed her coat and hat. She shot Bea a look.

'Speaking of boyfriends, Bea, when are we going to meet this young lad of yours?' Harry asked.

Ruth looked at her sister. 'It's time to tell them,' she said.

Bea climbed up on their parents' bed, just like they used to do when they were children. Ruth pulled a chair from the table and brought it to sit at the bedside. Bea held her mam's hand as she told them the truth. The words came slowly, hesitantly.

Jean took the news stoically, not moving, letting it sink in, but Harry was furious. The smile he had been wearing when Ruth and Bea returned home vanished into thin air.

'Where is he, this Jimmy Tate? I'll smash his bloody face in!' he growled.

'No, Dad,' Ruth said. 'Let Bea finish what she's got to say. There's more.'

'There is?' Bea said, confused.

'What we talked about in the yard just now, remember?' Ruth prompted.

'I'm going to get married,' Bea said with as much conviction as she could muster.

'Too bloody right you are,' Harry yelled. 'No daughter of mine is having a baby out of wedlock!'

'Has Jimmy proposed to you, pet?' Jean asked.

Bea shook her head. 'No, but he will. I'm going to see him tonight to tell him we're getting married.'

'And I'm going with her,' Ruth said. 'I'll make sure he knows what's expected.'

'Aye, and tell him from me I want a word with him,' Harry said. 'I want him here, in this room, standing in front of me where I can see the whites of his eyes.'

Ruth began her chores, bringing in buckets of coal for the fire and stoking it high enough to cook on. She brought in a bucket of water. She began chopping leeks, and the room was filled with a strong, distinctive smell that made her stomach growl with hunger. She peeled potatoes and boiled stock. Around her, Harry continued to seethe with anger at what he'd been told, while Bea cuddled in Jean's arms.

Ruth turned to face her. 'When you marry Jimmy, it's going to mean you giving up your job at the mill, you know that, right? Married women aren't allowed to work at Grange Paper Works, and I don't see that changing any time soon. We'll lose your wages once you're wed.'

Her words hung heavy over them all.

Chapter Seven

Later that evening, Ruth and Bea walked in silence to Railway Street. It was one of the mucky pit rows tucked behind the coal mine, the closest street to the pit's noise and grime. The pit rows were owned by the Ryhope Coal Company, and Ruth knew the area well, for the Hardy family had lived in a row close by before Harry's accident. He had made a fuss, demanded compensation after the accident left him crippled. But it was deemed to be his own fault for not securing his workspace securely. When a pit prop gave way and a wall fell, his workmates feared the worst. But Harry had survived.

'You're lucky to be alive,' he was told, but Ruth knew that her dad didn't feel lucky. He felt bitter and angry at not being able to walk unaided any more. She wondered if the soldier who'd be coming to work with her in the rag room would be feeling the same.

She couldn't believe her eyes when she saw the state of the house where the Tate family lived. Houses in the pit rows were lime-washed once a year to stop them from becoming decrepit. But even by pit-row standards, this one was in a perilous state. It was a two-storey cottage, with one window downstairs at the front. The window directly above was smashed, the hole covered with wood to keep the rain out. Each house in the row had its own front garden, where miners grew potatoes and leeks. Some grew flowers in the summer, dahlias and roses to enter in the show at the working men's club. But nothing good grew in the Tates' garden. The soil was choked with weeds, some as tall as Bea. Ruth wondered if the inside of the house would be as uncared for as the garden. She glanced up at the broken bedroom window. The state of the outside of the house didn't fill her with confidence at what, or who, she might find indoors.

'Let me go in first,' Bea said as they walked down the path.

The front door was opened by Jimmy himself. Ruth saw a lecherous grin cross his face when he clapped eyes on Bea. She also saw how quickly it disappeared when he realised that she had arrived with reinforcements.

'What's *she* doing here?' he spat in Ruth's direction.

'She's my sister. She needs to talk to you,' Bea said. 'We both do. It's important.'

Ruth was impressed by the direct way her sister spoke to Jimmy. It was a different side to her, one Ruth didn't see often.

'Well, are you going to invite us in or what?' Bea added.

Jimmy stood to one side and held the door open. As Ruth passed him, she paused and said in a quiet voice, 'I'm watching you, lad. You'd be wise to remember that.'

As she followed Bea into the front room, she took in her surroundings. From the little she could see, the Tates' house was a lot smaller than the pit house the Hardys had lived in. At the end of the short hallway was a tiny scullery. The stairs led off the hallway. No mats covered the bare wood floors. The paintwork was chipped and dirty. And there was a stench like rotten meat. Ruth followed Bea and Jimmy into the front room where there was a table and three mismatched chairs.

'You live here with your mam and dad?' Ruth asked.

'And my two brothers,' Jimmy said insolently. 'Not that it's any of your business.'

'Oh, it is my business if we're to be related,' Ruth said firmly.

Jimmy laughed. 'Related?' He turned to Bea. 'What's she on about?'

Bea laid a hand on her stomach. 'I told her, Jimmy. I had to. I had no choice. My mam and dad know, and Dad says I have to take you home to meet him, or he'll come looking for you.'

Jimmy laughed in her face. 'I hear your dad's a cripple who can't leave the pub.'

Ruth stepped forward. 'Don't you dare say things about our dad,' she hissed. 'If he says he wants to meet you, then the least you can do is get your backside to the Guide Post Inn.'

'I don't have to do anything I don't want to,' Jimmy sneered.

Bea put her hand on his arm. 'Jimmy, please.'

There was a noise in the hallway. Ruth turned to see a thin woman with the same dark hair as Jimmy, and the same haunted look in her eyes. She had sallow skin and her hair was greasy and unkempt. The strong resemblance to Jimmy left Ruth in no doubt as to who she was.

'You must be Connie,' she said. She tried to keep her

voice friendly, but there was nothing friendly about the look in Connie's eyes. 'I'm Bea's older sister, Ruth. We've come for a word with your Jimmy.'

'What do you want with my son?' Connie said. Ruth noticed the slur of her speech.

'Our dad needs to have a word with him about his future with Bea after what's happened between them,' Ruth said.

'A word? What *has* happened? Jimmy?'

Ruth saw Connie and Jimmy exchange a look. Jimmy looked away unable to look his mam in the eye. Connie shook her head as realisation dawned.

'No . . . she's not pregnant, is she? Oh for God's sake, lad!' she yelled. She glared at Bea's small frame, hidden under her black coat. 'Well, you're not showing yet. It can't be too late to get rid of it. Are you trying to trap my Jimmy?'

'Trap him?' Ruth cried. 'It's our Bea who's caught in this. Our Bea who'll lose her job at the mill when they find out.'

She decided to keep quiet about Mrs Pike's threat to throw them out if Bea didn't get married. She didn't want Jimmy or Connie to know how much her family were depending on Jimmy to do the right thing. She knew she had to approach the situation carefully. She looked at Connie again, properly this time. It was clear she was three sheets to the wind. Well, she'd been warned that Connie Tate liked her ale. She felt herself being appraised as Connie greedily eyed her boots, skirt and coat, all the way up to her hat.

'What's your surname, lass?' the woman asked.

'Hardy,' Ruth said. 'We live in the Guide Post Inn.'

Connie let the information sink in. 'Hardy, eh? Are Harry and Jean your mam and dad? I went to school with Harry Hardy.'

'That's him,' Ruth said.

Connie turned her attention to her son. 'Jimmy, get yourself to see Harry, and don't act up when you're there.'

'But Mam, he'll make me marry her, and I don't want—'

Bea gasped. 'But you told me you loved me!' she cried.

'Get your coat, Jimmy,' Ruth said. 'We're going now. Dad's waiting.'

As Jimmy and Bea headed out to the hallway, Ruth could hear bickering, Bea crying and pleading.

'They can't move in here when they're wed, mind. I've no room and no money to feed extra mouths,' Connie said.

Ruth looked around the dirty front room. It wasn't fit for a dog to live in, never mind her sister and a newborn baby.

'They'll have to live with you lot in the pub,' Connie slurred.

There wasn't room at the Guide Post Inn for Jimmy to move in, and even if there was, Ruth would fight against having him there.

'They can live separately, just like they're doing now. But it'll be respectable, at least. She'll be Mrs Tate for appearances' sake. And if she wants Jimmy to stay the night when the baby's born, he'll be welcome. We'll sort something out. You'll be welcome to see the bairn too.'

'Generous of you, I'm sure,' Connie sneered.

Ruth and Bea stepped outside and waited for Jimmy

on the front path. Despite the black, smoky air from the pit, Ruth breathed deeply. It was a damn sight better than the stench in Connie's front room.

Ruth heard raised voices from indoors as Connie scolded her son.

'You stupid boy! How many times have I told you to be careful? You're going to end up married to that stuck-up bitch's little sister, and you haven't got a penny to your name.'

Then a door slammed and Jimmy walked from the house and followed Ruth and Bea to the pub.

Left alone in the house on Railway Street, Connie Tate cracked open another bottle of stout. She shook her head at the thought of Jimmy getting a lass pregnant. But then she thought of the girl and her sister, of the Hardy family, who lived in a pub. They must be worth a bob or two, surely? An evil smile made its way to her lips.

Chapter Eight

Two weeks later, on a cold October day, Bea and Jimmy were married at the register office. Ruth had been unable to secure the day off work despite pleading with Miss Wagstaff, and had to miss the service. Jean was unable to leave her bed, too weak from the illness that racked her body and shook her bones. The Hardy family was represented by Harry. He walked to the register office in Ryhope village, every step an agony for him. But as he told Jean, no matter how painful it was for him to get there, he needed to make sure that Bea was made respectable and Jimmy was called to account. None of the Tate family were at the register office, and Jimmy offered no explanation for their absence.

After the short service ended, Harry collared Jimmy on the path outside. 'I've got my eye on you, lad,' he warned. 'Our Ruth's told me things about you, things she's seen that Bea doesn't know. When the bairn comes, you'll pay your way, you hear? You'll give Bea the money she needs to feed it and look after it.'

Jimmy glanced away and took an unusual interest in the gravel path.

'Look at me when I'm talking to you, lad,' Harry said firmly.

Jimmy slowly raised his eyes to meet his father-in-law's stern face.

'You're a mess, lad. Where's your pride? Now listen, before you come to the Guide Post Inn next time, get your bloody hair cut first, smarten yourself up.'

Jimmy skulked away with Bea at his side, steadfastly refusing her requests to hold her hand. Meanwhile, Harry made his slow, torturous way back to the pub to give Jean the news. He knew she'd be waiting to hear all about it.

When Ruth came home from work, she was disappointed to hear that none of Jimmy's family had turned up for the wedding, though from what she knew of the Tates, she wasn't too surprised. The more she mulled this over, however, the more a thought gripped her.

'Are you sure there was no one there, Dad?' she asked.

'Course I'm sure. I'm not blind,' Harry huffed.

'Lil Mahone wasn't there?'

Lil Mahone was Ryhope's worst gossip.

'I've just told you, there was only me. What's got into you, girl?'

Ruth thought for a moment. 'We can keep quiet about Bea being married for now, you know,' she said. 'It'd mean she can stay on at the mill until she begins to show. I'll talk to her when she comes home from Jimmy's.'

'No, lass, the Hardys don't lie,' Jean said. 'And what about the Tates? Just because they weren't at the wedding doesn't mean they won't know Jimmy's a married man now.'

'We can't starve, Mam, and that's what'll happen if Bea

leaves the mill. We can hardly manage with two wages coming in, never mind one.'

Jean raised her eyes towards her husband. 'Harry? What do you reckon?'

'I don't like telling lies, not one little bit.'

'What choice have we got?' Ruth pleaded. 'The only people who know Bea's a married woman are us lot in here. If we keep quiet, there's no problem. Connie's a drunken lush and Jimmy's brothers and his dad don't care. If they did, they'd have been at the register office today.'

Harry and Jean were silent a long time.

'Look,' Ruth said. 'It's unlikely that news of Bea's wedding will make its way around Ryhope. If it does, and word reaches the mill, we'll face the consequences. Until then, she can continue to work and collect her wages each week until her pregnancy shows.'

Harry sighed. 'It doesn't look like we've got a choice.'

In the coming weeks, autumn turned to winter and a sharp frost set in. Trees on the village green shed their leaves and the sky grew grey and dull. The weather was vicious, sleet blew in sideways and daylight disappeared into dark. Life for the Hardy family carried on as usual, with Ruth eking out a living from the meagre earnings she and Bea made at the mill. Harry grumbled more often in winter than he did during the long summer days.

Bea was often sick in the morning before she walked to work. By the time she and Ruth arrived at the mill after their long walk along the clifftop, she was done in. Ruth's heart went out to her.

'Remember, you're not to say a word about the wedding or the baby at work,' she warned. 'Keep it to yourself.'

'Who is there to tell?' Bea sighed. 'I don't have any friends in the machine room. You know fine well it's just men who work there. None of them give me a second glance. I'm just little Bea with my sweeping brush.'

Ruth glanced at her sister. Bea's black coat hung loosely over her stomach. She didn't look to be carrying a bairn. Not yet, anyway.

'Keep your coat on at work,' Ruth advised. 'You can get away with it for a few more weeks.'

'And then?' Bea said.

They both knew exactly what would happen the minute Bea started showing. She'd have to leave work and then there would be only Ruth's wages to keep the Hardy family fed and warm. It wouldn't be enough. The winter months meant more coal for the fire. Her mam's health had worsened since Bea's wedding, and Ruth wondered if the stress of it all was lying heavily on Jean's mind.

'You can take in sewing at home,' she suggested. 'It won't bring in much, but it'll be something. And it'll give you something to do. Mam'll love to watch you work.'

'And Dad?' Bea said.

'Dad . . .' Ruth sighed. 'Dad is going to have to get used to things. He's still angry at being forced out of our old home. Just make sure he doesn't direct any of that anger at you. If he does, leave him be until he calms down. I'll deal with him when I get home.'

'And Jimmy will come to see me too,' Bea said. 'He's trying to find another job. He'll help with money for coal, I know he will, just as soon as he gets work.'

Ruth wasn't so sure. 'He's looking for another job? What happened to the one he had before?'

'The gaffer laid him off, said he didn't need him any more.'

Ruth had heard rumours around Ryhope, rumours that came into the Guide Post Inn that Harry picked up and passed on. By all accounts, Jimmy had been caught stealing beer bottles from the yard at the Colliery Inn.

'Be careful with Jimmy,' she warned her sister. 'When he comes to see Mam and Dad, tell him to be respectful, and to take his cap off when he comes through the door.'

Bea stopped dead in her tracks. 'You're doing it again, Ruth. Stop it!'

Ruth spun around. 'Stop what?'

'Stop telling me what to do! I know Jimmy's not your cup of tea. I know Dad doesn't like him and I know Mam wants better for me. But he's different when he's with me. You don't know him like I do. He's kind and funny and gentle.'

This didn't sound like the Jimmy Tate that Ruth knew, that was for sure. But there must be some good in the lad if Bea was so determined to protect him. Ruth softened towards her sister when she saw tears in Bea's eyes. She went to put her arm around her shoulders, but Bea stepped away and Ruth's arm dropped to her side.

'I'm a married woman now. You can't talk to me like I'm a little girl any more.'

Ruth swallowed hard. The last thing she wanted was to upset Bea, and it was clear she'd gone too far. She opened her mouth to apologise, but Bea wasn't finished with her yet.

'Things have changed, Ruth. *I've* changed.' Bea put her hands to her stomach. 'I've got this one to think about now. Jimmy will do his best. He'll pay his way with the baby, our dad'll make sure. All Jimmy needs is to find another job.'

Ruth had wondered many times why Jimmy wasn't working down the coal mine with his dad and two brothers. It was hard, dangerous work, but it paid. It would put pennies on the table to feed Bea and Jimmy's bairn.

'There's always jobs at the pit,' she said as they walked.

'He's tried asking there a few times. Says the gaffer doesn't like him or something.'

Ruth wasn't surprised to hear that. She wondered if there was anyone in Ryhope who did like Jimmy Tate, apart from Bea.

They were nearly at the mill yard. Ruth knew they'd have to be careful about what they said when they were in earshot of the workers. The last thing they wanted was for gossip to be spread about Bea's baby.

Just then she felt Bea's small hand slip into hers, and a smile made its way to her face.

'I'll always love you, Ruth. And I'll always be proud to be your sister. But I'm respectable now and you mustn't keep thinking that you know what's best for me. I know what I want. I want my own home, my own family. I've got a baby in my belly and I'm married now, to Jimmy. I know we're not living together as man and wife, but don't you ever forget he's my husband.'

'Bea, please, I'm sorry.'

'Do you know what your problem is, Ruth?'

Ruth was startled at Bea's tone. It was so unlike her sister to challenge her.

'What you need is a fella of your own. A life of your own, outside of the Guide Post Inn.'

She felt her stomach churn. 'And when am I going to meet someone, or have time to spend with them if I did?' she said. 'I've got Mam and Dad to look after, the room to clean, and I'm exhausted after work at the mill.' She shook her head. 'I'm no catch, Bea. Not like you with your fair hair and pretty face. Not like Edie with her confident ways.'

'Stop feeling sorry for yourself,' Bea snapped.

Ruth felt as if she'd been slapped across her face. 'I'm not,' she said.

'Oh you are,' Bea replied. 'You're as pretty as any of the girls at the mill. And you've got something about you, too. Why else did Waggy tell Mr Hewson you could be trusted? She must think a lot of you.'

'And how's any of that going to land me a fella?' Ruth said.

Bea smiled at her. 'Oh Ruth, open your eyes and start looking. What about Mick in the rail yard? He's been interested in you for weeks now, but you've barely given him the time of day.'

'I'm not chasing after him at work,' Ruth said forcefully.

'Then when will you? When will be a good time for love to come calling on you, Ruth Hardy?' Bea crossed her arms across her belly and faced her sister. 'When will you realise that you can't sit around and wait for things to happen to you? If you want something enough, you've got to go and get it. And by *it*, I mean Mick Carson. Let him know how you feel about him.'

Ruth opened her mouth to reply, but couldn't find the words. She knew Bea was right and she snapped her mouth shut.

Ahead of them, the machine room loomed, and their conversation came to an end.

'Come here,' Bea said, and she held her arms open to

Ruth. The sisters hugged warmly, then went their separate ways.

A familiar face was waiting outside the rag room, and Ruth beamed when she saw who it was. She hadn't spoken to Mick since the day he'd given her the leeks. As delighted as she was to see him there, she knew she daren't be late for work for fear of getting another black mark from Miss Wagstaff. As she drew closer, she saw a smile on his face and a sparkle in his eyes. Bea's words were uppermost in her mind, and she was pleased that Mick seemed as happy to see her as she was to see him. The two of them seemed drawn to each other by an invisible force pulling them together. Ruth wanted to put her arms around his neck, to hug him, thank him for turning up to greet her. She wanted to tell him how happy she was to see him again, but all she could do was give him a soppy grin. She hoped she didn't look as gormless as she felt. She took heart from Bea's words about her being as pretty as any of the girls at the mill.

'Leeks all right, were they?' Mick asked.

'Perfect, thank you,' Ruth said. But then quickly she added, 'I can't stop to talk, Mick. I don't want to be late. I have to go in.' Oh, if only time would stand still, she thought.

'Ten seconds, that's all I need,' Mick said.

There was something about the way he was standing, with his arms crossed, that didn't seem right. Ruth wondered if he'd injured himself at work. Underneath his black railwayman's coat, something moved at his chest. Ruth was startled. She stepped back.

'What is that?' she said.

He glanced around to ensure no one was watching. 'Button.'

Ruth was confused. 'A button? On your jacket?'

'No.' He shook his head. 'Button. My dog. I'm not supposed to bring him into work, but he keeps me company in the engine. He loves it. But I have to keep him out of sight of the gaffer. I smuggle him in inside my jacket.'

Ruth stared in astonishment. Two tiny brown ears appeared from under Mick's chin as Button made his way out from the coat. Two round glassy eyes popped up next, followed by a velvety black nose and a mouth with tiny teeth. Ruth thought the dog looked like he was grinning. Button had a thin blue collar around his skinny neck.

'Get back in,' Mick whispered, and the dog dutifully disappeared. The whole scene made Ruth giggle.

'I was just on my way home from shift, but I wanted to see you, Ruth. I wanted to ask you something.'

Ruth cast an anxious glance into the rag room, where the girls were heading to their seats. 'I've got to go, Mick. Waggy'll have my guts for garters.'

Mick coughed nervously and stood up straight. Inside his jacket Button began to whine. 'I was wondering, like . . .' he began hesitantly. 'I was wondering if I could take you out.'

'On a date?' Ruth said, surprised. A million thoughts were whirling in her mind, not least that she'd be getting another black mark against her if she didn't go into the rag room immediately. But then Bea's words from earlier that morning came to her again, telling her that she needed to find a life of her own. Hadn't Edie told her exactly the same thing before, many times?

'Well, yes, I suppose it would be a date,' Mick said.

Ruth glanced shyly at his face and wondered if he was

feeling as nervous as she was. 'I'd like that very much,' she said, then turned and ran into the rag room just as Miss Wagstaff was poised with her black pencil. Was she mistaken, or did the supervisor look disappointed that she wasn't going to be marking Ruth down?

Ruth slid on to her seat between Edie and Jane. As she did so, Jane moaned softly and shifted a few inches along the bench.

'Do you need more space?' Ruth asked. 'I can ask Edie to shuffle the other way.'

Jane shook her head. 'No, it's all right.'

Ruth glanced at her friend's ashen face and noticed how thin and pale she was looking.

'Me and Edie are going for a walk at dinner time,' she said. 'Want to come?'

Jane concentrated on the work in front of her, avoiding Ruth's eyes. 'I'd better not,' she said. 'Davey doesn't like me leaving the rag room at dinner time.'

'What's it got to do with him?' Ruth demanded.

'Girls!' Miss Wagstaff yelled. 'Let's have less chatting and more work! Please!'

Ruth playfully nudged Jane in the ribs as they returned to their work. But when she did so, Jane gasped. Ruth shot her a look, but Jane said nothing more under Miss Wagstaff's steely gaze.

Each morning after that, when Ruth arrived at work, Mick was waiting at the rag room door. He brought gifts for her too. One day there was a bag of potatoes from his dad's garden. Another day he brought more leeks. Ruth was grateful for his support and found herself looking forward to seeing him. It was during one of their morning chats that they arranged their first date for Sunday, Ruth's next day off. Mick was working the morning shift that day and they agreed to meet at the mill in the afternoon. He promised her a ride on the steam engine from the mill to the docks. He even offered to show her around the port, where he spent much of his working day.

When Sunday came around, Ruth woke with a happy heart. She was excited about the day ahead and eager to see Mick. Each time she thought of him, it was his polite ways that came to mind, how courteous and kind he was. And as for that comic little dog he carried inside his jacket, it just made him seem even more friendly. She was curious to know more about him, about his family and where he lived.

Sundays at the Guide Post Inn were always a quiet affair, as the Hardys weren't a religious family and there was no need to head out to church. Ruth's day off usually meant doing chores at home, seeing to her mam and placating her dad. Rarely did it coincide with Bea's, so the girls took it in turns to sit with their parents. On this particular Sunday, Ruth had a spring in her step and it didn't go unnoticed by Harry and Jean. She'd already told them about Mick – well, she'd had to explain where the vegetables were coming from. Bringing home an armful of fresh leeks or a bag of potatoes pulled that day from the soil didn't go unnoticed in the room the Hardys shared. Besides, she'd never kept anything from her mam and dad before.

She prepared cold meat for them all, brought in coal from the yard and made sure her mam was settled.

'You'll bring this lad home to meet us soon, Ruth, won't you?' Jean asked.

'She'd bloody better,' Harry growled. 'We don't want her ending up in the family way like our Bea.'

'Dad!' Ruth admonished. She turned her head away, her face burning with embarrassment. She'd not so much as held hands with Mick Carson, never mind anything else. Well, today might be the day when they'd hold hands for the first time. The thought of it made her smile.

'Seems a shame to be heading back to the mill to go on a date,' Jean said as Ruth prepared to leave.

Ruth didn't see it like that. 'Seems fitting to me, since the mill is where we met.'

She kissed her mam on her cheek. Weak winter sunshine filtered through the window that looked out to the pub's yard. She kissed her dad too.

'Watch what you're doing,' Harry warned.

Jean tutted loudly. 'You can trust our Ruth to behave herself, Harry. She's a grown lass, leave her be.'

Ruth headed out of the pub and walked towards Ryhope village green. From there, she began the long trek to the mill. It was another cold day; winter had gripped Ryhope with force, and she pulled her collar up. The wind rustled the leaves still clinging to the trees. She had walked the same route for years, since her first day at the mill. But this was the first time she'd walked it not to go to work, but for a very different purpose. Beyond the fields was the sea, grey under the winter sky. Trams trundled by, but Ruth didn't have money to spare for a ticket.

After ten minutes' walk along Ryhope Road, she reached the Toll Bar hotel. It marked the spot where a toll gate had once stood, in the days long before Ruth was born. The hotel had a fearsome reputation, and word had spread that bare-knuckle fights took place on a patch of rough ground at the back. Ruth walked quickly past. Beyond the hotel, the landscape changed, with furrowed rows of farmers' fields. On Ruth's left was Ryhope Grange, with its farm buildings and fields, and then Grangetown cemetery appeared. Angels carved in stone stood guard.

On past the mission room she walked, until she reached Ocean Road, where she turned right to head to the sea. Another pub, the Hendon Grange, with its domed roof, lay ahead. It was a large pub, a drinking palace for the paper-mill men and twice the size of the Guide Post Inn. It was solid-looking and grand. She carried on past the pub to the clifftops, passing the reservoir. She could smell the mill before she could see it. Smoke belched from its tall chimneys.

In the mill yard was an enormous white-faced clock. Sturdy black iron hands ticked away time. Ruth was early; she and Mick had planned to meet on the hour, and it was still just a quarter to. Walking to the machine room to check on Bea, she stood at the door, scanning the vast room for her sister, but Bea was nowhere to be seen.

She walked slowly to the rail sidings at the back of the mill. Here the paper mill's railway merged with the North East Railway's Sunderland to Hartlepool line. She heard a shout and saw Mick walking towards her with his arms crossed. She saw the familiar squirming as Button made his way up and out of his jacket.

'Ready for a ride to the docks? I'm all set to take the Hylton engine back, then I can clock off, have a quick wash in the railwaymen's executive bathroom and I'm all yours for the rest of the day.'

Ruth gasped. 'Is there really an executive bathroom?'

'It's a quick rinse with a flannel in the office at the docks, if I'm lucky,' he laughed.

She felt heat rush to her face at her ignorance. She knew little about the mill outside of the rooms she'd worked in.

Mick shifted the small dog inside his jacket. 'We'll walk Button as soon as we get there. Stop wriggling, lad.' He gently pushed Button's head down inside his jacket and turned to Ruth.

'Come on, Hylton's just over here. She's a smart little engine. You'll enjoy the ride, I hope.'

It was only a short trip to the docks from the mill. So short that Ruth could see the industry of the docks along the coast before they even set off. In the railway sidings a dark green engine was steaming and ready to go. A thickset man in a dark uniform and cap waved to Mick.

'She's all yours, Mick. Good to go,' he called.

'Cheers, Bob!' Mick replied.

He held his hand out to Ruth to help her up on to the footplate. There wasn't a lot of space, and the two of them had to stand close together, which Ruth found she enjoyed. She felt safe with Mick, content. And boy, was this an adventure, her first time on a train and riding in the engine! The heat was like nothing she had felt before, with the fire burning right in front of her.

'All aboard, ready to go,' Mick called.

Slowly, carefully, the engine inched its way from the siding. Ruth's heart sped up as the train hissed and screeched from the mill to the main railway line.

'Hold on tight,' Mick warned.

She grabbed hold of a metal ring attached to the door

at her side. The train rattled and jerked as it joined the main line, and she felt her heart flutter with fear. Was it about to leap off the rails? It certainly felt that way. But one look at Mick and she felt safe again. Everything was under control; he knew what he was doing. The train ran along the clifftop, smoke billowing, filling the air with the dark scent of burnt coal. It was an exhilarating ride, thrilling for Ruth, and it was over much too soon. The docks appeared quickly, a maze of tall buildings, warehouses and ships, and oh, the noise! Men shouting, calling to each other, unloading boxes from ships to be taken to Sunderland's paper mill, shipyards, glassworks and mines. It was a different world to anything Ruth had ever experienced. A heavy smell of oil was in the air, not a smell she liked, and she put her hand to her nose.

'You get used to it after a while,' Mick said.

He brought the train to a dead stop, leapt from the footplate and held his hand out to help her down. Three men walking past caught sight of them and began teasing Mick about his 'lady friend'.

'Ignore them, they're not used to seeing women down here,' Mick said. 'I've to drop off my paperwork, but I'll not be gone long, ten minutes at most.'

He loosened the buttons on his coat and lifted Button out, handing the tiny dog to Ruth. 'Would you mind taking him? I can't let the gaffer see him.'

Ruth took the dog, surprised at how light he was. Button cocked his head to one side and eyed her suspiciously.

'Stroke him under his chin, he loves that,' Mick said.

Ruth did as instructed, and Button's tail wagged like mad.

'Here,' Mick said. He handed Ruth a length of rope. 'Use this for a leash.'

Ruth fastened the rope loosely, but the dog strained at it when Mick disappeared into a warehouse. Ruth stood with her back pressed against a wall and watched the industry around her. This was heavy work, men's work, cranes unloading cargo from ships. But the noise and smell of it all! She didn't think she could get used to it. Thank heavens for the quiet and calm of the rag room. She wouldn't trade places with any man working at the docks.

There was shouting to one side, and she was horrified to see two men arguing, yelling and swearing. One man was using the worst words she had ever heard, his temper flaring. She saw he had a wooden crutch held tight in his armpit to keep himself upright. He had his back to her, so she couldn't see his face, but she could hear his fury. Men working around them stopped what they were doing and watched as the argument continued. Some hollered and jeered; others egged the fighters on. Ruth pressed her back further into the wall and Button began to shake. She picked the tiny dog up – he was no bigger than the coal bucket at home – and tried to calm him as the fight became louder and then Ruth watched in horror at what happened next. The man with the crutch hopped on to his good leg, let the crutch drop from his armpit, then picked it up with both hands and crashed it down on the head of the other fella, striking him hard, over and over again.

'Hey, get off him!' men called as they piled in to help. Mick came running from the warehouse. Ruth watched as he dived straight into the fray and grabbed the crutch. The fella let rip with a stream of words so vicious that she buried her face against Button's furry head. The man was whippet-thin, wiry, but it still took Mick and a much bigger fella to pull him away from the fight. Ruth looked up and flinched when she saw his face. A red-raw scar ran under his right eye.

Ruth and Mick's afternoon together started dramatically with the fight by the docks. But once they escaped the noise and stench they walked to Hendon beach. It was too cold to sit on the sands, even in the shelter of the rocks where Ruth and Edie sat at dinner time. Ruth shivered as they walked. She gathered her thin jacket around her and pulled her hat down on her head.

Mick offered his arm in a gesture of friendship. Ruth had walked arm in arm with Edie before, with Jane and with Bea. She'd walked arm in arm with her mam before Jean had taken poorly. But she'd never walked that way with a boy. She hesitated for a second before she took his arm. She felt the warmth from his body as they walked on the black sand. Button scampered at their feet, barking at the waves and running to Ruth and Mick when the waves threatened to catch him.

'Is he a Yorkshire terrier?'

'He's a bit of a mix-up,' Mick replied. 'He's half Yorkie and half something else, I've never been sure what. He's a lovely little fella. Keeps me company at work and sees off the rats at home.'

Ruth wrinkled her nose. 'Rats?' It wasn't a problem they suffered with at the Guide Post Inn. But the unkempt garden at Railway Street where the Tate family lived flashed through her mind.

'Dad sees them in the garden sometimes. He's a stickler

for his garden, as Grandad Stan was before him. My grandad worked at the paper mill, you know.'

'As a train driver, like you?'

Mick shook his head. 'He was a papermaker. This was back in the days before the machines came in, when the paper was still made by hand.'

'I can't imagine how hard that must have been,' Ruth said.

'Strange thing is, he loved it. He still enjoys telling stories about getting his hands in the pulp and turning it, running it through his fingers. Then he'd lay big sheets of it on the press to get the water out before hanging the sheets to dry. I feel connected to him, you know, every day at work. The warehouse at the mill where I deliver the grass from the docks is the same building that Grandad worked in.'

Ruth was intrigued. She'd heard of men making paper by hand, but this was the first time she'd talked to someone who knew how the process worked.

'The top floor, where Grandad worked, is just storage now, though, old boxes and a paper press they don't use any more.'

'You've been in there?' Ruth asked.

'Couldn't resist a look. And when Grandad wasn't at work, he was in his garden. Guess my dad's taken over from him with his talent there. Dad grows all kinds of vegetables. You should come and see it sometime.'

Ruth turned to smile at him. Was this an invitation to meet his parents? To visit his family, his home? She was relieved that he seemed to like her as much as she liked him.

* * *

The date ended with a polite handshake, which left Ruth surprised and disappointed. She'd wondered if they might share a kiss. She would have accepted Mick's lips on hers; she knew she was ready. When she was with him, emotions she'd never experienced before flooded her body and mind. She found herself thinking about him when she was at home with her family. And as the weeks turned towards Christmas and she spent more of her free time with him, Harry insisted she should bring him home.

On the last Saturday before Christmas, Ruth met Mick at the village green. He had brought Christmas gifts with him: a fat stalk of juicy, sweet sprouts from his dad's garden. When they reached the Guide Post Inn, Ruth took hold of his hand. Harry was in his chair by the fire, reading the *Sunderland Echo*, and Jean was propped up in bed. Bea and Jimmy were there too, together on the sofa, although Jimmy looked as if he wanted to be somewhere else.

'Mam, Dad, this is Mick, the lad I've been telling you about,' Ruth said proudly.

Mick whipped off his cap and strode towards Harry. 'It's good to meet you, sir,' he said.

Ruth watched as he shook hands with her dad. She saw the way her dad gave him the once-over, taking in everything from his shoes all the way up to his dark eyes and hair. Then Mick greeted Jean with a polite handshake too. He even tried to get a conversation going with Jimmy, though he didn't make much progress, with Jimmy grunting rudely in reply to his questions.

Ruth and Bea served a tea of beef sandwiches with pickled onions. It was a cosy night with everyone around the fire, talking happily together. Mick slotted right in, as if he'd always known the Hardy family, as if he'd always been a part of Ruth's life. And later that evening, when the Saturday-night singer started up in the pub, he asked Harry's permission to take her for a drink.

At the end of the night, Ruth went with Mick to the tram stop. They walked hand in hand, happy and proud to show each other off.

'I've met your mam and dad and now I've been for tea. I suppose this means we're courting,' Mick said when they reached the stop.

'I suppose we are,' Ruth replied coyly.

She stepped closer to him and he slipped his arm around her waist. She turned her face to Mick, brought her lips close to his and they kissed for a very long time.

The next morning, Ruth was still floating on air. She and Bea made their way to work in the frosty morning. Bea wanted to know all about Mick, buzzing with questions that Ruth was happy to answer. When they reached the mill, she kissed Bea goodbye and headed to the rag room. But the minute she stepped inside, she knew that something was wrong. A man stood beside Miss Wagstaff.

'Miss Hardy,' Miss Wagstaff said firmly. 'This is Mr Hepple, the gentleman Mr Hewson spoke to you about. You will show him how the rag room operates.'

Ruth recognised the man immediately and her stomach filled with dread. She knew exactly where she'd seen him before. He was a thin, wiry man with a wooden crutch under one arm and a deep, raw scar on his face.

Chapter Nine

John Hepple was not an easy man to get along with. However, Ruth didn't have any choice but to do as she'd been told and show him how the rag room worked. Her instructions had come from the mill owner himself.

In the first few weeks of working together, she was wary of him. What if he turned violent against her or the girls? Plus, it was unheard of to have a man working in the rag room, never mind a wounded ex-soldier. His presence proved unsettling, and it was Ruth's job to keep the gossip down. But just as Bea had warned, it was easier said than done. The girls stared at the scar under his eye, a war wound they supposed. John was sullen and quiet when he worked. Ruth had a quiet word with Miss Wagstaff one day and suggested that she move him to the end of a bench so that getting into his seat was easier for him with his crutch. Miss Wagstaff agreed, even thanked Ruth for her suggestion, and John was moved. But if he was grateful for this, he never said thank you to anyone. Ruth tried to engage him in conversation, but he wasn't interested in small talk. He didn't even answer her cheery 'Good morning!' when he came into work each day. He was moody, as if a quiet anger seethed through him. Ruth wondered what he made of working with the girls, but he never said a word. She sensed his pride had been hit hard.

Once he'd got the hang of tearing and ripping rags, slicing hems open and cutting them through, Ruth left him to his work. She no longer felt she had to try to make conversation. But the atmosphere in the rag room changed. Even Miss Wagstaff seemed on edge having a man there. Ruth confided in Mick, told him that John was the same fella he'd had to pull from the fight at the docks. Mick warned her to take care, as if Ruth wasn't already aware how dangerous John could be.

Ruth and Mick continued meeting daily. Mick would be waiting each morning by the rag room door for her to arrive and would greet her with a kiss. By now, their courting was a topic of gossip at the mill, their relationship out in the open. No one was surprised to see them chatting or sharing a hug. Meanwhile, at home in the room at the Guide Post Inn, the bitter cold of winter did its worst. Jean suffered greatly and her coughing kept all the Hardys awake.

As winter began to release its icy grip and the weeks gave way to spring, Jimmy was rarely seen and Bea was too sick, too exhausted to go chasing after him. She called at the Tates' house a few times on her way home from work, but he was never there, or so Connie told her when she asked. And when her pregnancy could no longer be hidden, she had no choice but to leave the mill. Her wages stopped the day she left work. The only money coming in now was Ruth's wages, and every penny was spent on food and coal. Ruth approached Mrs Pike one day to ask if there was any cleaning work going that Bea could do, but the landlady shook her head.

'Not in her condition,' Mrs Pike said firmly. 'Not when she's carrying a bairn. And speaking of which, when's it due?'

'May,' Ruth replied.

Mrs Pike tapped her fingers against the bar. 'Aye, well, you'd better think about what you're going to do when it comes. I can't have a screaming bairn putting my customers off their beer.'

'Babies cry, Mrs Pike. What are we supposed to do?'

'There was never anything in our agreement when you moved in about a baby living in that back room. The walls are thick in this old place, but not so thick that a crying bairn won't be heard in the lounge. It'll be bad for business.'

Ruth tried to keep her tone even. She was angry with Mrs Pike, but knew she'd have to play things carefully. 'Are you saying you'd throw us out?'

'Of course not,' Mrs Pike replied. 'What do you take me for? Me? Put a newborn bairn out on the street? That'd be cruel, that would.'

'Then what *are* you saying?'

'I'm saying we'll have to come to some agreement with the rent. Extra noise from the back room might need extra money if you want me to turn a deaf ear to what's going on.'

Ruth stared at her. 'You're a hard woman. You know how we're fixed now Bea's out of work. We're worse off than ever. Dad can't return to the pit and Mam won't recover. When Bea's baby comes, we'll have an extra mouth to feed. How are we supposed to pay you more rent?'

'Bea's married, isn't she? Get her in-laws to pay. The Tate lads are all working.'

Ruth wondered how far she could push her luck. She

looked around the bar where she and the landlady stood. Each night the pub was full of miners and farmers coming in after work. When the Saturday-night singers were on, the place was packed out. No, Mrs Pike didn't need more rent from them. She was being greedy, that was all. Her pub was a gold mine. Ruth decided to carry on.

'You know Jimmy Tate isn't working. All of Ryhope knows the lad can't hold a job down,' she said. 'We'll not be relying on the Tates for money, Mrs Pike. But I was hoping we could rely on you for the kindness everyone respects you for.'

Ruth saw a twitch appear at the corner of the landlady's mouth. The stern set of her face changed, just briefly, and she sighed heavily. And in that moment, Ruth knew she'd won this little war.

'We'll see how it goes,' Mrs Pike said with a resigned air. 'But consider this a warning, Ruth.'

After Bea left the mill, life for Ruth became even busier. Bea's pregnancy made her ill, drained her of energy. She was laid up in bed with nausea. Ruth began to dread walking in through the door. Her mam was getting worse. Bea was either too weak or too sick to help with the chores. And as for Harry, the whole situation was becoming unbearable for him, spending his days in the same room as two women who were ill. Ruth knew that he was suffering. He was barely able to watch as the love of his life wasted away in front of his eyes. And there was his daughter, growing larger every day with the baby of her good-for-nothing husband.

The back room at the pub was turning into an unpleasant place to be. When Ruth returned home exhausted after long hours at the mill working alongside John's seething anger, her day turned from bad to worse. The stench of Bea's vomit filled the air. Jean's bedpan needed emptying. Harry's resentment and bitterness had left him a shell of himself. He was often in tears when he wasn't asleep. It was becoming impossible for Ruth to keep herself cheerful. She went from Bea to her mam to her dad, caring for them, wiping up after them, cooking and feeding them. She wondered if this was all there would ever be. Maybe when the baby was born things would be different, better somehow. But hanging over Ruth's head were Mrs Pike's words about the noise of the newborn's cries. Life in the pub was so demanding and draining both physically and mentally that it was almost a relief to leave each morning for the mill. At least there she had Mick to talk to.

The burden of looking after her family began to take its toll. She complained bitterly to Mick outside the rag room door each morning. At first he would hold her in his arms, comfort her and tell her everything would be all right. But with each passing day, a distance began to creep in between them. Ruth was so wrapped up in her own life, that of looking after the Hardys, that all her talk was of the Guide Post Inn. If she wasn't telling Mick how anxious she felt about the outstanding rent owed to Mrs Pike, she was worrying about Bea and her mam, or asking for advice on her dad. She didn't notice Mick's sighs or his eyes glazing over as he hugged and kissed her. She didn't realise that not once had she thought to ask him how *he* was and what was going on in his life. She was obsessed with doing the right thing for Bea, for her mam and dad, but not, it seemed, for Mick. Ruth couldn't see what was happening, but Mick felt it keenly. When her exhaustion became too much to bear, she began cancelling her dates with him. She couldn't even spare the time to speak to him at the rag room door any more. She tried to get to work early so that she and Mick had time to talk. But when the sleepless nights caught up with her, it was all she could do to get herself to work before Waggy rang her bell.

'Is there anything I can do to make things easier for you?' Mick asked.

Ruth shook her head. 'I can't ask you for help with my family; it'd be unfair. They're my responsibility.'

'You're not asking, I'm offering,' he said.

But she couldn't let him help, not with her mam and Bea. There were things she did for her mam – washing her, brushing her hair – that only another woman could do. And as for Bea, Ruth couldn't expect him to soothe her sister's fevered brow when the nausea came on her. But there was one thing that ran through her mind, and she wondered if she dared ask him. It would mean they'd miss yet another date and a chance to spend time together. But she needed assistance and he'd offered and she had no one else. She decided to take the plunge. If she didn't ask, she'd never know and as her mam often said, 'shy bairns get nowt'.

'There is something you can do, if you're sure.'

'Course I'm sure. I wouldn't have offered otherwise.'

'Could you take my dad for a drink?' she asked. 'The money you'd spend taking me to the pictures tonight, use it to keep Dad company instead. Take him to the pub for an hour or two. That way I'll be able to see to Mam and Bea. I'll get hot water boiled on the fire to give Mam a bath.'

She studied Mick's face carefully as her request sank in. She knew she was asking a big favour of him, perhaps more than he'd expected. She was asking him to become involved in the domestic life of her family when all he wanted to do was take her to the cinema, or out for a walk. She looked for signs of disappointment in his rugged face and dark eyes, but saw nothing that gave her cause for concern. Not then, anyway.

'Of course I'll take your dad to the pub,' he said. 'It'll give me a chance to get to know him better. We'll have a good chat.'

'And you don't mind missing out on our date? I won't have time to say more than hello and goodbye when you call in to collect him.'

Mick sighed deeply. Then he took Ruth's hands in his and kissed her lightly on the lips. 'You're an angel, Ruth Hardy. You know that? You care for everyone else and take nothing for yourself. I don't know how you do it.' And with that, he turned and walked to the rail sidings.

Ruth watched him go. How she longed for him to return and fling his arms around her. She craved reassurance that she was doing her best and that things would get better some day. Mick had called her an angel, but she knew she was no heavenly spirit. She was flesh and blood and needed to be looked after, cared for and loved just as she cared for others. And yet there she was, lonely and cold, standing outside the rag room, with Waggy and sinister John Hepple waiting for her inside. Her back and shoulders were already aching and she hadn't even begun her day's work. She sank to the ground and buried her face in her hands, and cried tears that had threatened for weeks.

Chapter Ten

Ruth struggled on. At home, Bea managed to take in sewing work, but it earned little more than pennies. She was no seamstress, and even with Jean's guidance, progress was slow. Money coming in was reduced to a trickle. Ruth was forced to ask Mrs Pike if she could wait for the rent, and offered Bea's help for free, washing glasses and pots in the bar. Mrs Pike agreed as long as the heavily pregnant girl stayed out of sight of her customers.

Jimmy called into the Guide Post Inn only once to see Bea, while Ruth was at work. Harry told her about his visit when she returned home.

'He just sat in the chair, took a cup of tea Bea offered him and barely spoke a word. Not once did he even ask our Bea how she was.'

'Is he working?' Ruth asked.

'Said something about being laid off after the gaffer took a dislike to him.'

Typical, thought Ruth.

As the days went on, Bea reluctantly gave up on any future with Jimmy. When his name was mentioned, Jean shook her head woefully and Harry thumped his fist on his chair. It was a scene Ruth observed many times.

'If I had the energy in me, I'd get myself down to Railway Street and drag that lad up here by his bloody hair!' Harry growled.

'No, Dad, leave him be,' Bea said. 'He's shown his true colours. He's let me down badly. I've been a stupid fool for ever thinking he might love me.'

'Love?' Harry snorted. 'You don't know the meaning of the word, lass.'

'Dad, listen,' Bea pleaded. 'If Jimmy doesn't want me and his child, we'll go it alone.'

'Don't be so bloody heroic!' Harry yelled. 'Where's the money to feed your bairn going to come from?'

'I'll go back to work as soon as I can,' she said.

Ruth kept quiet. Both she and Bea knew full well that it would be impossible to leave the baby at home with her mam and dad. Her mam was too ill and her dad didn't have the first clue about looking after a baby. They certainly couldn't ask Mrs Pike, and they knew no one else. Even if they found a woman to look after the baby while Ruth and Bea worked, she'd want paying, and there wasn't any spare cash.

In their bed at night, Ruth clung to the mattress as Bea tossed and turned. While their parents slept, the sisters whispered about what they would do when the baby arrived. An idea had been forming in Ruth's mind for some time. She decided to tell Bea.

'You don't have to keep it, you know,' she said. She was grateful for the dark, for she didn't want to see Bea's face as her words sank in. She could imagine it, though;

she knew Bea would be horrified. Still, desperate times called for desperate measures.

'What are you saying? You know I'm too far gone to get rid of it.'

'That's not what I mean, Bea,' Ruth said. 'There's women in Hendon, down by the market, who buy and sell bairns.' She reached for Bea's hand. Bea snatched it away.

'Never,' she hissed. 'I couldn't. It's part of me, Ruth.'

'Then what about Jimmy's mam? Couldn't she look after it?' But even as the words left Ruth's lips, she knew she'd never allow drunk, unstable Connie to be left alone with Bea's baby.

Bea shook her head, and so Ruth tried again, desperately trying to think of someone who might look after the child.

'Have any of Jimmy's brothers got a girlfriend from a decent family we could ask?'

'They're all single lads and big drinkers, just like their mam.'

Ruth heard Bea gasp.

'What's the matter?'

'Oh . . . it's moving. Ruth, it's moving!'

She felt Bea take her hand and place it gently on top of her swollen belly. She could feel the baby moving under her sister's skin.

'Can you feel it?' Bea asked.

Ruth couldn't speak. She couldn't get her words out in the joy and the shock of the moment.

'Well, can you?'

She felt tears prick her eyes. She swallowed hard. 'Yes, I can feel it. It's kicking!' she said at last.

'Now you know why I can't get rid of it, Ruth. I can't sell it. Tell me you'll never ask me again.'

Ruth kept her hand on Bea's stomach, feeling the flutter each time the baby moved. It was right there, under her hand, a new life breathing and moving. She wondered if this was as close to motherhood as she would ever come. For when would she ever get married or have her own bairns when her life was spent caring for her mam and dad? She thought of Mick and wondered if they might have a future together. Might she one day carry Mick's child? The thought seemed ludicrous, nothing more than a silly dream, and it disappeared as quickly as it had arrived.

'Tell me, Ruth,' Bea begged. 'Tell me you'll never again talk about selling my baby.'

Ruth closed her eyes tight and slid her hand away. 'I promise with all my heart.'

Chapter Eleven

Through the spring weeks of March and April, the weather turned brighter, the days longer. Even Harry perked up a little in the room at the back of the pub. When Ruth walked to the mill, she passed hedgerows where bright yellow daffodils poked through the mud. She had seen less of Mick in the last few weeks. She kept looking for him at the mill, hoping to spot him in the yard, but their paths, which once used to cross often, barely brought them into contact any more.

'You need to watch out, he'll think you're taking him for granted,' Edie warned Ruth as they ate their dinner on the black sands at Hendon.

'I think he's avoiding me. He never comes to the rag room any more,' Ruth said.

'Then you need to go and find him, make him feel special, as if he's the only man in the world.'

'And how am I supposed to do that with my mam and dad to look after and Bea's baby on its way? Food doesn't put itself on the table. You know I've got responsibilities at home. I can't leave them to look after themselves,' Ruth answered firmly.

She saw a look cross Edie's face, one she hadn't seen before. She was taken aback when Edie laid her sandwich down, crossed her arms and began to speak in measured tones.

'Now listen! How many times have I told you to get your own life? Bea could've helped out with your mam and dad much more than she ever did.'

'But she's pregnant . . .' Ruth protested.

'Pregnant? My mam's constantly pregnant! As soon as she pops one bairn out, she's got another in the oven warming up. And she still works scrubbing doorsteps for money, pregnant or not.'

'But Bea's weak, you don't understand,' Ruth said. She thought of how sick Bea had been throughout her pregnancy. Jimmy Tate had a lot to answer for. And no one had seen hide nor hair of him in weeks. The last Ruth had heard was that he'd been chased out of Ryhope by a couple of fellas after he'd borrowed money from them and not paid them back.

'What I'm saying, Ruth, is that you've been given a chance with Mick. He's a lovely fella and he thinks the world of you. He could be the making of you. Just what you need to take you out of yourself and live a bit. Go to the pictures with him, go dancing; just give yourself a break from looking after other people for a change. It's time to look after yourself.'

'But—' Ruth began.

Edie placed a finger on Ruth's lips. 'No buts. He's a nice lad, Mick Carson. You'd best do something soon, because he won't stick around if you're ignoring him. Just you mark my words.'

Ruth gazed out to sea. She could feel Edie staring

right at her.

'Have you met his mam and dad yet?' Edie asked.

Ruth shook her head. 'He sort of invited me to see his dad's garden, ages ago, but he never asked me again.'

'And you haven't pushed him on it? He's been to your house and met your family. What's so wrong with you meeting his?'

Ruth was about to speak, but Edie continued. 'Oh I know, don't tell me . . . you didn't want to leave your mam and dad and Bea?'

Ruth nodded. 'Exactly.'

'You've made a rod for your own back, Ruth,' Edie said harshly. 'They're taking the mickey, the lot of them; they've been treating you like a skivvy for years.'

Ruth scrambled to her feet and brushed the black sand from her skirt. She stared down at Edie, furious.

'That's my family you're talking about,' she hissed. 'How dare you? How bloody dare you say that about them?'

'Ruth, please,' Edie cried.

Ruth stormed away from her friend, heading back to the rag room with tears in her eyes. It was all getting too much. Edie was only trying to be kind, but there was a truth in her words that had been hard to hear. She loved her family and would do anything for them, but she knew she'd been doing too much. Yet she'd kept going willingly. Her family relied on her wholly, waiting at home for her to come in and start cooking and cleaning. But what else could she do? Her dad was wounded, with his bad leg and dark moods. Her mam spent her day in bed, unable to move from the pain that racked her body. And Bea, sweet little Bea with a bairn in her belly, was weak and sick and . . .

'Ruth! Wait!'

Ruth turned to see Edie running to catch up with her.

'I'm sorry,' Edie said. 'I went too far and said too much. My big fat mouth's always getting me into trouble.'

Ruth wrapped her arms around her friend and the girls hugged tight. She looked deep into Edie's eyes.

'You're right, Edie. I know I need to spread my wings and live my own life. But you know how I'm fixed. I can't just up and leave them at home. They need me.'

She linked her arm through Edie's and they headed to the rag room together.

'Mick Carson needs you too. Your friends need you,' Edie said. She nodded towards the rag room door. 'Him in there, the odd-bod soldier with the scarred face. He needs you.'

'He does not,' Ruth laughed.

'And Waggy, she needs you.'

The two girls dissolved into giggles.

Just then Ruth caught sight of the mill owner in the yard. It was his suit she recognised first, the light grey jacket with matching waistcoat and patterned tie. In the lapel of his jacket was a vibrant yellow rose. Once again she thought how odd it was for a rose to bloom out of season. And then she noticed a well-dressed young woman at his side. The girl was no mill worker, she could tell that immediately by the cut of her clothes and her delicate, clear skin.

Ruth stiffened when Mr Hewson began striding towards her with the young woman in his wake.

'You all right?' Edie asked. 'You look like you've seen a ghost.'

Mr Hewson greeted Ruth with a smile. 'Why, it's Miss Hardy, isn't it?'

'See, even the mill owner needs you,' Edie said under her breath, before disappearing into the rag room, leaving Ruth on her own.

'Yes, sir,' Ruth said shyly. She glanced at the young woman at Mr Hewson's side. She was wearing a hat, the type Ruth only ever saw Ryhope women wearing for weddings or Easter Sunday service at St Paul's church. It was wide-brimmed, in a delicate blue, with a navy ribbon around. Her long, thick dark hair was tucked up underneath. She wore a pale blue jacket over her skirt and a silver chain with a daisy pendant at her neck. Ruth was relieved to see her smile. If she had been forced to guess, she would have said the girl was about the same age as herself, perhaps a year or two older. She was surprised when she thrust out her hand.

'Sarah Hewson, pleased to meet you. Father's told me a lot about you, Miss Hardy. I understand you're helping a family friend of ours in the rag room.'

So the girl was the mill owner's daughter, Ruth thought. She could see the resemblance. Both of them were tall and slim, with kind, open faces. She took Sarah's hand and was surprised by the strength in her handshake.

'Father's giving me a guided tour of his mill,' Sarah said proudly. 'Would you care to show me the rag room, Miss Hardy? I'd like it very much if you would.'

'Me, miss?' Ruth said, surprised. Surely a duty like this should fall to Waggy, who was the supervisor there after all. She turned to face Mr Hewson. 'Sir? What about Miss Wagstaff?'

'Just leave Eleanor to me, Miss Hardy. Now, if you'd

like to lead the way . . . I'm showing my daughter the papermaking process from beginning to end. What better way to begin than at the point where raw materials are brought in. We're off to see the esparto grass warehouse next.'

Ruth's heart leapt into her mouth as she turned towards the rag room. In all the years she'd worked at the mill, she'd never known Miss Wagstaff's first name. Well, just wait until she told Edie and Jane! She felt nervous walking into the room with the mill owner. Having his daughter with her made her more nervous still. She clocked Miss Wagstaff's face when she caught sight of the three of them, and oh, it was a picture! Miss Wagstaff's jaw dropped before she leapt from her seat, rushed over to Mr Hewson and shook his hand.

'Sir, what an honour,' she said.

As Ruth watched, all she could think was that the woman she had always known as Waggy, Miss Wagstaff, had a first name. Eleanor. It made her seem human, almost.

All eyes in the room turned to Mr Hewson and his daughter. He introduced himself to those in the room who didn't yet know who he was, and then introduced his daughter. No fuss was made of John Hepple; not even a mention or a special hello. But that was exactly how Mr Hewson had wanted it, Ruth recalled, when he'd first told her that a man would be joining the rag room. There was to be no special treatment, no gossip or fuss. Still, the whole experience left her feeling odd. She caught Edie glaring at her and knew her friend would be dying to know what was going on.

Miss Wagstaff began explaining to Sarah how the rag

room operated. Just as she was getting into her stride, Mr Hewson chipped in to bring Ruth into the conversation and encourage her to take over. Ruth saw the look that clouded Miss Wagstaff's face, but knew she couldn't refuse a request from the mill owner, no matter how much she would suffer Miss Wagstaff's sharp words later. She told Sarah about the rag and bone men with their horse and carts who came to the door selling rags. She told her about the sorting machine, about loose buttons and hems having to be ripped on the bench with sharp knives. She didn't have to tell her about the stench in the room. It was obvious enough, although Sarah never once put her hand to her nose. Neither did she mention how backbreaking the work was, how repetitive and dull. She kept quiet about how cold the room was in winter, so cold that fingers turned blue. She also made no mention of the air, thick with dust that made its way into the girls' lungs with every breath they took. If they stayed in the rag room at dinner time and ate bread or pie brought from home, every bite, every mouthful would carry particles of dirt and hair.

She watched as Sarah glanced around the room, taking it all in. John Hepple kept his eyes on his work and didn't look up to acknowledge Mr Hewson or his daughter. But Sarah definitely saw him. Ruth clocked the look she gave him and saw Sarah's face take on a look of distaste. In that instant, she wondered whether Sarah knew the same thing about him that she already did. For under his quiet, sullen, seething presence in the rag room, Ruth was aware of how evil he was.

Chapter Twelve

When Mr Hewson was certain that his daughter had seen enough of the rag room, he ushered her out into the open air. He beckoned Ruth to accompany them, and Miss Wagstaff's face darkened again. She clearly wasn't happy that Ruth was being given special treatment by the mill owner; treatment she obviously felt should have been given to her.

Out in the yard, both Mr Hewson and Sarah shook Ruth's hand and thanked her for her time. How different they were to the previous owner, she thought, who had never made himself known to his workers. In the short time she'd been speaking to the two of them, she had forgotten all about her hardships at home. She'd forgotten about Mick and having to cancel their dates. Forgotten about Edie's warning that she'd lose him if she wasn't careful. She'd been Miss Hardy of the rag room, explaining to the mill owner's daughter how her job worked and what it entailed, speaking with pride about her role in the papermaking process. For although it was hard work, Ruth always kept in mind how important it was. Paper was needed more than ever now the war was over and the country was open for business again.

Before she returned to the rag room, she watched Mr Hewson and his daughter head to the esparto warehouse. Two men from the machine room were walking towards them. Ruth recognised the shorter of the pair, Alan Murphy. He was the machine room supervisor, a fair-minded man whom the others respected. Both men doffed their caps and said good morning to Mr Hewson and Sarah. Then Alan Murphy smiled at Sarah, and Sarah blushed in return. Intrigued, Ruth headed back into the rag room, ignoring the hard stare from Miss Wagstaff.

As the warm spring days continued, Ruth became even busier at home. Bea's baby was due any day and there was still no money for a doctor. Neither was there spare money for more food. One evening there was a knock on the door at the back of the pub. Ruth opened it and saw an odd little man in front of her.

'Big Jimmy,' the man said. 'Pleased to meet you. I was hoping for a word with Harry, if he's in.'

Ruth looked at the man in front of her. Big Jimmy was a joke of a name, as he was one of the shortest men she'd ever seen.

'Dad? There's a fella called Big Jimmy at the door,' she said.

'Let him in,' Harry said. 'It's Jimmy Tate's dad.'

Ruth couldn't see any likeness between the man at the door and Bea's husband. She wondered whether the man was Jimmy's real dad, for his size and colouring were nothing like Jimmy's. She watched as Big Jimmy walked towards Harry and shook his hand, then brought out a handful of coins from his pocket.

'It's the best I can do,' he explained. 'I'm giving it to you now before Connie can find it and spend it on ale. I know it's not much, but it's all I've got.'

It hurt Harry's pride to be reduced to taking money from Big Jimmy. They'd worked together at the pit, hewing coal from the earth. But the Hardys needed money, it was as simple as that. He had no choice but to take it.

Ruth began to struggle with her workload both at home and at work. On the days when she saw Mick waiting for her outside the rag room on her way to work, her heart leapt. How she missed spending time with him. How she longed to kiss him again and feel his lips on hers. How she wanted to hug him, confide in him and tell him what was on her mind. But when he asked when he might see her again, she told him the truth. She couldn't spare the time.

'You understand, don't you?' she said.

Mick fell silent and crossed his arms. Ruth could see Button wriggling inside his jacket.

'When will there be time for us, Ruth?' he asked.

'I don't know,' she said sadly.

Mick turned towards Ruth. Softly, slowly, he lifted her chin with his fingers. 'When, Ruth?'

She tried to wrap her arms around him, but he took a step back. Her heart dropped. Was she about to lose him as Edie had warned?

'Everything will be all right, Mick. We just have to give it time,' she said.

'No, Ruth, it won't be. And I don't know if I can wait.'

Ruth was confused and upset. 'Wait for what?'

'For our future to begin,' he said firmly. 'What'll

happen when Bea's baby arrives and you've another mouth to feed, another person to look after?'

She was shocked by the flash of anger in his reply. This wasn't the Mick she thought she knew, the Mick she was falling in love with.

'Mick, please!'

He shook his head. 'No, Ruth. I thought I'd found a good 'un when I found you. But I realise now that I'll always come second best to everyone else.' He kissed her gently on the cheek. 'I'm sorry.'

Ruth felt her eyes prick with tears. 'Just like that? We're done?'

Mick bit his lip and walked away.

Chapter Thirteen

Ruth felt her heart break into pieces. Every fibre of her being was telling her to run after Mick and beg him not to go. But she didn't. She forced herself not to. She might not have much in life, but by God, she had her pride. That was something her mam had instilled in her and Bea from an early age. A pride that meant she would stand on her own two feet and do things her own way. A pride that meant she would never beg for the company of anyone, whether man, woman or child. Even if it meant watching Mick, the best thing that had happened to her, walk away and out of her life.

She bit her lip and forced herself not to cry. She had to go into the rag room and deal with Miss Wagstaff's hard stare and the brooding presence of John Hepple. She put her hands to her face and slapped her cheeks.

'Come on, Ruth Hardy. Pull yourself together,' she said out loud. 'He's just a fella. There'll be others.'

She tried to believe her own words but knew she'd have to go a long way to find another kind, loving and courteous man like Mick.

She pulled off her woollen hat and replaced it with her

work cap, pushing escaping wisps of long brown hair under it. She squared her shoulders, ran the back of her hand across her eyes to wipe her tears away, then walked slowly towards the door of the rag room, her head bowed, not wanting to catch Miss Wagstaff's eye. She didn't want to look at Edie or Jane either, as they'd be concerned when they saw she'd been crying. She couldn't face telling them what had happened yet, or letting Edie know that she'd been right after all. Edie had warned her many times to nurture her relationship with Mick, to cherish him.

As she stepped into the room, she became aware of an unusual silence. Normally there was the swish of cloth as seams were ripped open. Even the rag-sorting machine was still. Confused, she looked up and gasped when she saw the tall, well-dressed figure of Mr Hewson standing next to Miss Wagstaff.

'Ah, Miss Hardy! Just the girl we were hoping to talk to,' he said.

Ruth looked at the girls on the benches. They were staring directly at her, as dumbfounded as she was. She gulped, her heart pounding. Had she done something wrong? What on earth was going on? She glanced at Miss Wagstaff and saw that her face was set like stone. It was a sharp contrast to the cheerful way Mr Hewson had greeted her.

'Sir?'

'I have news for you, Miss Hardy,' he said. 'Now that I've been running the mill for a little while, I've decided to make a few changes.'

Ruth felt her head spin. Surely this could only be bad news? But hadn't Mr Hewson given her his assurance when they'd first met that no jobs would be lost?

'I have had a private meeting with Miss Wagstaff and she was just about to explain to the girls here that she is being moved to the clerical side of the mill's operation.'

Ruth gasped. The rag room without Waggy? It was unthinkable. She'd worked there forever!

'She will begin work in the mill office, where I hope to make the most of her exceptional numerical skills,' Mr Hewson explained.

Ruth's mouth dropped open in shock.

'And I'd like to appoint a new supervisor in her place,' he continued.

He smiled broadly at Ruth, waiting for the penny to drop. When it did, Ruth's heart hammered so hard she was afraid the men in the machine room might hear it.

'Me, sir?' she said quietly.

'You indeed, Miss Hardy,' he replied.

She heard a voice cry out from the back of the room. 'Yes!' She didn't need to turn to see who it was. She'd recognise Edie's voice anywhere.

'Girls!' Miss Wagstaff said sternly. 'That's quite enough of that. I am still your supervisor and you'll do well to behave yourselves accordingly.'

Ruth looked into Mr Hewson's kind face and saw a mischievous sparkle in his eyes. The white rose in his lapel caught her eye.

'I don't know what to say, sir,' she said. 'Are you sure I'm up to the job?'

'I'm certain,' he said firmly. 'You'll be earning more money, of course, at the supervisory rate.'

'And working longer hours?' Ruth asked.

He shook his head, and she felt a rush of relief. The extra money was more than welcome.

Ruth looked from Miss Wagstaff to Mr Hewson. 'When do I start my new job?' she asked.

'I'll be in touch very soon to let you know,' Mr Hewson replied. 'I'll leave you to it, Miss Wagstaff.' He offered his hand to Ruth. 'Welcome aboard the Grange Paper Works supervisory team, Miss Hardy.'

Ruth shook his hand heartily, just as his daughter Sarah had shaken hers when they'd met. 'Thank you, sir. I won't let you down.'

When Mr Hewson had left, Ruth stood face to face with Miss Wagstaff at the front of the rag room.

'Get back to work,' Miss Wagstaff hissed.

Ruth hesitated a moment, just enough to let the supervisor know that she was not to be treated like a wayward child any more. She had power now, even if it was just a tiny amount. She headed to her seat on the bench with a huge smile on her face. And as she did so, another cry went up from Edie.

'Yes!'

Ruth couldn't wait to get home to share the news that night and ran almost all the way. She was so excited that she barely felt the rain on her face as she hurried past farmers' fields on the clifftop. When the spire of St Paul's church came into view, she slowed down to calm herself. The excitement of the day had almost pushed her heartbreak over Mick to the back of her mind. Almost, but not entirely. Every time she thought about him, she felt sick to her stomach. Had she really lost him for good?

She walked past Ryhope Hall and the big, fancy houses on the village green. She walked past the Uplands and peered through its windows, as she'd always done. But there was nothing and no one to see. She wondered who lived there, for she rarely saw anyone inside. She'd heard that a family from Scarborough on the Yorkshire coast owned the place and used it as their holiday retreat. She rounded the corner and walked past the church, the police house and the cinema. On the opposite corner stood the Guide Post Inn.

She picked up the hem of her skirt so she could run across Ryhope Street to the back lane behind the pub. She lifted the sneck on the gate and walked into the yard. It was empty, as she'd hoped. She didn't want to bump into Mrs Pike and be kept making small talk when all she wanted to do was burst in and tell everyone her news. She whipped off her hat and pushed at the door with her hand. She was excited, the words ready on her lips. She'd be bringing in more money! How happy her mam would be. She imagined seeing Jean's face light up with a smile like summer sunshine. And her dad, he'd be proud of his elder daughter, coming on at the mill, making something of herself. Bea would want all the gossip and news about Mr Hewson: what he said, what he wore and what colour rose he wore in his jacket. Bea would also be her confidante for her news about Mick, when she was ready to share. It was still too raw, too painful to think about, and she pushed him to the back of her mind, for now.

She bounded into the room, ready to explode with her news. And then she saw Bea lying on the floor.

Ruth stopped dead in her tracks. Her sister was curled up, gripping her stomach, crying, groaning, rocking from side to side. Ruth dropped her hat and ran to her side.

'Mam?' she implored. 'What's happened?' She saw tears streaming down her mother's face.

'Dad's gone to get a doctor. He couldn't find Mrs Pike – she must've gone out. He had to go himself,' Jean wept. 'Bea's waters broke.'

'But she's not due for another couple of weeks,' Ruth gasped.

'You can't tell a baby that, love. They come when they're ready. She's been in agony for hours. I'm so bloody useless. I'm her mam! I should be able to help my own bairn.'

Ruth tore her coat off and threw it to the ground. Then she rolled her sleeves up and pushed her hair behind her ears.

'Tell me what to do, Mam. You've been through this before with me and Bea. Think, Mam! What do I have to do?'

'You're never going to deliver her bairn yourself, are you?' Jean cried. 'Your dad'll not be long. Dr Anderson should be on his way by now.'

Ruth managed to move Bea so that she was lying on her back. She knew enough to do that much at least. Bea was groaning louder as the pain gripped her body. Ruth got down on her hands and knees and lifted her sister's skirt.

'Never mind Dr Anderson. The baby's on its way, Mam. You've just said they come when they're ready. It's not going to wait for the doctor.'

'Ruth,' Bea implored. 'Ruth, help me. It hurts, Ruth. It really hurts.'

'Mam?' Ruth yelled. 'You're going to have to guide me, you hear? Shout out anything I should look for. Anything I should do. Tell me, Mam! Now!'

'Ruth!' Bea implored.

'It's all right, Bea. I'm here. I'm going to deliver your baby. Just do what me and Mam tell you.'

'I need to push, Ruth,' Bea gasped. 'It feels like it's coming, I need to push it . . .'

'Push down!' Jean called.

'Push, Bea. Push!' Ruth urged.

Bea screamed. It was a sound like Ruth had never heard before, a noise feral and wild. She screamed again, harder and louder. From her bed, Jean yelled instructions. Ruth could see the baby's head, red and bloody, inching its way from Bea's body.

'That's it, Bea, good girl. Keep going,' she said.

'Hold it steady,' Jean called. 'Don't pull. Let Bea's body do the work.'

'GET IT OUT OF ME!' Bea yelled.

The baby's head was completely out now and lying in Ruth's hands. And now its shoulders, arms and hands were coming, its tiny torso, legs and feet.

'It's a girl, Bea!' Ruth cried. 'A girl!'

'You need a knife to cut the cord,' Jean commanded.

'Where am I supposed to get a bloody knife from? I can't let go of the bairn!'

There was a knock at the door, a hard knock, three times.

'What's going on in there? What's all the noise?'

It was Mrs Pike. Ruth had never been so relieved to hear their landlady's voice.

'Come in!' Ruth screamed.

Whatever Mrs Pike had expected to find when she walked into the room, the scene in front of her gave her the biggest shock of her life.

'Holy Mary, Mother of God!' she cried when she saw Ruth on her knees with the bloodied newborn in her hands.

'Mrs Pike, we need to cut the cord. We need a knife,' Ruth cried.

Mrs Pike disappeared and returned seconds later with a meat cleaver. 'It's the first one I could lay my hands on,' she said.

'Throw me a blanket from the bed,' Ruth said.

The landlady did as requested and then stood to one side as Ruth cut the cord and wrapped the baby tightly in the blanket. She handed the child to Bea, expecting, hoping that her sister would take it to her chest and hold it. But Bea kept on screaming, and when Ruth saw what was happening, her stomach turned over with dread. Bea was bleeding profusely. The blood pooled underneath her, around her, it wouldn't stop. Ruth gripped tight to the baby as it began to cry.

'Mam! Mam, I need to know what to do,' she yelled. 'She's bleeding, it's coming out heavy, Mam, it won't stop. I don't know what to do!'

At the sound of footsteps at the door, she looked up to see Harry and Dr Anderson. A rush of relief went through her at the sight of the doctor. He'd know what to do. He'd help Bea.

'The baby's safe, Doctor,' she said. 'But Bea won't stop bleeding.'

'Everyone out,' Dr Anderson demanded.

'Mam's bedridden, she'll have to stay,' Ruth said.

'You stay too, Ruth. I might need you. Harry, go into the pub. You don't want to see this. Mrs Pike, put plenty of water on to boil and bring clean towels.'

'Yes, Doctor,' Mrs Pike said obediently.

Dr Anderson immediately got down to business. Ruth watched in silent horror as he tried to stem the blood. She saw her mam say a silent prayer.

Dr Anderson stayed with Bea and worked long into the evening as the light began to dim. Mrs Pike went back and forth with hot water and towels. She brought brandy for Jean and Ruth's nerves. She served Harry pint after pint in the bar. But in the end, there was nothing the doctor could do. He dropped his head, defeated, as Bea's final breath left her body.

'No!' Ruth cried. 'No, Doctor. She can't die, she just can't!'

'Not my little bairn!' Jean called out in shock and disbelief. 'She can't be dead, no!'

Dr Anderson closed his eyes. 'I'm afraid she's gone,' he said. 'There's nothing else I can do.'

Ruth hugged Bea's baby to her heart. Dr Anderson stood over Bea's body and closed his eyes for a few moments. Then he took the baby from Ruth's arms. Ruth let the child go willingly, her heart breaking over her sister. She was in shock, and couldn't trust her arms to hold the precious bundle.

Dr Anderson laid the baby on the floor and opened the blanket. He examined the child and counted her fingers and toes.

'She's got a good pair of lungs on her,' he said. 'You'll need to clean her up, get the blood off her. Do you have milk to feed her?'

There was an urgency to his voice that Ruth didn't pick up on at first. How could she think about milk when

Bea was lying dead in a puddle of blood? She felt Dr Anderson's hands press firmly on her shoulders.

'Ruth, listen to me.'

She tried to focus on the doctor's kind face, but her head felt foggy with shock.

'You need to feed the child, Ruth. You need to look after it.'

'Bea . . .' Ruth whispered.

'Bea's gone,' Dr Anderson said softly. 'I'll arrange to have her body taken this evening. She haemorrhaged.'

Ruth looked at him, puzzled by the unfamiliar word.

'She had a ruptured blood vessel,' he explained. 'Ruth, I need you to concentrate on what I'm going to tell you next. Are you listening to me?'

She swallowed hard and nodded her head. Dr Anderson picked up the crying baby and wrapped it in the blanket again.

'Bea's baby is well, a healthy little girl. But she will need constant attention, feeding and cleaning. Are you willing to take her on?'

From the corner of the room, Ruth heard her mam's sobs.

'There is a place I can take her, if this is not to be her home,' the doctor continued.

Ruth knew about the institution Dr Anderson was referring to. It was where unwanted children were left. She shook her head.

'No. She's no orphan; she has us,' she said firmly. 'It's what Bea would want.'

As the words left her lips, she knew that keeping the baby was not just what Bea would want, but what *she* wanted too. She'd lived side by side with her sister every single day of her pregnancy. She'd suffered when Bea was ill and sick. She'd taken care of her when she couldn't sleep at night. It didn't feel right to do anything other than take her child in her arms and accept it into her life.

Dr Anderson passed her the baby, and Ruth cradled her to her chest. As the doctor laid a blanket over Bea's body, she closed her eyes and wept, rocking back and forth.

The day after Bea died, Ruth stayed at home with her mam and dad. She'd never missed a day of work at the mill and knew that Miss Wagstaff, Edie and Jane would be curious to know where she was. She'd lose a day's pay, but with everything that was going on – her shock and grief at her sister's death and her fears for the baby – money was the least of her worries. Harry and Jean were in shock, Jean constantly sobbing and Harry staring into space from his chair. Harry refused to have anything to do with his new granddaughter. He wouldn't hold her or even look at her. Jean, however, welcomed the baby into her arms, and together she and Ruth cleaned and fed her.

'She'll need a name,' Jean said.

It was something Ruth had been wondering about.

'How about calling her Maude after Grandma Hardy?' her mam suggested.

'What do you reckon, Dad?' Ruth asked. She secretly hoped that naming the baby after his mam might make Harry warm to the baby.

Harry sighed heavily. 'Maude Hardy, eh?' He blinked back tears. 'The newest member of our family. I think my old mam would approve.'

'Shouldn't she be Maude Tate?' Jean asked. 'Our Bea and Jimmy were married after all.'

'While I'm looking after her, she'll be called Maude Hardy, never Tate,' Ruth replied firmly.

Bea's funeral was held two days later, in the early hours of a Thursday morning. It was a pauper's funeral, conducted by Reverend Daye at no charge. He knew only too well how men who had lost their jobs at the pit were fixed. Ruth and Harry were there to say their goodbyes, Bea's sleeping baby nestled in Ruth's arms.

Ruth had given the news of Bea's death to Big Jimmy Tate and asked him to tell Jimmy. But none of the Tate family turned up in the church. Ruth hadn't mentioned the baby when she'd spoken to Big Jimmy, for Bea's feckless husband had never shown any interest in his child. But word soon got out. Mrs Pike mentioned it to a customer in the pub one night. The customer told Lil Mahone, the worst gossip in Ryhope. Once Lil had the news, it wasn't long before everyone in the village knew.

In the following days, with the Hardys lost in their grief, it was Mrs Pike of all people who proved surprisingly tender towards the baby, and far more supportive than Ruth could ever have imagined. However, what none of the Hardys, and few people in Ryhope knew was that the landlady had lost bairn after bairn when she'd been a young woman and married to the love of her life. She'd been unable to carry a baby full term, and the heartache had never left her. The emptiness she felt, especially since being widowed, was filled by running her beloved pub.

Each day she brought a pan of warm milk for the baby. 'Well, it would just go off in this weather if I left it,' she told Ruth. And it was true, the days were getting warmer, the air giving up its cold sting. 'But just remember what I said about the noise,' she added. 'I don't want business to suffer. If customers hear a bairn crying, it'll put them off their ale, and that would never do.'

On her way to work each day, Ruth remembered the times she and Bea had walked to the mill together, hand in hand, laughing, joking and sharing secrets. She remembered Bea teasing her about Mick being her boyfriend before Ruth even knew herself that that was what he would become. Should she seek him out at the mill and tell him the sad news about her sister? She was grieving so much that she couldn't think any further than putting one foot in front of the other. She wouldn't allow herself to think any more about Mick. It was Bea she was mourning. Pretty, delicate Bea.

She wondered how her family could carry on. Some days felt impossible, harder than ever to cope with their loss. And just when Ruth thought that her grief couldn't get worse, pain seemed to find a raw spot to gnaw in her heart. She cried herself to sleep. Jean did too. Harry remained closed, his heart turned to stone. And between them all was Bea's baby, who cried and mewled at all hours of the day and night. While Ruth was at work, Maude was left with Jean in the back room at the pub. Jean coddled the child, fed her, kept her clean. Caring for the baby seemed to give her a new lease of life, and even Harry began to ask to hold his granddaughter. But their grief at losing Bea was never far from the surface and their tears often fell.

At the paper mill, Ruth took over from Miss Wagstaff

as supervisor in the rag room. She was nervous about the change, and wondered how Edie and Jane might behave towards her. Would they be angry at having her as their boss when she'd always been one of the girls? But hadn't Edie cheered on learning the news? Ruth knew she was worrying needlessly. Sure enough, during her first week as supervisor, Edie gave her a bunch of wildflowers she'd picked on her way to work. Both Edie and Jane were supportive and sensitive to her grief over Bea, and when Ruth told them what had happened between her and Mick, they offered nothing but kindness.

'You were right,' Ruth told Edie one dinner time. 'If I'd spent as much time caring about Mick as I do for my family, he wouldn't have left me.'

'Love's a learning game,' Edie replied sagely.

'Not one I want to play any more,' Ruth said sadly.

Despite the support of her friends, the change wasn't easy for Ruth at first. She now had to deal with the rag and bone men who came to the mill, and she had to learn to barter for their rags. She was firm with them, determined to start as she meant to go on and let them know they couldn't take advantage of her just because she was new to the job. She'd watched Miss Wagstaff deal with them in the past, and had learned how much rags were worth. The extra money that came with her new role wasn't a huge improvement on her wages, but it was better than nothing, and she was grateful for every penny.

She had responsibility now; the rag room was her domain, and one she presided over with efficiency and concern for the girls. She sat alone, facing the others, at the table Miss Wagstaff had once occupied. Working at her own table meant she missed out on the shared secrets that ran along the bench. She missed talking to Edie and Jane. But she didn't miss sitting with John Hepple. He remained a thorn in her side, though he kept quiet and did his work. This was more than could be said for Claire, who was one of the youngest in the rag room. Claire had almond eyes and long brown hair. She'd joined the mill straight from school, as had many of the girls, but Claire was noisy and lively, a little bit cheeky. She needed more supervision than most.

With each passing day, as Ruth settled into her new role, baby Maude grew stronger at home. However, while looking after the baby had begun as a joy for Jean, it quickly began to take its toll. She wasn't up to holding Maude or feeding her for too long when she didn't even have the energy to dress or feed herself. Harry offered to help, but constantly had to ask what to do. He'd never been involved in raising Bea and Ruth as babies; he'd never changed a nappy or bathed his daughters. His role as a dad had been as provider and protector. He'd offered a sturdy knee for his daughters to sit on. He'd sung songs to them and run with them on the beach as they splashed in the waves. But as far as the practical aspects of child-rearing were concerned, he didn't have a clue.

As the baby grew and thrived over the summer, Ruth worried for her mam's health. She knew that looking after Maude wasn't easy for Jean, but she had no other option than to leave the baby with her mam and dad. At the mill, she kept her mind on her work as much as she could, aware that she needed to focus on what she was doing. But even with the extra responsibility at work and much on her mind at home, there was still something she longed for. Each morning when she walked towards the rag room, she held out hope that Mick might be there. She longed to see him again, to see Button wriggling under his jacket. She wanted to tell him about losing Bea, about baby Maude and about her new job. But Mick was never there.

One morning at the mill, a rag and bone cart arrived filled with rags to sell. Ruth recognised the old horse, Stella. She belonged to Ernie Sutcliffe, whom Ruth had dealt with before. But it wasn't Ernie sitting on the cart this time. In his place was a beauty of a girl with dark hair. Ruth knew that this was Ernie's daughter Meg, who had often visited the mill with her dad. She'd heard gossip around Ryhope that Ernie had passed away and Meg had taken on his rag and bone round. She knew how dangerous a profession travelling the back streets was, especially for a young girl, and a beauty like Meg. It meant dealing with traders at the East End market, which was no place for a woman and certainly not a girl on her own. Behind Meg on the cart, a skinny white dog stood guard, glaring at Ruth.

'Come on in,' Ruth said, beckoning to Meg.

Meg jumped from the cart and followed her.

'Welcome to the rag room! Or as I like to call it, my little palace.' Ruth smiled.

'And I'm her little princess!' Edie called out. The other girls roared with laughter.

'Calm down,' Ruth ordered.

It was Meg's first time inside the rag room, and Ruth was aware that she was taking it all in. She saw her watching the girls cut and tear the old clothes.

'What've you got for me, Meg?' she asked, eager to get her hands on more rags.

Meg pointed to her cart. 'There's white cotton at the front,' she said. 'And canvas and cord at the back.'

'Smashing,' Ruth said. 'They'll go to make white and brown paper.'

She handed payment to Meg, then took a notebook and pencil from her pocket and marked down the transaction. She handed the book to the mill office at the end of each day and collected it again the next morning. She took pride in her work and made sure her figures were entered as neatly as possible.

'Have you always worked here?' Meg asked.

'Always. Started off in the machine room, sweeping cuttings from the floor, and then moved here. I was made supervisor not so long ago.' Ruth eyed Meg. 'Why do you ask? Are you interested in working here? It's hard work, but you'll be used to that after being out on the horse and cart. The girls start at six thirty each morning and work until six at night. They get a full day off once a week.'

Meg shook her head. Ruth should have known that a lass like Meg wouldn't want to be stuck inside six days a week from dawn to dusk. The rag and bone round offered a freedom that Ruth envied. A pang went through her as she thought of Meg spending her days outside.

'I'll bear it in mind,' Meg said politely.

The two girls walked to the door. Together they pulled the piles of rags from the cart and moved them into the rag room. When they'd finished, Ruth watched Meg climb up on to her cart, gee her horse and leave for the open road. She sighed as she watched her go. What she wouldn't give for the feel of the wind on her face and the freedom of being at no one's beck and call.

The whistle in the mill yard sounded, marking the dinner break. A cry went up from inside the rag room.

'Ruth!'

She turned and walked back inside. Edie was standing at the bench.

'Ring your bell, Ruth!' she laughed. 'I'm so hungry my belly thinks my throat's been cut.'

'Sorry, girls,' Ruth said. She reached under her seat until her fingers found the brass handbell. She pulled it out and rang it heartily. With each clang of the bell, more girls stood from the bench.

The day was warm and still, perfect for getting away from the dusty room. Some of the girls ran straight down to the beach or found a spot on the clifftop to sit. Even John limped his way to the door with a cigarette in his hand. But Edie and Jane didn't run; they waited for the room to clear and then approached Ruth.

'You're coming to have your dinner with us on the beach,' Edie said.

Ruth shook her head. 'I can't.' She pointed at the piles of rags she'd just bought from Meg Sutcliffe. 'These need sorting before they go in the machine. I have to do it.'

'Can't you spare just ten minutes?' Jane implored. 'It feels like we've not had a good gossip in ages.'

'We want to know all about baby Maude,' Edie said. 'Come on, Ruth. Spare us a few minutes, that's all. We're your friends, remember?'

Ruth linked arms with the two girls. 'How could I ever forget?'

The three of them walked together, chatting and gossiping all the way to the beach. Edie had her usual ham sandwich for dinner, Ruth had a boiled egg.

'Want to do a swap?' Ruth asked. 'Half of my egg for half of your sandwich?'

Edie agreed and ripped her sandwich in two. Ruth offered her the boiled egg and Edie bit into it greedily.

'I can't afford to buy meat for sandwiches any more now my wages are the only money coming in,' Ruth said. 'Maude's being fed by the kindness of Mrs Pike bringing milk, while Mam and Dad are eating slim pickings from whatever I manage to buy.'

'I'll see if I can sneak out something from Mam's kitchen for you,' Edie said.

Ruth was surprised to see Jane with no dinner at all. 'Aren't you hungry?' she asked.

Jane shrugged. 'Davey says I'm turning fat.'

'But there's nothing on you, you're as skinny as a rake,' Edie cried. 'Anyway, when did you start doing what Davey says? If he said go and jump off a cliff, would you?'

'Edie, leave her be,' Ruth said.

The girls sat in silence a few moments, enjoying the warmth from the sun. Edie removed her shawl, exposing her bare arms. Ruth did the same, but Jane kept her woollen jacket on.

'Aren't you boiling up wearing that?' Edie asked.

'The sun feels gorgeous on my skin,' Ruth said, hoping it would encourage Jane to remove her jacket. But Jane still kept it on.

When Ruth had finished her boiled egg, she made her apologies and said she had to get back to work.

'All work and no play, that's your trouble; always has been,' Edie said.

Ruth was stung by the remark, even if it had been said

in jest, for it was what Mick had said too. She stormed back to the rag room, expecting to see John inside. He rarely left at dinner time. Sure enough, he was there, but he wasn't alone. Ruth was shocked to see that Claire was with him. Neither of them was aware of her presence, they both had their backs turned to her. Ruth knew immediately that something was wrong. She heard Claire's voice raised in distress, saw her batting at John, trying to punch his arms and chest. She rushed to Claire's side, and when John saw her, he let rip with a stream of abuse. She immediately saw Claire's blouse had been ripped. It didn't take much to put two and two together.

She pointed at John. 'You! Get out. Now!' she yelled.

'It was her! She wanted it just as much as I did!' he growled.

Ruth pulled Claire to her side. Claire's hands went to her breast as she sobbed.

'Did he hurt you?' Ruth asked.

'No, but he tried to.'

Ruth glared at John. 'Get out! Or God help me, I'll do something I'll regret.'

John sneered. 'You're just a lass. What could someone like you possibly do to an ex-soldier like me? I fought for king and country, girl! What have you ever done with your life?'

'Out!' Ruth screamed.

This time, the force of her voice seemed to shock John into silence. She watched, seething with fury, as John gathered his crutch and limped out of the room.

Chapter Fourteen

John was subdued for the next few days. Ruth moved him away from Claire and kept a watchful eye on him. When she had a moment of privacy with the girls, she warned them to stay away from the man in their midst and never be alone with him. She couldn't say more as Mr Hewson had told her he wanted no gossip spread.

In all the time he'd worked in the rag room, John had done nothing to make himself likeable. He didn't greet the girls at the beginning of the day, or smile in reply to their cheery hellos. He just seethed with an anger directed at his work. The force of his bitterness worked its way out of him as he ripped the rags on the knife. Ruth stood her ground with him; she knew she mustn't show weakness. When he challenged her with a scornful look or a snarl, she straightened her shoulders and looked him directly in the eye, forcing him to turn away. She'd been entrusted by the mill owner to take on the role of supervisor in the rag room and she was determined not to let John undermine her.

It was a role she was growing into, a job she was loving more with every passing day. The girls trusted and respected her in a way that none of them had Miss Wagstaff, as Ruth had risen through the ranks from working on the bench. She knew what she was doing and instilled her own work ethic in her girls. Productivity went up, the piles of rags were cleared faster and the girls were happier. John remained an irritation, but Ruth had no choice other than to keep him in the rag room, since he'd been placed there at the request of Mr Hewson.

After work was done at the end of each day, she always took a moment to collect herself before she walked out through the door. Standing in the empty, quiet room after the girls had left to run home, memories of Bea flooded back. Oh, Bea was always on her mind, every morning, every night. But it was when she headed out of work that Bea's absence hit hardest. She would find herself searching for her sister in her black coat and hat by the gates. Then she'd shake her head, tell herself to pull herself together. But she would have given anything, everything, for Bea to be waiting by the gate.

As days turned into weeks, the pain in Ruth's heart over losing Bea didn't ease. There was plenty to keep her busy, but there was an emptiness in her life now. She missed her sister every single day.

In those warm days of summer, Ruth's walk home from the mill was a pleasant meander along the clifftop. She trailed her hand through the long grass and turned her face to the sun. Some days it was hot enough to take off her woollen jacket and carry it over her arm. How she longed on those days to sit a while and gaze out at the sparkling blue sea. But she couldn't. She had to get home to cook dinner and clean.

Her dad's mood had become brighter, helped by a welcome offer from Mrs Pike.

'It doesn't pay much, but I need a hand with pot-washing in the pub,' she told him. 'And there'll be a free beer in it for you at the end of each night.'

Harry jumped at the chance of helping. It wasn't a demanding job and didn't need him to walk. He pulled up a stool at the end of the bar and carried out Mrs Pike's commands.

When Ruth was out at work, the door in the back room was thrown open to let in the air. On one such day in July, as she approached the pub on her way back from the mill, she heard yelling, angry words. A woman's voice. She knew immediately that it wasn't her mam, as Jean hadn't the strength in her to shout. Neither did it sound like Mrs Pike. She ran inside, stopping dead in the doorway when she saw who was there. It was Connie Tate. Beside her stood Big Jimmy, who was pulling at his wife's arm, begging her to quieten and leave. Harry sat in his armchair and Jean was in bed with baby Maude at her side.

'What's going on?' Ruth demanded.

Connie spun around. Ruth saw immediately she was drunk. She could hardly stand up, and if it wasn't for the little fella at her side, she would have fallen flat on her face.

'Jimmy was just about to take Connie home, weren't you, lad?' Harry said impatiently.

'Aye, Harry, I was. Come on, lass. Let's get you out of here. I told you not to come, but you wouldn't listen to me, would you?'

But Connie was not for leaving. 'I'll be back for my

grandbairn!' she shouted. 'You can't stop me seeing her. I want her. She's mine as much as yours! I'll take the little bugger, I swear!'

'Now, you'll do no such thing,' Big Jimmy said firmly. Ruth watched as he tried to steer his wife towards the door.

'You hear me? I want that bairn!' Connie yelled.

'Connie!' Big Jimmy snapped. 'Will you stop making a show of yourself and get yourself home. Now!' He gave her a gentle push in the direction of the door and she half fell, half stumbled through it.

Ruth was bemused, but disturbed too. What did Connie mean about coming back to take Maude? The Tates had no claim on Bea's baby, surely? As Big Jimmy manoeuvred his wife out of the yard and into the lane, she followed to make sure they left.

'Keep Connie away from us,' she said. 'My mam's not well, she doesn't need more stress.'

Big Jimmy sighed. 'Don't worry, lass. You won't have any more bother from her. She's been on the ale all day. Gets it into her head that she wants our Jimmy's baby for herself. But I keep telling her the bairn's better off with you lot. She's in no fit state to look after a dog, never mind a bairn.'

Ruth was about to head back into the yard when Big Jimmy put his hand on her arm. She turned in surprise.

'I'm sorry, lass,' he said. 'I'm sorry about the whole flamin' mess our Jimmy caused your Bea. And I'm awful sorry for your loss.'

Ruth felt herself soften at the little man's kindness. 'Look, when Connie's sober . . .' she began.

Big Jimmy shook his head. 'No chance of that, pet.'

'. . . but if she is, ever, she'll be welcome here to see her granddaughter. Don't you want to see the bairn too?'

'I've got enough on my plate looking after this one,' Big Jimmy said, and he put his stocky arm around Connie's tiny waist to stop her from falling.

Ruth watched as they slowly walked away, with Connie swearing and yelling. She felt uneasy about Connie. The woman was a drunk, a ruined soul, but she was still Maude's grandma whether Ruth liked it or not.

'What was all that about?' she asked when she returned to her mam and dad.

'Ah, it's just something and nothing,' Harry replied with a dismissive shake of his head.

'It was more than that and you know it,' Jean reprimanded him.

Ruth looked from her mam to her dad. 'Well, who's going to tell me the truth?'

She sank on to her mam's bed and lifted Maude into her arms. The baby's eyes were open, and she felt as if she was looking at Bea. Maude had Bea's cheeky smile and the same sparkle in her eyes. Ruth traced her cheek with her finger.

'She's her mother's child all right. She's the spitting image of Bea.'

'Aye, but never forget she's got Tate blood in her,' Jean said warily.

'What happened with Connie, Mam?'

'She was drunk, love. You saw that for yourself. She comes in here saying these things about taking the baby, demanding the right to her own flesh and blood.'

'Do you mean this isn't the first time?'

Jean sank back against her pillow. 'I wasn't going to

tell you, love, but me and your dad have had a few run-ins with her since Maude was born. It's taken either her husband or one of her sons to get her out of here and away home.'

'One of her sons?' Ruth said. 'The only son who should be taking an interest in Maude is the baby's dad, and he hasn't been seen in ages.' She glared at Harry. 'Why didn't you tell me?'

'Ask your mother. She wanted it kept from you.'

'Mam?' asked Ruth.

'You're busy, love, with the mill and your new job and all,' Jean said.

'Nothing is as important as Maude. You should have told me you'd been having trouble with Connie. I could have gone and had a word with her.'

Harry shook his head. 'She won't listen to anything you say. I worked with Big Jimmy at the pit for years. I know what Connie's like. I've heard the very worst about her from him.'

Ruth cradled the baby. 'And what if she comes here again while you and I are at work and Mam's asleep, or too unwell to stop her from taking Maude?' She glanced from her mam to her dad, her thoughts working overtime, fear running through her. 'What if she's even more drunk next time? What if her husband's at the pit? Her sons won't always know where she is. Who knows what she might have done if Big Jimmy hadn't controlled her today?'

'Ruth, love—' Jean began.

'Mam, we need to face up to the fact that Connie has a right to see her granddaughter, but if she comes in here drunk and screaming, threatening to take her, then what'll we do?'

'We'll keep the door locked,' Jean said.

'On a day like today?' Ruth replied. 'You can't get your breath at the best of times, Mam.' She stood and paced the floor. 'I can't let Connie take her. I won't.'

Harry banged his fist against his chair. 'That bloody woman!' he yelled.

'We could ask Mrs Pike,' Jean offered.

'No, we couldn't,' Ruth said quickly. 'She's letting us slide with the rent as it is. And she's already offering milk and food. We can't ask for more.'

'Then what are we supposed to do?' Harry cried.

Ruth paced the floor between her dad in his armchair and her mam in her bed. An idea had been brewing in her head for some time. It was a daft idea and she knew it. So daft that she'd kept it locked in her heart. She hadn't dared say a word. But it might be the only way to keep Maude safe from Connie's clutches. What did she have to lose? If she wanted to protect her family, she had to make an impossible choice.

She stopped pacing and took a deep breath. 'I'm going to take Maude to the mill.'

Chapter Fifteen

Harry laughed out loud.

'Don't be daft, lass.'

'Ruth, you can't,' Jean pleaded.

'I can and I will,' she said firmly. 'It's the safest place, away from Connie.'

'Think of the dangers there. And who'll look after her when you're working?' Jean said.

Ruth sat on the edge of the bed with Maude in her arms. She locked eyes with her mam. 'I won't keep her in the rag room. I'd never subject her to that.'

She thought of the buildings at the mill, the machines and the reservoir, the bleaching house and railway tracks. Danger was everywhere. But there was somewhere she'd been thinking of, somewhere she hadn't yet seen. It was the old drying loft Mick had told her about, the room where his grandad once worked. It was where paper had been hung in the days when it was made by hand, before the machines came in. Hadn't Mick said it hadn't been used in years? Could she leave Maude there? But if not, then where? What other choice did she have?

'There's a quiet place, somewhere Maude will be safe

while I'm working. I'll check on her once an hour.'

'Once an hour? That's nowhere near enough,' Jean said. 'Ruth, no, this is madness. You haven't thought it through.'

It was true. She hadn't thought about the practicalities of taking Maude to the mill. She'd never looked after a baby full-time before; she didn't know exactly what Maude would need. But she was determined to get her away from Connie by any means she could, and her mind whirred with possibilities.

'I'll tell Edie and Jane, ask for their help; the three of us can look after her between us. We'll work out a rota. I'm supervisor, after all. I can leave the rag room as often as I need to and authorise regular absences for Edie and Jane. No one will find out, Mam, I promise you. I'll take a bag each morning with food and clean nappies, and I'll bring the dirty ones home. I can do it, Mam, with the help of my friends, I know I can.'

Jean shook her head. 'I won't allow it, love, no.'

'Let the lass speak, Jean,' Harry said.

Ruth glanced at her dad, taking courage from his words and his confidence in her. Taking Maude to the mill was a crazy idea and she knew it. But so was leaving the baby with her mam ill in bed and at the mercy of drunken Connie. Who knew what might happen if the woman got her hands on her? It didn't bear thinking about. She had to do something to ensure Maude's safety, no matter how drastic it seemed.

She had seen the way baby Maude had brightened her mam and dad's world, a ray of sunshine in their otherwise desperate lives. She was the reason they were able to cope with their grief at losing Bea. But while Maude had put a smile on Jean's face, Ruth knew that caring for the baby had become nigh on impossible for her. Her mam wasn't getting any better; every day her breathing worsened. She was immobile, wholly confined to her bed, while her dad remained indifferent to the baby's needs. Bairns were women's work as far as an ex-pitman like Harry was concerned, though Ruth saw the look in his eyes on the rare occasions he held his granddaughter. She saw the smile that played over his lips and the tears in his eyes. He missed Bea as much as anyone, but he could never say it out loud.

'I'm going to do it, Mam,' she said firmly. 'I'm going to take her to the mill. No one will know except Jane and Edie.'

Jean bit her lip. 'And what if one of you gets caught?'

Ruth thought of Mr Hewson. She remembered his kind face, the rose in his lapel, the proud way he'd spoken of his daughter. 'The mill owner's a family man. I can only hope he'd understand.'

'But if he doesn't, you're out of a job,' Harry warned. 'And then where will you be? Scrounging for work in Ryhope pubs like your dad. There's pride to be found in having good, honest work and you know it.'

Ruth glanced into Maude's tiny face. 'Trust me, I know what I'm doing.'

Though she wished she felt more sure.

The following morning, Ruth set off on the long walk to work carrying Maude. It wasn't an easy journey, much more difficult than she had thought. For although Maude was small, she cried and squirmed and in no time at all Ruth's arms were aching. She was also carrying a bag containing milk, clean nappies and a blanket. She had to stop often to reposition the baby and make sure she was safe. Doubts clouded her mind. Had she done the right thing taking Maude from her mam and dad? But any uncertainty soon vanished each time Connie came to mind.

As she walked past the buildings of Ryhope Grange, she glanced across to the farmhouse. Was she mistaken, or was that the twitch of a curtain as the farmer's wife watched her go by? She felt nervous, as if she was being judged. When Grangetown cemetery came into view, she walked quickly past the stone angels. Their empty stares sent a chill right through her.

She arrived at the mill an hour before she was due to start work. There was activity all around her; production never stopped, no matter the time of day. Ruth walked quickly with her head bent low. Baby Maude was covered by a shawl and held at her chest. Although Maude was nothing but a tiny scrap of a baby, it had been a long walk and Ruth's arms ached. She scuttled along the side of the esparto warehouse, her heart hammering. She hoped that if any of the men working there saw her, they would think she was one of the mill girls and pay her no mind.

She had never been inside the warehouse before. She looked around for the stairs, then, holding Maude tight, ran swiftly up one flight then another. The last staircase was old and worn. She had to pick her way carefully, avoiding holes in the treads. She held tight to the handrail with one hand and cradled Maude against her chest with her other.

When she reached the top, she gasped. It was exactly as Mick had told her. There was nothing in the room except packing crates and boxes. She felt sure she could create a cradle from an old box, and line it with the blanket. Light flooded in through a bank of windows at one end. She knew those windows faced north, for she'd heard that in the days of handmaking paper, the light couldn't be too strong. Newly made paper had to be protected from the sun. The room was certainly light and airy. She was also struck by how quiet and warm it was.

The roof of the loft arched upwards. At either side of the room, thick wooden poles were attached to the walls. Sturdy honey-coloured beams ran from the poles across the room, some with rope still attached. Ruth wondered if this was where the paper had been hung to dry. There was a calm about the place that she liked; it made her feel safe. She walked towards the boxes and crates, determined to find a safe place. She'd have to tell Edie and Jane – she'd need their help in looking in on the baby – but she knew she could trust them. They'd have to be careful, though. They didn't want to raise the suspicions of any of the workers downstairs. Maude would need feeding and changing. There was a lot to think about. But for now, Ruth's priority was finding somewhere warm and dry; a box that wasn't dirty or rotten.

As she walked towards the boxes, she heard a noise. Her heart sank. Rats? She stood still, alert. The noise came again, a scraping sound from behind the boxes. She inched forward. If there were rats, what then? She'd have to take Maude all the way back to Ryhope. She wouldn't leave her with vermin and the disease they might bring. She was ready to kick out at anything that might run at her as she stepped close to the boxes. But then she heard another sound. This one was different: a voice. Human. A murmur of voices, hushed and low. She heard a man's voice then a woman's. She didn't know what to do. She couldn't move. She didn't want to be found with a baby in her arms, but neither did she want to return to the staircase and run. Yet how could she stay when there were people in the loft? Were they thieves? She dismissed the thought. There was only one thing a woman and a man would be up to in such a private space.

Just then, Maude wriggled and began to cry. 'Shush, little one,' Ruth whispered. But her cry became louder, began to echo around the room. In sheer panic, Ruth turned and walked quickly to the staircase. She had to get out. She couldn't risk being caught. She was just about to start down the steps when a man's voice called out sharply.

'Who's there?'

Ruth gasped. She spun around and saw Alan Murphy, supervisor of the machine room. He was pulling at a cotton scarf at his neck with one hand and fastening his waistcoat with the other.

'You, girl! What business do you have here?'

Ruth could have asked him the same question, but she kept her mouth shut. Maude continued to cry.

'The child, sir . . . I apologise. I was just . . . I mean, I was trying to . . .'

And then Ruth watched in astonishment as a tall, slim young woman with a kind, open face stepped out from behind the boxes and made her way towards Alan. She smoothed her skirt as she walked then ran a hand through her hair.

Ruth fell silent. She was too shocked to say more. The woman was Sarah Hewson.

Chapter Sixteen

Ruth locked eyes with Sarah. She didn't know what to say. It was Sarah who spoke first.

'You won't tell Father, will you?'

Ruth couldn't believe what she was hearing. Here she was, standing in an abandoned room at the mill, holding a baby. And yet Sarah Hewson was the one concerned that she was in the wrong place. It was all Ruth could do just to shake her head. She was afraid she wouldn't be able to speak.

Alan stepped forward. 'I've got to get back to work,' he said stiffly.

He turned to Sarah, and Ruth saw the smile that passed between them. It was the same look she'd seen them exchange in the mill yard some time ago. Then he headed towards the staircase, pausing when he reached Ruth. 'Please don't breathe a word about this.'

And with that he was gone, and Sarah and Ruth were left facing each other across the big empty room. Maude continued to cry.

'Is the child yours?' Sarah asked.

Ruth swallowed hard. She knew that Sarah Hewson

had the power to have her sacked. All it would take would be a word in the ear of the mill owner. But there was little point in lying. Ruth had been caught red-handed.

'She's my sister's,' she said. 'She died.'

'I'm sorry to hear it,' Sarah said.

They stood in silence a moment, staring at each other, both unsure what to say next. Ruth decided to press on with the truth, knowing full well that she couldn't improve the situation by lying.

'Miss, I know I shouldn't be in here, but I had nowhere else to take her.'

'You can't leave her at home?'

'No.'

'You have no family to look after her?' Sarah asked, surprised.

'No,' Ruth replied. She didn't elaborate; it was no one else's business but the Hardys' what was going on at home.

Sarah took a tentative step towards her. When she was within a few feet of Ruth, she stopped.

'May I see her?'

Ruth swallowed hard. Her heart was going like the clappers. The morning had taken an unexpected turn and she wasn't sure how it would end. Would she be sent home without a job, turned out from the mill? But there was something in Sarah's voice and in the friendly, informal way she spoke that gave her heart. She carefully laid her bag on the floor, then turned her arms towards Sarah so that she could see the baby. Maude was quiet now, and her eyes were tight shut in her tiny pink face.

'She's called Maude, miss,' she said proudly.

'She's beautiful.'

More beautiful than the brightest rainbow over Ryhope colliery, Ruth thought. More precious than a diamond in a seam of coal. 'Yes, miss,' she said.

'Miss Hardy,' Sarah began. 'Ruth . . . could you call me Sarah, rather than miss?'

Ruth was surprised to be asked. 'But you're the mill owner's daughter, miss. It wouldn't be right.'

Maude began to squirm, and she struggled to hold her. Her arms were burning with the ache in them. Sarah seemed to pick up on her distress. She pointed to the north-facing wall under the windows.

'Why don't we sit down over here for a while and talk.'

Ruth felt a stab of anxiety. She was aware of time passing; she needed to begin work soon. That was, if she still had a job to go to after Sarah had finished with her. Sarah settled on the floor, paying no heed to the dust and dirt on her pretty skirt. Ruth sat beside her with Maude in her lap.

'Were you really going to leave the baby in the loft?' Sarah asked. 'You know, some of the men come up here at dinner time. They bring their newspaper and cigarettes; they say they like the peace and quiet. Your baby might have been safe, but she wouldn't have gone unnoticed.'

This was news Ruth didn't know. How foolish she'd been thinking she could leave Maude here.

'Miss . . .' she began.

Sarah laid a hand on her arm. 'Call me Sarah, please.'

Ruth looked at her shyly. 'You asked me whether I would tell Mr Hewson about finding you here with Alan Murphy.'

'And you won't, will you?' Sarah pleaded.

141

'No, of course not!' Ruth cried. 'But what about me and Maude? Will you tell him about finding me here with the baby?'

'No,' Sarah said firmly. 'It'll be our secret, just yours and mine. As long as you keep to yourself what you saw just now. You must never tell a soul about Mr Murphy and myself. Do you promise?'

Ruth breathed a sigh of relief. 'I promise.'

Sarah thought for a moment. 'I can stop the men from coming here at dinner time. I can make sure your baby is left alone. I'll have a word with my father.'

'Won't he question your request?'

'I'll tell him it's unsafe. I can get one of Alan's men to speak to Father if he needs to know more.'

Ruth's eyes widened. 'Alan Murphy would do that for you?'

A mischievous smile played around Sarah's lips. 'Oh, there's not much that Alan Murphy wouldn't do for me,' she said. 'We've been close since Father bought the mill.'

'Then why keep him a secret?'

Sarah gazed out across the drying loft and took her time before she replied. 'Because Father wants only the best for me. The best clothes, the best education.'

'And the best husband?' Ruth dared to ask. She noticed Sarah's face cloud over.

'Father wants the man I marry to be someone other than a mill worker. But Alan and I, we're in love. I don't want anyone else.'

'Can't you stand up to your dad and tell him that?' Ruth asked.

'I've been trying to pluck up the courage to speak to

him for weeks.' Sarah reached to the sleeping baby and stroked her hand. 'Father respects you, Ruth. It's why he made you supervisor in the rag room. You're one of the hardest-working girls at the mill. I respect you too. For not being shocked at what I've told you. And for keeping my secret safe, just as I will keep yours.'

'If Maude stays in the drying loft, I have two friends in the rag room who'll help me keep watch over her during the day.'

'You're lucky to have such good friends,' Sarah said. Again Ruth saw a sadness flicker across Sarah's face. 'I'll look in on her too. Perhaps if you show me what to do, where her food is kept, I can feed her if she's hungry.'

'There'll be her nappy to change too,' Ruth said.

Sarah wrinkled her nose at the thought. 'Perhaps your friends could assist you with that,' she said. 'But I promise I'll call in on her each time I'm at the mill to see Father . . .' She raised her eyes to meet Ruth's. '. . . or Alan.'

'Thank you, miss . . . Sarah,' Ruth said. 'I can't tell you how much I appreciate your help. And I swear I'll keep your secret. I'll not say a word.'

'I hope this might make us friends, Ruth,' Sarah said with a smile. 'What do you say?'

Ruth offered her hand, and the other girl shook it heartily.

'I say we're friends,' Ruth replied.

Chapter Seventeen

Ruth and Sarah worked quickly to find a suitable box to use as a crib. Ruth lined it with the blanket and laid Maude inside. Then she lifted the box and moved it out of sight, behind a stack of boxes and crates. If Maude cried, she wouldn't be heard on the floor below. The noise of the men working there, unloading esparto grass from the train, sorting it into batches, moving it from one end of the warehouse to the other, would cover any sound.

Once Maude was settled, Sarah began to walk towards the staircase, but Ruth couldn't take her eyes off the baby. So many doubts whirled in her mind. Was she really doing the right thing leaving her? She'd be safe, yes, but alone. Oh, how she wished she had another choice. There'd be no cuddles for Maude, or milk when she cried. She would have to wait until Ruth, Edie or Jane could slip away from the rag room on the pretence of heading to the netty. Ruth looked at Maude's tiny face. The baby was sleeping, unaware of what was happening. She swallowed a lump in her throat.

'She'll be safe,' Sarah said. 'I promise.'

Ruth looked at Sarah's kind face. 'I still don't know if

I'm doing the right thing. It feels very wrong. Bea would never forgive me.'

'This place is quiet and warm,' Sarah said. 'And it has something special about it, doesn't it? It feels safe. Don't you feel that yourself?'

It was true. Ruth had felt something the moment she'd reached the top of the staircase earlier. There was something welcoming about the room that was hard to put into words. Perhaps it was the north-facing windows that flooded the room with delicate light. Or the honey-coloured beams that ran across the ceiling.

'It's the only empty room at the mill,' Sarah said.

Her words helped to quell Ruth's doubts. There was nowhere else she could have left Maude.

'Alan told me that his father worked here, making paper by hand. It was a happy room; men sang as they worked. Their legacy lives on.' A blush spread across Sarah's face. 'I'm sorry,' she said. 'I get carried away sometimes. My father says I'm too romantic for my own good.'

'It still feels wrong to leave Maude here,' Ruth said quietly.

Sarah laid her hand on Ruth's arm. 'I won't pry, Ruth. But you strike me as a determined young woman with fight and spirit in you.'

'I could say the same about you,' Ruth said with a smile.

'A girl like you wouldn't leave her sister's child here if there wasn't a good reason to do so. Whatever that reason, you must take heart from knowing you're doing the right thing, the only thing you can do.'

Ruth straightened her spine. She knew what she was doing was right, but oh, the pain in her heart at leaving Maude alone even for a few hours was almost too much to bear.

'Come.' Sarah took her by the arm as they walked towards the staircase. But before they left the loft, she had a question. 'I understand you're now supervising John Hepple in your rag room?'

Ruth stopped in her tracks. 'Yes, I am,' she said firmly. She wondered why Sarah had brought up the man's name.

'Has he settled in?' Sarah asked. 'Is he working hard?'

'Yes,' Ruth said. Well, at least her answer to the second question wasn't a lie.

She wondered how much to tell Sarah. John had after all been placed in the rag room at the request of the mill owner. Hadn't Mr Hewson said that he was a friend of the family? Ruth didn't want to upset Sarah; she couldn't risk losing her friendship after everything that had just happened. She needed Sarah on her side to allow Maude to stay. But her hesitation in answering seemed to make Sarah determined to enquire further.

'I know John can be a little . . .' She paused, and Ruth picked up on her hesitation, alert. She wondered if perhaps Sarah knew just what John was capable of. 'I know he has his *difficulties*,' Sarah continued.

Ruth noticed the emphasis she placed on the word. 'Difficulties?' she repeated.

'In getting on with people,' Sarah said slowly. 'How is he with the girls?'

'Well,' Ruth began, 'there have been some, as you say, difficulties.' She thought of Claire in tears, with her blouse torn. She thought of the fight she'd seen at the docks.

'If you have any more of these problems,' Sarah said cautiously, 'come to me, let me know.'

'Thank you,' Ruth said. 'I'm very grateful.'

'And I'll speak to Father about allowing children on

the works outing this summer. You could bring Maude.'

'A works outing?' Ruth asked. She was surprised to hear this. There'd never been a works outing before in all the time she'd worked at the mill.

'It was my idea,' Sarah said. 'Father is going to announce it this week. Those who are invited will travel in charabancs for the drive to Seaburn sands.'

'Charas?' Ruth said excitedly. 'I've never ridden in a chara before.'

'Keep it quiet from the rag room girls for now, until the news makes its way around the mill.'

Ruth and Sarah walked down the stairs together and out through the warehouse. Ruth noticed men raising their caps when they recognised the mill owner's daughter. Sarah took it all in her stride. How different their lives were.

Bidding farewell to Sarah, Ruth headed to the office to collect the rag room key. She tried to appear as if everything was normal; as though it was just a day like any other. But her legs were shaking with nerves mixed with guilt at leaving Maude in the loft. She took the heavy key and signed the ledger for its receipt, then walked to the rag room and unlocked the door. She had a lot on her mind. The first thing she needed to do was to speak to Edie and Jane and ask for their help with Maude.

As she busied herself setting up for the day, tidying the bench, she heard footsteps at the door. It was still early and the girls were not due to start work until the clock in the yard struck the hour. Ruth was surprised. None of the girls ever arrived early. She looked up to see who was there, and was shocked to see Jane, cradling a bloodied hand and in tears.

Chapter Eighteen

'Jane? What's happened?'

Ruth ran to her distressed friend. She couldn't ever remember seeing her in such a state before. Jane was always the one who kept her emotions in check and her problems to herself.

'It's nothing. I fell, that's all.'

Ruth looked at Jane's hand. It was badly scraped; dirt and grit mixed with blood covered her fingers and wrist. 'You fell? Where?'

'On the road by the gate,' Jane said.

There was a dullness to her words that Ruth put down to the shock of what had happened. She took Jane's hand, turning it over to inspect her friend's injury.

'It looks worse than it is. It doesn't even hurt much now, although it did when he . . .' Jane stopped herself, but Ruth picked up on the word immediately. She glared at her friend.

'Who's *he*?' she demanded. 'Who did this to you?'

Jane turned her face away. 'No one. I told you, I fell.'

Ruth laid both hands on Jane's shoulders. 'Look me in the eye and tell me the truth.'

She waited for her friend to tilt her head up and look at her. It took a while, but Jane finally did as she asked. 'I fell,' she repeated.

Ruth took a deep breath. 'If that's what you're telling me, that's what I have to believe. But you're my friend, Jane. You can come to me and tell me anything. You know that, right?'

Jane nodded.

'Get yourself to the first-aider across the yard,' Ruth said. 'Don't come back until your hand's cleaned up. And remember, if you want to talk, I'm here. Me and Edie will listen, we'll help.'

Jane walked from the rag room in silence. Ruth sank into her seat. She wondered how much of what her friend had said was true. She thought of the Jane she'd known before her engagement to Davey. She had never been an outgoing girl; she'd always been quiet. But since Davey had come into her life, she'd been a shadow of her former self. Ruth resolved to speak to Edie; perhaps the two of them together could encourage their friend to open up. Until she did so, they wouldn't know what was going on and wouldn't be able to help.

Ruth returned to her work as the girls began to file in ready to start the day. Behind them, two men she recognised from the machine room walked in. This was most unusual. One of them carried a square table with a knife placed in the exact spot for cutting rags.

'Can I help you?' Ruth demanded.

'Where do you want him seated?' the taller of the men asked. He was a stringy fella, with a mop of greasy dark hair that fell over his eyes.

Ruth was confused. 'Who?'

'Mill owner's sent us to set up a separate work space for John Hepple.'

'Mr Hewson's sent you? But why? Hepple sits at the back of the room.'

'Not any more,' the man said. 'Hewson wants him at the front, on his own, under your direct supervision.'

'But he's fine as he is,' Ruth cried. 'I don't understand.'

The man carrying the table dropped it in front of Ruth's work station. Ruth's mouth fell open. All the girls in the room were watching.

'He's to sit there, in the middle, on his own. That's the instruction from Mr Hewson.'

'This isn't right,' Ruth said. 'I'm going to see Mr Hewson, find out what's going on.'

She felt a hand on her arm and the bulk of a man near her.

'I wouldn't do that if I were you,' he said. 'We understand that there's been some problems with Hepple. Best if you leave things the way Mr Hewson wants them.'

The two men walked out, leaving Ruth in a state of shock. She knew immediately who had been responsible for having John moved. Sarah was the only one who knew there'd been a problem. She must have told her dad. Well, Ruth didn't relish telling John about the new arrangement when he arrived that morning. But if he moaned about it, she'd simply tell him that the order came from Mr Hewson's office. That ought to shut him up.

She greeted the girls as more arrived for work, until the room was full and busy. John, as always, was last to arrive. Ruth was surprised when he took the news about being seated in front of her without comment. He kept his head low and his hands busy. When Jane returned from the first-aider with her hand bandaged, no one said a word. Ruth gave Edie a look that told her friend she'd tell her everything when she could.

As the morning wore on, Ruth slipped out often to check on Maude. She noticed the inquiring looks Edie and Jane were shooting her way each time she returned to the rag room. When the morning break bell was rung and the girls could finally talk, Ruth took Edie and Jane to the old drying room and explained all about leaving Maude there. Edie sucked air through her teeth and grimaced, while Jane took the news in her stride. Both of them promised Ruth that they'd help as best they could. And during the remainder of the morning, Edie and Jane left the rag room at intervals to check on Maude. Each time either of them returned to the rag room, they gave Ruth a thumbs-up sign to let her know all was well. The baby was sleeping, and Ruth was relieved and heartened to know she was safe. But she still had her doubts, and spent the morning feeling sick with guilt. She was exhausted after spending nights trying to get Maude to sleep. Her back and arms ached, and tiredness dulled her mind. Without Bea around to help, caring for her mam now fell entirely to her, and there were still her dad's moods to contend with. And now Jane's injury darkened her thoughts.

Apart from Maude's smile, which melted Ruth's heart, there was little to brighten her days. Most of the time she accepted this; she knew her lot in life would never be more, or better. But on days like today, how she wished she had someone to take care of *her*.

* * *

After checking on Maude mid afternoon, Ruth was on her way back to the rag room when the stern features of Dorothy Smith the mill clerk came into view. She was walking from the office waving a sheet of paper.

'Here! Got a bit of good news. There's to be a works outing.'

Ruth took pride in being in Sarah's confidence and already aware of the news. She took the paper from Dorothy and read the details printed on it.

'I'm handing these to the supervisors of those invited to the first outing,' Dorothy said. 'Not everyone at the mill is allowed to attend, for production here is non-stop, as you know. I need a list of names of who's going from the rag room by four o'clock sharp so I can get the charas organised. It's a half-day outing, pick up at two o'clock. No shirking allowed in the morning; no dinner break that day either.'

Ruth watched as Dorothy scuttled away with the papers in her hand, eager to give the news to the men in the machine room, the esparto warehouse, the bleaching room and all the other rooms at the mill. She glanced again at the paper and a smile made its way to her face. An outing to the seaside, an afternoon with friends. Maybe this was just what she needed.

Chapter Nineteen

On the morning of the outing, Ruth had trouble getting the girls to concentrate. Everyone apart from John was animated, chatter at a level she had never known. She had to calm them, tell them to be quiet, which was difficult when she was just as excited. Many of the girls had brought their best hats to wear on the outing. They hung them on coat hooks on the wall, and with their colourful ribbons, they brightened the rag room.

Ruth had checked with Dorothy in the mill office that she was allowed to take her sister's baby on the outing. Dorothy had grudgingly approved her request.

'Looks like you've been given special permission from Mr Hewson,' she huffed. 'No one else is being allowed to take children on the chara. Those who want to take their bairns are being asked to go by tram.' She leaned across her desk and glared at Ruth. 'I don't know what makes you so special, Ruth Hardy. But there's something going on, I can tell. I've worked at the mill my whole life and I know when something's awry.'

Ruth kept her face straight and gave nothing away to the woman in front of her. It was no one else's business that she and the mill owner's daughter were friends sharing secrets.

'Tell Mr Hewson I'm very grateful,' she said.

Dorothy sniffed. 'You can tell him yourself. He's put you in the chara with the supervisors. You'll be sitting with them and Mr Hewson.'

Ruth felt a pang of disappointment. 'But I want to sit with my girls.'

'You'll sit where you're put,' Dorothy said sharply. 'If Mr Hewson wants you in the supervisors' chara, that's where you'll go.'

'With the baby too? The top brass at the mill won't be happy about that, surely?'

Ruth watched as Dorothy appeared to give this some thought. 'I'll see what I can do,' she said eventually. 'If I can rearrange the list of who's going in which chara, I will. But I can't promise anything.'

Ruth left the office with a spring in her step. She'd known stern-faced Dorothy Smith since the day she'd started work at the mill. Everyone knew the clerk was a stickler for lists, charts and columns of figures. But underneath that hard exterior, Ruth was beginning to wonder if she'd finally found Dorothy's heart.

At two p.m., a whistle blew in the mill yard. It was the signal for work to stop, where it could. Esparto grass, wood pulp and rags continued to be swallowed up at one end of the mill. Sheets of newly made paper still needed to be counted into reams by nimble-fingered women in the counting room. Finished paper still needed to be transported from the mill to the docks. It was a lucky few who were able to attend the first outing, and the girls in the rag room were among them. When the whistle blew, they leapt from their benches, pulled on their hats and ran out to the yard. Ruth didn't stop them, didn't tell them to slow down; she was happy and excited too.

Edie and Jane came with her to collect Maude from the loft, both girls more than willing to help. Edie, with her many younger brothers and sisters, was a natural with the baby; she was confident in holding her, knew how to feed her, how to get her wind up. Ruth learned a lot from her friend.

Jane, however, was more reticent. 'I'm frightened I'll break her,' she said when Ruth laid the baby in her arms the first time. 'She's so precious and tiny.'

'She's our Bea's bairn; she's got a lot of fight in her,' Ruth said.

The three of them made their way to the mill gates, where a line of charabancs was waiting. The girls stood admiring the carriages, eyeing the drivers in their smart black hats. Edie gave a long, low whistle through her teeth.

'Have you ever seen the likes of it before?'

Ruth and Jane had to agree that they hadn't. Ruth looked along the line of charabancs, all the way to the front. She saw Mr Hewson standing at the roadside, opening the door to allow Alan Murphy inside. She saw Sarah take her seat next to Alan as the chara filled up with supervisors, all men. Ruth was the only female supervisor at the mill. She was grateful to Dorothy for changing the list of who was sitting in each chara so that she could travel with the rag room girls instead of in the supervisor's chara.

'Is John Hepple coming?' Jane asked.

'He didn't put his name on the list,' Ruth said. 'And for that we can all be grateful.'

They walked towards an empty chara, and when the driver saw them approach, he leapt down to the pavement, opening the door with a flourish.

'Ladies, your carriage awaits.'

Edie stepped up inside; once she was seated, Ruth handed Maude over before she clambered aboard. Jane was next, and then the rest of the rag room girls climbed in. When they saw Ruth with a baby in her arms, some of them were shocked into silence. They clearly didn't know what to think. Others began gossiping about the child, wondering whose it might be. Ruth ignored them, happy to let them chat. She didn't want to spoil their outing by telling them off, but Edie had heard enough. She stood up and clapped her hands.

'Now, listen, you lot!' she yelled. The girls snapped into silence. 'I've got two things to tell you. Yes, there's a baby in our chara. And no, it's none of your business.' She sat down and brushed her hands together as if dismissing further talk.

'Well done,' Ruth laughed. 'Are you sure you wouldn't fancy having a crack at being the supervisor one day yourself?'

'Not on your nelly,' Edie replied.

The girls were subdued for a moment or two, but they were too excited to stay quiet for long. They were soon singing, laughing, carrying on and joking. Ruth felt a happiness the likes of which she'd not felt for a long time, not since Bea died.

Suddenly she felt a sharp nudge in her side as Jane was pushed into her. She instinctively gripped Maude tightly. 'What the . . . ?' she cried.

She looked past Jane to see what was happening. Davey

Winter had pushed his way on to their chara when it was already packed full and had squeezed in beside Jane. A heaviness settled in Ruth's heart.

'Shove along, lasses,' he demanded.

'Oh no, not him,' Edie whispered. 'What's he doing here? He should be on the chara with the machine room men.'

Ruth and Edie shifted along the bench as far as they could. It had been a tight squeeze even before Davey got on, and with his added bulk, the three girls were pinned tight. Ruth didn't smile or say hello to him, but she locked eyes with him for a second, letting him know she'd seen him. Her stern expression, she hoped, would tell him all he needed to know about what she thought of him.

She watched as he took one of Jane's hands. But what should have been a romantic gesture quickly turned sinister. There was no mistaking Davey's words, even though he spoke quietly, for Ruth and Jane were squashed together and she could hear him clearly.

'You weren't thinking of heading off on the outing without me, were you, Jane?'

'No, Davey.'

'It's just as well I found you before you set off then, isn't it? If I didn't know better, I'd think you were trying to avoid me, to spend the day with your friends. And what sort of friends are they? One's got a bairn and the other's well known at the mill for being a tart.'

'Davey, please,' Jane urged.

'Haven't I told you not to go anywhere without me now we're engaged? We do things together or not at all. Isn't that right?'

'I'm sorry, Davey.'

Ruth felt her blood run cold at the big man's threatening tone. 'Are you all right, Jane?' she asked. She made sure Davey could hear her. She wanted him to know she was aware of him controlling her friend. She thought again of Jane's bloodied, scraped hand, and her reluctance to talk about it.

She felt another uncomfortable bump as Davey put his arm around Jane's shoulders.

'Should be a smashing day, this,' he said with forced cheer.

'It was before he turned up,' Edie muttered to Ruth.

Their conversation ended when the engine roared into life and the chara slowly moved away from the mill. Within minutes, it was making its way towards the bridge that spanned the River Wear. Ruth had never been across the river before. The furthest from Ryhope she'd been was only as far as the mill. There'd been no reason to go into Sunderland town centre, for she couldn't afford the tram fare, never mind goods from the shops. She'd heard about the shops, though. Edie had told her about walking around the magnificent Binns store with her mam, looking at things they'd never be able to buy. It sounded like a different world to anything Ruth had seen. Edie had also told her about the museum, with its glass-covered winter gardens looking out to a lake. Ruth hoped they would pass this on their way through the town, and she kept her eyes peeled. She felt her excitement build, and kissed Maude on her cheek as the chara sped on to the bridge, with the wide river flowing below.

'Look, baby,' she cooed. 'It's Sunderland, the land cast asunder by the Wear.'

She marvelled at the structure of the bridge, which

loomed high above, intricate and delicate, like a lace pattern forged from steel. Rumour had it that one of the rivets was made from pure gold. Ruth glanced around her, taking in the splendour. Behind her, the rag room girls had quietened, and she wondered if they were awestruck too. Certainly the sights had taken their minds – and gossip – away from baby Maude. On the river below, ships of all sizes lined the quays and docks. And beyond was the sea, sparkling in the sunshine. Ruth saw a lighthouse, two piers curving towards each other, welcoming ships into the docks.

At the end of the bridge, the chara carried straight on, then turned right towards Roker.

'We're nearly there,' Edie said, her eyes wide with excitement.

Ruth sat up straight in her seat, trying to jostle for space to hold Maude. But the bulk of Davey on their seat made it impossible to get comfortable. She glanced at Jane. Where Edie and Ruth had talked excitedly all the way from the mill, their friend had been silent, despite Ruth's best efforts to include her in conversation. She noticed that Jane's hand was still gripped by Davey's fat fingers.

Finally the chara pulled to a stop outside the tea room at Seaburn. Davey was the first to leave the chara, and relief rushed through Ruth when she could finally breathe again. Jane stepped out next, and Ruth saw Davey roughly grab her as they headed off together. Ruth called to her and Jane turned round briefly, but then Davey said something that Ruth couldn't hear and Jane turned her back on Ruth and Edie.

'I thought the three of us were going on the sands together,' Edie said.

'Looks like Davey's got other plans for Jane,' Ruth said. 'We should have talked to her ages ago. We kept saying we would. I feel like we've let her down.'

'Don't be so hard on yourself. You've had a lot on your plate, what with Bea and Maude and everything else you've got on at home. Jane's a big girl. She can look after herself.'

But Ruth wasn't so sure.

Ruth and Edie alighted from the chara, each of them taking a turn to hold Maude. The summer day had been warm and still when they'd set off from the paper mill, but at Seaburn, the wind whipped in from the sea.

'Will I buy us a pot of tea to take on the sands?' Edie asked.

Ruth hesitated. There was nothing more she wanted than a cup of hot tea, but she couldn't afford it.

'It's all right, I'll pay,' Edie said, picking up on her unease. 'And I'll ask for a cup of warm milk for Maude.'

'You're a good friend, Edie,' Ruth said.

There was a long queue of people lined up to be served at the tea room.

'I might be some time,' Edie said.

Ruth nodded towards the beach. 'I'll wait by the steps, then we'll go and find a nice spot.'

She walked across the road to where a flight of stone steps led down to a broad sweep of golden sand. How beautiful the beach was, how different to the coal-blackened stretch at Hendon where she and Edie sat at dinner time. Ruth tucked her skirt under her legs and sat on the top step, gazing out to sea. The tide was far out, further than she'd ever seen it at Hendon. There were no rocks on this beach, and no dramatic cliffs either, not like at Ryhope.

Maude began to cry and Ruth tried to shush her. 'Milk's coming soon, Maude,' she said. 'Edie's bringing milk.'

She turned her head to see if she could spot Edie in the tea-room queue. When she returned her gaze to the sea, a small dog ran past her. He wore a blue collar, and his little brown ears and tiny mouth with its crooked grin looked familiar. Ruth's heart leapt.

'Button?'

The dog stopped, looked towards her and ran up the steps to her side. She stroked him with her free hand. She hadn't let herself hope that Mick might be on the outing, for what good would it do her to allow herself to dream? He had made it clear that things were finished between them, and she'd struggled to accept it. But now suddenly there he was, as large as life, as handsome as ever and walking straight towards her.

A brief look of confusion crossed his face when he saw Maude.

'Mind if I sit here?' he asked.

Ruth shifted along the step, clearing a space. Button lay down between them. Ruth cradled Maude to her shoulder to ease her cries. So many times she'd wanted to see Mick since he'd given her the brush-off. At first she'd felt the loss of him acutely, her heart aching for his touch. But now? Had too much water flowed under the bridge? She hadn't seen him in ages. Their paths had never crossed at the mill. She wondered if he'd deliberately kept out of her way.

'Thought I'd lost Button for a second,' Mick said cheerily. 'He's always running away on the beach; he loves it here.'

Ruth smiled weakly. If Mick was making the effort to

make polite conversation, the least she could do was respond.

'Did you bring him on the chara?' she asked. She was certain Dorothy Smith wouldn't have allowed that when she'd given instructions as to who should sit where.

'No, I walked here,' Mick said.

'All the way from the mill?'

'It's not far, four miles or so. Button needed the exercise, and to tell you the truth, so did I. How are you, Ruth?' he asked. 'And who does the little 'un belong to?'

Ruth wondered where to begin. A lot had happened since she'd last seen Mick. She began, hesitantly, to tell him about Bea. But she kept quiet about leaving Maude in the loft. That was her secret, with Sarah, Edie and Jane. The fewer people who knew about it, the better. Besides, Mick wasn't her confidant any more, she reminded herself.

When she'd finished speaking, Mick was silent, stroking Button's ears. The two of them gazed out to sea. They were sitting close together, close enough almost to touch. Close enough for Ruth to hear and feel Mick's breath.

'I was thinking, Ruth . . .' he began. He stopped and began to stroke Button's ears.

Ruth's heart leapt. She swallowed hard. She couldn't let herself get caught up in some romantic notion about Mick, not again. He'd broken her heart once and she'd thought she'd never recover. She couldn't let him do it again.

'I was thinking maybe I'd not treated you well, last time.'

Ruth bit her tongue. Last time? Was he hinting there'd be a next time? She couldn't go through with a next time, not with Mick or anyone. Love seemed to have a nasty way of making itself felt in hurt and despair. She'd suffered tearful sleepless nights since Mick had ended their relationship. The loss of his friendship had hit her hard, right when Bea had died. She'd have given anything to have had him to talk to then. But she'd held firm, her pride intact. She hadn't made a fool of herself going chasing after him. She decided to stay quiet, but was curious to hear what he had to say.

'And I was feeling,' he continued, 'that I've been too harsh. You're a wonderful girl, Ruth. I know that now. I was selfish, expecting you to give all your attention to me when you had your parents to care for and Bea to look out for. And I see the way you are there with Bea's baby – you look like a natural, lass. To think I could have . . .' He paused. 'We could have had our own bairns one day, even got married. I kick myself daily for what I said to you back then. I've been a fool, Ruth. A stupid, thick-headed fool who let the best thing that's happened to him slip through his fingers. Worse than that, I pushed you away.'

Ruth felt tears prick her eyes. But still she kept quiet and stared ahead. How easy it would be to turn to Mick, to take his hand, to kiss him, to tell him she forgave him. How easy it would be to take up where they'd left off. But he'd said hurtful things. He'd expected her to put him above looking after her poorly mam and dad, above Bea. No, she couldn't thaw towards him, she mustn't. And yet her heart screamed for him to take her in his arms and kiss her and tell her everything would be fine. Could she dare try another time with him? Should she? She felt conflicted.

She reached a hand towards Button's ear and scratched

him. Button whined with pleasure, with Ruth rubbing one ear and Mick the other. And then Mick's little finger made its way across the dog's head to where Ruth's hand lay. His touch sent a shockwave direct to her heart, and she allowed her fingers to be gently caressed.

'Ah, so that's where you are!'

Mick pulled his hand away. Ruth looked round and saw a young woman standing behind them. She was a bonny lass, with a round face and freckles across the bridge of her nose. Her long fair hair fluttered in the breeze and she wore a hat printed with a band of daisies.

'Are we going for a walk on the sand then, or what?' she demanded.

Mick stood up. 'I was just talking to a friend,' he said.

The girl nodded towards Ruth. 'Pleased to meet you, I'm sure.' She slotted her arm through Mick's, and the two of them stepped down on to the sand, with Button following.

'Who was she, Mick?' Ruth heard her ask as they walked away. 'You two looked very pally there, if you don't mind me saying. I hope I haven't got competition for my new fella.'

Her heart dropped when she heard Mick's reply.

'She's just a paper mill girl.'

Ruth held her head high and swallowed the lump in her throat that threatened to overwhelm her. Tears filled her eyes and she turned her face to the sun, willing them away. But if she had glanced towards Mick, she would have seen him turn around and look back. And she would have noticed regret, love and tenderness etched all over his face.

Chapter Twenty

Ruth felt something nudge her side and was relieved to see Edie, carrying a tray with a small silver teapot, two porcelain cups, a jug of milk and four lumps of sugar.

'My word, that queue was long. Looks like all the charas turned up at the same time and everyone had the same idea. People were bursting for a cuppa.'

Ruth slowly and carefully stood from the step with Maude in her arms.

'Who was that fella you were talking to?' Edie said. 'I saw you when I was walking towards you.'

'Mick Carson,' Ruth said. The words felt heavy on her lips. His name had been constantly on her mind and in her heart, but she hadn't said it out loud in months.

'No!' Edie cried. 'What did he want? Ruth? What did he say?'

Ruth began to walk down the steps. She wasn't ready to talk about Mick, about what had almost happened between them, about their hands touching, about what he'd said. Instead she pointed to the sands, changing the subject. 'Look! Some of the mill lads have brought a football. Let's watch them play.'

The two girls headed to where men from the mill had set up a game of football. They settled themselves on the sand. Ruth took off her woollen jacket and placed it between her and Edie, laying Maude there to protect her from the wind.

Edie lifted the teapot. 'It was a whole shilling's deposit for this,' she said. 'I'll get it back when I return the tray before we go home. Speaking of which, we mustn't forget to be at the chara by five o'clock. Mr Hewson's arranged for a photographer to take a picture before we go back to the mill.'

Ruth didn't need reminding. She looked at her worn skirt and her boots with the holes that let in the rain. How she wished she had something else, something better to wear for the photograph.

'Shall I be mother?' Edie said, as she poured milk into cups.

Ruth looked at Maude lying beside her. 'Yes, you be mother,' she said. 'I don't think I'll ever make a good one. I can't even look after my own niece properly. It still doesn't feel right leaving her on her own.'

'Ah, don't beat yourself up, Ruth,' Edie said breezily. 'You're doing a fine job and Bea would be proud. Maude's been all right in the loft, hasn't she? No rats have come to nibble her toes, no tinkers have come to thieve her.'

'Oh Edie,' Ruth laughed. 'What would I do without you? How will I manage when the weather turns cold, though?'

'That's not for months yet. Something might turn up before then,' Edie said.

'I wish I knew how,' Ruth sighed.

Edie handed her a cup of tea. 'There's plenty of milk

166

left for Maude. The woman behind the counter didn't charge me when I told her it was for a bairn.'

Ruth dipped her hand into her pocket and brought out two slices of bread.

'What have you got there?' Edie asked, opening her bag. 'Want to go halves on mine? I brought gooseberries for us too.'

'There's a lot of them,' Ruth laughed when she saw the box of berries.

'I thought Jane would be here to help us eat them,' Edie said.

Ruth peered at Edie's food, a slice of meat pie. 'I'll swap you,' she said. 'Half your pie for a slice of my bread.'

Edie tore the pie with her fingers and handed half to Ruth.

'You don't mind sitting here watching the lads playing football, do you?' Ruth said.

Edie watched the men running about in front of her. Some of them had removed their jackets to use as makeshift goalposts, and many had loosened their ties. One or two of them had even rolled up their trouser legs and taken off socks and boots.

'You're asking if I mind watching a bunch of half-naked fellas running around?' Edie said mischievously. 'Oh, I think I can cope.'

The two girls giggled as they watched the game. Ruth quickly noticed that one of the men kept looking over at Edie. He even waved and smiled at her every now and then.

'He's got his eye on you, that one,' Ruth said.

'Who, Ted? He's one of the Lumley brothers,' Edie said. 'He's on my top-ten list of good-looking fellas I know.'

Ruth laughed at the notion of Edie keeping such a list. 'Would you go out with him if he asked you?'

Edie shrugged. 'Might do. Depends if he asks. Anyway, what were you and Mick Carson chatting about? Come on, Ruth, tell me.'

Ruth avoided Edie's stare and looked out at the men running, shouting and kicking the ball. She still wasn't ready to talk about Mick. She wanted to think about what he'd said earlier; she wanted to go over his words one last time before she let him go from her mind.

'He's got himself a girlfriend,' she said.

'Anyone we know?'

Ruth thought of the pretty girl in the hat. 'I didn't recognise her.'

'Was he chatting you up?' Edie asked hopefully.

'Edie . . . don't, please,' Ruth said. 'I'll tell you what he said, I promise. But not yet. I need time to think.'

She sipped her tea and fed milk to Maude. Edie untied her boots and pulled them off, then stood, burying her feet in the sand and wiggling her toes.

'Oh, that feels good, Ruth. You should try it. There's no feeling like having sand between your toes. Can I take Maude to see the sea?'

Ruth wrapped the baby up in her jacket and handed her over to Edie's safe arms, then sat back on the sand and watched as her friend made her way to where the waves kissed the shore. As she walked past the men playing football, Ted Lumley peeled away from the game. His absence was met with shouts of derision from the rest of those playing. A few catcalls and whistles went up when his teammates saw him walking with Edie. Ruth wished she had half of Edie's confidence. Edie could talk to anyone, get along with everyone where Ruth was shy and guarded.

A woman's voice pulled her from her reverie. 'Hello there. Are you on your own?'

Ruth spun around and was surprised to see Sarah Hewson. At her side was a man Ruth had never seen before. He didn't look like one of the men from the mill. He appeared more delicate than that, as if he'd never done a hard day's work. He was as tall as Sarah and his skin was ghostly pale. Ruth's first thought was that if the wind got a little stronger, it might blow him away.

'Ruth, this is Henry Wood, a friend of the family,' Sarah said. 'Henry works in my father's solicitor's office. Henry, this is Ruth Hardy, one of the hardest-working girls at the mill. And she's a supervisor too.'

Henry doffed his hat. 'Pleased to meet you,' he said.

Ruth was surprised at his deep, powerful voice, which was at odds with his frail appearance. She looked into his face and saw his blue eyes sparkle. A smile made its way to his lips, and at the sight of it, she felt a heat rise in her neck that ran all the way up to her cheeks. She doubted very much that Henry Wood would make his way on to Edie's list of good-looking fellas, yet there was something about him that Ruth was drawn to. His blue eyes and sandy hair gave his face an open, honest look. She offered her hand.

'Nice to meet you too,' she said.

She had expected Henry to shake her hand. Instead, he gently brought it to his lips and planted a soft, warm kiss. She was shocked to the core. No one had ever kissed her hand before, and she wasn't sure how to react. Was he flirting with her? Was he poking fun? She pulled her hand away from Henry's and then Sarah broke the silence. 'Come along, Henry,' she said firmly.

Ruth was taken aback by her tone. Had she done something wrong, overstepped an invisible line in letting Henry take her hand and kiss it? It hadn't been her decision, and yet Sarah seemed rattled. Ruth felt uneasy.

'Must we go?' Henry asked, keeping his eyes fixed on Ruth.

'Yes, we must,' Sarah said. 'Bye for now, Ruth.'

'Bye,' Ruth replied.

Henry winked at her. 'Goodbye, Miss Hardy, I hope our paths might cross again.'

Ruth watched the pair of them walk away along the sands, all the while thinking what an unusual man Henry was.

Chapter Twenty-One

The week after the works outing, the photograph of the mill workers went on display in the office. Ruth allowed groups of excited girls from the rag room to go and look at it. She was as keen as they were to see the photograph framed and hung. She knew the girls would search the picture to find themselves there. They wanted to see how pretty they looked, if their best hat flattered their face as much as they hoped. They all wanted a reminder of their carefree afternoon on the sands.

'One at a time, girls!' Dorothy Smith called when the girls piled into her office.

Ruth and Edie were first in the queue. Jane, however, seemed less interested and hung back at the end. Ruth searched the photograph to find herself, but it was Mick's face that jumped out first. He was beaming at the camera. She searched for the girl he had been with at the beach. She wasn't at his side, nor in front or behind him. When she finally found her, standing at the back of the group, she was surprised how relieved she felt that she and Mick hadn't been pictured together.

'There we are!' Edie cried. She was pointing at the end

of the third row. The first row of girls were seated on the sands, the second kneeling behind, the third standing. Ruth was right on the end of the row, with Maude hidden behind a wide-brimmed hat worn by a girl in the row in front of Ruth. Those behind them were standing on the steps leading up to the prom. The effect was a small mountain of hats, heads and arms. Everyone was looking at the camera, at the funny little photographer with the curled moustache who'd kept waving his arms around and calling for them to be still. Everyone was smiling. Everyone, that was, except Jane.

Ruth gasped when she found Jane in the photograph and saw the expression on her face. She turned to look at Edie and saw that her friend was open-mouthed. She knew Edie had seen what she had too.

'Look at Davey, behind her,' Edie said, nodding at the picture.

Davey was staring at the camera as if challenging it to a fight. Jane was in front of him, with her head turned to one side as if she wanted to be somewhere else. But it wasn't just the expression on her face that caused alarm bells to ring for Ruth and Edie. It was the sight of Davey's hand on her neck. It was obvious to anyone who cared to look that he was holding her just a little too tight.

'She was trying to move away from him,' Edie said. 'He was hurting her. Look! It's right there in front of us. We're going to have to have it out with her. Today.'

'Dinner time,' Ruth whispered. 'We'll go to the loft as if we're going to check on Maude. It's time we got to the bottom of this.'

* * *

At dinner time, the three girls sat together in the drying loft. Ruth had Maude in her arms. Edie opened her bag to reveal a boiled egg and two cold potatoes. Ruth and Jane each had a crust of bread scraped with beef paste.

'Anyone want to swap dinner?' Ruth asked. She was eyeing one of Edie's potatoes.

'I'll give you a bite of potato for a bite of your bread,' Edie offered.

Ruth didn't need asking twice. The floury potato melted on her tongue.

'I'm all right with what I've got,' Jane said.

'How's your Davey doing?' Edie asked casually.

Ruth shot her a look. She hadn't expected her to bring the subject up in such an obvious way. She'd hoped they could get Jane to talk about the outing first, to say what she'd enjoyed and perhaps what she hadn't. Typical Edie, she thought, rushing into things head-first without pausing to think. There was nothing Ruth could do now, though. Edie's words were out and Davey's name hung over them like a bad smell in the air.

Jane shrugged. 'He's all right,' she replied sullenly.

Ruth raised her eyebrows.

'I know you don't like him,' she said. 'I can tell. But Davey looks after me. He's a good man. I wouldn't be planning to marry him if he wasn't.' But even while she was singing Davey's praises, she couldn't look Ruth and Edie in the eye.

'We're just worried about you, that's all,' Ruth said. 'You seem different since you met him, not as happy as you used to be.'

Now it was Edie's turn to join the conversation, putting her foot right in it again. 'Look, Jane, we saw the photograph in the mill office this morning. Was he hurting you?'

Jane dropped her sandwich.

'And when you hurt your hand and had to have it bandaged in the medical office, did he cause that?'

'Edie, please,' Ruth begged. She felt Edie had gone too far with her questions. She would have asked a lot more subtly if it had been just her and Jane. But maybe, she thought, it was what Jane needed, someone to demand the truth. She looked at Jane and saw her cheeks flush red. Was it anger or embarrassment? And then Jane's eyes welled up with tears, and she began sobbing on Edie's shoulder.

'I don't know what to do,' she said softly in between her tears. 'I'm stuck with him now.'

'You're not stuck with him, love,' Ruth said. 'Tell us and we'll help you.'

Jane shook her head. 'I *am* stuck. We're engaged and our families are planning the wedding. I can't stop it now.'

'Do you want to stop it?' Edie asked.

'Yes,' Jane sobbed. 'I should never have let it get so far.'

'Does he . . .' Ruth began. She paused a moment before she continued. 'Does he hurt you, Jane? With his fists?'

Jane nodded. Ruth and Edie shared a concerned look.

'Jane? Can I ask you something?' Jane wiped the back of her hand across her eyes as Ruth carried on. 'That day on the beach, when it was hot, do you remember? Me and Edie were sunbathing, with our bare arms in the sun. We asked you if you were boiling up in your jacket. I mean, you must have been, but you wouldn't take it off. And then there was a day in the rag room when you moved away from me on the bench when I sat too close to you. What was all that about? It was out of character for you.'

Jane closed her eyes tight and took her time before replying. 'He hurt my arm; there were bruises. I couldn't let you see them, that's why I kept my jacket on. I was ashamed. I didn't have the strength to tell you. I was frightened you'd think badly of me.'

Edie held her hand. 'Oh Jane. We're your friends, you must never think that.'

'And I moved away from you on the bench for the same reason. I had a pain in my side.'

'Davey caused that too?' Ruth asked.

Jane nodded. 'He says he's sorry, every time he hits me. Sometimes he cries and swears he'll never do it again, but then he does. And I don't know how to leave him. I *can't* leave him. My mam and his mam know each other, they'd be upset.'

'Never mind your mam. You've got to think about yourself,' Ruth said.

Edie shot her a look. 'Says you, the woman who runs around doing everything for everyone else.'

'Edie, this isn't the time or the place. This isn't about me.'

Edie squeezed Jane's hand. 'Jane, if you're not happy with the lad, getting married won't make things better. If anything, they'll get worse. If he treats you badly now, how do you think he'll be once he puts a ring on your finger?'

'I want to leave him,' Jane cried. 'But I don't know how. He's threatened to follow me home if I do. I've tried to cool things with him, but he won't leave me alone.'

'We'll help you,' Ruth said firmly. 'Won't we, Edie?'

'Course we will,' Edie replied, planting a kiss on the side of Jane's head. 'You can come and stay at ours for a few days if you like,' she offered. 'It's not much, but there's a houseful of kids and it'll take your mind off Davey. He'll not find you.'

Jane remained quiet while Edie's offer sank in.

'I'd offer you to stay at ours, but you know how we're fixed in the pub,' Ruth said. 'But there is something I can do for you.'

Jane raised her tearful eyes towards Ruth, desperate to hear what her friend had to say. Ruth knew she had to choose her words carefully, she didn't want to arouse any suspicions in her friends about the secret she shared with the mill owner's daughter.

'I've got a bit of influence with the supervisor in the machine room. I can ask him to keep an eye on Davey and make sure he doesn't come near the rag room at work.'

'No!' Jane cried. 'I don't want Davey to know I've told anyone about him. He'll punish me, I know. You can't tell his supervisor, Ruth, no!'

'You'll be safe with us when you're at the mill,' Ruth assured her.

Jane bit her lip, lost in thought.

'And after work you can come to mine, even if it's just for an hour or so,' Edie chipped in. 'Mam won't mind having another mouth to feed. She cooks for that many of us anyway, she'll barely know there's another person at the table.'

'We'll keep you away from Davey and we'll keep Davey away from you,' Ruth said. 'That is . . . as long as you're sure it's what you want?'

'All right, I'll take what help you can give. But please, don't let him know I told you any of this.'

Jane choked back more tears. 'I thought I loved him, you know? And he said he loved me.'

'Love isn't being given a scratched, bleeding hand, Jane,' Ruth said. 'Love isn't being held so tight that it hurts or being told what you can and can't do or who you can and can't speak to. Love isn't selfish and nasty.'

Jane searched her face. 'Then what is it?' she pleaded. 'How do any of us know when we've met the right one? The one we'll marry and have babies with?'

Mick's face flickered through Ruth's mind and she had to close her eyes. It was too painful. She chided herself for allowing the memories to come so easy. She couldn't stop them, though, no matter how hard she tried. Mick had taken her heart, shown her affection like she'd never known. Despite it all, she knew there was still a part of her that missed him dearly.

'I don't know what love is,' she said at last. 'I just wish that I did.'

The sound of footsteps on the stairs caused the girls to spin around to see who was coming into the loft. At the sight of Sarah Hewson, both Edie and Jane stood and smoothed down their skirts. Edie was still eating. She stood with her hands behind her back, hiding the remains of her food from the mill owner's daughter.

'Oh, there's no need to be formal, girls. Please sit,' Sarah said as she walked towards the three friends. 'I didn't mean to intrude. I just wanted a quick word with Ruth, if I may?'

'We need to get back to the rag room anyway,' Edie said.

'I'll follow you as soon as I've settled Maude,' Ruth told her.

She felt conflicted watching Edie and Jane scuttle away. It made her uncomfortable knowing there was a divide between her new friend and those she had known for years. As the two girls left the loft, she saw Edie take Jane's arm, and chided herself yet again for letting things go on so long. She braced herself to ask Sarah to speak to Alan about Davey. She'd promised Jane, after all.

'How's the baby?' Sarah asked. She sat down at Ruth's side, paying no heed to the dust as her skirt spread on the floor.

'Coming on a treat,' Ruth replied. 'Despite being left alone in here for most of the day.' She immediately realised how ungrateful her words sounded. 'What I mean is . . . I'm sorry, Sarah, that came out all wrong. She's safe here, and warm, and I appreciate your help more than you'll ever know.'

Sarah stroked Maude's tiny fingers. She appeared not to be offended by Ruth's clumsy words. After a moment she glanced up.

'Are you friendly with Dorothy Smith, who works in the mill office?'

Ruth thought this an odd question and wondered what lay behind it. 'Not particularly,' she replied. 'I know who she is, of course. She's efficient at her work, but apart from that, I don't really know her at all.'

A playful smile made its way to Sarah's lips as she ran her hand along Maude's chubby arm. The baby gurgled with glee. 'Well, I've got to know Dorothy well,' she said. 'Father's encouraging me to learn the business, and I'm taking it one step at a time. I find the women easiest to speak to and I've spent a lot of time talking to Miss Smith.'

Again, Ruth wondered what any of this had to do with her. She kept quiet, waiting for Sarah to explain.

'It turns out that Dorothy has a sister, Amelia,' Sarah said.

Ruth was even more perplexed.

'Amelia's a widow woman. Well, as good as. She planned to marry, you see, hoped that one day she'd walk down the aisle at St Paul's church with the man she loved on her arm. But he died in the war, killed in France by all accounts. And now she's settled herself into a lifetime of widowhood without even being married. It's the saddest tale I've heard.'

Ruth shifted Maude from one arm to the other. 'Sarah, I should really return to the rag room,' she said. Her half-hour dinner break had ended more than five minutes ago. Despite Sarah being the mill owner's daughter, Ruth still reported to Mr Hewson himself, and she didn't want to be disciplined for being late for work.

'Don't worry, I'll cover for you if anything's said about you taking a long break,' Sarah said. 'Because I have news you might like. You see, Dorothy's sister takes in bairns.'

Ruth gasped. It was the very same thing she had once suggested to Bea: that she should sell the baby once it was born. Bea had shown her then what love was, had laid Ruth's fingers to her skin so that she could feel the new life moving inside her. Now that Ruth understood that love, she was horrified at what Sarah seemed to be suggesting.

'I won't give Maude up!' she cried. 'I won't sell her. I couldn't, ever. This is Bea's bairn. Mam and Dad would be as heartbroken as me.'

179

Sarah laid her hand on her arm, and Ruth saw a flicker of confusion in her eyes.

'Sell her?' Sarah was shocked.

'Our lives are different to yours,' Ruth said. 'Poverty takes its toll on us all. And there are women who buy babies for cold, hard cash.'

Sarah shook her head. 'No, Ruth, please. That's not what I mean. Listen to me.'

Ruth sat stock still, taking in Sarah's words as she told her about Dorothy's sister. With no other work available to her, Amelia Smith took bairns into her own home and looked after them while their mothers were at work. The house was clean and safe, Sarah reassured Ruth, and best of all, Amelia Smith lived in Ryhope.

'She's got two rooms in a house beyond the coal mine. It's a big place called Tunstall Terrace; do you know it?'

Oh, Ruth knew it all right. Tunstall Terrace wasn't actually a terrace at all; rather, it was a grand detached building, surrounded by lawns and tucked away behind a high wall. It had been built for the manager of the Ryhope Coal Company to live in when the pit was sunk in the 1860s. Now it had been converted into three large homes.

'I know where it is. I've seen it from the road,' she said.

'Amelia feeds and cares for the children who come to her.'

Ruth sighed. It sounded too good to be true. 'And how much does she charge? You know I can't afford it.'

Sarah fidgeted with the delicate sleeve of her blouse. 'That's where I might be able to help.'

'No, I won't take your charity,' Ruth said firmly.

'You've been more than helpful already, letting me keep Maude in the loft.'

'It's not my idea, it's Father's,' Sarah said shyly. 'In reward for . . . well, let's say those difficulties brought into your life by John Hepple that we have already discussed.'

This news took Ruth by surprise. Being rewarded privately for staying silent about menacing behaviour from one of the mill's employees didn't sit well with her. She also worried how much Sarah had told Mr Hewson about Maude. However, she couldn't afford to take the moral high ground and turn down such an offer. Mr Hewson regarded himself as a forward-thinking mill owner, one of the new breed her dad read about in the *Sunderland Echo*. If she wanted Maude cared for properly, safely, she had no choice but to accept his generosity.

She opened her mouth to reply, but snapped it shut again. 'I don't know what to say,' she said at last.

'Just say you'll visit Miss Smith and talk to her. If you choose not to leave Maude there, it will be your decision. But if you employ her services, I'll see that Father pays each week for as long as you need it.'

Sarah reached into her pocket and brought out a piece of paper, which she handed to Ruth. 'Miss Smith's address in Ryhope,' she said.

'Thank you,' Ruth said. 'Now I really should be going back to work.'

'One more thing, Ruth,' Sarah said. 'Father's invited some of the supervisors to join him for drinks. He's asked me to invite you too.'

'Me?' Ruth said, surprised.

'Friday night at eight. Will you come?'

Ruth's mind whirred with anxiety and she felt a heaviness in the pit of her stomach. She had nothing suitable to wear. And where would she leave Maude? She'd need to speak to her mam and dad about Amelia Smith.

'I'd like it very much if you did,' Sarah added.

'Where, here at the mill?' Ruth asked.

Sarah laughed. 'No, not here. It's an informal event, at our home. You see, Father's keen to break down barriers between his workforce and management. Some say he's too progressive for his own good. But I admire him for it.'

Ruth's mouth dropped open in shock. 'You've inviting me into your home?' she said.

'We live in St Bede's Terrace. It's at the edge of Mowbray Park, on the outskirts of Sunderland town centre. Here, take this. I've written the directions for you.' Sarah handed Ruth a second slip of paper. 'Please say you'll come, otherwise I'll be the only woman in a room full of men.'

Ruth knew she couldn't refuse. After Mr Hewson's generous offer of paying for Maude to be looked after by Amelia Smith, she had no right to turn down such an invitation. But still doubts played heavy on her mind.

'I've never been invited to such an event before,' she said. 'Are you sure I'll fit in? My clothes, Sarah . . . I have no smart dress I can wear.'

'Don't you worry about that,' Sarah said. 'Father's invited you because of your quick mind, and your ability to run his rag room efficiently and with kindness. He's not concerned about what you wear; it's not a fashion parade. Oh, and Henry will be there,' she added with a glint in her eye.

Ruth thought of the man with the fair hair she'd met on the day of the outing. He'd seemed pleasant enough, friendly and kind, if a little odd in his behaviour towards her.

'He took a shine to you,' Sarah said. 'He told me.'

'He did?' Ruth was surprised and flattered to hear this.

'Mind you, Henry's always been the sort to quickly lose his head over a girl.'

'He sounds like just what I need,' Ruth said quietly.

'Be careful with him,' Sarah warned. 'As much as I love him, he can be a wolf in sheep's clothing where girls are concerned. One minute he's charming; the next he's moved on to someone else.'

'Don't worry, I wasn't intending to do anything more than be friendly with him,' Ruth said. She appreciated Sarah being so honest with her.

'Alan will be there too,' Sarah continued. 'He's hoping to become more friendly with Father. There's something he wants to ask him in the coming weeks.'

'About you?'

Sarah beamed. 'Would you like to hear another secret?' She didn't wait for Ruth's reply before carrying straight on. 'He's going to ask Father for my hand. He's already proposed.'

'And you've said yes?'

'I've said yes.' Sarah nodded. 'With my heart and my head and with everything I am, I've said yes. I love him, Ruth. There's just the small matter of getting Father to understand.'

'But you said your dad was progressive, intent on breaking down barriers.'

'At work, yes,' Sarah sighed. 'At home, he's very

183

traditional. But I know my father. I'm his only child; it's just the two of us. I'll figure out a way to make him accept Alan.'

'Just the two of you? What about your mam?'

Sarah paused. 'Mother died last Christmas, from the Spanish flu.'

Ruth watched as the other girl closed her eyes. 'I'm very sorry to hear that,' she said.

Sarah gave her head a little shake as if to pull herself together. 'Come on, I'll walk you back to the rag room. Maude looks like she's sleeping now.'

'Sarah? Before we leave, there's a favour I hope I might ask.'

Sarah's eyebrows shot up.

'I realise I'm in no position to ask for anything more after the generosity of your offer today,' Ruth apologised. 'But it's not for me. It's my friend Jane, the girl who was just here, the one with the fair hair.'

'She looked rather sad,' Sarah said. 'I'm intrigued to know what I could possibly do to help.'

And so Ruth began to tell Sarah about Davey Winter. Once they were done, she wrapped Maude in her woollen jacket and settled her inside her box crib. Her heart felt heavy every time she walked away from the child, and this time was no exception. But at least there was now a flicker of hope, if Amelia Smith turned out to be half the woman Ruth hoped.

Chapter Twenty-Two

At home that evening in the Hardys' room at the pub, Ruth scraped potatoes and boiled them in a pan of water on the coal fire. Slices of cold beef waited on plates next to a jar of pickled onions, three cups, a milk jug and the teapot. Jean lay in her bed, in surprisingly good spirits, with Maude at her side, as Jean was now too weak to hold her granddaughter. Harry was in his armchair, reading the day's newspaper and complaining loudly.

'Listen to this, Jean, you'll never guess what's happened now,' he said as he snapped the paper open.

Ruth sat by the fire, keeping an eye on the water, making sure the potatoes didn't boil over. She loved these moments in their room, just the three of them together, with the baby quiet. Perhaps now was a good time, she thought, to broach the subject of Amelia Smith. Plus she needed to talk to her parents about the party on Friday night. She knew she couldn't take Maude with her, but would she dare leave her with her mam if her dad was working in the pub? She gave this some thought. Connie had come looking for Maude a few times since Ruth had taken her to the mill. She'd caused a scene, shouted the odds in her drunken state and demanded to take the child. She'd threatened to sell Maude at the docks, and her words had horrified Jean, though Harry had brushed them off.

'It's just the ale talking,' he'd said.

Sober or drunk, Ruth didn't trust Connie one inch. With her mind made up, she decided to speak to her mam and dad about taking Maude to stay with Amelia on the night of the party. It would give her a chance to meet the woman and see the state of her rooms at Tunstall Terrace. If the place was acceptable, she would decide whether to take Maude there while she worked.

She had expected her mam to try to persuade her to leave Maude at the pub, but there was a resigned air about Jean. She'd finally accepted she could no longer look after the child. Harry was realistic about the situation, although he was suspicious as to why the mill owner had offered to pay for Maude's care. Ruth had kept the subject of John Hepple to herself – she hadn't wanted to upset her mam and dad – but she decided that now was the right time to tell them. And once Harry heard about John's violent temper, his attack on Claire, and how Ruth managed his seething anger in the rag room, it went some way to helping him understand Mr Hewson's generosity. Ruth just wished she understood it better herself, for it seemed more than the situation deserved. With the evening meal of potatoes and beef eaten, she set to boiling up water again to wash plates and cups. Once her chores were done, she sat at the end of Jean's bed, with her legs crossed and her feet tucked under the eiderdown.

'Mam?'

'What, love?'

'You know I said I'd take Maude to visit Tunstall Terrace on Friday night to see if it's suitable to leave her there with this Smith woman?'

'Mmm?' Jean replied sleepily.

'If it's all right there, I was thinking about leaving her. Just for the evening, for a few hours. I'd collect her on my way home.'

'Back home from where?' Harry barked.

Ruth looked from her mam to her dad. 'I've been invited out,' she began hesitantly.

'By a fella?' Jean asked.

Ruth's heart fell at the hopeful tone of her mam's voice. How she wished there was a fella to tell her mam about. Henry's pale face and odd behaviour flickered across her mind.

'No, not a fella.'

'Now that's a shame,' said Jean.

'I've been invited to a party,' Ruth said. 'Mr Hewson's daughter invited me. It's being held at their house.'

Jean raised her eyebrows. 'A party in his own home?'

'And he's invited you?' Harry said. 'My word, the fella really is an advocate of social reform, just like it says in the newspaper.'

'All the supervisors have been invited,' Ruth said.

'Then you must go,' Jean said. 'Oh, you don't half make me proud, love.'

'I want you home before ten,' Harry said.

'Leave the lass alone,' Jean chided. 'She's a grown woman. You can't go telling a supervisor what time she has to come home from a party.'

'I'll not be late, Dad,' Ruth promised.

'What'll you wear to this party, love?' Jean asked.

187

Ruth sighed heavily. 'I've been thinking about that a lot. I haven't got anything suitable. I can just about get away with putting my work skirt and blouse on if I rinse them through first.'

'Nonsense!' Jean said.

Ruth was surprised at the force with which the word left her mam's lips. She hadn't heard her speak so loudly in months.

'What about Bea's clothes?'

'They're too small for me, Mam.'

'Her skirts and blouses might be,' Jean said, 'but you can still wear her lovely blue scarf.' She pointed to the wooden ottoman at the end of the bed, where blankets and old clothes were kept. 'Have a look in there, see what you can find. Oh, and Ruth . . . ?'

'Yes, Mam?'

Jean slowly turned to her bedside table, where there was a small diamond-shaped black lacquer box. She picked up the box and with some trouble, for her fingers were frail, she lifted the lid. Inside was a pair of clip-on earrings made of tiny clusters of what Bea and Ruth used to call pearls when they played with their mam's jewellery as children. But it wasn't the earrings Jean handed over. It was a brooch, one that Ruth and Bea had always been forbidden from touching.

'Here, you can pin this to Bea's scarf,' Jean said.

Ruth turned the brooch over in her hand. It was a tiny bouquet of flowers, with sparkling stones of pink and green. The bouquet was tied with a twist of gold-coloured metal. It wasn't real gold, of course, and the stones weren't real gems. The Hardys could never have afforded such riches. There was no value to it other than the memories it held. But it was the prettiest, most colourful thing they owned.

'Grandma's brooch? Are you sure?'

'I'm sure,' Jean said. 'It's not every day my daughter gets invited to a party, and as a supervisor no less.'

Ruth leaned across to her mam and planted a kiss on her cheek.

On Friday afternoon, Ruth left the rag room as soon as the whistle blew in the mill yard. She collected Maude and headed home quickly. She had a lot to do before attending the party. She had to cook dinner, get dressed and brush out her hair. And then she had to walk to Tunstall Terrace to meet Amelia Smith. If she was satisfied with what she saw there, and only if she was certain, she would leave Maude and take a tram into town. How she hated spending money on the tram when she could ill afford it. But her dad insisted. He wanted her kept from harm and wouldn't hear of it when she told him she could walk.

'Be careful,' he warned. 'They're not like us out there.'

Ruth laughed. 'Out where, Dad?' she asked, puzzled.

'Outside of Ryhope,' Harry replied sagely.

'Oh Dad, you're so old-fashioned,' Ruth teased. 'You can't spend your life looking inwards; there's more to life than the confines of Ryhope, you know.'

Harry rattled his newspaper and raised it in front of his face, putting an end to the conversation.

'Just ignore him. He's always been a silly old fool,' Jean said.

Ruth glanced at her mam, and for the first time in a long time saw the faint trace of a smile on her ashen face.

She pulled a brush through her hair and tied Bea's scarf around her neck. It was a beautiful pale blue, soft and delicate, just like Bea herself.

'Come here, let me pin the brooch to the scarf,' Jean said.

Ruth watched as her mam's frail, papery hands took the coloured brooch out of the box, but when Jean tried to open the catch at the back of the brooch, she didn't have the strength to do it. Ruth cradled her mam's hands and kissed her fingers. Then she took the brooch and pinned it herself.

'You look a picture,' Jean said as she kissed Ruth goodbye. 'Enjoy your party, and remember, I want to hear all about it when you come home tonight.'

Ruth picked Maude up and cradled the sleeping child to her breast.

'I'll walk out with you,' Harry said. 'Mrs Pike's expecting me to clean some glasses in the bar.' He limped alongside Ruth to the back yard of the pub and waved her off into the night.

Ruth set off towards Tunstall Terrace. She felt apprehensive about leaving Maude with a woman she didn't know, but knew it was safer than leaving her at the mill. Miss Smith had come recommended, after all, and by Sarah Hewson no less, which meant that Ruth's fears were somewhat allayed. She walked quickly from the Guide Post Inn, past the Church Institute. Ahead of her was the colliery bank that climbed up to the coal pit. Pubs lined the colliery bank, one after the other, a total of fourteen in less than a mile, catering for the thousands of men and boys working at the coal pit. Well, mining was thirsty work.

Ruth walked up the bank and noted the passing place for trams where the road widened in front of Double Ryhope Street. That was where she would need to take the tram after she'd safely delivered Maude. On she walked, up past the Ryhope & Silksworth Co-operative Society, where many people in Ryhope shopped. Further on, she passed even more pubs lining Ryhope Street North. Finally the Colliery Inn came into view, the last pub at the top of the bank. Here she crossed the road. Ahead of her loomed the high wall that guarded Tunstall Terrace.

She didn't know how to reach the front of the house; there was no gate she could see. She walked as far as she could until the wall turned down the side of a field. She followed the uneven ground and ended up on a sloping lawn. Flowers bloomed in borders, a pretty sight indeed. She picked her way carefully along the edge of the lawn; she didn't feel it right to march up the middle. She was arriving uninvited and needed to have her wits about her. She wondered how much Amelia Smith knew about her other than that she worked at the mill. The sweet smell of honeysuckle filled the air as she walked towards the open back door. She stepped gingerly into the doorway.

'Hello? Miss Smith?'

'Just a minute!' a voice called.

Ruth glanced around, taking in her surroundings. She had entered a sitting room by the looks of things, or was it a kitchen? It was a little hard to tell. A coal fire burned in an enormous black hearth. Above it, pots and pans hung from a bar that ran the length of the fireplace. Three blue pairs of drawers and a pair of black stockings also hung there to dry. Ruth was embarrassed to find herself staring at Miss Smith's underwear before she'd so much as met the woman. In a corner of the room a solid-looking tall and imposing grandfather clock ticked the minutes away. When she saw the time, she gasped. She needed to get a move on if she was to catch the tram, or she'd be late. Then she pressed her feet to the floor, calmed her racing mind and kissed Maude gently. She knew she wouldn't be going anywhere if Miss Smith turned out to be an ogre.

There was a window in the room that looked out to the garden. Under it was a wooden table with a candle in a holder sitting next to a pair of knitting needles poking through a skein of wool. On the mantelpiece above the fire was another clock. Ruth thought how odd it was that anyone would have two clocks in the same room. Both of them ticked loudly, but far from being noisy, the sound was soothing and cosy. On either side of the mantel clock were two china dogs facing each other, keeping watch. A wooden clothes horse leaned at one wall. The floor was swept clean, and Ruth was relieved to see the place tidy.

A woman came scuttling into view. Ruth knew immediately that this was Amelia Smith; she was the absolute double of her sister. She had the same stern expression as Dorothy, and the same dark hair tied in a bun, but she looked younger than her sister. She was wearing a green-checked apron over her clothes, on which she wiped her hands before addressing Ruth.

'What can I do for you, miss?'

'My name's Ruth Hardy and this is Maude. I work at Grange Paper Works.'

Amelia eyed her keenly and Ruth was aware she was

being appraised. She straightened her spine.

'So you're the paper mill girl,' Amelia said. 'I've heard all about you from Dorothy. She tells me you've been keeping the poor bairn at the mill.'

Ruth was horrified. That was supposed to be her secret with Sarah.

'Oh don't look so worried,' Amelia said sharply. 'Dorothy's middle name is discretion. But lass, the paper mill is no place for a bairn. What on earth were you thinking?'

Ruth kept quiet about her mam and dad and their dire situation in the pub. The Hardys had never been a family to air their dirty laundry in public. 'My circumstances left me with no other choice,' she said. 'I was told you might be willing to help.' She felt a nervous flutter in her stomach. What if Amelia refused to take Maude?

'Let me see the bairn,' Amelia said.

Ruth passed her over. 'She's called Maude Hardy,' she said. She would never name the child Tate and acknowledge the child was Jimmy's when he'd shown no interest in her at all.

Amelia held Maude at arm's length, inspecting her. 'She's a good weight. Does she cry much?'

'Yes, I'm afraid she does,' Ruth said.

'Good. Quiet babies aren't happy babies. A good cry gets their lungs working, brings oxygen in. I'll take her. When do you want to start bringing her in?'

'I was thinking . . . hoping really . . .' Ruth began. She took a deep breath. 'Could I leave her tonight for a few hours?' she said at last.

She saw Amelia glance at the clock on the mantelpiece. 'Tonight? Now?'

Ruth lifted her chin. 'I have a function to attend on behalf of the paper mill,' she said.

Amelia gave this a moment's thought. 'Aye, I can keep your bairn tonight. I'll have to charge, of course; I understand from what Dorothy's told me about the situation that my fee is being covered. Now go to your function and let me and little Maude become friends.'

'Thank you,' Ruth said.

She kissed Maude on her cheek and headed out to the garden. She followed the stone wall round to the road, then walked out into the night, heading to the first party of her life.

Chapter Twenty-Three

Ruth left the tram at the end of Toward Road. She'd been given directions by Sarah about how to find the Hewsons' home. She must have read Sarah's words ten times already, but now she studied them again, making certain she knew which way to go.

Looking up, she took in the sight in front of her. It was the museum and winter gardens she'd heard so much about. A magnificent sweep of glass curved out over a lake. The beauty of it gladdened her heart, but she didn't have time to stare. She followed the directions in her hand. Along Toward Road she walked, with the lush green gardens, fountains and statues of Mowbray Park at her side. After a few minutes, she arrived at a crossroads, with Peel Street to her left and Park Road to her right. Here she glanced at Sarah's directions again. She turned into Park Road and walked past the grand avenues of Park Place East and Park Place West, where the houses were the size of three Ryhope pit cottages.

Despite the warm summer night, she felt the cold at her back. She glanced down at her worn boots and old skirt. She wouldn't fit in at a house as grand as these!

What on earth had she been thinking? She hesitated a moment and looked around. Some of the houses were three storeys high, with long, thin gardens at the front. Doubts rushed through her mind, but she forced her feet forward. Sarah had invited her, hadn't she, and at her father's request too. Hadn't she told Ruth that her clothes didn't matter? She'd been invited because she was a mill supervisor. What on earth was she scared of? Sarah had promised that she would look after her at the party, and it sounded as if she had a friend in Henry too.

But even as Ruth was giving herself a pep talk to quell her fears, all she really wanted to do was run to the tram stop and head back to Ryhope. Her dad's words came to her about taking care of herself in the town. She wasn't in Ryhope any more. She knew her place there. Here, in this world of big houses, she felt alone and afraid. She shook her head. She couldn't leave now, not after she'd come this far. Maude was settled for the night, her dad was at work in the pub and her mam was resting. No one needed her at home. This was her night and hers alone. What was the point of giving up now?

She glanced again at the note in her hand. Sarah's neat handwriting advised her to turn left into St Bede's Terrace. Ruth saw the street name etched in a large white stone at the end of the terrace. She gulped as she turned the corner. St Bede's Terrace was even grander than the two previous streets. Large, imposing houses ran down both sides of a wide street. Black iron railings stood guard in front of neatly tended gardens that sloped to the road. Ruth stood and gazed up at the house on the corner. This was it, the house where the mill owner lived.

She let out a long, low whistle between her teeth. She

could see three storeys, and when she looked closer, she saw a fourth, a basement, with windows peeking out to the lawn. She wondered if anyone lived in the house other than Sarah and her dad, for it was a big place for just two people. She lifted the sneck on the gate and pushed it wide open, then walked slowly along the garden path. Trees and shrubs that she didn't know the names of lined the path to her left. To her right was a wooden fence behind a neat flower bed. She recognised the tiny red and white flowers as busy Lizzies. On she walked, trying to calm her mind. Ahead was a tall, wide door painted red. Above the door a sash window looked down to the garden, and to the left of it was a bay window, curtains draped at each side. The same windows were repeated on the floors above. And at the top of it all, five chimneys, straight and tall.

Ruth peered into the bay window on the ground floor. She saw men standing with drinks in their hands, cigars. They were talking, laughing, slapping one another on the back. She didn't recognise any of them, and her stomach flipped again. It wasn't too late to run away, and she was sorely tempted. But she would never forgive herself if she did such a cowardly thing. She thought about what Bea would have told her to do. Her sister would have urged her on. If Bea had been there, right at that minute, she'd have been running up the steps and banging hard on the door, demanding to be let inside. Ruth smiled at the thought. If she headed home now, her mam and dad would be disappointed too. Ruth hadn't been brought up to run away from difficulty but to face it head on. She took another step forward.

To reach the front door meant walking up a short

flight of steps. At either end of each step were pots with red busy Lizzies inside. The whole effect was pleasing and welcoming, and it gave Ruth some comfort. It was a reminder that this was a family home and she'd been invited by a friend. But still she was nervous.

She knocked three times at the door. An unfamiliar face greeted her when the door swung open. It was a girl, much younger than Ruth. She wore a maid's uniform of white pinafore and cap over a long green skirt and dark blouse. She had a plump, round face and auburn hair that she wore in a wave. Ruth took a step back and almost lost her footing. As if she wasn't nervous enough! She didn't know how to behave; she'd never encountered a maid before. But she needn't have worried, for the maid stood back and invited her in, and Ruth stepped hesitantly into the wide hallway.

The walls were painted a muted yellow, and this, together with the oil lamp burning on a side table, gave the hallway a warm, cosy feel. Ahead of her was a flight of stairs, with a patterned carpet runner leading up and away to unseen rooms. The staircase was fancy, with a curved wooden handrail. Ruth saw a wide landing lit by the last of the day's sunlight streaming in through a tall arched window. On each side of the hallway, pictures hung on the wall: framed paintings of ships. One picture in particular caught her eye, and her hand flew to her heart. It was a painting of a handsome, strong woman looking directly at the artist who had wielded the brush. At first glance Ruth thought it was a portrait of Sarah, but the woman's face had more years of life etched into it, especially around her eyes. She looked a lot like Sarah, too much of a resemblance for there to be any doubt about who she was. This could only be Mrs Hewson, Sarah's mam. She had the same look about her, the same curve to her chin and the same glint in her eye.

'May I take your . . .' the maid began to say. Ruth felt the girl's eyes resting on her drab, worn clothes. Ruth had no formal jacket, which must surely be appropriate for this type of event. Her only jacket was the woollen one she wore for work. '. . . your scarf?' the maid offered.

'No, thank you, I'll wear it,' Ruth said quietly.

'That's ever such a pretty brooch, Miss Hardy,' the girl said.

Ruth's fingers fluttered to the stones of her grandma's brooch. 'Thank you,' she said.

She wondered how the maid knew her name. It added to her sense of unease and put her on the back foot. But hadn't Sarah told her she would be the only other woman at the party? So it wouldn't have been difficult for the maid to deduce who she was. Ruth gave her head a shake and told herself not to be nervous. She had to keep reminding herself she'd been invited and wasn't trespassing. But still her stomach turned at the thought of entering a room full of important men. She reminded herself she was an important woman, the only woman supervisor at the mill. She had as much right to be there as any of the men. But still, she felt her legs shake.

'This way, miss. Mr Hewson and Miss Hewson are expecting you.'

The maid extended her arm to a room on Ruth's left. It was the room with the bay window that she had seen from the path, the room where the men were drinking and talking. She could hear chatter and laughter, but she didn't dare move.

'Miss?' the maid said in an encouraging tone. 'They're waiting for you inside.'

The nerves that Ruth had been suffering from since the minute she'd been invited to the party finally got the better of her. She leaned towards the girl.

'Can I use the netty before I go in?'

The maid smiled at her. 'The lavatory, miss? Of course, follow me.'

The maid bustled along the hallway and headed up the stairs. Ruth followed her. She had expected to be shown into the yard, for she'd never known a netty be inside a house before. In Ryhope, it was either in the back yard, or, for those less fortunate, shared on the pit lane with neighbours. Up a second flight they went, past the landing and the tall arched window where the sunlight streamed in.

'It's there, miss,' the maid said, pointing towards a blue door. 'I'll wait downstairs in the hall.'

Ruth entered the room and closed the door behind her. She hadn't expected to feel so overwhelmed by the grandeur of the Hewsons' home. She needed to take a moment to pull herself together. She sank on to a wicker chair with her head in her hands. When she raised her eyes, she found herself looking at the most opulent room she'd ever seen. She was gobsmacked. It was almost half the size of the Hardys' room at the Guide Post Inn. Slim white and green tiles decorated the walls, and she ran her hand over them, tracing the edges with her fingers. A bathtub with iron claw feet took pride of place. The taps were silver. Were they real silver? she wondered. Surely not, they couldn't be! Her eyes widened. There was a washstand with a basin and the same silver taps. Oh, wait till she told her mam and dad about this. And if this was just the netty, what splendours must there be in the rest of the house?

She stood and gazed into the mirror above the wash basin. The coloured stones of her brooch sparkled in the light. She studied her reflection. Her hair was tidy, her face clean, and Bea's blue scarf at her neck complemented her colouring.

'Come on, Ruth, you can do this,' she said out loud.

In reply, Bea's voice came to her unbidden, almost taking her breath away. *You're as pretty as any of the girls at the mill. And you've got something about you, too. Stop feeling sorry for yourself.*

She headed out to the landing. As promised, the maid was waiting in the hall. Ruth swept down the stairs, Bea's scarf floating at her neck. She allowed herself a moment to dream. Many times when she'd walked past the Uplands in Ryhope, the grandest house in the village, she'd tried to peek in through its windows. She'd wanted to see how the other half lived. And now here she was, experiencing it for herself. She could hardly believe it.

She reached the bottom of the stairs.

'Ready to go into the party, miss?' the maid asked.

Ruth pushed her bare feet forward in her boots. 'I'm ready.'

Chapter Twenty-Four

When Ruth stepped into the front room, the first thing that hit her was the fug of smoke coming from the men who stood around holding drinks and cigars. She hovered near the door, looking about her, hoping to find someone she knew: Sarah, Mr Hewson or Alan. For although she might recognise some of the supervisors from the mill, she didn't know them to speak to. She felt someone at her side and turned to see the maid holding a tray of drinks. She knew she was expected to take a glass, but had no clue what the drinks were. The maid, well trained, took her lead.

'The sherry's on the left, miss, and the whisky's on the right,' she said politely.

Ruth would have given anything for a cup of tea after the tram ride and the walk to the party, but she didn't dare ask. She took a glass of sherry and held it with both hands as the maid walked into the throng of men. She felt less nervous now that she was finally in the room. She looked around her. It wasn't as grand as she'd expected, but it was large, running from the front of the house all the way to the back. Despite its size, however, it felt homely and comfortable. The walls were painted the same subtle yellow as the hall, and the floor was laid with a patterned mat that reached all the way to the walls. Ruth lifted her heels and placed them firmly on the thick tufts, enjoying the springy sensation. Flowered curtains hung all the way to the floor at either side of the window. She looked at the folds of material that seemed to have no purpose other than to pool on the floor. Why, she could make two dresses and a dozen cushion covers from that!

There was an unlit fireplace in the centre of the long wall of the room, and above it a mantelpiece. Ruth thought of Amelia Smith's mantelpiece with its clock in the middle and the two china dogs. She felt yet another pang of guilt about leaving the baby with a woman she didn't know. There was only one item on the Hewsons' mantel: a globe of the world that sat under a painting of a mountain and stream.

She felt the eyes of some of the men turn towards her, appraise her and then turn away. She still couldn't see anyone she recognised. She didn't know what to do. She couldn't approach someone she didn't know and start talking to them; she didn't feel confident enough. She thought of Edie, and a smile played on her lips. Edie would know exactly what to do in a roomful of men. She'd walk up to the most handsome man there and smile at him, start flirting. But Ruth wasn't Edie.

She pressed her back against the wall and gazed past a plump sofa and two armchairs to a window that looked out on a garden with trees. She wondered who looked after it all when Mr Hewson and Sarah were working. She reckoned if they could afford to hire a maid, they might well employ a gardener too. She stepped further into the

Glenda Young

room, no longer searching for a friendly face, but curious to see more of the garden. As she inched her way past the men, she caught the eye of Alan Murphy, who was talking to a man she didn't recognise. He nodded towards her in acknowledgement.

When she reached the far end of the room, she realised that what she had first thought was a window was actually two large doors. As she stood looking out, she slowly brought her glass to her nose and sniffed it. She'd never drunk sherry before, nor whisky or brandy. She'd only ever had a small glass of beer, in the Guide Post Inn. The dark liquid in her glass smelled of spice, ginger wine, and Christmas cake like her mam used to make before she took ill. She swirled it and watched the way it clung to the inside of her glass. Then she took a tiny sip. The sherry warmed her lips, her throat, the inside of her mouth. It wasn't unpleasant, but it wasn't as sweet as the smell suggested.

'Ruth! I'm glad you could make it!'

She was relieved to see Sarah walking towards her.

'I'm sorry I wasn't here to welcome you when you arrived.'

Ruth was about to say there was no need to apologise, but the words got stuck in her throat. All she could do was stare. Sarah looked immaculate in a white patterned dress and beaded shawl. Ruth found the whole effect dizzyingly beautiful. She felt more keenly than ever the drabness of her own clothes, and took a step back as if to distance herself from such finery.

'My, that's a beautiful brooch,' Sarah said, admiring the coloured stones.

'Thank you,' Ruth replied. 'You look very nice too.'

Sarah gazed out through the glass doors. 'I saw you admiring the garden just now,' she said. 'It was Mother's pride and joy. She laid out the lawns, dug the holes for the trees and planted all the flowers. Father and I try to tend it, but neither of us has green fingers like Mother used to have.'

'It's very pretty,' Ruth said.

'Would you like to see the hothouse?' Sarah asked.

Ruth had never heard of such a thing. She wondered if it was something to do with the kitchen. It would have been impolite to say no, though, as it seemed important to Sarah.

'I'd love to,' she replied, intrigued.

Sarah took Ruth by the hand and the two girls threaded their way through the throng. Several men wanted to stop Sarah to talk to her. She was polite with them, but firm.

'I have business with Miss Hardy at the moment,' she said to one man. She turned to another who was demanding her attention: 'I'll return soon and we'll have that chat I've been promising.'

Ruth was impressed by Sarah's assertive manner when she spoke to the men. She had admired this before when she'd walked with Sarah through the mill. Would men ever treat *her* with so much respect at work? she wondered. For although she was a supervisor, she seemed invisible to many of the important men there. Apart from Mr Hewson, of course.

Finally the two girls escaped from the room. Ruth followed Sarah past the staircase to the back of the house, through the scullery and kitchen. And there, between the kitchen and the back garden, was a most peculiar small room. It was almost as if it was half garden, half house, neither indoors nor out, and Ruth couldn't make sense of it. It had a sloped glass roof and a stone floor. A glass door led out to the garden, and around the walls was a bench at waist height. It was the scent, though, that Ruth noticed above all else. A sweet, familiar smell. Rows of pots in all sizes were neatly lined up on the bench. A rose bush grew in each one, with small, delicate blooms in all colours. She didn't know where to look first. There were tiny red roses, others with petals of pink, white, yellow, even orange. It was a feast for the eyes. She breathed in the sweet smell. The powerful scent made her feel as if she could float right up to the roof.

'It's beautiful,' she said.

Sarah beamed. 'Isn't it? It was Mother's. I keep it going in her memory. I seem to have developed her knack for growing roses indoors, although I'm less successful with the gardens.'

'So this is why your father has a fresh rose in his jacket each day at the mill,' Ruth said. It all began to make sense.

'We can grow them all year round in this little room. It gets the direct sun. Even in winter there's enough warmth to keep some of them flowering.'

Ruth bent low to take in the scent of a pink rose that caught her eye. 'You must miss your mam a great deal,' she said.

Sarah took a rose petal between her fingers and caressed it.

'We've both suffered loss, Ruth,' she said. 'You with your sister and me with my mother. It doesn't get any easier, does it?'

Ruth ran her hand along Bea's scarf at her neck.

Sarah let the rose petal go free from her hand. 'Come

on, let me introduce you to some people,' she said. 'Henry's looking forward to meeting you again, though remember what I said about him. Don't let his charm fool you.'

Ruth let Sarah lead her by the arm and they returned to the room full of men. She was still puzzled about Henry, and wondered why on earth a man of his standing would be interested in a mill girl like her.

'Ah, Miss Hardy!' Mr Hewson beamed when he caught sight of her. He looked more dapper than ever in his charcoal-grey suit, and his eyes twinkled merrily. Ruth shook his hand, and as she did so, she took in the tiny white rose in his lapel. She knew now how significant the roses were.

A short, fat man waddled towards them. He had a cigar in his wet mouth that he appeared to be chewing rather than smoking.

'Ruth, I'd like to introduce you to Mr Thomas Hepple,' Mr Hewson said.

Hepple? A shiver ran down Ruth's back. Was this man connected to John Hepple working in her rag room? she wondered.

The short man extended his hand to Ruth. His fat fingers were clammy to the touch, and when Ruth brought her own hand away, she felt as if she needed to wipe it clean and dry. Instead, she gripped her sherry glass tightly.

'Mr Hepple is one of the most influential men in Sunderland,' Mr Hewson continued, with a mischievous tone in his voice.

'Now, now, Oswald, I wouldn't go so far as to say that,' Thomas laughed. Ruth saw spittle at each side of the man's rubbery lips, which turned outward like a petulant child's. There was something about his features that she recognised, and the more she looked at him, the more she realised he must be related to John at work. Was he his father, perhaps, or his brother?

Mr Hewson leaned in conspiratorially towards him. 'Ruth here is one of the hardest workers at the mill. Supervisor in the rag room, no less. I'm going to leave you two to become acquainted.'

Thomas's eyes widened. '*You're* the girl in the rag room?' he said sharply.

'Yes, sir,' Ruth replied.

'What does your father do?'

'He was a miner.'

She watched as Thomas's gaze took in her old boots, skirt and blouse. His eyes lingered on her grandma's brooch.

'A miner? Not for diamonds or gold, I assume from the imitation jewellery you wear.'

Ruth was affronted by the man's words. Was he playing a game with her that she didn't understand? She raised her glass and took a long sip of sherry. Then she looked Thomas Hepple in the eye. 'He was a coal miner.'

Thomas gave a curt nod. His gaze didn't waver from Ruth's face. 'My son tells me all is going well in the rag room,' he said.

'Your son?' Ruth felt sick when the realisation hit. Now it all made sense. The man's features, his sharp way with words, his rudeness. 'Your son is John Hepple?'

'He is indeed. My splendid boy did his duty for the King, and now he's destined for great things at the paper mill.'

Ruth bit her tongue. She didn't know anything about

John Hepple's work other than that he turned up each day sullen and angry and with violence on his mind. She caught Sarah's eye across the room, and within seconds her friend was at her side.

'I hope you two are getting to know each other.' Sarah spoke politely to Thomas, but Ruth noticed that her lips were set tight and she wasn't her usual friendly self.

Thomas took a sip of his drink, stuck his cigar in the corner of his mouth and sucked loudly. Then he removed it and blew smoke at Ruth's face. Her eyes stung, and she wanted to cough, but she forced herself to remain still. She wasn't going to give him the satisfaction of knowing he'd upset her. He smiled a rubbery, wet smile towards Sarah.

'I was telling the paper mill girl here—'

'Miss Hardy is one of our supervisors,' Sarah interrupted. But her words had no effect on Thomas Hepple.

'I was telling her about my son John. He fought for his country, as you well know.' Thomas glared at Ruth. 'Women who know their place have returned to working in the home since peace was declared.'

'And as *you* well know,' Sarah said pointedly, 'my father believes in equal access to jobs for all, whether men or women. He believes in appointing the hardest workers to the role. And Miss Hardy is a dedicated employee.'

Thomas chewed his cigar. 'That she may be. But does she know what changes are planned for the rag room?'

Ruth swallowed hard. She'd been told of no changes. She kept quiet, but inside she felt hurt that news had been kept from her, by Sarah of all people, someone she trusted.

Thomas Hepple raised his chubby hand and waved to someone across the room. 'Excuse me,' he said, giving a brief nod towards Sarah and ignoring Ruth completely as he turned away.

The minute he was out of earshot, Ruth leaned towards Sarah. 'What changes?' she demanded.

Sarah laid her hand on Ruth's arm. 'I'd planned to speak to you about it tonight,' she said. 'I had hoped to do so before you heard it from someone else. We need to speak in private.'

Ruth's stomach felt heavy. Speaking in private meant that whatever Sarah had to say would not be good news.

Chapter Twenty-Five

Sarah led Ruth along the hallway and into a room dominated by a large oval table framed by twelve chairs. Sarah pulled two of the heavy chairs out from the table.

'Sit down, Ruth, please.'

Ruth put her glass of sherry on the table and sat up straight in the chair. She placed her feet solidly on the wooden floor and looked Sarah in the eye. 'What's going on?' she demanded.

'I want you to know this is Father's idea, not mine. I've tried to talk him out of it.'

'Sarah? Tell me what it is,' Ruth said. She tried to keep her voice as calm as she could, which wasn't easy as her heart was hammering.

'It's John Hepple,' Sarah said. 'Father will be promoting him to supervisor in the rag room.'

The news hit Ruth like a bullet to her heart. She wanted to scream, to beat her fists on the table, to throw the glass against the wall. She lifted the glass to her lips and swallowed her sherry in a single gulp. But when she looked at Sarah, she saw there were tears in the girl's eyes. Whatever had gone on had clearly caused

Sarah as much pain as it was bringing to Ruth. So many questions ran through Ruth's mind, but only one word left her lips.

'Why?'

'You deserve an honest reply,' Sarah said. 'And I beg you to hear this in confidence.'

Ruth watched as Sarah composed herself and began to talk. She told Ruth that Thomas Hepple worked in the River Wear Commissioners Office, responsible for overseeing ships allowed into the port. The Grange Paper Works were wholly reliant on the Commissioners for their licence to import raw materials to make paper. Without esparto grass from Africa and Spain and wood pulp from Scandinavia, the mill would come to a standstill within days, production would stop and hundreds of men and boys, women and girls would be without work. Sarah explained how Thomas Hepple had requested that a role be found for his son at the mill when John returned injured from war.

'And he's worked there ever since, under my supervision,' Ruth said. She felt a hot rush of anger rising from her chest to her neck and spreading to her face. Not only was her job being taken from her, but it was to be given to someone as evil as John.

'I don't trust John Hepple to run the rag room,' Sarah said. 'I've spoken to Father about him many times. He wanted to teach John a lesson once he found out you'd been having problems with him. That was why he placed him at the front of the rag room at his own bench. I've tried to talk Father out of putting him in charge. But he has no choice.'

'What do you know about John that makes you

distrust him?' Ruth dared herself to ask the question in the privacy of the quiet room.

'I've seen the way he is with Father, with other men at the mill,' Sarah said. 'I've seen how he acts in private, away from them, too. He's been here in our home before. Father invited him and Thomas one evening, and made the mistake of leaving me alone with John, just for a few moments.'

Ruth's eyes opened wide. 'What happened?'

Sarah glanced at the door. She shook her head. 'No, I won't say. But I think you know what he's capable of. When we talked that day in the drying loft, we both knew there was evil in the man.'

Ruth nodded. She knew only too well.

'But the future of the mill relies on a solid relationship between Father and Thomas Hepple's office. Thomas has requested that John now be given the supervisor's role.'

'*My* role,' Ruth hissed.

'Father can't refuse him. You must see that, surely?'

'Oh, I see it. But I don't like it one little bit.'

'We'll find another role for you,' Sarah said quickly. 'Father won't expect you to return to working on the rag bench after being supervisor. There are opportunities in the counting room.'

Ruth knew that Sarah was hoping she'd see her point of view. But she was angry, trying to make sense of the situation.

'As long as you don't mind the paper cuts to your hands,' Sarah added with a forced lightness.

Ruth chose to ignore the comment. 'It's not my own future that concerns me if I leave the rag room to work elsewhere at the mill,' she said at last. 'It's the girls I leave behind I'm worried about. What will happen to them working under John?'

Sarah leaned closer and cast a glance at the door before carrying on. 'You told me you had difficulties with the man. Is that what you're referring to when you say you're concerned for the girls?'

This time, Ruth told Sarah everything she knew about John. No more veiled allusions, no more blurring the edges of what she knew he was capable of. She told her about him attacking Claire, about his fight at the docks, about his moods and his violent temper that he kept just barely concealed. Finally she'd rid herself of the burden she'd carried around for months.

When Ruth was done, Sarah sank back in her chair, taking it all in. 'John's father demands he takes up his new role immediately,' she said. 'But after all that you've said, I will speak to Father again.'

'I don't want to cause trouble,' Ruth said. 'But I had to tell the truth.'

'Of course,' Sarah said. 'We might be able to postpone the change until the turn of the year. I can't promise, but I'll do all I can to convince Father to hold off for as long as he can. But it will happen, Ruth, mark my words. The future of the mill depends on it.'

Ruth raised her eyes to meet Sarah's. 'And if I move to the counting room, will I become just one of the girls again? Will I lose my supervisor's wage? You know that I've excelled in my work in the rag room.'

'I will do all I can for you,' Sarah said. 'Trust me.'

The dining-room door flew open, startling Ruth and Sarah as they sat with their heads bent together. It was Henry.

'Here you are,' he beamed. 'Found you at last! What are you two conspiring about?'

Ruth knew she should greet him, smile at him at least. It was the polite thing to do. But after what she'd just learned, she wanted to run out of the room and head home.

Sarah rose and brought Henry to her in a warm embrace. 'Lovely to see you,' she said. 'You remember Ruth Hardy, don't you?'

Ruth stood and looked at Henry's delicate, slim face. He took her hand, and this time he shook it heartily.

'Remember her? Why, Ruth Hardy, you made a pleasant day at Seaburn one that I couldn't forget.'

How Ruth wanted to be swept away by Henry's friendly words and warm greeting, but her stomach was in knots after her conversation with Sarah.

'Shall we have a drink?' he asked.

'I'd love to,' Sarah said. 'Ruth?'

Ruth forced a smile. 'Yes, please,' she said.

Henry slipped one arm through Sarah's, the other through Ruth's, and the three of them headed sideways through the dining-room door. Sarah burst out laughing at the ludicrous way they were walking like crabs along the hallway, and Henry joined in. Soon even Ruth felt a bubble of laughter rise up inside, displacing the anxiety she'd felt before.

Once they reached the living room, the three of them composed themselves. The men in the room were still smiling and talking, but this was no party, Ruth realised. There would not be dancing or laughter. This was a business meeting as serious as any other, the only difference being that it was held away from the mill.

She allowed Henry to bring her another sherry and she sipped this one slowly. She was getting used to the taste of it now, and found that it warmed and relaxed her. Sarah's warning rang loud in the back of her mind at first. However, after her second sherry, unused as she was to drinking, the warning became muted. Henry was attentive to her and she enjoyed his company. He was funny and quick-witted and didn't falter in conversation, though he didn't once ask her about her work at the mill, and neither was he curious to know about where she lived.

'Have you ever been to Ryhope?' she asked.

Henry shook his head. 'Never. My family live in Ashbrooke; they have investments in property.'

'Investments?' Ruth gulped. 'Well, my dad was a coal miner and my mam a seamstress,' she said.

Henry's face never flickered. He didn't seem in the least bit interested in what Ruth had to say. Harry's words from earlier that night ran through her mind. Perhaps those who lived outside of Ryhope were different after all. Henry's eyes fell to her bosom.

'Would you like to visit Ryhope?' Ruth asked, her voice a little louder than normal. She fully intended to return Henry's gaze to her face. Her question did the trick and his eyes lifted. 'I could show you around, give you a guided tour. There's the coal mine and farms, the beach and the cliffs, the railway. We've two railway stations, you know.'

She thought of her mam and dad. They'd be waiting for her to return home to tell them about the party. Well, there was unwelcome news about the rag room she'd be taking home too. She wondered if she would tell them about Henry, and if so, how much she would say.

Henry slipped his arm around her waist. She didn't move, and let his hand stay where it was. Was it the sherry, she wondered, that was making her feel wanton and brave? Or was it a reaction to her earlier distress at Sarah's news about her job in the rag room? Well, whatever it was, she welcomed his touch and inched closer to him. She felt his hot breath on her neck, and he began to nibble her ear. Sarah's warning was still there in the back of Ruth's mind, but it seemed a long way away as the blood coursed through her veins. She'd never been kissed this way before.

'Who needs Ryhope when I could show you around Ashbrooke?' he cooed.

'I've heard it's pretty,' she said.

'Not as pretty as you.'

Ruth felt a heat rise from her neck. In that moment, she wished that the man standing at her side was a taller man, with dark hair and dark eyes. She wanted Mick more than ever. She closed her eyes. Mick was in her thoughts, her heart, in her dreams at night, and yet it was Henry by her side.

Around them, men were turning to see what was going on between Henry and Ruth. Some laughed, some nudged a friend and nodded in Henry's direction.

'With a paper mill girl? How common!' one said.

Sarah too had seen what was happening, and she walked from the room, disgusted with Henry, disappointed in Ruth.

Ruth thought of Henry's family, living a very different life to hers. Try as she might, she couldn't envisage Henry waiting outside the rag room with an armful of leeks. And if she took him to Ryhope to show him how and where she lived, what then? He would laugh at the state of the Guide Post Inn. The likes of him, a gentleman, would consider living in a pub indecent, unclean. As the thoughts turned in her mind, Henry's lips brushed her neck and she melted. No one had ever been so intimate with her before.

'So, Ruth Hardy,' he murmured against her soft skin. 'Would you like to see Ashbrooke? My parents are away on business. Come for dinner one evening next week.'

Ruth's body was screaming yes while her head was saying no. She wanted Mick, just Mick.

'Will you come?' Henry breathed in her ear.

Ruth felt his fingers tighten at her waist. Could she love Henry and finally put Mick from her mind? There was only one way to find out.

'I'll come,' she said at last.

Chapter Twenty-Six

The tram rattled its way back to Ryhope, and Sunderland disappeared from view. The light of the summer night was beginning to fade, but what a night it had turned out to be. A night that had ended with Henry's urgent kisses and an invitation to visit his home. Ruth laid a hand on her forehead; her head was hurting in a way she'd never experienced before. Was it the effects of too much sherry? She thought of the party, and her heart melted at the thought of Henry's touch. And yet when she tried to bring Henry's face to mind, it was Mick's handsome, rugged features that appeared.

The tram made its way to Ryhope village green and then on to the stop outside St Paul's church. Ruth watched the Guide Post Inn come into view, but she couldn't head home just yet. First there was Maude to collect from Amelia Smith, who lived another tram stop away. Leaving Maude had proved less difficult than she'd expected, and she hoped that Bea, rest her soul, would forgive her. There had been something about the woman that had made her feel certain that Maude was in good, safe hands. Amelia had a no-nonsense way about her and her rooms at Tunstall Terrace felt cosy and warm. But now Ruth was longing to hold the baby, cuddle her and take her home to her mam and dad.

When she arrived at Tunstall Terrace, she could hear a woman singing. She walked along the side of the lawn to the back of the house. The voice was soft and low, the words of the song about a man lost at war. She stood a moment and listened. The door of Amelia's room was open to the garden, and the notes floated out on the air.

Only when the song ended did Ruth announce her arrival with a knock at the door. Amelia was sitting in a rocking chair by the fire, cradling Maude. The ticking of the clock on the mantelpiece and the grandfather clock by the wall was as regular and comforting as a heartbeat.

'Come in, dear,' Amelia said.

'Has she been good?' Ruth asked.

'As good as gold. She slept most of the evening. Here, take her.' She offered Maude to Ruth. 'You'll bring her back in the morning,' she said.

It wasn't a question, Ruth knew that. 'Yes, I will.'

Amelia nodded her head. 'Good. I won't hear of you taking her back to the mill.'

'I'll bring her every day while I'm at work,' Ruth said. 'And I want to thank you for looking after her.'

'Don't thank me, thank Mr Hewson. He's the one paying.'

Ruth thought of what she'd learned that night about John taking her job at the mill. She wondered if Mr Hewson's offer to pay for Maude's care was in some way an apology. Perhaps he had known it would happen? Well, whatever the case, Maude was her priority, and it didn't matter whose pocket the coins came from.

'I trust your sister won't mention this at the mill?' she said.

'I've already told you, lass. Dorothy won't say a word.'

Ruth held tight to Maude, ready for the walk home down the colliery bank. Before she left, she glanced from the grandfather clock to the small clock on the mantelpiece.

'You're wondering why I need two,' Amelia said.

Ruth gasped. 'Sorry, I wasn't prying. I was curious, that's all.'

'Dogs like them.'

Ruth was confused. 'Dogs?'

'Stops them crying when they're moved from their mother's side. The steady sound of a ticking clock next to a newborn puppy makes them think their mam's beating heart is close by. The noise calms them, you see.'

'And it works for babies too?'

'Seems to do the trick,' Amelia said. 'Now go on, get yourself home and get the little 'un settled. I'll see you both in the morning.'

Ruth stepped back outside, and walked away down the lawn and around the stone wall to the road, tucking Maude under her jacket to protect her from the cold night air. She walked past the working men's club, the string of pubs on the colliery bank, the miners' hall and the Co-op. When she drew close to the Prince of Wales pub, she heard a commotion. The pub door flew open, and there was a scuffle. Ruth stepped to the other side of the road, away from whatever trouble was brewing. Men were shouting, vicious words were flung into the night, then she heard a woman's voice in the midst of it, cursing louder than any man there.

'Get away with you, woman!' a voice called.

The rabble quietened and disappeared back inside. Ruth picked up her pace. She didn't want to get caught up as a witness to a fight. But she couldn't resist a quick glance to see if she knew who had been causing the fuss. If she told her mam and dad about the fight, they'd be wanting details and names. She saw a woman in a black coat and hat slumped on the ground. Standing over her was a young man. He was trying to pull the woman up, but she was drunk and slipped from his hands. Ruth watched as the man and woman performed their strange dance of pulling and pushing. They were swearing and laughing as if it was a game. Their voices were slurred, but what she heard sent a chill down her spine. She knew who they were.

Her stomach turned with unease and she gripped Maude tight. She forced her feet forwards, no longer walking, almost running. She had to get away. But it was too late, she'd been spotted.

'Oi! Come back here with our bairn!' the woman called.

Ruth glanced behind her. She saw Jimmy Tate pull his mam to her feet. She was shocked to the core to see Jimmy again. He hadn't once called at the pub to give his condolences over Bea or express any desire to meet his daughter.

'Come back here, you little whore!' Connie screamed.

Ruth tried to run, but it didn't feel safe with Maude in her arms. She picked up her pace, her heart hammering, and only when the Guide Post Inn came into view did she give a sigh of relief. But her nightmare was far from over. Connie was screaming abuse at her and her voice was getting louder.

'I've got a right to see my grandbairn!' she yelled.

'Think you're above us Tates, do you? I'll get my hands on that baby if it kills me. It needs its dad, my Jimmy.'

'For God's sake, Mam, will you just shut up about the bloody bairn?' Jimmy said. 'You know I don't want it, I never have! It was a bloody mistake!'

Ruth walked quickly to the pub and let herself in through the back gate, closing it firmly behind her and standing with her back against it, her breath coming from her thick and fast. Outside in the back lane she heard a scuffle of feet as Connie and Jimmy followed. She threw the bolt into the lock just as Connie started banging on the gate.

'You won't get away with this,' Connie's voice slurred.

'Come on, Mam, let's go,' Jimmy said. Ruth heard the lazy way he spoke, the beer slowing his words. 'She's gone now.'

Connie rattled the gate. Ruth cupped her hand protectively around Maude's tiny head, then put her ear to the gate and listened.

'What on earth do you want the bairn for anyway?' Jimmy said.

Connie laughed. 'What? You think I want to keep it? Think again, lad. I know people who'll pay good money for a bairn like that. It's healthy, got all its limbs.'

Ruth's heart caught in her chest. So that was Connie's plan all along; she'd never felt anything for Maude!

'I just need to get my hands on it, and I will, I promise you that. That's our bairn she's got in there. And we've got just as much right to it as the flamin' Hardys.' Connie paused. 'I need another drink, son,' she said. 'Come on, buy your old mam another drink.'

'The Albion will still be open,' Jimmy slurred.

'Aye, the Albion it is,' Connie said. 'You're a good lad.' Their voices faded as they disappeared down the lane.

Ruth kissed Maude and headed inside. Her dad was in his armchair by the fire, eyes closed, snoring heavily. Her mam was asleep in her bed. Ruth was relieved to see them like that, for she hadn't been looking forward to telling them about her night. When the time was right, she would describe to her mam the splendour of the Hewsons' home, Sarah's beaded dress and the roses in the exotic hothouse. She would tell her dad about the men she'd met there. But there was more from the night that she would keep to herself for now. She wouldn't worry them about John taking over her job at the mill. It would mean less money coming in, as she was sure to lose her supervisor's bonus. Neither would she tell them about her run-in with Connie and Jimmy. And she wouldn't mention Henry. She didn't think her mam and dad would understand about her kissing him at the party. She was troubled enough by it herself and vowed never to drink so much alcohol again. She might be starved of affection, but she knew she didn't want empty kisses and even emptier promises.

She settled Maude into bed, then slipped on her night-gown and brushed out her hair. Finally she fell into her own bed and closed her eyes. The evening danced through her mind. Henry's kisses had provided an excitement she'd never felt before. She thought of his hand on her waist and how her heart had skipped at his touch. But each time she tried to bring his face to mind, his delicate pale features were replaced by Mick's dark eyes staring into her soul.

Chapter Twenty-Seven

The next morning, Ruth dressed quickly, fed Maude, helped her mam with her bed bath and cooked a breakfast of oats. She kissed her parents farewell and headed out with Maude for the walk to Tunstall Terrace.

It was a fine day with a clear blue sky. She was more pleased than ever with the arrangements for Amelia to take care of Maude, and walked up the colliery bank with a spring in her step. She felt no fear of meeting Connie or Jimmy that morning, sure that they'd be sleeping off their hangovers from the night before. Connie's words, however, remained heavy in her heart. How dare she think of selling Bea's baby? Now that Ruth knew the truth, it was more important than ever that Connie was kept away from Maude. It was unlikely that any of the Tate family would find out where Maude was being looked after, but she thought it best to warn Amelia, just in case.

When Ruth delivered the baby to Amelia's cosy living room, she was surprised to see three empty drawers on the floor. Amelia was busy arranging layers of blankets in each one.

'Just getting beds ready for the bairns coming today,'

she said breezily when Ruth appeared.

'You look after three babies each day?' Ruth asked. She was surprised to hear this; she'd thought Maude would be Amelia's only charge and receive her undivided attention.

'Not three, lass, five, but I've only got three spare drawers. There's enough room in each one for at least two bairns, sometimes three. I've got Billy MacDonald's twins coming this week. His sister normally looks after them, but she's gone on holiday to Scarborough for the week. His wife died not long since, and he has no one to help him.'

'You provide a good service,' Ruth said.

Amelia stopped what she was doing and looked at Ruth. 'The best,' she said. 'I love all the little 'uns who come into my care. Now come on, pass her over. Has she been fed this morning?'

Ruth handed Maude into Amelia's welcoming arms. 'She's had some milk.'

Amelia glanced at her grandfather clock. 'Then I'll feed her mid morning and mid afternoon. It's all part of the service; there's no need to thank me. I do what I'm paid for.'

'Amelia . . .' Ruth began hesitantly. 'If another person, a woman, say, came calling for Maude or for any of the children you look after—'

Amelia cut her short with a look that could have curdled milk, then put her hands over Maude's ears as if to prevent the child from hearing. 'How dare you?' she hissed.

'I'm concerned for her safety,' Ruth said. 'Surely I have a right to ask you now that I'm trusting you with my flesh and blood?'

'No one comes in here while I look after other people's bairns,' Amelia said. 'No one! I stake my reputation on it. And if you've heard otherwise, tell me who told you and I'll have their guts for garters!'

Ruth was relieved to hear the woman speak so passionately. But still she needed to press home her point, for when Connie Tate was drunk, who knew what she might stoop to in order to steal Maude.

'There's a woman who thinks Maude should belong to her,' she said.

Amelia's eyebrows shot up. 'A relative?'

Ruth nodded. 'Her grandmother. She's a drunk. She's threatened to steal Maude and sell her.'

If Amelia was shocked by what Ruth told her, she made a good job of cloaking her reaction. She simply stared at Ruth, waiting for her to continue. But Ruth said no more. The women looked at each other as the two clocks ticked in the room.

'I've been looking after bairns ever since my Sidney passed,' Amelia said. Her voice held pride tinged with sadness. 'And I have never . . .' she paused, 'not once, allowed anyone inside my home who hasn't the right to be here. When the children are in my care, I dedicate myself fully. I feed them, bathe them and sing them to sleep.'

'I wasn't being critical,' Ruth began. 'But this woman is dangerous—'

Amelia held her free hand up to silence her. 'If a mother brings her bairn here, I expect her to collect it. I won't even hand it over to its dad, its grandma, an auntie or a friend without the express permission of the mother. Do you understand what I'm saying?'

'I do,' Ruth said firmly.

Amelia's stern expression softened. 'Then get yourself to the mill to do your job, and I'll do mine.'

Ruth kissed Maude on her rosy cheek and headed out for the walk to the mill.

The day was still, the sky blue, with just a few clouds scudding by. But the air held a nip of autumn, a hint of cold, dark days to come. Ruth pulled her jacket tight and walked quickly to warm up. Down the colliery bank she went, around the village green and on to the main road through Grangetown.

As she walked, she thought of the party. Henry's words played on her mind, his offer of dinner at his home. She couldn't quite fathom him out and wondered what he saw in her when he could have any woman in Sunderland. Men like Henry didn't need to cavort with the likes of Ruth. She knew what she was: just a girl from a pit village. What was he up to? He wouldn't know what it felt like to live hand to mouth as Ruth did, going hungry some nights after she'd cooked dinner for her mam and dad, feeding Maude and leaving little for herself.

Perhaps he was toying with her, intent on having his way and discarding her like an old shoe. She remembered Sarah's warning. Did he kiss and canoodle with every girl he met, whatever their social class – mill girl or mistress of the manor? Was Ruth just another in a string of girls? She should have heeded Sarah's warning more closely. But oh, when he'd kissed her! She shivered at the memory of his lips on her neck. Mick had never been so forward while they were courting. He had had more respect for her and was happy to let their relationship move at its own speed, with friendship first and foremost.

She walked faster, her strides longer, as if she was trying to leave Henry behind. However, no matter how fast she walked, Henry stayed in her mind, but it was Mick who remained in her heart. And then she thought of John Hepple, and an icy chill ran through her. She would face whatever came her way at the mill with as much bravery as she could muster. She would brave it out; she had to. She needed the money. Her mam and dad depended on her, Maude too. But still it rankled with her to be losing her job to John Hepple of all people.

That morning at the mill, the girls complained of the nip in the air and rubbed their hands together to get the blood going. John was as moody as ever, sitting in front of Ruth like a school dunce in front of his teacher, casting sour glances towards her. Did he know, she wondered, that his position and hers would soon change? If he did, he made no mention of it, and Ruth was grateful for that. But then John rarely spoke about anything. He was as brooding and silent as always, as if biding his time.

As the girls worked, Ruth glanced at Claire, the youngest of them all. How would she manage if John tried it on with her again, and next time there was no one to stop him? It didn't bear thinking about. Ruth ripped harder at the seam she was cutting on the knife.

When the whistle in the yard blew for dinner break, some of the girls stayed inside the rag room, clustering around the bench to eat sandwiches their mams had made and to catch up with friends. Despite the cold day, however, Ruth wanted to get out for some fresh air. She linked arms with Edie and Jane and they walked to the coal-blackened beach. They chose their spot carefully, sheltered from the wind. Ruth took a meat-paste sandwich from her skirt pocket. Edie had two boiled eggs wrapped in paper with a twist of salt. Jane had an apple and a slice of beef pie. Ruth was pleased to see her friend eating again. Jane looked better, happier.

'Who wants to do a swap?' Jane asked. 'Edie? I'll give you some pie in exchange for a bite of your egg.'

'I'll stick with my meat paste sandwich,' Ruth said.

'How are things with Davey?' Edie asked.

'I haven't seen him in a while,' Jane said. 'He keeps turning up outside our house, but Dad sees him off.'

'You told your mam and dad the truth?' Ruth asked.

Jane nodded. 'Davey's mam's fallen out with mine now, though. They don't see each other no more. But Dad's been really great. He threatened to call the police on Davey if he turns up again. Thanks, Ruth, for all you did to help. And you, Edie, thanks for letting me come to your house for tea after work. Both of you have helped me feel safe.'

They carried on eating in silence. Ruth steeled herself to tell Edie and Jane about the party. She didn't mention Henry, or Sarah's dress, or the hothouse. That all seemed irrelevant, fanciful given the news she had to share about John. When she'd finished speaking, Edie and Jane sat quietly for a while, letting it sink in.

'Sarah's hopeful her dad can postpone the change, maybe into the new year,' Ruth said.

'We'll miss you if you leave the rag room,' Edie said. 'It won't be the same without you.'

'The girls need you, Ruth,' Jane added.

Edie nodded in agreement. 'We all need you. Can't we

complain to Mr Hewson about John? What he did to Claire was wrong!'

'I know,' Ruth said sadly. 'And he must never get away with doing it again. I'm relying on you both, as the eldest in the room, to keep an eye on the young 'uns. Don't let them be alone with the man.'

'And if he insists? He could threaten to sack us,' Jane said.

Edie popped a whole boiled egg into her mouth. Ruth and Jane watched as her cheek bulged out.

'Good old Edie,' Ruth laughed. 'Always biting off more than she can chew.'

Edie put her hand to her mouth, trying to suppress her giggles while she chewed.

'Jane's right,' she said once she'd swallowed. 'We could lose our jobs if we challenge him. What do we do then? Tell Mr Hewson?'

Ruth thought for a moment, then shook her head. 'Tell Dorothy in the office,' she said.

'That hatchet-faced old bat?' Edie asked. 'Why her?'

'Because I've discovered that she's got more power at the mill than the three of us knew. She'll have a private word with Sarah, who will pass the news to her dad. Don't go direct to Mr Hewson; he'll not appreciate tittle-tattle from the rag room. He's got higher things on his mind. Dorothy will help, I promise, and she'll be discreet.'

They continued eating in silence.

'Come on then, Ruth, tell us more about the party,' Edie said with a cheeky smile. 'It can't have been all bad news.'

'Tell us about the Hewsons' house,' Jane said. 'Was it posh?'

Edie shuffled forward. 'Never mind the house, tell us about the men. Were they handsome? And rich? Come on, Ruth, spill the beans and tell us what we've been dying to hear.'

'They were rich all right,' Ruth said, thinking of Henry. 'And handsome if you like that sort of thing.'

'What sort?' Jane asked.

'Pale and thin and weedy,' Ruth laughed.

'Weren't they tall and strong with shoulders so broad you'd want to wrap your arms around them and squeeze the living daylights out of them?'

'They were kind, that's all. Pleasant.'

'Pah!' Edie said. 'What's the use in that? Fellas should be muscly and romantic and sexy and gorgeous. Who wants pleasant and kind?'

'I do,' Jane said softly.

Ruth laid her hand on Jane's arm. 'And you'll find him one day.'

'Wasn't there anyone who turned your head at the party?' Edie continued.

Ruth thought of Henry's kisses like butterfly wings on her skin, and Sarah's warning flooded back.

'There must have been someone you liked the look of, surely?' Edie persisted.

Ruth gazed out to sea and shook her head.

That evening Ruth rang her handbell to dismiss the girls from the rag room. Another day was done and the workers headed home. As always, she tidied the room before she left so that it would be in a fit state the next morning. Then she locked the door behind her with the big iron key and delivered it to the office, where

Dorothy signed for its receipt in her ledger.

In the yard, girls and women were streaming from the mill, chatting, linking arms, catching up with friends, sisters, mams and aunties after a day spent working indoors. Ruth walked towards the gates, working her way along the edge of the throng. Suddenly she stopped dead in her tracks. Waiting by the gate was a girl in a black coat. She was standing exactly where Bea used to, wearing the same hat. She was the same size, the same height. Ruth's stomach flipped with fear. Was she imagining things, going mad?

All around her, girls hurried past, bumping into her, some apologising, others elbowing her out of the way in their rush to get home. Ruth stood still, her heart pounding. She took a tentative step forward, and at that moment the girl turned her head and Ruth saw the truth. She had no freckles like Bea. She had no sweetness to her features like Bea used to have. How foolish Ruth felt. It wasn't Bea. It could never have been Bea. But just for a second, Ruth had tricked herself into believing it was.

The deadness in the pit of her stomach gave way to an overwhelming sorrow, and she pushed her way through the girls, desperate to get home. She walked back to Ryhope with tears in her eyes and a yearning in her soul for her sister who she missed every day.

Chapter Twenty-Eight

Ruth heard nothing more from Henry Wood. His invitation to join him for dinner at his parents' house in Ashbrooke seemed to have disappeared on the autumn breeze. She felt relieved at not having to meet him, for what on earth did she have in common with someone like him? Their only connection was that they both knew Sarah Hewson. And while Ruth felt at ease in Sarah's company, she couldn't have said the same about her brief time with Henry. He lived a different life in a different part of town that might as well have been another world.

She remembered the look that had come over his face at the party when she'd talked about her parents. He hadn't pressed her for more or asked her where she lived or what she did at the mill. She was just a miner's daughter and of no interest to him other than getting her alone to kiss her. Not that Ruth hadn't enjoyed his attentions. But surely there had to be more to the start of a relationship than kissing and canoodling? No matter how many times she told herself not to compare Henry with Mick, she couldn't help it. Mick was the only boyfriend she'd ever had, and his face came to her unbidden. He was often the last thing she thought of when she went to sleep at night and the first when she woke the next day. If only Henry's words, his invitation to dinner, had come from Mick. If only Henry's kisses on her neck had come from Mick's lips too.

Ruth sighed heavily. What was the use of thinking of a future with Mick when he'd made it more than clear that he hadn't the stomach to take her on? Hadn't he complained that she cared too much for her mam and dad and Bea? And now there was Maude to look after, and Mrs Pike to appease because they were so far in arrears with the rent. How could she dedicate her life to any man when she would always put her family first? She shook her head. Mick had already told her he couldn't bear to come second in her life, and had left her to cope on her own. Though hadn't he given her some hope that day on Seaburn sands? And what if he *did* want her back, what then? No, she decided. She had too much pride to go running after him. But then why did she continue to miss him so much?

One dinner time at work, Ruth, Edie and Jane were walking back to the rag room arm in arm, three friends sharing secrets and laughing as they walked. From the doorway of the machine room, the brooding figure of Davey Winter loomed, unseen by the girls. He kept his eye on Jane, watching her and biding his time.

The days shortened and grew colder, and summer became a distant memory. At the paper mill, Ruth waited with a knot in her stomach for the day when John would take her place. But each time she asked at the mill office if there was news, Dorothy shook her head.

'I'll tell you when they tell me,' she said.

'They? Who are they?' Ruth demanded.

'Mr Hewson, of course,' Dorothy replied sharply. 'Now get back to work and keep your rag room in order, while you've still got it.'

'And will Mr Hewson tell you where I'm likely to be moved to?' Ruth asked.

Dorothy shook her head again. 'You'll find out in good time.'

'Will it be the counting room?'

She raised her stern face and glared hard at Ruth. 'Don't push me, Ruth Hardy. When I have something to tell you, I will.'

Ruth left the office with her shoulders slumped. She walked back to the rag room with a heavy heart. She had no idea what lay ahead and didn't like feeling unsettled. At home, Maude was being safely looked after by Amelia. Her dad's spirits had improved since he'd started helping out in the pub. And her mam . . . well, her mam was getting worse, there was no two ways about it. Ruth kicked at the cobblestones with her worn boots as she headed back to the rag room, and crossed her arms to keep herself warm.

'Ruth?' a voice called.

She looked across the yard. It was Sarah. Ruth hadn't seen her since the party, and her heart leapt at the sight of her. But the smile was wiped from her lips when she saw Henry behind.

She stood still, waiting for the two of them to approach. She pushed her shoulders back and stood tall, avoiding Henry's gaze, giving her full attention to Sarah. But it was Henry who pushed forward with his hand outstretched in greeting. Ruth shook it; she didn't want to appear impolite.

'We've been visiting Father in his office,' Sarah explained. 'It's good to see you. Are you well?'

'You look well,' Henry interrupted, over keen.

Ruth locked eyes with him then his gaze fell to her boots before moving up over her skirt, her breasts, her cold, pinched face and her hair tucked under her cap. She didn't enjoy being appraised, especially not by someone like Henry with his airs and graces and broken promises. She would give him no encouragement this time. She wondered what she had ever seen in him to allow herself to be seduced so easily. Drinking too much sherry had a lot to answer for. She knew she'd never do it again. She thought of Edie and what she would say if she was giving a fella the brush-off, especially one as wealthy as Henry. But Ruth was more interested in life's heartstrings than purse strings.

'I'm fine,' she said coolly.

'And how is Maude?' Sarah asked.

Ruth's face broke into a smile at the mention of her niece's name. Maude was growing strong now, taking after Bea with her rosebud lips and tiny nose, though her dark curly hair was just like Jimmy's.

'She's a little beauty,' she said. 'And being well cared for.'

Sarah acknowledged their secret arrangement with an imperceptible nod.

'Maude? Who's Maude?' Henry demanded.

His question hung in the air. Ruth felt it was none of his business who Maude was. He'd never expressed any interest in her family when they'd spoken at the party, and she certainly wasn't going to enlighten him now. She saw Sarah shift uncomfortably; she was clearly waiting for Ruth to reply. When Ruth kept quiet, Sarah spoke up.

'Maude is Ruth's baby,' she said quickly. 'Well, what I mean is, she's not exactly Ruth's baby, but she's—'

Henry rocked back on his heels. 'A baby?' he said. A horrified expression clouded his pale face.

Ruth pressed her feet hard to the cobbles. 'Yes, a baby,' she said, trying to keep the anger from her voice. 'My sister's, if you must know. She died. I bring up Maude as best I can, all things considered, and I'm grateful for any support I get.'

'I didn't know you were lumbered with a . . .' He paused, as if he could hardly bring himself to spit out the next word, 'a baby.'

Ruth glared at him. She had to restrain herself from slapping him across his soft pink face. 'Lumbered?' she growled.

'Well, I . . .' Henry began.

'Lumbered?' Ruth said again, louder this time. 'My sister's baby is not a hindrance.' She locked eyes with him. 'Sir.'

'Surely you could send the child to the Sunderland orphanage?' he said. He offered the words as if it was an obvious solution, as if Maude was a problem to be solved.

'I could, sir, that's true.' She looked him straight in the eye. 'But I would never be so cruel.'

How dare he say such a thing about her beloved niece? His reaction on learning she had a child to look after had certainly given his true feelings away.

Just then a movement outside the machine room caught Ruth's eye. Sarah had seen it too, and she excused herself and headed to meet Alan Murphy. Ruth and Henry stood in silence. Henry pulled awkwardly at his shirt collar and studiously avoided looking in Ruth's direction.

'Your parents are well, I hope?' Ruth asked. She kept her tone calm and even; she wanted her words to hit the spot. She wanted to let Henry know she hadn't forgotten about his invitation to join him for dinner. His blank expression confirmed that his offer had meant nothing to him and had slipped his mind completely.

'My parents?' he said.

She took her chance to twist the knife. She doubted very much she'd ever see him again, and if she did, it wouldn't be of her choosing. How foolish she'd been to let a man like Henry try to seduce her. Take away his smart coat and shined shoes and his heart was rotten to the core.

'Did you ever intend for me to visit you at Ashbrooke?' she asked.

He looked over to where Sarah and Alan were talking.

'No, I thought not,' Ruth said. 'Well, if you'll excuse me, I need to get back to work.' She turned on her heel and headed back to the rag room.

Just before she reached the door, she saw Sarah hurrying towards her.

'Underneath all his bluster, Henry's a good man,' Sarah said quickly, nodding towards Henry.

'But not one I care for, I'm afraid,' Ruth replied.

'What if I give him the chance to apologise to you in person, at my home, a more relaxed setting than the mill?' Sarah offered. 'Henry is my friend, one of my oldest, and you're my friend too. I can't bear to think that you can't get along with each other.'

Ruth could think of nothing she wanted less than to

meet Henry again, but neither did she want to upset Sarah especially when she'd been so generous to arrange for Maude to be cared for by Amelia Smith.

'When's your next day off?' Sarah asked.

'Tuesday.'

'Come to tea, just the three of us. Please say you will.'

Just as Ruth disappeared into the rag room, Jane came into the yard. She was only halfway across when she stopped dead in her tracks and her hand flew to her heart. Davey was walking towards her, his face set firm, unsmiling.

'Where do you think you're off to?' he demanded.

'Leave me alone, Davey. You can't talk to me now. My dad'll get the police on you, remember?'

'And your dad's here at the mill, is he?' Davey sneered. 'You think you're free of me, don't you, Jane? But I'll always be here, always lurking, watching, always ready to get you back with a snap of my fingers.'

Jane swallowed hard. She wanted to run to the rag room, but her legs were shaking so much she wasn't sure they would carry her.

'What's going on here?' a voice called.

Jane swung around to see Alan Murphy approaching.

'Davey, are you shirking again?' Alan asked.

'No, boss.'

'Then get yourself back to work, lad. You and I will have words later about this.'

Davey didn't move an inch.

'Now!' Alan yelled.

Davey spat on the cobbled yard, wiped the back of his hand across his mouth and ambled away back to work.

As soon as he was out of sight, Alan turned to Jane.

'Are you all right, Jane? He didn't harm you, did he?'

Jane shook her head.

'Sarah told me what's happened between you and Davey. She asked me to keep an eye on him, and I've learned there's another side to that fella. He's not the man I thought he was.'

'We were just talking, sir,' Jane said.

'Talking, eh? Well, whatever he said has put you in a bit of a state, lass. You're shaking.'

'I'll be fine, sir, honest I will.' Jane reached her hand to the wall to steady herself as her legs turned to jelly. She hadn't seen Davey in days, not since her dad had threatened him with the police. She'd thought she was rid of him once and for all, and now he'd followed her into the mill yard. His threatening words had sent a chill down her spine.

'He's a strong lad, that Davey, and a bit too handy with his fists,' Alan went on. 'I've been thinking for some time I might move him out of the machine room to somewhere like the docks, where brawn rather than brain is what's needed.'

'He'd be away from the rag room then?'

'He'd never have reason to come up to the mill yard again,' Alan said. 'And if you ever see him, or if you've got any cause for concern, just tell me, you hear?'

Jane nodded.

'Now then, get back to work, the rag room is waiting.'

Alan turned and began to walk towards the machine room, but was stopped in his tracks when Jane finally plucked up the courage to say something she'd been thinking for some time.

'Mr Murphy, sir, Sarah Hewson's a lucky lady.'

Chapter Twenty-Nine

Tuesday dawned with rain pelting against the windows of the Guide Post Inn. Ruth lay in her bed, eyes open, listening to the wind and rain. Inside the room, her dad was snoring, her mam wheezing and baby Maude was crying.

'Come on, little 'un,' she said. 'Let's get you fed.'

She set to lighting the fire in the hearth, and as the flames licked paper and wood, she dressed quickly before laying a shovelful of coal on top. She helped wash her mam and made her comfortable. She gently brushed her mam's hair then softly stroked her hands.

'You look sad, love,' Jean said.

'Oh, it's something and nothing,' Ruth replied.

Jean lifted a finger to her daughter's face and laid it gently on Ruth's cheek. 'Penny for them?'

Ruth sighed. 'How do you know what love is, Mam? How do you know when it comes?'

'Love? Now there's a question!'

'You and Dad, you're like two halves of the same person. How did you know he was the one for you?'

'It's not always been easy; love never is,' Jean sighed.

'Are you having trouble with a fella at the mill?'

'Not exactly,' Ruth said. 'It's more complicated than that.'

'Well, let me tell you this. Love isn't complicated. When you meet the right man, and you will, talking to him will feel as easy as putting on your favourite pair of slippers, and as welcoming.'

'Slippers, eh?' Ruth laughed. 'I'll bear it in mind.'

She glanced out of the window and saw the rain easing. She was desperate for some time on her own. She needed to think about Sarah's offer to meet Henry at St Bede's Terrace that day; she had a decision to make. Should she really allow him another chance after his reaction when he'd found out that she looked after Maude as her own child? She was curious, that was for sure, but she also had her pride. But if she turned down the invitation, might Sarah think badly of her?

'I thought I might head out for a walk when the rain stops, Mam,' she said.

'Wrap up well and take Maude with you,' Jean said. 'It'll do her good to get some fresh air.'

Ruth's day passed in a blur of cleaning, washing and cooking. She called to see Mrs Pike to hand over two shillings towards the rent. The landlady was in good spirits and sang Harry's praises.

'Your dad's proved a good worker, and he gets on well with the customers, although he's limited in what he can do, of course.'

'His bad leg still gives him trouble,' Ruth said. 'It won't get any better.'

'Well, I've got him seated behind the bar most days,

serving from his bar stool and chatting with those who come in for a beer. They like him and he seems to enjoy the work.'

'It's a far cry from his work at the pit, though,' Ruth said.

'And it doesn't pay anywhere near as much as he's used to,' Mrs Pike said. 'But desperate times call for desperate measures.'

'Is that how you see us?' Ruth asked. 'The desperate Hardys?'

Mrs Pike beckoned her to a table in the quiet, empty pub. She pulled out two stools and encouraged Ruth to sit down.

'I'm prepared to let you stay, Ruth, all of you.'

Ruth's heart lifted at the words. This was a welcome surprise indeed.

'And the rent we owe you?'

'Pay it when you can. As long as your dad keeps working, as long as the occasional shilling comes my way, I'll say no more about it. I'm not a hard woman, Ruth.'

Ruth bit the inside of her mouth. Mrs Pike was well known as one of the toughest women in Ryhope when it came to business. Ruth felt privileged to be seeing a side to her that few others saw.

'I admire you, Ruth. I saw how you dealt with Bea's passing and how you're looking after little Maude. It can't be easy and I have no wish to make things worse.'

'Thank you, Mrs Pike.'

The landlady stood and laid her hand on Ruth's shoulder. 'Just remember, keep those shillings coming and we'll remain on good terms.'

Ruth sat a while in the silent pub as Mrs Pike went

about her business. Outside, the rain eased and the beginnings of a blue sky appeared between the grey clouds.

Ruth hung the washing in the yard and settled her mam and dad. Then she wrapped Maude in a shawl and set out towards High Farm. That was as far as she planned to go, but as she began walking, the sun peeked out from the clouds and a warmth spread across her face. Maude was quiet, nestled against her chest. With the day brightening, and a lot on her mind, when Ruth reached High Farm she carried on. She walked along the path that skirted the village green, past the cattle market and Ryhope Hall. From here she followed the track to the beach.

There were no roaring waves, no crashing at the cliffs, which meant the tide was out. The golden sands were streaked with black lines of sea coal washed to the shore. Men were shovelling coal into barrows and carts to wheel it home. One man even used a battered old pram. Even in its ruinous state, Ruth would have welcomed the luxury of such a carriage for Maude. The bairn was getting heavy.

She picked her way along the sand, taking care to watch the stones, for one twist of her ankle and she'd fall. Her own pain she could bear, but she would never forgive herself if anything happened to Maude. Far ahead of her, she could just make out the figures of two men digging in the sand. This time it wasn't sea coal they were after, but worms to use for fishing bait.

She found a low, flat rock and made herself comfortable. Then she placed Maude in her lap and turned the baby to the sea. They sat a while under the endless sky, watching waves break on the shore. Ruth let her worries drift like clouds, trying not to grip tight to any of them. John Hepple floated through her mind and she let him go, sending him out to the waves. She thought of Sarah Hewson and Alan Murphy, but their relationship was not her concern and she dismissed them as easily as throwing a pebble. And then there was Henry, for he was the reason she needed to think. Should she accept Sarah's invitation to tea? All she had to do was get to know him better, if only for Sarah's sake. She kissed Maude gently on the top of her head. She was torn over what to do and knew she couldn't leave the beach until her decision was made.

The sun was shining. Ruth's gaze focused on the waves and Maude was soon asleep. The two men digging for bait began walking towards her, making their way to the track through the cliffs. Both wore black caps, shapeless black jackets, loose trousers. They trudged along with their heads bent. As they neared her, she saw a dog running rings around them. It was a small dog, and she knew she'd seen its blue collar before. Her heart leapt, and she peered at the men, her heart pounding. One of them was middle-aged, greying, but with the dark features she recognised immediately. She stared at the younger man at his side, her heart pounding. Then she sat up straight.

'Hello, Mick,' she said.

The men stopped in their tracks. Neither of them had noticed Ruth and Maude on the rock. They had been deep in conversation, heads down, their black caps almost touching as they walked.

'Ruth?' Mick said.

Ruth saw the look of surprise on his face. Was it good surprise or bad? she wondered. She saw his eyes flicker towards Maude.

'I'll catch you up, Dad,' he said to the older man, who doffed his cap to Ruth.

'Nice to meet you, miss.'

Mick waited until his dad was out of earshot. 'Can I sit down?' he asked.

'It's a free country,' Ruth said. She tried to keep her voice calm, but it was hard when her heart was jumping. She'd expected, hoped, to bump into Mick at the paper mill, but their paths hadn't crossed since the day of the works outing to Seaburn.

Mick settled himself on a rock, and Button flopped on to the sand at his side.

'Didn't expect to see you down here,' Ruth said coolly.

'It's my day off. I'm going fishing with Dad when the tide's in tonight.' He nodded towards Maude. 'Do you take Bea's baby everywhere you go? Last time I saw you, you had the bairn then too.' There was a pleasant tone to his voice that Ruth enjoyed hearing.

'Our Maude? We're inseparable,' she replied.

'She's a little smasher,' Mick said.

Ruth looked out over the waves. She took heart from the fact that Mick was sitting beside her, that he'd broken his walk with his dad just for her. There were questions burning in her mind and she came straight out with the one uppermost.

'Not with your girlfriend today?'

'Girlfriend?' Mick asked.

'The lass you were with at Seaburn.'

'Oh, her.' Mick sighed. 'She wasn't my girlfriend. She thought she was, like. Took a while to shake her off. She wouldn't leave me alone.'

'Seems like you shake a lot of girls away from you.'

He hung his head, started poking his finger in the sand. 'I deserve that comment. What I did to you, Ruth, what I said, it was all wrong. I thought I knew what I was doing, but it turns out I hadn't a clue.'

Ruth sat still and stared ahead. Her insides were churning like the frothy white sea ahead of her. She didn't know what to say.

'I'm sorry,' he said. 'I regret it all, every word.'

She felt a lump in her throat, and forced herself not to cry. 'Sorry? What for?' she said. If he was going to apologise to her, she wanted every last word squeezed from him. She needed to know exactly where she stood before she let him back into her heart.

Mick stared ahead too, and Ruth felt the heat from his body next to hers.

'I'm sorry for losing the best thing that ever happened to me.'

'What do you want, Mick?' She needed to know, needed to hear it from his lips. She turned her face to meet his.

'I want you back, Ruth. I want *you*,' he said. 'And Maude, and your mam and dad.'

'Changed your mind about my family then?' she asked, as casual and cocky as she could.

'Ruth, don't . . .' Mick said.

'Don't what? Don't remind you of everything you said you didn't want when you dumped me? You said you didn't want to come second to my family. They'll always come first, Mick. Always.'

'I want us to be together, Ruth, if you'll have me. If you'll forgive me.'

Ruth's heart thumped. She felt sick with nerves. Those were the words she had longed to hear.

'I want us to help each other,' he continued. 'Be a team, the two of us against the world. We'll look after our families, your mam and dad, mine.'

Ruth held her head high. 'And the baby?'

'I'd be proud to take her on as my own.'

Ruth was shocked. 'Take her on? But I wasn't talking about marriage!'

'I was,' Mick said quietly.

Ruth thought her heart would burst with happiness, yet her mind was raging with confusion. There were still questions that she needed answers to. 'You've changed, Mick,' she said warily. 'How do I know you won't get a notion in your head when we're back . . .' She paused, corrected herself. '. . . if we get back together? How do I know you won't change your mind again?'

He laid his hand on hers. She didn't move away.

'Because ever since that day at the mill, I've thought about you all the time. I've been a fool, Ruth, a damned fool. Sometimes you don't appreciate what you've got until you lose it.'

'And if I take you back?' she asked.

'I'll do everything in my power to never lose you again. It's as simple as that.'

Ruth lifted her free hand and covered Mick's fingers with hers. 'You say it's simple, but it's difficult for me. How do I know you won't break your promise?'

'Because I swear, Ruth, on all that is sacred to me, on my mam and dad's lives, that I will love you till my dying day.'

Ruth leaned towards Mick and looked into his dark eyes. They moved closer to each other until Mick's lips were on hers, where they stayed for a very long time.

At last she pulled slowly away. 'What time are you going fishing with your dad?' she asked.

'Fishing?' Mick laughed. 'We'll head out at seven, but what's that got to do with anything I've just said? I lay my heart on the line and you ask me about fishing?'

'Well,' Ruth said as a smile played on her lips. 'Before you go, how would you like to come for tea?'

Mick arrived at the Guide Post Inn later that afternoon with a newspaper parcel in one hand and a bottle of ale in the other. He handed the beer to Harry, who accepted it gratefully. Mick gave the newspaper parcel to Jean. 'These are for you.'

Ruth watched as her mam peeled back a layer of paper. She saw green leaves inside, and hoped it would be leeks, for they couldn't afford to buy fresh vegetables. Eggs, bread and pies kept them going.

'Help me, love,' Jean begged. She was struggling to remove the paper. Ruth went to her mam's bedside and pulled the paper away to reveal a bunch of frilled yellow flowers.

'Dahlias from Dad's garden,' Mick said proudly. 'Do you like them?'

'I love them, lad. Thank you,' Jean said.

Ruth took the flowers and filled a bucket with water. 'I'll find something better to put them in later,' she told Mick. 'I'm sure we've got a vase somewhere.' She felt heat rise in her face at the little white lie. They had no vase in the room. The Hardys owned nothing frivolous or decorative any more. Everything had been sold when they'd been thrown out of their pit house.

In his armchair by the fire, Harry poured his beer into

a glass. It caught the colours of the flames, honey and red. 'Cheers,' he said as he lifted the glass towards Mick. 'Not having one yourself?'

'Not tonight. I'm going fishing with dad at the beach. But I'll share a beer with you another time, Harry. That is, if I'm invited back.'

Ruth watched the exchange with interest. She appreciated Mick's honesty, and the fact that he'd accepted her invitation to return to the Guide Post Inn and make amends with her family after what had gone before.

'It's not me you need to ask about being invited back, lad,' Harry said sagely. 'As long as our Ruth's happy to have you here, then me and Jean are happy too. Isn't that right, Jean?'

Silence. Ruth looked across at her mam. Jean's eyes were closed to the world.

'Your mam's not getting any better then?' Mick asked quietly.

'She slips away more each day. Little by little we lose her.'

'What does Dr Anderson say?'

Ruth and her dad shared a look.

'We can't afford the doctor, lad,' Harry said. 'We keep Jean as comfortable as we can. Ruth looks after her well.'

'But surely there must be something the doctor can do to help?' Mick asked.

'There's no money, Mick,' Ruth said. 'Everything I earn is spent on feeding us and paying the rent. There's not a penny left over.'

Mick reached for her hand. 'Would you let me help?' he asked.

'We don't want your charity, lad,' Harry said firmly.

'Not charity, Harry. I didn't mean to offend you. I don't earn so much myself at the mill that I can spare money to help. But I can bring vegetables from Dad's garden, potatoes and onions. We've got sprouts coming through; they'll be ready by Christmas. And if we catch fish, I can bring any Mam doesn't need. What do you say, Harry?'

'Aye, lad. I daresay a bit of fish would go down nice with a plate of potatoes now and then.'

'Ruth?' Mick pleaded. 'Will you let me help?'

Ruth thought of her mam's words earlier that day, about love being as comfortable as putting on a pair of favourite slippers. She gently squeezed Mick's hand.

Meanwhile, in a high-ceilinged drawing room of a terraced house in a leafy street, Henry paced the floor. Sitting on the sofa, Sarah sipped tea from a china cup.

'I told you she wouldn't come,' Henry said. 'It was a stupid idea to invite her.'

'I had to try to redeem you somehow,' Sarah said. 'You treated the girl rotten, Henry. Kissing her one minute then dropping her like a hot stone the next. Inviting her to tea so that you could apologise was the least I could do.'

'You knew I had no fancy to see her again.' Henry stood by the fireplace and rested his arm on the mantelpiece. 'Although she had a bit of grit about her, I liked that. Saucy, too, after a glass or two of your dad's best sherry,' he added.

'Henry, don't,' Sarah pleaded.

'Don't what?'

'Don't get that lecherous look on your face. It happens

every time you talk about girls who catch your eye. It's not respectful. If you're to find a decent girl, the kind your mother hopes you will, you're going to have to stop being so free with your kisses. I saw you and Ruth at the party.'

Henry stuck out his chin. 'She enjoyed it as much as I did,' he said.

'I'm giving you advice, as your only friend,' Sarah said. 'Ruth might be just a paper mill girl but she deserves better than you.'

Henry sniffed. 'I was only having a bit of fun.' He sighed heavily and gazed from the window out to the tree-lined street. Then he sat down on the sofa beside Sarah and she poured him a cup of tea.

'Do you think your father will ever approve of Alan Murphy?' he asked.

'I daresay he won't. Every time I try to bring Alan into a conversation, Father changes the subject.'

'Then what will you do?' Henry asked.

Sarah bit her lip. She and Alan had made a pact to tell no one of their plan to elope. She took another sip of her tea.

'I'm certain love will find a way,' she said.

Chapter Thirty

Over the coming weeks, Ruth and Mick grew close again, much closer than before. He visited her often at the Guide Post Inn and each time brought gifts from his dad's garden: carrots, potatoes and cabbages. Ruth confided in him about Mr Hewson paying for Maude's care and told him about John taking over as supervisor. She had still not received confirmation of when this might happen, although Dorothy had hinted that the change might take place at the end of the year.

Each morning when Ruth arrived at the mill, Mick was waiting for her, just as he used to do. Button was always with him, tucked inside his jacket out of sight. Some days Mick presented her with a flower or two, picked from his dad's garden. Some days he handed her a couple of onions or a loaf of freshly baked bread from his mam. And there was always a hug and a kiss.

'Mam's invited you to tea on your next day off,' he said one day. 'She hopes you'll bring Maude with you.'

'She doesn't mind that I've as good as got a bairn of my own?'

'Mind? She admires you for taking Maude on.'

'You mentioned inviting me to meet your mam and dad before, if you remember,' she reminded him. 'But it never happened. Why now?'

'Because I wasn't sure what I felt back then. I didn't think I was ready to settle down, to belong to someone else's family.'

'And now?'

He kissed her on the lips. 'Do you know how many times I stood here, outside the rag room, trying to pluck up the courage to tell you I was sorry?'

'You did?'

'I'd say the words out loud, begging you to forgive me and give me another chance. I had my hand on the door a couple of times; almost pushed it open, but in the end, I couldn't do it. I was a coward, Ruth. I hate myself for what happened. And that's why I'm going to make the most of every minute we've got together. I want you to be part of my family in the same way that you want me to belong to yours. Come and meet Mam and Dad, bring Maude, and we'll have tea and cake.'

'Cake, eh?' Ruth said. 'Now that's a luxury I haven't enjoyed for some time.'

Mick's face clouded over. 'And I want to help find the money to have the doctor look at your mam.'

Ruth sighed. 'I've told you, Mick. I haven't a penny to spare.'

'Me neither,' Mick said. 'But we'll work something out, you'll see.'

On the day Ruth was due to go to Mick's home for tea, he came to the Guide Post Inn to collect her. She wore Bea's blue scarf and her grandma's coloured brooch. She

255

brushed out her long hair and wrapped Maude in a woollen blanket. Mick had brought Button with him, and the dog ran alongside, staying close to his side.

Mick's family lived in George Street, a row of lime-washed cottages running parallel to the railway lines near Ryhope East station. As they walked there, he once again brought up the subject of paying for the doctor. It was almost too much to bear for Ruth, being given hope that money might be found to ease her mam's pain. Mick talked the problem over; he wouldn't let it go. He wasn't yet ready to admit what Ruth and Harry had long ago accepted: that the money was simply not there. And even if it was, would it make any difference now? Jean's illness had gone on too long and robbed her of her life.

They walked past Ryhope Hall and the cattle market, past the chapel and village school. At the bottom of the village green was Watson's Grocers. Mick's eyes widened at the sight of the little shop.

'I've got an idea,' he said.

He began to stride ahead of Ruth, leaving her behind. She walked as quickly as she could to catch up. When he reached the shop, he walked around to the yard at the back. Ruth watched carefully. What on earth was he up to? The yard was protected by a stone wall no higher than her waist. Inside were boxes of apples and cherries. A long, skinny dog lay sleeping in one corner. She guessed it was there to guard against anyone stealing the goods. But it didn't stir when Mick approached.

Mick turned to her and put his finger to his lips. 'Shh.'

'No, Mick!' Ruth hissed when she realised what he

was up to. But he took no notice and jumped up on to the wall.

The dog in the yard was still sleeping, its legs twitching as if dreaming of chasing a hare. Mick balanced on the wall and then dropped into the yard. He kept as far away from the dog as he could, just in case it woke and turned on him.

'Mick, no!' Ruth repeated.

Mick didn't seem to hear. Keeping his eyes fixed on the dog, he tiptoed across the yard and picked up a box of red apples. It was heavier than expected and Mick struggled to lift it. Slowly he turned with the box in his hands, ready to make his escape. The dog was snoring now, oblivious.

Ruth couldn't believe her eyes. She felt a sharp pang of disappointment. Was Mick nothing but a common thief? He'd always acted so upright and truthful in all the time she'd known him. Now he was proving himself no better than someone like Jimmy Tate. And to think of all the times she'd warned Bea about Jimmy being a low-life thief! But any disappointment and regret she felt quickly gave way to the realisation that what he was doing was for her. He was taking a huge risk. For that she felt grateful, despite her misgivings at him stealing, even if it was just a box of fruit. Fresh fruit was a luxury the Hardys could no longer afford.

As Mick made his way over the wall, Ruth looked around. She was terrified that someone might have seen him. And if he had been seen, then so had she. She felt as much to blame. If they were caught by the village coppers, she'd be locked up, or at least given a talking-to at the station. She could imagine only too easily how angry and disappointed her mam and dad would be. And what if word got back to the paper mill? Was a box of apples worth losing their jobs for?

Mick was back beside her now, and whispered in her ear, 'Run for it!'

He set off with the box in his arms, Button scampering after him. Ruth followed as quickly as she could, cuddling Maude to her chest. She couldn't run, for Maude was heavy and Ruth's legs were weak with shock. Her heart was beating so hard she thought it might leap from her chest, and she couldn't catch her breath. Maude began to cry at being jostled.

Mick ran around the corner of the Railway Inn. Ruth followed, and they stood together, panting, by the back wall of the pub.

'You stole them,' Ruth gasped. She was having trouble making sense of what had just happened, and why. 'You're nothing but a thief!' Her anger left her in short bursts. 'What else don't I know about you?'

'I did it for your mam, Ruth. For the doctor's fee. You know that.'

'That doesn't make it right,' Ruth cried.

'Then do you have another idea?' Mick said. 'Because if you do, let's hear it. Let's see where Ruth Hardy can get money from out of nowhere to look after her mam who's lying ill in the back room of a pub.'

'Mick, don't,' she pleaded. 'It's the shock, that's all. I'm not used to things like this. I've never stolen anything in my life.'

'And you think I have?' he hissed. 'This box of apples, it's money to help your mam. I'll sell them at the docks tomorrow and we'll get Dr Anderson to look at her.'

'I still don't like it, Mick, it scares me.'

Mick was silent for a few moments. 'Me too,' he replied eventually.

Ruth was terrified they'd be caught, but she also knew they needed the money. She had no choice but to trust Mick on this.

'Promise me something?' she asked.

'Anything,' Mick said.

'Don't ever do it again.'

'I promise,' he replied.

On the other side of the wall, in the yard of the Railway Inn, Connie Tate was at work. She had run up a bill for ale at the pub, and for the first time in their married life, Big Jimmy had put his foot down. He refused to cover her debt, and the only way for Connie to pay the money she owed was by cleaning the pub yard and mucking out the stables.

Now she stood with her hands clasped at the top of her broom handle, listening to a conversation on the other side of the wall. She recognised the girl's voice only too well, although she'd be hard pressed to say who the boy was. Mick? She didn't know anyone called Mick. But whoever he was, his words told her all she needed to know. Fancy that, she thought. Ruth Hardy, stealing. An evil grin spread wide across her face. Oh, this was news that she could make something of.

Chapter Thirty-One

The afternoon tea with Mick's mam and dad passed as pleasantly as Ruth had hoped. Their small cottage on George Street was squashed in the middle of a tightly packed row opposite the railway line. Before they walked in through the front door, Mick laid the box of apples behind a metal drum used to collect rainwater.

'What'll you tell your mam and dad if they ask where the apples came from?' Ruth asked.

'I'll probably not tell Mam; it's best she doesn't know,' Mick replied warily. 'I'll have a word with Dad when I can. He'll understand when I tell him about your mam.' He ushered Ruth and the baby indoors.

Mick's dad, Bobby, was the double of Mick, with the same bushy hair and dark eyes. His mam, Gloria, was a short, energetic woman, stocky around the hips, with firm calves and thick wrists. She spoke her mind and didn't mince her words. Ruth decided then and there that she never wanted to get on the wrong side of Mick's mam. Both Bobby and Gloria adored Maude instantly. Gloria insisted on holding her and making a fuss of her. She wanted to know all about Ruth; asked about her mam and dad and gave her condolences over Bea.

'I hope our Mick's not going to let you slip through his fingers this time,' Bobby said.

'He told us what happened last time,' Gloria added. 'I told him he was a fool to let you go, and that was before we'd even met you. Now that we have, I can see why you're such a catch. You're a supervisor at the mill, our Mick says.'

'That's right,' Ruth said, although she wondered how much longer her role would be secure.

Conversation flowed easily and Gloria served her home-made vegetable soup, although what kind of vegetable it had once been, Ruth would have been hard pressed to say. But as she ate, something niggled all the while. Knowing how easily Mick had stolen the box of apples didn't sit easy with her. Although he'd promised he'd never do it again, she was learning things about him that she hadn't known before and she wasn't sure she liked what she was finding out. She tried to square it with herself. It was only a box of apples. It wasn't as if it had been a crate of beer stolen from a pub. And he had taken them to help her, doing it out of the goodness of his heart, nothing more. Wouldn't it all be worth it when Dr Anderson called to see her mam?

But still she felt uneasy. She vowed to put right Mick's wrong the minute she could afford to do so. She'd even confess all to Mr Watson, the grocer. And she'd take Mick with her when she did. If the two of them were going to spend their future together, she had to do this. And woe betide Mick if he ever put another foot wrong, because Ruth knew she wouldn't forgive him for stealing again.

* * *

Ruth and Mick walked back to the Guide Post Inn as darkness began to fall. They kissed goodnight in the back lane and Mick waved to Maude, who gurgled in Ruth's arms. Ruth lifted the baby's tiny hand and waved it back. With her free hand, she pushed the gate open and walked into the yard.

'Thought you'd seen the last of me, I bet?' sneered a voice from a hidden corner.

Ruth peered into the darkness. 'Who's there?'

When she saw Connie Tate emerging, she brought Maude tight to her chest. Her first instinct was to scream. Mick might hear her from the back lane and come running. But she didn't scream. She wasn't afraid of Connie for herself. Her only fear came from what the woman might do to Maude.

'What are you doing here?' she said. She stared hard at Connie, and what she saw surprised her. The woman was standing steady, not rocking from foot to foot as she normally did, or shouting and causing a scene. Ruth had never seen her sober before and had no idea what she might do.

She watched as Connie walked across the yard to stand in front of her, blocking her entry to the room where her mam lay in bed. Her eyes flickered to the back door of the pub, where her dad would be working. If if wasn't for Maude, she might have been able to run past Connie into the pub. If Connie had been drunk, she would have done it, but she knew that sober, the woman's reflexes would be sharp. She wouldn't risk Maude being caught in a fight.

'What do you want?' she asked, louder.

'I thought I'd call in to see if you had anything for me,'

Connie said. She stepped across the yard like a tiger ready to strike. Ruth backed away.

'There's only one thing you want from me and you're not having her. Now get out of here before my dad finds you. He's just in there, you know.'

'Your dad with his gammy leg?' Connie laughed. 'I doubt very much he'll come galloping out. He can hardly move, that fella.'

'I'll shout for Mrs Pike,' Ruth said, although she felt uncertain whether anyone would hear. The noise from inside the pub was building with the more ale people sank.

'Oh, I want the bairn,' Connie said. 'I'll never stop wanting the bairn.'

'You don't love her like I do,' Ruth said. 'I know what your plans are. You'd sell her the minute you got your hands on her.'

'Sell her?' Connie laughed.

'I heard you and Jimmy talking,' Ruth said. 'You'll never get her.'

Connie eyed her warily. 'So you heard me and Jimmy?' she said. 'There's no point in lying, then. You're right, I'd pass her on for money. I can't be doing with another greedy mouth at home. Anyway, we've got no proof she's even our Jimmy's. Your little sister was a whore. That bairn could belong to any lad in Ryhope.'

Ruth took a deep breath and replied as evenly as she could, even though her instinct was to lash out at Connie. 'Bea was not a whore. But I'll tell you this. I wish with all my heart that this bairn didn't have Tate blood in her veins.'

'Aye, well, it's not the bairn I've come for.'

Ruth's heart hammered. 'Then what is it? Beer? Is that what you want? A couple of bottles to send you back to oblivion, where you belong?'

Connie swallowed hard, and she licked her lips. 'I've got a taste for the beer. So what?' she hissed. 'But it's not beer that I've come for either. I was hoping for something else, Ruth Hardy. I hear you've got something that doesn't belong to you. Apples, eh? A full box of them stolen from Watson's Grocers.'

Ruth gasped. How on earth did Connie know? She kept silent and pressed her feet to the cobbled ground. Connie took another step towards her, until they were just inches from each other. Her foul breath landed on Ruth's face.

'Now, I can do one of two things,' Connie said. There was a malicious tone to her voice that filled Ruth's stomach with dread. 'I can call at the police station. Why, it's practically on my way home. I'm sure they'd be interested in what I've got to say. Mr Watson might not want to press charges; he's as soft as they come. But his wife will demand justice. You know what she's like.'

Ruth knew only too well. Everyone in Ryhope knew how bitter Renee Watson was. She stayed perfectly still as Connie continued.

'Or I could keep quiet. Course, I'll need something in return for my silence.'

'You're not having her, Connie. Maude is our Bea's bairn and she lives with us here.'

'Tsk, lass. I've already told you, I don't want the flamin' bairn. If I had her, I'd sell her, you're right, but it's too much trouble dealing with the women down in the East End. No, it's money I need, and fast.'

'You know how we're fixed. We haven't got two ha'pennies to rub together.'

'Then you'd better find it. Because if you want me to keep quiet and the police away from your door, I want five pounds by the end of the week.'

Five pounds? Ruth had never had five pounds in her life! How on earth was she going to pay?

Chapter Thirty-Two

The next morning, Ruth found Mick waiting outside the rag room in the pouring rain. He had his collar pulled up to protect him from the miserable weather. As she walked towards him, they both ran to take shelter at the back of the machine room. Ruth leaned in close and told him what had happened with Connie the night before.

'We could lose our jobs if she starts gossiping about the theft. It won't be long before word reaches the mill,' she said.

'Lose our jobs over a box of apples? The police don't arrest folk for that.'

'How can you be sure?' Ruth asked. She narrowed her eyes. 'Are you being honest with me, Mick? *Have* you done this before?'

He shook his head. 'No, Ruth, I swear. And I've already told you I won't do it again. It was an impulse, I don't know what came over me. I was thinking of getting money for your mam, that's all I wanted to do.' Button's furry head appeared from under his collar.

'Mrs Watson's a nasty piece; there's no telling what

she'll do when she finds out who robbed her shop,' Ruth said.

'Is she really that bad?'

'She's worse. She looks down on Ryhope folk, thinks she's above us. She'll be looking for any excuse to tar and feather the culprit. I feel bad for her husband. He's a lovely fella; you couldn't meet a nicer man. When all this is over and we can afford it, we're going to pay him for those apples.'

Mick nodded. 'I know it doesn't make things right, but I sold them first thing this morning.' He dug his hand into his pocket and pulled out a handful of coins. 'I'll drop this at the doctor's house and ask him to visit your mam.'

Ruth was torn. She looked at the money in Mick's hand. She'd not seen so much in a long time, not since she and Bea combined their wages at the end of each week.

'No, Mick . . . it's wrong.'

'Well, I can't give it back, lass.'

'We should give it to Connie, see if she'll take it as part of the five pounds. It might be enough to keep her quiet.'

'No,' Mick said firmly. 'Connie Tate can rot in hell as far as I'm concerned. Your mam needs this.'

Just then Alan Murphy and three of his men from the machine room walked by. Mick pushed Button back inside his coat.

'Morning, Alan!' he called.

'All right, Mick?' Alan shouted back.

Mick turned back to Ruth. 'Now listen. This money's going to the doctor. I said I'd look after you and your family, and I will.'

'But Connie—'

'Never mind Connie. Leave her to me. We'll find her five pounds.'

'How? By stealing more apples, a few turnips, some sprouts?' Ruth hissed.

'I know a fella,' Mick began hesitantly. 'He knows someone who lends money. I could ask him if he'll give us five pounds. We'll use it to get Connie off our backs.'

'How much will this moneylender ask for in return?' Ruth said. 'And if he's so generous with his cash, why didn't you go to him first, instead of stealing from Watson's?'

'I didn't think, Ruth. I saw the shop and . . . I don't know, something came over me. It was an easy steal. The sleeping dog, the low wall, it was too easy.'

'Well, you've ended up in a right mess now. Both of us have. We could be facing arrest if Connie does what she threatens. And then we'll both lose our jobs.'

'What if we tell the police Connie threatened you with violence?' Mick said. 'They know she's a drunk.'

'You're suggesting we lie to cover a theft?' Ruth said. 'Mick Carson, I'm surprised at you. Disappointed, too.'

Mick sighed. 'You're right. We've got to face up to this.' He pocketed the coins and Ruth was glad they were out of her sight. 'I'll go to Dr Anderson now, pay him what I can and get your mam seen.'

'And then?' Ruth asked.

'And then I'll have a word with my mate who knows the fella who lends money.'

'We need to wait until Connie's sober before we hand it to her,' Ruth said. 'Otherwise she'll be screaming blue murder that she never received it.'

'How will we know when that'll be?'

Her face clouded over. 'I suspect she'll be back at the end of the week. For someone who spends much of her time rolling drunk, she sobers up quick enough when there's money involved.'

'I'll sort it out, Ruth. Don't worry.'

Mick wrapped his arms around her and hugged her, then Ruth pushed her hair behind her ears and set off to the mill office to collect the rag room key.

'It's already been signed out,' Dorothy said.

'Who's taken it?' Ruth demanded. 'I'm the only one allowed to have it.'

Dorothy closed her eyes. It was as if she couldn't bear to say the name. She turned the ledger so that Ruth could see the signature. Ruth's mouth fell open. She forced herself to look at Dorothy, who shook her head, slowly, sadly.

'When did this happen?' Ruth said.

'About half an hour since, right after Mr Hewson left on business with his management team. They're travelling to Apsley to visit the paper mill at Frogmore.'

Ruth stormed from the office, slamming the door behind her. John Hepple must have arrived in the small hours of the morning to arrive at the mill before she did in order to get the key. She marched across the yard, not even stopping when she heard someone call her name. She pushed the rag room door open and came face to face with John Hepple.

He was sitting in her seat at the front of the room. Ruth seethed with an anger she had never felt before. She wanted to lash out and knock the stupid grin from his scarred face. But she knew better than to do anything rash if she wanted to keep her job, any job at the mill.

'You're late, Miss Hardy,' he sneered. 'Sit down and start work.'

Ruth looked out into the sea of faces in the room. The girls looked to be in as much shock as she was. She clenched her fists.

'Sit down, Miss Hardy, or I'll sack you. It's as simple as that. I'm in charge now.' Ruth caught Edie's eye, and Edie beckoned to her. Ruth slid on to the bench between her two friends, feeling sick to her stomach. Yet there he was, John flamin' Hepple, lording it over the girls in the rag room. Ruth was fizzing with anger and humiliation. Why hadn't Sarah told her the change was taking place so soon? She hadn't seen Sarah since the day she'd been invited to tea with Henry. Was this her way of punishing her for not turning up that day? No, Ruth thought; from what she knew of Sarah, she wouldn't be so petty.

'You all right?' Edie said.

Ruth glanced at John, who was staring right at her. She shook her head. 'No, I'm not.'

'We'll talk at dinner time,' Jane whispered.

'You three!' John barked. 'Separate yourselves from each other. Now! I will not have talking in this . . .' he paused, and leered at Ruth, '. . . in *my* rag room.'

The room fell silent. Ruth stood.

'Ruth, no,' Edie said.

'Don't worry about me,' Ruth replied. 'I'll move to the bench behind.'

'You'll move here,' John demanded. He was pointing to the chair in front of his own, where he'd once sat under Ruth's watchful eye.

Ruth stuck out her chest, held her head high and thought of her mam and dad. She took a step forward to the seat where John demanded she sit. And with each step she took, she thought of the shillings and pennies she needed to pay for coal to keep her mam warm. She thought of the food she needed to buy to keep her dad fed. Every step was painful, awkward, humiliating. But she would not let John know he'd defeated her. She knew her way around the rag room with her eyes closed. She didn't need to look where she was going. She locked her gaze on his as she walked from the back of the room to the front. When she reached John, she kept her eyes on him. She felt she'd won a small battle when he looked away first.

'Get to work, now,' he hissed at the girls. No one moved. The air hung quiet and still.

Before Ruth slid into her seat, she turned to the girls behind her.

'Back to work, girls,' she said in as friendly a tone as she could. She glanced at John; he was red in the face, the scar under his eye angry and raw. Ruth couldn't tell if it was rage or embarrassment or a mixture of both.

'Call this your rag room?' she said quietly. 'It'll never be yours.'

Only when Ruth began her own work did the others get down to theirs, pulling and ripping cloths on the knives. Ruth's hands, hard-working and strong at the best of times, were extra forceful that morning as anger worked its way out of her on to the knife. When the whistle in the mill yard sounded the noon break, the girls waited for John to ring the handbell to dismiss them. It was cold out, but that wouldn't stop Ruth from leaving the room as quickly as she could. Still she waited for the bell to be rung. When John showed no sign of picking it up, she finally snapped.

'For God's sake, man, what's got into you? Power gone to your head already? Give the girls their break.'

'Sit down,' John yelled. 'Sit down! You don't stand up until I ring the bell, got it? You're not dismissed until I say you're dismissed.'

Ruth heard a gasp from one of the girls. She put her hands on her hips and cocked her head on one side. 'It's dinner time. We need a break. The girls need the netty and something to eat. The rag room's always run to time with the mill yard whistle.'

'I'm in charge now,' John said. 'You'll do as I say.'

Ruth spun around. 'Girls? Everyone file out for your break.'

No one moved.

'Stay where you are,' John hissed. 'Anyone who moves gets the sack. I'm the supervisor now and it's my word that goes.' He pointed at Ruth. 'Not hers.'

Ruth waved her arm towards the girls. Some of them looked fearful, some were hiding behind others. None of them dared look her or John in the eye.

'Well, I'm going out,' she said calmly. 'Anyone want to come?'

Edie's hand shot up. 'I'm coming,' she said, stepping forward.

'And me,' Jane said.

'Me too,' piped up a voice from the back. Ruth recognised the voice as Claire's; she was happy to hear it, for she feared what might happen to Claire under John's watch.

Slowly but surely the girls began to walk forward, keeping their gaze on the floor. Ruth held the door open and watched as they filed past her and out into the wintry day. Every single one of the girls left the room until just Ruth and John were left. Ruth let the door close. She took a step towards him.

'I know what you are,' she hissed. 'And if you ever take advantage of any of the girls in here again, I'll have you sacked. You hear me?'

He spat on the floor at her feet. 'You'll never do it. Lass like you? Who'd take your word over mine?'

'I've got friends at the mill.'

'Friends?' John laughed. 'I've got family. I've kept quiet for too long, Miss Hardy. I've bided my time, made to sit in front of you for long, humiliating months. Well, now I'm in charge. I'm talking and it's your turn to listen. I understand you've met my father. And as you've met him, you'll know how influential he is.'

Ruth swallowed hard. She knew only too well how important Thomas Hepple was to the mill. 'You've been warned,' she said, surprised how calm her words sounded, because inside she was shaking and her legs felt in danger of giving way.

'I'll consider myself terrified, shall I?' John mocked. 'Now get out and stay out. You took the girls out of the rag room for their dinner break; well, you can all bloody well stay out in the cold. See if I care. I'm locking the door and not letting anyone back in until the mill whistle goes again.'

'You can't do that,' Ruth said quickly. 'It's against the rules.'

'Watch me,' John said.

He marched towards Ruth, but she stood her ground. He grabbed her arm with one hand and with the other yanked the door open. Ruth struggled, but she was no match for him and she found herself pushed outside. She heard the key turn in the lock. The girls were all huddled outside, waiting for her to speak.

'I'm sorry, lasses,' she said. 'It's as much a shock to me as it is to you. I only found out this morning what was going on.'

'I want to go in for my dinner,' Claire said. 'My mam's packed me a pie and a slice of bread. I'm starving, Ruth. Please let us back in.'

A murmur rose amongst the girls. Despite everything, they wanted to go back into the warmth. Their food was locked inside while their bellies rumbled with hunger. Ruth felt dejected. She'd tried to help the girls but had ended up causing trouble for them. She banged on the door with her fist.

'Open up, you bastard!'

A look passed between Edie and Jane. They'd never heard Ruth swear before.

'Open up or else!'

'Or else what?' John yelled from the other side of the door. 'You'll go and tell Mr Hewson? He's away on business, lass. He's left his precious mill behind. That's how much he thinks of this place. And who's running it while he's away? No one, that's who!'

Ruth bit her lip. She could head to the mill office and ask Dorothy if there was a spare key to the rag room. But she didn't want news of this to reach Mr Hewson, not when she was the one responsible for having the girls locked out. There was nothing else for it but to call for help from someone she trusted.

'Go and get Alan Murphy,' she instructed Edie. 'Tell him I need him here.'

Edie ran to the machine room while Ruth and the girls waited. The younger ones huddled together, arms around each other, trying to keep warm. Some of them shot daggers at Ruth for stranding them out in the cold. The wind howled, and what had started as drops of rain now fell as sleet, lashing sideways on the wind. The girls dropped their heads, turning their faces away from the sleet that fell on their skin like pin pricks.

After an anxious wait, for Ruth wasn't at all certain that he would come, she spotted Edie running out of the machine room, and was relieved to see Alan walking behind.

'What's going on?' he demanded.

Ruth told him what had happened. She tried to keep her voice calm and measured, but inside she was quaking, as much from the cold as from fear of what might happen if Mr Hewson got to hear of events. Alan banged at the door.

'Hepple! Open up! It's Alan Murphy.'

Ruth heard the key turn but the door stayed closed. She put her hand to it and pushed it hard. She nodded towards Claire and the younger girls.

'Get inside and dry off,' she said. 'Quickly now.'

She watched as Alan and John exchanged words by the door. They spoke in low voices and she wasn't able to hear what they said. But she saw the look that clouded John's face and guessed that Alan had brought his seniority to bear. She wondered if Alan knew who John's dad was and how important he was to the mill.

'Ruth?' Alan called.

She walked to his side and he bent towards her conspiratorially. 'I suggest you head to the mill office before you leave tonight, find out what's going on. Hepple says he was told just yesterday evening that he was the new supervisor.'

'Sarah never told me things would be changing so soon,' she said.

At the mention of Sarah's name, Alan's eyes widened. 'Sarah? You've seen her?'

Ruth shook her head. 'Not for a while. If you see her, would you tell her I'd like to speak to her?'

'I could ask the same of you,' Alan said.

Ruth noticed a sadness as he spoke. 'You haven't seen her either?' she asked. She was confused. Surely Alan and Sarah were as tight a couple as any with their engagement looming? That was what she'd been led to believe by Sarah, and she wondered what might have happened.

'No,' Alan said. 'I . . . Well, her father is against us, as I think you might know. I understand Sarah thinks highly of you. She regards you as a friend. She's told me you know about us, about her dad; that there are some . . . problems to be overcome.' He gave a little cough. 'I've said too much. I must get back to work.' He cast a glance towards John. 'I suggest if you have any more problems with him, you have a word at the office. Speak to Dorothy; she's got Mr Hewson's ear and she'll know what to do.'

Ruth headed towards Edie and Jane, ignoring John completely. The three of them huddled together, swapping bites of bread, boiled potatoes and eggs and whispering between themselves, Ruth passing on to them what Alan had told her. However, she kept quiet about what he'd said about Sarah.

As they finished their meal, John crossed the room and stood near them, brooding and silent.

'What do you want?' Ruth asked when she caught sight of him.

He looked across the room towards Claire, who was sitting with the younger girls, but said nothing.

Ruth stood up and faced him. 'I'll ask you again. What do you want?'

He stepped forward and poked her hard on the shoulder. 'I want you to remember something,' he said. He poked her again, almost knocking her off her feet this time. 'I want you to remember whose rag room this is.'

Edie shot out of her seat. 'Leave her alone, you big bully. You're not our supervisor; we'll do what Ruth tells us, not you.'

'Disobey me and I'll sack you,' John said coldly. 'Do you hear me, the lot of you? You stinking bunch of stupid girls. Disobey me and you lose your jobs. Got it?' He glared around the room.

Some of the girls sniffed back tears; others remained rigid, quiet, scared.

John took another step towards Ruth and hissed in her ear, 'Got it?'

She turned her head sharply from his rancid breath.

'Say it,' he demanded. 'Say, "I get it, Mr Hepple."'

She closed her mouth and bit her tongue.

'Say it, you bitch,' he hissed. 'Say it, or by God I'll sack them, one by one. Your mates here, they'll be all right. They can get another job. I daresay there'll be work for them whoring on the pit lanes. But what about the young 'uns? I'll start with them, shall I?'

'You wouldn't dare,' Ruth said.

John glared at her. 'Try me.'

From the corner of her eye, she saw Claire's hand fly

to her eyes to wipe away tears. She couldn't do it to them, not to Claire, not to any of the girls. She mumbled something under her breath.

John put his hand to his ear. 'What was that, Miss Hardy? Did you say something?'

'I said, I get it,' Ruth said loudly.

John laughed in her face. 'It's my rag room now. Mine. And don't you forget it.'

Ruth sank into her seat, pressed her eyes tight shut and willed herself not to cry.

Chapter Thirty-Three

When Ruth had worked as the supervisor in the rag room, she always made sure the girls left on time at the end of each day, and that they remembered to take their hats and scarves with them. She held back any of the girls who'd been quiet during the day and asked what was on their mind, staying for as long as it took to listen to their concerns. Usually it was a problem at home, and she offered advice where she could. Once all the girls had left, she swept the floor, piling the dust to one side. She liked a tidy room; it made coming to work the next morning more bearable, knowing that she didn't have to start cleaning the minute she walked through the door.

But on that first day with John in charge, she hurried out of the room without even putting her coat on. As she ran to the mill office, the rain and wind bit her bare arms. However, Dorothy couldn't answer her questions about John, although she told Ruth she wished to high heaven she could.

'I've heard bad things about Hepple,' she said. 'That's all I can say. I don't envy you a jot having to work for him.'

'How has he received Mr Hewson's permission to take over my role when Mr Hewson isn't even here?' Ruth demanded.

Dorothy shook her head. 'It's most unusual. There's no memo like there should be.'

'Something's not right.' Ruth sighed. 'This happens while Mr Hewson's away, the minute he leaves? It doesn't make sense.'

Dorothy raised her eyebrows. 'If I hear anything, I'll tell you,' she said. 'Now go home and get your lovely little bairn from my sister. I hear Maude's a settled soul; she rarely cries these days, although Amelia said she used to scream the place down at first.'

Ruth's heart lifted, and for the first time that day she smiled. She always loved seeing Maude at the end of her day, picking her up and taking her home to the Guide Post Inn. Her sweet little niece was getting bigger every day. Ruth could have sworn she grew in the hours between leaving her in the morning and collecting her after work.

'Night, Dorothy. See you tomorrow,' she said.

Feeling disheartened after her upsetting day at work, she made her way into the throng streaming from the mill. Another shift was coming in and there was a crush at the gates. Once again a girl in a black coat and hat caught her eye. This time she didn't look. She knew it wasn't Bea; it was her grief making her see things that weren't there. She wouldn't be fooled again.

She walked quickly, head down against the wind and rain. All she wanted was to be at home in front of the fire, cooking tea, singing songs to Maude and hearing about her mam and dad's day. Her mam! In all the commotion and upset of the day, she'd forgotten that Dr Anderson was coming out to visit her. But while her heart leapt at the thought of Jean finally being seen by the doctor, her stomach plummeted as she remembered how he would be paid. It was money that still didn't sit easy on Ruth's conscience. Money that had come from the sale of stolen goods, even if they were only apples. Money that had landed her and Mick in more trouble than they could have imagined. And now Mick had to find five pounds to secure Connie's silence to stop them being arrested as thieves. How much they'd have to repay a moneylender didn't bear thinking about. They'd be in the man's debt for months. Owing money and having Connie blackmailing them was hardly the best start to their life together, if that was what it was going to be. She shook her head to dismiss her doubts. They'd get through this together. They'd pay off the debt, no matter how long it took. It would be worth it to cut Connie from their lives.

The thought of Dr Anderson calling to see her mam spurred Ruth on. She picked up the hem of her skirt with one hand and ran as fast as she could. By the time she reached Tunstall Terrace, she was soaked through. Amelia helped her dry off, but there was little point really, as she needed to head back into the driving rain.

Maude was as unsettled as the weather. She cried and screamed as they headed home, which added to Ruth's already dark mood after her day at the mill. But as always, before she headed into the room where her mam and dad would be waiting, she plastered a smile on her face, then took a deep breath and tried to compose herself. For if her dad's mood was dark and her mam was in pain, they'd be relying on her to bring in a ray of sunshine, no matter how bleak she felt.

Ruth pushed the door open. She wiped the rain from her face and tucked her wet hair behind her ears. Her dad was sitting on her mam's bed. She stopped, rain dripping from her clothes, and watched. Harry was leaning across the bed, his back towards Ruth. It was as if her parents were kissing or sharing a hug. Ruth felt embarrassed. Her mam and dad had never been a couple for outward displays of affection. Their love was in the small details, the soft touch of her mam's hand at her dad's neck when he came home from the pit, every inch of him black with coal. Washing him in the tin bath by the fire, scrubbing coal dust from his skin.

'Don't wash my back,' he would warn.

'But it's filthy, Harry.'

'Leave it, woman. It's there to strengthen my back. It's unlucky to remove it.'

'It might be unlucky, but it doesn't half make a mess of my clean sheets,' Jean would reply.

Their love was there in Harry's smile, a warm, loving smile when Jean cooked him a leek pudding, his favourite. Yet here in the room, right in front of Ruth's eyes, she seemed to have interrupted an intimate moment between her parents. She coughed to announce her presence, but Harry still didn't move.

'Dad?' she said softly to get his attention. 'Potatoes for tea? I'll get the water boiling.'

Still nothing.

She took a step forward, keeping her eyes on the back of her dad's head. And it was then that she realised he wasn't holding her mam, or kissing her, as she had first

282

thought. His body was slumped across hers and his shoulders heaved. It was the first time in her life Ruth had seen him cry.

'Dad?'

The horror of what had happened began to sink in. Ruth gripped Maude tight.

'She's gone, love,' Harry said.

'But the doctor came, surely?' Ruth said. She laid Maude in her bed and walked towards her dad. She knelt at her mam's bedside and held Harry's hand. His hard, calloused fingers curled around hers.

'The doctor did come,' he began. His face was raw with pain, eyes red from crying. 'Said nothing could be done. I think we always knew that. Hours after he left, she slipped away. She was sleeping, eyes closed; I was in my chair by the fire. When I woke up, I asked her if she wanted a cup of tea and she never replied. She's gone, Ruth. She's with our Bea now.'

The pain of watching her dad suffer was overwhelming, and Ruth felt her heart break. She looked at her mam's face, her waxy skin. She touched her hand. It was stone cold. It was as if her mam was sleeping, but this time she'd never wake. Her passing had been a long time coming. Ruth had thought she'd prepared herself for this moment many times, gone over in her mind what she'd need to do. What she had never planned for, what she'd never expected, was how much love she would feel for her dad. He was the one who needed protecting now.

'She's with Bea, Dad, you're right,' she said.

Ruth and Harry sat together a long time, holding hands, eyes closed, saying their goodbyes to Jean. Ruth wished, oh how she wished, that she could be certain her mam was with Bea. Outside, the wind howled at the window and the rain lashed from the dark sky.

'Dad? I need to tell the doctor what's happened,' Ruth said at last. 'I'll feed Maude and then go.'

'Will you tell Mrs Pike I won't be at work tonight?' Harry said.

'Course I will. She'll understand.'

Harry looked around the room. 'What is it with this place, eh?' he said softly, shaking his head. 'First it took Bea and now your mam.'

Ruth headed back into the rain, running as if her life depended on it all the way to Dr Anderson's house on Stockton Road. And it was while she ran, while her feet pounded the pavement, that the shock of her mam's passing finally left her. She'd been numb at the pub, her instinct simply to protect her dad. Now the shock was settling into something else, something painful and raw. Dr Anderson's house was up ahead, Ruth saw an oil lamp burning in the hallway. She staggered towards it, every step painful, every step breaking her heart. To say the words out loud, to tell the doctor that her mam's body lay cold in her bed, was too much to bear. Inside the grounds of the doctor's home, Ruth slumped against a wall and began to cry.

Jean's funeral was held early on a winter's morning, when the ground was hard with frost. Ruth had taken the day off work at the mill, which had incurred John's wrath. There was little he could do, however, as Dorothy had rightly pointed out that she was allowed the day to bid farewell to her mam.

Ruth and Mick hardly spoke as they prepared to leave

the pub to head to the church, Ruth too lost in her grief. But Mick had something to tell her, something important that she needed to know.

'I've paid Connie the money she asked for,' he said.

Ruth closed her eyes, swallowed hard and turned her face away. Today was not a day to think about Connie and her feckless son.

'She's out of our lives at last,' she said.

Mick put his arms around her and hugged her.

It was agreed by all who attended the funeral that Reverend Daye gave Jean a wonderful send-off. In the front pew of St Paul's church, Ruth sat with Maude in her arms, Harry on her left-hand side and Mick on her right. Mrs Pike sat behind with Mick's mam and dad. A few of Jean's friends, and friends of Harry's from his pit days, turned up to pay their respects. Ralphie Heddon from High Farm was there too, wiping the back of his hand across his eyes. The Lord's Prayer was read, Jean's favourite. Lil Mahone, who was well known and little liked, being the village gossip, sat at the back to ensure she had the best view of those who attended.

With the funeral over, hymns sung and Jean's body buried, Mrs Pike invited everyone back to the Guide Post Inn. It was a quiet, sombre group who walked the short distance from the church to the pub. Harry hadn't spoken all day, his mood blacker than Ruth had ever known. Ruth felt a darkness inside that threatened to overwhelm her. She could only imagine what hell her dad was going through. Mick proved a godsend, saying all the right things, just enough, one man helping another to struggle through a difficult day.

When the mourners reached the pub, Mrs Pike insisted

on everyone going through the front door. 'The coppers won't disturb us if they see us opening up early,' she said. 'They'll understand, today of all days.'

'I want to settle Maude,' Ruth said. 'Let me take her into our room, and then I'll come through for a drink.' The baby would be perfectly safe; the room would be locked while Ruth raised a glass to say goodbye to her mam.

She watched Mick take Harry's arm to help him into the pub. But when she turned the corner, ready to head into the yard, she stopped dead in her tracks. Two men were loitering by the gate, one of them smoking, the other with his hands in his trouser pockets. Both wore flat caps pulled low. One had the beginnings of a moustache, dark fluff on his top lip, while the other looked too young to try such a thing. They were just boys, she realised, not men. The one with the moustache swaggered towards her.

'Are you Mick Carson's lass?'

Ruth looked from one lad to the other, trying to work out what was going on. 'Whose business is it?'

The boy who was smoking coughed loudly and threw the burning cigarette to the ground. He stepped forward. 'Tell him Dicky Brown wants the first instalment of his money paid by the end of this week.'

'What money?' Ruth said. But with a sinking feeling in her stomach, Ruth knew exactly what he was talking about. Was one of these lads really the moneylender that Mick had borrowed the five pounds from?

The boys stood tall, looked at each other.

'Yeah, tell him we want the money,' the one with the moustache repeated.

'Who are you?' Ruth asked.

'I'm Arthur—' the smoker said.

The other lad clipped him around the ear. 'Shut your bloody mouth! Dad said not to give anyone our names, remember?'

Any fear that Ruth had felt when she'd first clapped eyes on the boys disappeared. She almost had to stop herself from smiling.

'Don't you hit me, Billy!' Arthur cried. He shot his fist out and smacked the other lad on the side of his face. It wasn't long before the two of them were swinging punches at each other as they tumbled away along the back lane and out of sight.

Chapter Thirty-Four

In the weeks after Jean died, Harry sat all day long in his chair, barely speaking. He stopped reading the newspaper Mrs Pike brought in. He had no desire to catch up on the news. Ruth did all she could. She cooked for her dad and cleaned the room as always. She sat by the fire with him each evening, with Maude in her lap. But Harry was unresponsive, lost in his thoughts as he struggled with grief.

Christmas came and went, unmarked for the first time by the Hardys, for there was little to celebrate. Mick's mam had invited them to their tiny home for Christmas dinner, and while Ruth was grateful for the invitation, Harry didn't want to leave his chair by the fire, so she stayed with him. The Saturday-night singers at the Guide Post Inn were full of festive cheer, the pub enjoying its busiest time of year. But in the back room of the pub, Ruth and Harry sat in silence.

The new year turned and the dark days continued. Ruth read stories to Maude, played with the growing child. But not even Maude could put a smile on Harry's face. It was a dark and difficult time. Without her mam, without Bea, Ruth felt more alone than ever. Even with

Mick by her side, supportive and helpful, she felt lost and in need of advice. Her mam and Bea had been her friends, her confidantes.

It was Edie and Jane who stepped up and took her under their wing. One cold January day, after the rain had eased at dinner time, the three girls walked from the mill to Hendon beach. Ruth eyed Edie's cold potatoes and Jane's raw carrots and bread.

'Who fancies doing a swap? I'll swap you a bit of my sandwich for half a carrot,' she said to Jane.

'I'll have half a carrot too, Jane, if you've got more than one,' Edie said. 'You can have some of my potato.'

The girls swapped food, eating slowly, savouring the little they had.

'Ever since we've known you, you've looked after us,' Edie said to Ruth.

'You saved me from Davey's fists,' Jane added. 'I'll always be grateful for that. And now it's our turn to take care of you.'

'The last few weeks have been the worst of my life,' Ruth admitted.

'Spring will come, it always does,' Jane said. 'It's what my grandma says, anyway.'

Ruth took her hand. 'I appreciate the thought.'

She looked out to sea. Since John had taken over as supervisor in the rag room, her job at the mill seemed less important than ever. It was a means to an end, nothing more. She turned up each morning, suffered the humiliation of working under a man like John and took her money at the end of the week. Other than Edie and Jane, and her morning hug and kiss from Mick outside the rag room, there was little joy to her days at the mill. Her life at home wasn't much better. Since her mam's death, she'd been looking after her dad while coping with her own grief, and she and Mick were scrimping and saving to pay Dicky Brown each week. Since she'd been stripped of her supervisor's role, she'd lost the little extra cash she was paid. And still there'd been no word from Sarah or Mr Hewson about her being moved to a supervisor role elsewhere.

'I can't stand working for creepy John in the rag room,' Jane complained.

'None of us can,' Edie said. 'Isn't there anything you can do?'

Ruth thought of Sarah. She'd seen her twice at the mill since the day she was invited to take tea with Henry, and on both occasions Sarah had seemed in a hurry to get away. Not unfriendly, not exactly, but distracted certainly. The first time they'd met, she had given her condolences to Ruth about her mam's passing. She'd held Ruth's hand and told her she knew the darkness she was facing, having lost her own mam. But she'd also begged Ruth not to tell anyone the truth about Thomas Hepple and his relationship with the Hewsons and the mill. Ruth shook her head.

'No, there's nothing I can do,' she said sadly. 'Come on, we'd best get back to work.'

They walked arm in arm from the black sands. When they reached the rag room, they saw a group of girls huddled at the door.

'It's locked,' a small girl called Margaret shouted when Ruth came into view.

'Again?' Ruth cried, confused.

She ran to the door and shoved against it with all her

might. It didn't budge. She banged on it with her fists. 'Who's in there?' she asked the girls.

'Claire stayed inside. She wasn't feeling well,' Margaret replied.

Ruth banged on the door again, harder, faster. 'John Hepple! By God, you're for it this time! Claire? Claire, can you hear me?'

A girl's scream came from inside the room, a scream so loud that all of them around the door heard it.

'Margaret, go and fetch Alan Murphy!' Ruth commanded. She didn't care if she got into trouble from Mr Hewson; it was about time he found out the truth. 'Jane, go to Dorothy in the mill office. Ask if she's got a spare key.'

'What can I do, Ruth?' Edie asked.

'Get the girls away from here. I don't want them to see this.'

Edie spun around, desperately seeking a place of shelter she could take the girls to. Outside the mill, the road led to the Hendon Grange pub. It was common knowledge that the landlady there kept hours outside of the law. There was a chance it might be open.

'Follow me,' she cried as she led the girls out.

Ruth returned to hammering on the door. 'Hepple! Get this door open now!'

There was more screaming, shouts from John, and then the sound of a bench being moved, scraped along the ground, and something heavy being overturned. Claire screamed again.

'Claire! We're going to get you out!' Ruth cried.

She saw Margaret running towards her with Alan walking slowly behind. When he reached Ruth, he sighed. 'What is it this time?' he said.

Once Ruth explained what had happened, however, he leapt into action, kicking repeatedly at the door. But it was all to no avail, it still wouldn't open. Dorothy came scuttling across the mill yard carrying a large iron ring from which a dozen keys hung.

'One of these will fit, I know it,' she said breathlessly.

There was an agonising wait as she tried every key in the lock. From inside the rag room, Claire's screams continued. And then there was silence. Pure, evil silence.

'Hurry up, Dorothy,' Ruth urged. 'For God's sake, hurry up.'

Finally the right key found its way into the lock. Ruth stormed inside, followed by Alan and Dorothy. The three of them came to a sudden halt, and stood in shocked silence.

Dorothy put her hand to her heart. 'Jesus, Mary, mother of God,' she gasped.

In front of them, Claire lay panting on the ground. Blood was smeared on her arms. 'I didn't mean to . . . I didn't . . .' she pleaded.

Next to her, John was bent double, holding his stomach with both hands. Scarlet blood dripped to the floor. Ruth swung around towards Jane, who was hovering behind her with Margaret by her side. 'Get the young 'un out of here.'

Jane took Margaret's hand and led her away.

Ruth flew to Claire's side. 'Are you all right? What happened?'

Dorothy took a look at John. 'I'll fetch the first-aider.'

'Call for an ambulance,' Alan said.

'He tried to . . . he tried to touch me, Ruth. He locked the door and tried to hurt me,' Claire cried.

'Claire? Listen to me,' Ruth said. 'Are you in pain?'

Claire nodded. 'He was chasing me and I had to get away. I fell over the bench, hurt my back.'

'And the blood? What happened?'

'I pushed him. I had to get him off me, and he fell on the knife.'

'Oh, punishment indeed for the king of the rag room,' Alan hissed. 'The dangers of this mill aren't in the machinery; they're in the minds of men like you.' He pulled John to his feet. 'You disgusting piece of dirt,' he spat.

'Claire, can you stand up?' Ruth asked.

As the girl struggled upright with Ruth's help, Dorothy came bustling into the room with Clive Dixon, one of the men from the boiler room, a first-aider at the mill. Ruth saw his mouth drop open when he caught sight of John.

'Ambulance is on its way,' Dorothy said.

Claire began to cry. 'I'm sorry, Ruth,' she sobbed. 'I didn't mean to hurt him, I didn't mean to do it.'

Ruth put her arm around Claire's shoulders, and the girl turned her tear-stained face towards her.

'Will I get sacked?' she said in between sobs.

'No, love,' Ruth said. 'Trust me, it's not you who needs to worry about that.'

Later that day, in the bar at the Hendon Grange pub, a coal fire roared in the enormous black hearth. The paper mill girls sat in silence, listening as Ruth told them what had happened. Claire was with them. She was shaken but not seriously hurt. John, however, was on his way to hospital suffering a gash to his stomach.

The pub door swung open and Mr Hewson walked in. He was dressed as smartly as always, this time in a pale grey suit. A red rose was pinned to his jacket lapel. Sarah followed him into the pub and Ruth was glad to see her.

'Miss Hardy,' Mr Hewson said firmly. 'We need to speak about the incident.'

Sarah laid a hand on his arm. 'Father, let me speak to Ruth and the girls.'

'But this is mill business, Sarah.'

'No, Father, this is women's business.'

Mr Hewson bristled at his daughter's words. But then Ruth saw him glance towards Claire, who was still shaking and in tears after her ordeal. He nodded to Sarah and turned to leave.

Sarah pulled a stool from a table and sat between Ruth and Claire. The girls stared at her finery, her expensive coat and hat, her gloves and scarf of a quality none of them would ever be able to afford. She delved into her handbag and brought out a blue notepad and a pencil. She opened the notepad and turned to Claire.

'Tell me everything that happened. If we're to get rid of the disease in our midst that goes by the name of John Hepple, I need to hear every single word.'

Once she had the information she needed, the girls were dismissed and told to return home. The rag room would be closed for the rest of the day. Ruth told Claire to take the following day off too and stay at home with her mam. The girls headed off, some of them happy to have a free afternoon while others were more wary.

'Will we get paid for this afternoon if we go home?' Margaret asked. 'I can't afford to lose wages; my mam needs the money.'

Ruth opened her mouth to reply, but was cut off by Sarah. 'I'll arrange something with Father, don't worry.'

Jane took Margaret's hand and led her from the pub, while Edie walked out with her arm protectively around Claire's shoulders.

After all the girls had left, Ruth and Sarah sat in front of the roaring fire, while the rain lashed the windows outside.

'What'll happen to John?' Ruth asked.

'He should be sacked,' Sarah spat.

The two women looked at each other.

'But he won't be, will be?' Ruth said.

Sarah shook her head. 'His father holds too much influence over the mill. But I'm hoping that once Father hears what happened . . .' She lifted her notepad. 'It's all here. Once he knows the truth about the man, he'll have no choice but to tackle Thomas Hepple. He'll have the full support of the management committee, I'll make sure of it.'

Ruth raised her eyes shyly to Sarah. She had something on her mind but wasn't sure it was her place to speak of it. She broached the subject carefully. 'I hear that Alan Murphy has been nominated to join the committee. He's been very supportive in all that's happened with John.'

'Alan?' Sarah said quickly. 'You've seen him?'

'He helped at the rag room when John locked the girls out at dinner break, and he was there again today. He saw the state of Claire when we got in the room. He could prove a good witness, if you need one, for the testimony to your dad.'

Sarah's eyes lit up. She began to gather her handbag and jacket. 'Then I must go and speak to him.'

'I'm pleased to hear it,' Ruth said. 'And I know he will be happy to see you.'

'Father . . .' Sarah began, '. . . he doesn't quite understand how things are between Alan and me.'

'Well? How are they?'

'We love each other,' Sarah said softly. 'As I think you already know.'

'Then tell him straight that you've found happiness. No dad would deny his daughter that.'

'We were planning to elope,' Sarah confided.

'And rob your dad of the chance to dress up in his best suit and tie, wearing a glorious rose for your special day?'

'If only it was so easy.'

'It is,' Ruth insisted. 'Invite Alan to dinner, get your dad to meet him socially, just the three of you. How will he ever get to know him in the same way as you do if you don't give him a chance?'

'I'll think it over.'

'I need to get back to the rag room,' Ruth said. 'When the girls return tomorrow, I want all trace of John Hepple gone.'

Sarah laid her hand on Ruth's arm. 'Ruth, before we go, there's something I need to tell you,' she said. 'It's about Henry.'

Ruth's heart sank. 'Oh?'

'I want to apologise for him, for the way he behaved that night at the party. He's not always so uncouth.'

Ruth raised her eyebrows. 'Isn't he?'

A smile played around Sarah's lips. 'He's young and has a lot to learn. But I hope you won't hold what happened with him against me. I enjoy your friendship, Ruth. I'm grateful for it, too.'

'Henry is in my past now,' Ruth said. 'I'm courting someone new.'

Sarah's face lit up. 'You are? How wonderful. Does he work at the mill?'

'Yes, he's a railwayman.'

She thought for a moment. 'Surely it can't be Mr Steadman?'

Ruth laughed out loud. 'Heavens, no! He's far too old for me. It's Mick Carson, the man with the dark hair.'

'I've seen him, he's nice. Very polite, if my memory serves me right from the visit that Father and I made to the engine shed. Is it serious between the two of you?'

'As serious as you and Alan,' Ruth said. 'The only difference is that Mick and my dad get along with each other. They've met and Dad approves very much. Tell your dad about Alan, Sarah. You can't live a lie and elope; you'll regret it, I'm sure.'

'Oh Ruth, I know you're right. I need to speak to Father at home.'

Ruth stood. 'I really should get back to work now. There's a lot I have to do to get the rag room cleaned up.'

As the two girls headed to the door, ready to head out into the rain, Ruth spotted something on the floor. She bent and picked it up.

'Your dad's rose,' she said. It had been flattened and squashed by the girls' feet when they'd left the pub earlier.

'It must have fallen from his jacket,' Sarah said.

Ruth offered the tattered bloom to Sarah, but she waved it away. 'It's no good to him now. I'll pick another tomorrow.'

Ruth stroked the flower with her fingers. Although the rose had been scuffed and flattened, there were untouched velvety petals inside.

'Could I keep it?' she asked.

Her question seemed to amuse Sarah. 'Of course,' she replied.

Ruth and Sarah parted ways outside the rag room. While Sarah continued on her way to see Alan, Ruth headed inside to scrub the memory of John Hepple away. The room was quiet and still, the upturned bench a silent reminder of the horror that had taken place. Drops of John's blood darkened the floor. Three buttons from Claire's blouse lay scattered. Ruth laid the tattered red rose on a bench. She took a metal bucket, filled it with water and began scrubbing the bloodstains away. When she'd finished, she swept the cotton dust to one side and tidied the room for when the girls returned the next day.

As she sat, exhausted, looking around her, the door slowly opened, letting in a rush of cold air.

'Mick!' she cried. She was more than happy to see him.

He ran to her side and cradled her in his arms. 'I've just been told what happened,' he said. 'You're not hurt, are you?'

'No, not me. Just poor Claire, but she'll be all right.'

'And John Hepple?'

'He'll survive.'

'He's a bad 'un. You should hear what the lads on the railway have got to say about him. He's been found down by the docks drunk many times since that first day we saw him fighting.'

'I think I'd rather forget all about him. Have you finished your shift now?'

Mick nodded. 'Dropped off my paperwork at the office and I was just about to head home. But I couldn't leave without seeing how you were.'

'I'm done here now too,' Ruth said. 'Mr Hewson's closed the rag room for the rest of the day. Is it still raining outside?'

'Pouring.'

'We could sit here for a while till it eases,' she suggested.

Mick glanced around the room. The red rose on the bench caught his eye. 'Someone been giving you flowers?'

Ruth explained where the rose had come from. 'It's a bit tattered and torn, but I thought I could take it home. It might perk up if I put it in some water.'

Mick was silent for a few moments. 'I've got an idea,' he said at last.

He picked up the rose in one hand and grabbed Ruth's hand with the other. He was overtaken by an excitement that Ruth had seen once before, and she didn't like it. It was the same reckless spirit she had witnessed the day Mick stole the box of apples from Watson's. She pulled back, reluctant.

'We're not going to get into trouble, are we?' she asked.

'I promise you, Ruth, no.'

She still wasn't convinced.

'Come on,' he urged.

'Where are you taking me?'

'You'll see.'

'Ah, what the heck.' Ruth laughed. 'What have I got to lose after the day I've just had? All right, let's go.'

Mick was laughing and joking as they ran to the warehouse where the esparto grass was stored. Up the stairs they went, almost tripping over each over, all the way to the old drying loft on the top floor. They stood holding hands, looking out over the empty room. Ruth felt her heart skip. Had Mick brought her up here to do what she'd caught Sarah Hewson and Alan Murphy doing behind the wooden boxes the day she'd first taken Maude there?

'Mick, not in here,' she said quickly.

He looked startled by what she seemed to be suggesting.

'No, my love. No,' he reassured her. 'I want our first time to be somewhere special, not here at the mill.'

'Then why did you bring me here?'

Mick stepped confidently into the room and strode across the floor. 'My grandad worked here, making paper by hand.'

'You've told me that before,' Ruth said.

He turned towards her, his eyes bright with excitement, and held up the rose. 'And we're going to make our own piece of paper, with this.'

She laughed out loud. 'Making paper with a rose? Have you gone mad?'

Mick disappeared behind the wall of crates and boxes. 'Got it!' he cried.

Ruth followed to see what he was up to. He was holding a metal box stuffed full with torn-up scraps of paper.

'They call this making porridge,' he said. 'All we need is some water.'

'But we can't possibly make paper in here,' she said.

'Just watch me. I'll fetch water from the yard.'

He disappeared down the stairs and Ruth wandered the length of the loft. She tried to imagine rows of men and women working together making paper by hand. It was an image she conjured up easily. She'd always had a good feeling, a warm, safe feeling whenever she was in the loft. She heard Mick's footsteps on the stairs as he made his way back carrying a bucket of water. She watched as he knelt on the floor and poured water into the box of scrap paper. As the paper turned into mush, Mick crushed it repeatedly with his hand.

'A drying press,' he said, glancing urgently around the room. 'There must be an old one in one of those boxes. Grandad says not all of them were thrown out when the machines came in.'

After rummaging around, he found a mesh square moulded in a tight wooden frame. Ruth watched, entranced, as he poured the mush of water and paper in the mould. The water drained through the mesh into the bucket, leaving just the wet paper porridge inside.

'Now for the rose petals,' Mick said. 'Can you tear them up small?'

Ruth began to peel the scarlet petals from the tattered bud and tore them into tiny pieces. She placed the fragments of red on to the mesh, where they soaked into the freshly made paper.

'Course, there was a lot more to the process in Grandad's day,' Mick explained. 'But if we're lucky, if we leave this to dry, we'll have our own sheet of paper, hand-made, with rose petals in it.'

Ruth was curious. 'How did you know about adding the petals?'

'Grandad told me,' Mick said softly. 'He used to grow hydrangeas in his garden. He had the biggest blue hydrangea bush in Ryhope when everyone else's gardens would only grow pink. And he'd tell me about picking the blue petals and putting them in paper.' He cast a shy look towards Ruth. 'It's how Grandad met Grandma. He wrote a letter to her on paper he'd made specially for her.'

'Did she work at the mill?'

'In the counting room. She had the most nimble fingers of them all, Grandad said. What about your grandparents, are they still alive?'

Ruth shook her head. 'Both sets passed away a long time ago. Grandad Hardy was a miner, just like my dad used to be. Mam's dad was a gardener. My grandma Hardy was called Maude; that's where baby Maude's name comes from.'

Mick paused in what he was doing and looked at her. 'What a lovely thing to do, passing on your grandma's name,' he said, then returned his attention to the mould. 'Now we need to leave this for all the water to drain, then just the paper will be left, see, with the rose petals in it. And then we'll hang it in the loft to dry.' He laid the mould across the top of the bucket, where the water dripped slowly. 'We should be getting home,' he said.

Ruth got to her feet, and the two of them headed down the stairs.

The following morning when Ruth returned to the paper mill, she headed to the office for the rag room key. However, instead of being handed the key and the ledger to sign, Ruth was asked to wait until Dorothy finished her paperwork.

'Morning, Dorothy,' Ruth greeted the clerk when Dorothy finally turned her attention to Ruth.

'I've come for the key.'

'Not so quick, Ruth,' Dorothy replied sternly. 'Mr Hewson wants a word with you in his office. Now.'

Chapter Thirty-Five

This time Ruth knew her way to the mill owner's office. As she made her way up the stairs, she felt a flutter in her stomach. This must be about John and what had happened to Claire, she thought. She knocked at the door and entered when Mr Hewson called out.

'Ah, Miss Hardy,' he greeted her.

Ruth closed the door behind her.

'Take a seat,' he said.

She sat opposite Mr Hewson at his big, sturdy desk. In the lapel of his smartly pressed navy jacket he wore a single white rose. The flowers were no longer a mystery now that Ruth knew the secret of the hothouse.

'No doubt you'll be wanting to know what's happening with arrangements for the rag room after yesterday's incident?'

'Yes, sir,' Ruth said. She'd thought of little else the previous night and had slept badly with work on her mind.

'I'd like you to take on the role of supervisor again, Miss Hardy,' Mr Hewson said.

She had to stop herself from jumping up out of her

chair and hugging the mill owner. She gripped her seat tightly. 'Thank you,' she said.

'I understand that even while John Hepple was working in the room, you were responsible for much of the supervision.'

Ruth wondered how he knew this. Sarah couldn't have told him, for she didn't know what went on in the room. She wondered if one of the girls had spoken to Dorothy behind her back. 'Yes, sir,' she said.

'In which case, Grange Paper Works would like to reimburse you, at the end of the next financial quarter, for your work.'

Ruth was confused. 'Reimburse?'

'I understand that when John Hepple appointed himself supervisor in my absence, the bonus you were paid to manage the girls was cut from your wages.'

'It was, yes.'

'I'm a fair employer, Miss Hardy,' Mr Hewson carried on. 'And I want to make amends for all you've been put through. We'll see to it that you receive the money you should have been paid while John Hepple was in charge.'

'But sir . . .' Ruth began. 'I can't accept it. The money you pay to Dorothy Smith's sister for the care of my niece is already too generous.'

Mr Hewson folded his hands together and leaned across the table. 'Ah yes, about that,' he said. 'The arrangement with Miss Smith must come to an end, I'm afraid. Now that John Hepple will cause you no more difficulties, I can no longer compensate you.'

Ruth felt dizzy and sick. This was too much to take in. One minute Mr Hewson was offering her cash for work she'd already done, the next he was taking away the safety net of Maude being cared for. Many questions whirled in her mind but they all seemed stuck on her tongue. She could hardly complain about the arrangement ending. Maude's care had come as a godsend from Mr Hewson all those months ago. But where would she take the baby now? Whatever happened next, she knew she had to thank him, for without his kind offer, Maude would still be sleeping at the mill.

'I appreciate, very much, all you have done for my niece,' Ruth said.

Mr Hewson smiled at her. 'And I appreciate all you have done for my daughter.'

'Me, sir?'

Mr Hewson's eyes twinkled. 'Yes, you, Ruth Hardy. I understand you and she had words about Mr Murphy, the supervisor in the machine room.'

Ruth gasped. 'Not words, not exactly. I offered her advice, perhaps.'

'Advice that I've noted. You'll be pleased to hear that Mr Murphy is invited to dinner this weekend. For the sake of my daughter, I look forward to getting to know the man properly.'

'And what of John Hepple?' she said. 'If I'm to return as rag room supervisor, will I have to manage him again?'

'Hepple is no longer your concern, Miss Hardy,' Mr Hewson said firmly. 'He was discharged from hospital soon after being admitted. I tell you this so that you are fully informed and you can pass details to the girls who were affected by what went on. He suffered a flesh wound, nothing more. It has been recorded in the log book as an accident. Nothing more will be said about it and no charges brought.'

'Will he still have a job at the mill?'

Mr Hewson looked out of his window, taking in the expanse of the mill he owned. 'Yes,' he said, sadly. 'He'll be employed at the docks, in the loading bay. It's physical, tough work with tough men but he's recovering from his war wound now and should be up to managing the work. It should keep him out of mischief, away from . . .' He paused. 'Away from areas of the mill where he is no longer welcome.'

'Thank you, sir.'

Mr Hewson dismissed Ruth with a wave of his hand. She walked to the door, but before she pulled it open, she turned. 'Mr Hewson?'

'What now, Miss Hardy?'

'Alan Murphy is a good man. Sarah could do a lot worse.'

Before he could reply, she quickly pulled the door open and headed into the corridor. She knew she'd overstepped the mark with her parting shot, but it had to be said. Someone had to tell him, and if not her, then who? She walked quickly along the corridor and ran down the stairs.

'Ruth!' Dorothy called from her desk.

Ruth walked into the office to find Dorothy holding something in her hand.

'You're going to need this,' she said.

It was the key to the rag room door.

Chapter Thirty-Six

Ruth headed to work with a smile on her face. She wasn't the only happy one in the rag room that morning. Edie and Jane were in high spirits and the younger girls were pleased to have Ruth back at the helm. However, she felt a sense of dread in her stomach when she thought about Mr Hewson's words regarding Maude. Who on earth could she find to look after her niece?

At dinner time, she rang her handbell and the girls took their break to eat. Outside, a weak sun struggled to make its way through the clouds.

'Fancy a walk to the beach?' Ruth asked. Edie and Jane accepted without hesitation.

The three of them walked arm in arm, chatting and gossiping. When they were seated on the black sands behind the rocks, Ruth told her friends what Mr Hewson had said. Again she kept quiet about what he'd said about Sarah and Alan and her part in reuniting them. And again she felt a pang of guilt at hiding things from Edie and Jane. She was torn. Her loyalty to Sarah pulled her one way and her loyalty to her best friends the other. But just as she would never reveal any of Sarah's secrets to Edie and Jane, neither would she spread gossip about her friends to Sarah. The only time she'd ever betrayed Jane's confidence was when Sarah had helped to get Davey out of Jane's life.

'And how are you and Mick getting on?' Edie asked.

Ruth smiled at the mention of Mick's name. 'Just fine,' she said. 'I go to his mam and dad's house for tea once a week. They let me take Maude with me; she eats like a good 'un these days. She's crawling now. Too heavy by half to carry around. If you hear of any prams going, will you let me know?'

'Can you afford one?' Jane asked.

'As long as it costs next to nothing,' Ruth said.

'And how's your dad doing?'

Ruth looked out to sea. 'Not good,' she said. 'Mrs Pike comes in to see him each morning.'

'Is she the little fat woman who runs the pub?' Edie asked.

Ruth nodded. 'She calls on him after I've left for work. She sits with him and talks to him, even makes him a sandwich for his dinner.'

'Sounds like she cares about him,' Edie said.

'She does, she always has. She's been very good to us all. But Dad . . . I don't know, he's not himself. He's lost, you know? It's as if he's just existing, sitting in his chair, barely moving. He doesn't even work in the pub any more, says he can't face people asking about Mam.'

'Losing Bea and your mam, it hasn't been easy for either of you,' Jane said. 'Is there anything we can do to help him?'

'Help Dad?' Ruth shook her head. 'I don't think so. If I knew what to do, what to say, I'd do it, girls, honestly.

I'd give anything to see him smile again.'

'Doesn't Maude put a smile on his face? Surely he enjoys being with his granddaughter?'

'He says she reminds him of Bea too much, or he complains when she cries or needs changing or feeding. He's lost in a world of his own. I can't seem to reach him any more.'

'Is he eating all right? Sleeping okay?' Jane asked. 'That's the first thing Dr Anderson asks when you go to see him, no matter what you're suffering from.'

'He's sleeping too much and eating too little.'

'Do you think he's bad with his nerves?' Edie said.

'Can men be bad with their nerves?' Jane asked. 'I thought it was just women who suffered. My mam's friend Rose was bad with her nerves and they found her walking to the clifftop at Ryhope. She was going to throw herself off.'

'Dad wouldn't do that. He can't walk far, for a start, not with his bad leg.' Despite herself, Ruth smiled. 'Thank you both, I appreciate your support.'

'That's what we're here for,' Edie said. 'You've looked after us two from the first day we all started working in the machine room, sweeping up. Do you remember, Jane?'

Jane laughed. 'We were like lost little lambs, terrified walking in through the mill gates.'

'And then when we started work in the rag room, old Waggy scared us stiff,' Edie recalled. 'And it was you, Ruth, who took us for a walk that first day at dinner time. You brought us down here to the beach and told us everything would be all right, said that Waggy's bark was worse than her bite.'

'Don't know where we would have been without you,' Jane said.

Ruth took their hands. 'Thanks, girls,' she said.

'What's Mick's mam like?' Jane asked. 'Do you get on with her all right?'

'Is she friendly?' Edie asked.

When Ruth thought of Gloria Carson, it wasn't her friendly disposition that first came to mind. It was her strength of character, her forbearance, her stout hips and sturdy legs. She was built like an army tank, and to Ruth she seemed to be just as indestructible.

'Let's just say she's not the sort of woman who'd ever be bad with her nerves,' she said.

The girls fell about laughing.

'Mick's a nice fella,' Edie said at last. 'You two are good together. Think you'll get wed?'

Ruth shrugged. Marriage was something that she and Mick had touched on only once, on the day at the beach when they'd reunited. Mick had assumed they'd be wed one day and that he'd take Maude on. But he'd never actually asked her to marry him. He was down to earth and practical; he didn't seem the romantic sort.

'I suppose we'll get married one day,' she said quietly. First there was Dicky Brown's loan to pay off, but she kept quiet about that; there was no need for her friends to know how much debt she and Mick were in, or about Connie threatening to sell Maude. She wondered what secrets Edie and Jane kept from her.

'What about you and that fella from the machine room you had your eye on?' she asked.

'Ted Lumley?' Edie said with a cheeky smile. 'I've been out with him a few times. He's taking me to see a film at the Grand on Saturday night.'

'What about you, Jane?' Ruth asked. 'Any fellas on your horizon?'

'I'm leaving them well alone,' Jane said. 'After what happened with Davey, I don't think I want to get involved with anyone else.'

'Ah, you're saying that now, but just you wait until someone catches your eye,' Edie teased.

'Come on, lasses, we should be getting back to work,' Ruth said.

They stood and walked together arm in arm back to the rag room. Before they reached it, though, Ruth made her excuses and headed to the loft.

'I just need to check something in the esparto ware-house,' she said. She wanted to take a quick look at the sheet of paper Mick had made. She was curious to see if it was dry yet, and how the rose petals looked in the mould.

Up in the loft, she found the box Mick had used, exactly where he'd left it. But the mould with their rose petal paper had gone.

Chapter Thirty-Seven

'It's been stolen, Mick. Our piece of paper. Who could have taken it?'

Mick rested his arm against the rag room door. 'Who knows how many people go up there on their dinner break? I've heard fellas from the machine room head up there to smoke. Some of them go there to sleep. Any one of them could have taken it.' He shrugged.

Ruth felt saddened at the loss. It had been the first thing she and Mick had created together, and now she'd never know how it would have turned out.

Mick laid his arm protectively around her shoulders. 'Never mind, eh? It was just a daft piece of paper, that's all.'

'Mick . . .'

'What is it, love?'

'It's Maude,' Ruth sighed. 'I've got to find somewhere else for her.'

Mick's face clouded over as Ruth told him what Mr Hewson had said. He let out a long, low whistle. 'What are we going to do?' he asked.

Ruth snuggled against his warm body. 'We? She's my bairn to look after.'

Mick kissed the top of her head. 'When we get married, she'll be ours.'

Ruth pulled away from him. She put her hands on her hips. 'You're taking a lot for granted, aren't you?'

'What do you mean? I thought you wanted to get wed.'

She felt her heart skip. Of course she wanted to marry Mick. If she was honest with herself, it was what she'd wanted from the minute she'd first clapped eyes on him. But she'd hoped for a more romantic proposal than a peck on her head – and outside of the rag room of all places. There wasn't a less romantic spot in the whole of Sunderland!

'You know I want to marry you,' she said. 'It's just . . .'

'What?'

'Well, you could ask me properly.'

He looked at her, confused. 'Properly? I thought we'd arrange it one day when we feel the time's right. That's proper, isn't it?'

She crossed her arms. 'And that's it? That's your romantic proposal?'

Mick glanced down as Button made his way up through his jacket, the dog's furry head appearing at his neck. 'Get down, Button,' he said.

'Sometimes I don't think I know you, Mick Carson,' Ruth said.

'What have I done now?' he cried, exasperated.

Ruth sighed. 'Oh, nothing. Let's leave this conversation for another day.'

Mick leaned his back against the door and reached for Ruth's hand. Fingers entwined, they looked out at the mill yard, where men wheeled barrows in and out of the machine room. It was a fine spring day, with a hint of sunshine in a milky blue sky.

'Dicky Brown's coming to the Guide Post Inn tonight,' Mick said. 'He left word for me, said I've got to meet him with the next instalment of money.'

'Have you got it to give to him?' Ruth asked, worried.

'Most of it,' Mick said.

'I won't be able to contribute anything more, Mick, not when I start paying for someone to look after Maude.'

Mick rubbed his chin. 'We'll never get it paid off at this rate,' he sighed. 'We might as well hand over our wages to Dicky Brown every week.'

'The back pay Mr Hewson's giving me will go some way to helping,' Ruth said.

'That's true, it will,' Mick agreed. 'What are we going to do about Maude, though? That needs some serious thinking about.'

'Do you know anyone who could help? Someone who takes bairns in for women who work?'

He shook his head. 'I'll ask around. One of the fellas on the railway might know someone. Anyway, I'd best get back to the shed. I've got to run the engine down to the docks before I clock off and go home. Are you still coming to ours for tea tonight? Mam's looking forward to seeing you. And you should hear how she goes on about Maude. She's even been knitting for the bairn.'

'We'll be there,' Ruth said.

'Ask your dad if he'll come.'

'He won't, Mick. Even if he felt up to it, his bad leg wouldn't carry him that far.'

Mick kissed her on the cheek. 'I'm off, then. Promise me you'll think about what we talked about before.'

'About Maude, you mean?'

He gave a cheeky wink as he turned to walk away. 'About getting wed,' he shouted across the mill yard as he waved goodbye.

'Only if you promise to think about asking me properly,' Ruth shouted back.

Later that afternoon, in the back room at the Guide Post Inn, Ruth sat next to her dad by the fire. It was warm outside, too warm for a roaring coal fire. Yet Harry insisted on Ruth banking it up.

'We can't keep burning coal like this, Dad. We haven't got the money.'

Harry pulled his cardigan around him and shivered. 'I need the heat, lass,' he said.

Ruth sat opposite him with Maude on her lap. 'Why don't you come to Mick's mam's for tea? You're invited, they want to see you again. They haven't seen you since . . .' She stopped herself, not wanting to mention her mam's funeral. There were some words she didn't dare say for fear of sending her dad spiralling into another black mood. 'Come on, Dad,' she urged. 'It'll do you good to get out and meet people again. You can't lock yourself away for ever. Mrs Pike needs you behind the bar. She says the customers are missing you. They're all asking after you.'

'Let them ask, it's none of their flamin' business,' Harry retorted.

'Dad, please.'

He stared into the flames. 'And what if I did go?' he said at last. 'It'd take me ages to walk there and back.'

Finally! Ruth thought. The first tiny flicker of interest

her dad had shown in leaving the room. But any hope she felt was soon dashed.

'No, I'm not going anywhere. The cold gets to my leg, makes the pain worse.'

'It's warm outside, Dad.'

'Not warm enough,' Harry said grumpily.

'You'll come on a warmer day?'

He shrugged. 'We'll see.'

Ruth smiled. It was something, a start.

She warmed a pan of broth on the fire and left a bowlful for him.

'Promise me you'll try to eat something,' she said. 'I won't be out long. Mick's walking me back here after tea. He's meeting someone in the pub.'

She kept quiet about Dicky Brown and the loan. There were some things it was better for Harry not to know, although it pained her to keep secrets from him. Since her mam had died, it felt as if she and her dad were drifting apart. Jean had been the glue that had held them together. She kissed him on the cheek, then headed out for the walk to George Street.

When she arrived at Mick's house, it was Gloria who answered the door. Her eyes lit up when she saw Maude, and she opened her arms wide.

'Come on in and hand the little 'un over.'

Ruth was only too happy to pass Maude into Gloria's sturdy arms, for her niece was quite a weight now. She wanted to crawl and explore, and her constant squirming when Ruth carried her made it hard to keep her steady in her arms. She followed Gloria into the tiny room that doubled as kitchen and sitting room.

'How are you doing, Ruth?' Bobby asked.

'Not bad, Bobby. How's yourself?'

'Canny, lass. Canny.'

Mick pulled a chair from the table and Ruth sank gratefully on to it. Button lay under the table, his furry face peeking into the room.

'Put the kettle on, Mick,' Gloria said. 'I've got my hands full here with this lovely little bairn.'

Ruth watched as the domestic scene unfolded around her. Gloria was moving from foot to foot, singing a tune that Ruth didn't recognise but that Maude gurgled along to. Bobby too only had eyes for the bairn, and it was clear that he delighted in Gloria's enjoyment of having Maude at the house. Meanwhile, Mick took a large brown teapot and four mugs from a shelf.

'Brisket all right for you for tea, love?' Gloria asked Ruth. 'It's all we've got.'

'Perfect,' Ruth said. She thought of her dad, his bowl of broth, and hoped he'd made a start on it. He'd eaten so little that he was wasting away, just skin and bones inside clothes hanging loose. No wonder he was feeling the cold.

When the kettle finally boiled and tea had been brewed, Mick set the cups on the table. Gloria took her seat, still holding Maude. The baby was laughing and her tiny fists waved in the air. Ruth was so intent on watching her that she missed the look that passed between Gloria and Bobby. Bobby took a sip of tea, then cleared his throat.

'Mick's been telling us that your arrangement up at Tunstall Terrace is coming to an end,' he said.

Ruth bit her lip. The problem lay heavy on her mind. No matter which way she turned her thoughts, she couldn't find a solution. 'I don't know what to do,' she said. 'I've asked around, but no one seems to know anyone who takes bairns in for women like me. I mean, I could take her back to the mill; there's the drying loft, you see, though . . .'

'We'll do it,' Bobby said softly.

But Ruth didn't hear. She was upset and angry. Angry with herself, with the world. Truth be told, she was angry with Bea for leaving her, angry with Dicky Brown for taking money that she needed for Maude's care. Angry with Connie Tate for being a drunk and a blackmailer. She was even angry with her dad for not having the strength or the desire to look after his own granddaughter.

'. . . it's not ideal. We had something stolen from there, didn't we, Mick?'

'I said, we'll do it,' Bobby repeated.

Ruth sat up straight in her chair. Was she hearing things? She stared straight at Bobby.

'You?'

'Well, not me exactly. Both of us, like, though I'll leave most of the work to Gloria. It's been a long time since our Mick was a nipper.'

'And even then you never changed him or cleaned him,' Gloria said.

'I taught him to play football,' Bobby laughed. 'What more do you want?'

'Gloria?' Ruth said, confused. 'What's going on?'

'Listen, pet. Mick told us about the drying loft, and I daresay it's as warm and bright a room as he says it is. But a working mill is no place for a bairn. And soon she'll be crawling, then walking, and you can't leave her there then. So me and Bobby, we had a chat.'

'And we're willing to take Maude in,' Bobby added.

'Just while you're at work, mind,' Gloria said. 'On

your time off, she's yours. You drop her off here before you go to the mill and collect her on your way home.'

'But . . .' Ruth began. She didn't know what to say. 'Are you sure?'

'Oh, we're sure, lass,' Bobby said. 'Me and Gloria have talked about nowt else since Mick came home from work and told us.'

Ruth gasped. This was more than she could ever have expected or dreamed of. She'd trust Mick's parents with her life. It seemed the perfect solution. Well, almost.

'How much will you charge?' she asked.

She raised her eyes to see Gloria's mouth drop open. The woman looked like she'd been slapped.

'Eeh, pet! You don't think we'd charge you money to look after her? You're almost family!' She glanced at Mick. 'No, love, there'll be no charge. And frankly I'm offended that you thought there might be.'

'I'm sorry,' Ruth replied quickly. 'It's come as a shock, that's all. It's a lot to take in. I'm grateful beyond words.'

'Don't mention it,' Bobby said. 'You're doing us a favour. Having a bairn in the house brings a new lease of life to the pair of us.'

'It'll give us something to do other than bicker when he comes home from work; that's what he means,' Gloria said.

Ruth was relieved to see a smile on Gloria's chubby face. 'I didn't mean to offend you; that's the last thing I want.'

'It's all right, pet. Bring Maude to us the morning after your arrangement ends with the Smith woman. I'll feed her and look after her.'

'She'll enjoy having her,' Bobby added.

Ruth leapt from her seat and threw her arms around Gloria's neck.

'Now we'll have less of that,' Gloria said sternly.

'Well, I wouldn't mind a hug if the missus doesn't want one,' Bobby teased.

Ruth was only too happy to oblige.

Chapter Thirty-Eight

After tea, Ruth and Mick walked back to the Guide Post Inn. Mick insisted on carrying Maude, and Ruth was grateful.

'What's he like, this Dicky Brown?' she asked.

'Well, he's a big fella. Rough. You wouldn't want to mess with him. But he's not the brightest button in the box.'

'His sons weren't all that bright either,' she recalled.

'Bright or not, I have to pay him money tonight that I can ill afford. How are we supposed to save up for any kind of future when we're turning our wages over each week?'

'I can help pay when Mr Hewson gives me the extra wages he promised,' Ruth reminded him. She sighed. 'It seems as if we paid for peace of mind getting Connie out of our lives. And then we invited more trouble in from Dicky. The only consolation is that we will pay him back. One day we'll be free of him.'

'When?' Mick laughed. 'Nineteen forty-two?'

The Guide Post Inn came into view and Mick handed Maude over. The little girl was tired out after being made a fuss of by Gloria and lay against Ruth's shoulder in a contented sleep. Ruth kissed Mick goodnight and headed into the back lane.

When she pushed the door open, her heart skipped a beat. Her dad's chair was empty. And then she spotted him, lying on the bed that had been her mam's place of rest. He was sleeping, snoring loudly. It was a small thing, a tiny change in his behaviour. But moving from his chair to the bed was something important indeed. Since her mam had died, he'd spent his nights as well as his days in the blasted chair. It might just be a short walk to the bed, but Ruth believed it to be a significant step, though she knew she mustn't get her hopes up. It might be a long time till her dad's peace of mind returned.

She laid Maude in her bed, and then sat by the fire, watching the last of the embers die.

In the bar of the Guide Post Inn, Mrs Pike greeted Mick.

'Ruth not joining you tonight?'

Mick gave a nervous glance towards the door. Dicky Brown hadn't yet arrived. 'Not tonight,' he said.

'How's her dad today, have you seen him?' the landlady asked as she pulled Mick a pint of Vaux stout.

'She says he's much the same: quiet, still grieving.'

Mrs Pike handed Mick his pint and took his coins in exchange, then she pulled up a stool on the opposite side of the bar. It seemed she was in the mood for conversation, but Mick didn't feel much like talking. He had a lot on his mind. He wasn't looking forward to meeting Dicky again. And to add insult to injury, Dicky always insisted on Mick buying him a drink while he counted out the shillings he'd just paid over.

Mrs Pike began to make small talk about the weather. Mick ignored her, hoping she'd get the hint and leave him alone, but her words kept pecking at him.

'I call in every morning to see Harry, you know. He's not been himself since Jean passed away, God rest her soul. I was the same when my husband went. It takes a lot out of a person to lose their other half.'

'I'm sorry to hear that, Mrs Pike,' Mick said politely.

'I take him the paper each morning but I daresay he doesn't read it any more. I bring him some sliced ham or a bit of beef at dinner time and he's still sitting in that chair by the fire; he doesn't move. Still, it's the least I can do. Got to look after friends and neighbours, or else where would we be?'

Mick took a sip from his drink. 'Indeed.' He didn't want Mrs Pike to think him rude. He knew how good she'd been to Ruth, and especially to Harry since Jean died. But he was shaking inside, terrified about meeting Dicky and not in the mood for a chat.

Dicky wasn't a pleasant man; everyone in Ryhope knew of his fearsome reputation. People crossed the road to avoid having to face him. Mick often kicked himself for getting mixed up with him. But he'd have done anything to protect Ruth and Maude from Connie. Taking the money from Dicky had been the only way to get Connie out of their lives. He had worked out a plan to repay the money that would cover the steep interest charged. The repayments stretched all the way to Christmas. But at least there was an end in sight, no matter how far away. He'd get Dicky off his back eventually, and then he could start planning his future with Ruth.

'. . . and I said to him, Harry, I said, you've got to start facing people again, but nothing I say makes a difference.'

'Sorry?' Mick said. He was suddenly aware that Mrs Pike had been talking to him while his mind had been elsewhere.

Just then the door swung open and in walked Dicky Brown. A hush descended on the pub. From the corner of his eye, Mick saw two men at a table quickly down their pints and leave through the back door. He gulped. Dicky wore no coat; his bare arms, bulging from a short-sleeved shirt, were decorated from wrist to shoulder with tattoos. He'd fought in the war, and his tattoos carried his tale. On his head was a black cap. A ginger beard flecked with grey covered the bottom half of his face. His eyes were dark and menacing. He walked with his fists balled, glaring around the pub as he made his way to the bar.

'Pint of the usual, Dicky?' Mrs Pike asked.

'Make it three pints.'

Mick's heart sank. He could barely afford to pay for one pint, never mind an extra two.

Mrs Pike raised her eyebrows. 'Three?'

'My lads are on their way.' Dicky nodded towards Mick. 'He's paying for them all.'

He pulled a stool from the bar and fell heavily on to it, slapping Mick on the back by way of greeting. The slap was so hard and heavy that Mick couldn't catch his breath.

'Dicky, how are you?' he said as casually as he could while his heart was going nineteen to the dozen.

'Where's the money you owe this week?' Dicky replied, straight to business.

Mrs Pike's ears pricked up. She'd heard about Dicky Brown's foray into the world of moneylending. But surely a hard-working fella like Mick Carson wouldn't be daft enough to get caught up in that, would he? He must be desperate indeed if he had.

Mick put his hand in his pocket and handed over the coins. Dicky counted every single shilling, then pocketed them without a word.

'Dicky, I don't know what you're up to, but I won't have moneylending going on in my premises,' Mrs Pike said firmly.

Dicky ignored her and slurped his pint. Mrs Pike tutted loudly and shook her head, letting the two men know she didn't approve of whatever was going on.

The pub door flew open again and two gangly lads tumbled in.

'Arthur, Billy, there's a pint each for you,' Dicky growled.

Mrs Pike's eyes widened. 'Now listen to me!' she said sternly. 'They're far too young to be in here. You'll lose me my licence. Get them out. They're not stopping.'

'Stay where you are, lads,' Dicky Brown ordered.

Mick sat up straight at the bar. The last thing he wanted was to be caught up in any grievance involving Dicky Brown and his lads. Behind him, another fella left the pub through the back door, too scared to even finish his drink. On the other side of the counter, Mrs Pike pulled herself up to her full height, which was still no higher than Dicky Brown's broad shoulders.

'I said get your sons out of my pub! Now!'

'They're going nowhere,' Dicky replied.

Arthur and Billy stood behind their dad, their pints untouched.

'Dicky Brown, I've known you since you were no

taller than a pit shovel,' Mrs Pike said. 'Your mam was a good friend of mine, as you well know.'

'So?'

'So I'm asking you nicely for the sake of your mam's memory. Get your lads out of the pub, or I'll call the police. I'm not having you cost my precious pub its licence. If the coppers come in here and find I'm serving underage drinkers, it'll be me that gets it in the neck.'

'It's just a drink, for God's sake, woman!'

Mick gulped. He wished he felt brave enough to help Mrs Pike, although she seemed to be coping well enough on her own.

'I'll ask you one final time,' she said calmly. 'If you don't get those two out of the pub, I'll walk across the road to the police station myself and get the chief inspector in here right now.'

'You wouldn't dare,' Dicky challenged.

Mrs Pike stood with her hands on her hips. 'Try me,' she said. 'And while I'm at it, I'll tell them about your friend here.' She nodded towards Mick. 'I'm sure the chief inspector will be interested to hear what you're up to with moneylending and extortion.'

Dicky opened his mouth and tipped his beer into his big fat face. Almost half a pint disappeared in one gulp. 'It's nowt,' he growled. 'I'm helping folk who need money, that's all.'

Mrs Pike stepped from behind the bar. All eyes were on her. No one moved, no one spoke. Mick sat wide-eyed, watching the landlady as she took on Dicky Brown.

'She's a little fatty,' Arthur giggled behind his dad's back.

'Who's *she*? The cat's mother?' Mrs Pike said. As

she drew closer, she nodded her head slowly. 'I knew it was you, you little buggers!' she cried. She poked Arthur in the chest, and then did the same to Billy. 'The pair of you, last week, stealing barrels from my yard! I saw you, but I couldn't catch you. You two have a lot to answer for. Costs me a fortune buying them barrels from the brewery.'

'Lads?' Dicky said. 'What's gone on?'

'These two have been stealing from my pub, that's what's gone on,' Mrs Pike said grimly.

'We didn't, it wasn't us,' Arthur said, shaking his head. 'It wasn't, Dad, honest.'

'It wasn't,' Billy repeated. 'We weren't even here on Wednesday night.'

Arthur punched him in the arm. 'You bloody idiot. She never said what night it was.'

Dicky leapt from his seat. 'Is this true? You've been stealing from the only pub in Ryhope that I've not been barred from?'

'Dad, we were just—' Arthur began.

Dicky's large fist shot out and hit Arthur square on the jaw. Another punch caught Billy's nose. 'What have I told you both, eh?' he growled. 'You don't steal from your own bloody doorstep.' As he marched his sons to the pub door and threw them out on to the street, the remaining customers dropped their gaze to the floor. They wanted no part of this family dispute.

Dicky returned to his bar stool, but Mrs Pike stood firm.

'What's it to be then, Dicky? I can go to the police, or we can resolve things here and now.'

'What do you mean, woman? I've bleeding well

resolved it for you. The lads have gone. Your precious licence is safe.'

'I don't mean the lads this time.' She nodded towards Mick. 'I mean him and the money he owes.'

'It's a business agreement,' Dicky said.

Mrs Pike shook her head. 'It's extortion.' She eyed him keenly. 'So, you've been barred from all the pubs in Ryhope now?'

He grunted into his beer.

'I should kick you out of here myself.'

'Ah, Mrs P,' he moaned. 'You wouldn't do that, would you? Where's a working fella to get a pint from if I can't get one here? I'll have to go all the way to Silksworth or Seaham.'

'Well, I could let you stay,' Mrs Pike said. 'On one condition.'

Dicky sat up straight and took a long sip from his pint. 'Oh aye?'

'You let Mick Carson pay you back what he owes without charging him any more interest.'

Dicky spluttered into his beer.

'Take it or leave it. If you don't agree, get out now and never come back. And you can expect a knock at your door when the police come calling asking questions about those two lads of yours in connection with robbing my barrels. I've got witnesses here to confirm what they said.' Mrs Pike looked around the pub at her customers. All of them seemed to be taking an unusual interest in reading newspapers or studying beer mats, anything to avoid eye contact with her.

'You're a hard woman, Mrs Pike,' Dicky said, shaking his head.

'I have to be, running a pub like this in a village like Ryhope.'

Dicky nodded towards Mick and stuck out his hand. Mick took it warily and felt the weight of Dicky's fingers as they pressed into his.

'Pay me what you owe, forget the interest,' Dicky said through gritted teeth.

Mick felt light-headed with shock. He had to put his hand to the bar top to steady himself.

'I appreciate it, Dicky.'

'There now,' Mrs Pike said. 'All's well in the end. No need to get the police involved, see?'

She bustled back behind the bar. On the counter were the two pints she'd pulled for Arthur and Billy. She positioned one in front of Mick and the other in front of Dicky.

'Might as well have these,' she said.

Chapter Thirty-Nine

The next morning at the mill, Mick told Ruth what had happened.

'Dicky Brown? Frightened of Mrs Pike?'

'Oh, you should have seen her, Ruth,' he said. 'She wasn't in the least bit afraid.'

'She'd fight tooth and nail to protect her pub,' Ruth said.

'It means the end is in sight. We can give Dicky his five pounds back sooner than we thought. And once that's done, we'll have no one on our backs. We'll be able to start saving for our future.'

Ruth felt a lightness that she hadn't felt for a very long time. For the first time since she could remember, there was a lot to look forward to. A life with Mick and Maude. She glanced at the mill gate, where Bea used to wait for her at the end of the day. How she wished, more than ever, that she could have told Bea about Mick. She felt sure that her sister would have approved.

An idea came to her. 'Mick?'

'What, love?'

'Dad left his chair last night to sleep in his bed.'

'He did? That's good news.'

'A small step, but important, I feel. I was wondering . . . Well, he listens to you, Mick. How would you feel about coming to talk to him tonight? Maybe try to entice him into the pub for a pint?'

Mick kissed Ruth on the cheek. 'It'd be my pleasure,' he said.

Harry rejected Mick's offer that night of a walk into the front bar at the Guide Post Inn. He said he still wasn't ready to face people. But there was a glimmer of hope one evening when Mick brought a pack of cards with him.

'Fancy a game, Harry?'

Harry eyed the pack suspiciously. It took him a long time to reply, but when he did, Ruth's face lit up with glee. 'Aye, go on, lad. Let's see if I've still got it. I used to knock spots off the lads at the pit when we played cards at work.'

Ruth sat with Maude by the fire, watching Mick and her dad play their game. For the first time in a long time, she saw a smile on Harry's face. He was animated, laughing when he won a hand and throwing his cards to the table in mock disgust when he lost. At long last, Ruth felt her dad returning. It wouldn't be an easy process, with Harry still refusing to go through to the bar for a drink. But he did make it to the back door, where he stood in the pub yard, enjoying the warmth of the spring air.

When Ruth gave Amelia the news that Maude was to be looked after by Mick's mam and dad, Amelia took the news as if she expected it. She was used to the coming and going of bairns at her house and into her care. She hugged

Ruth and kissed Maude for one final time, then as soon as they left Tunstall Terrace, Amelia began preparing a drawer as a crib, ready to welcome the next baby who needed looking after.

Every morning Ruth walked with Maude to George Street and left her in Gloria's care. She carried on working hard at the mill, saving every penny she could to give to Mick to pay Dicky. The sooner they had him off their backs, the better, although there was still outstanding rent to pay. She gave Mrs Pike a few shillings at the end of each week, thanking her for her continuing kindness.

One summer evening, Mick called to see her. He brought onions and carrots from his dad's garden, and Ruth set to cooking up broth with barley.

'Fancy a pint, Harry, while Ruth's cooking?' Mick asked.

Harry shook his head sadly. 'Ah, lad, I'm not sure . . .' he began.

'It's on me,' Mick said. 'I'm not asking you to put your hand into your pocket.'

Ruth cast him a worried look. 'Can we afford it?'

'Dad's given me some money for a couple of drinks,' Mick said. 'What do you say, Harry? Come on, it'll do you good. If you start feeling at all uneasy, we'll ask Mrs Pike if we can bring the beers back here.'

Harry gave the offer some thought.

'Go on, Dad,' Ruth urged. 'The broth won't be ready for an hour.'

At last he smiled widely. 'Oh, you two,' he chided. 'You're in cahoots, the pair of you. Trying to get me out of this room.'

'Too right,' Ruth said.

She looked at Mick and nodded towards her dad. Mick read the gesture and walked across the room towards Harry, holding his arm out for the older man to grab hold of so that he could ease the pressure on his leg when he stood. He hooked his arm through Mick's and the two of them walked slowly from the room.

Ruth sat by the fire, stirring the broth. By her side on a rug, Maude was crawling.

'You look as happy as I feel, love,' she said. 'And one day, little Maude, I'll tell you all about your mam.'

Once Mick and Harry were out of earshot of Ruth, Mick leaned in conspiratorially. 'I've a feeling I'm going to enjoy this particular pint more than I've done in a while,' he said.

'Why's that, lad?'

'Because I've got an important question to ask you.'

A mischievous smile played around Harry's lips. 'A question that's not for our Ruth's ears, I gather?'

'You might be right,' Mick laughed.

'Well now,' Harry said. 'There's only one question a father gets asked in private when a young lad is in love with his daughter. I've been wondering when you'd come out with it. If you don't mind me saying, you've taken your time in pushing yourself forward.'

Mick smiled. Now that Dicky Brown's loan was about to be paid off and Connie was no longer in their lives, the time was right to think about the future.

'Well, now that you've got me on my own and it's clear what you're going to say, I'll save you the embarrassment. You don't have to ask, lad. My answer's yes.'

Mick's eyes sparkled with tears and a lump caught in

his throat. 'Ah, Harry, let me get the question out before you start answering,' he teased. 'I've been working myself up into a sweat all afternoon practising what I was going to say.'

'No need, Mick. If you want our Ruth's hand in marriage, I'll not stand in your way. You've got my blessing.'

Harry pushed the pub door open. A fug of cigarette smoke and stale beer wafted out. He held the door open and ushered Mick inside. As Mick walked past, he slapped him on the back.

'She's lucky to have you, lad. Welcome to the family. Now where's that pint you promised?'

Chapter Forty

The bells rang out loudly as Ruth walked down the church path on a warm summer day. She felt nervous, her stomach churning. At the door, the vicar was waiting to meet her. It was dark inside the church and it took a moment for Ruth's eyes to adjust. The organist was playing as she made her way inside. She didn't know where to go. She felt an anxious flutter as she looked around. Mick had promised he'd be waiting for her.

St John's Methodist Church in Ashbrooke Road was full of people Ruth didn't know. She searched for Mick and felt a rush of relief when she spotted his dark hair at the back of the church. She made her way over to him and slid on to the end of the pew.

'You look lovely,' he said.

Her hand flew to Bea's blue scarf, decorated with their grandma's brooch. Gloria had helped her do her hair that morning. Well, it wasn't every day that Ruth was invited to a wedding. And here she was with Mick, the two of them side by side. The invitation had read *Miss Ruth Hardy & Mr Mick Carson*, the first time their names had been joined.

The music from the organ stopped abruptly. Silence. And then it started up again with notes deep and true, filling the church all the way to the rafters. The congregation stood, and the groom waiting at the front gave a nervous cough. Ruth slipped her hand into Mick's. She was dying to turn around. How she longed to see her friend in her wedding gown. But she'd have to wait until the bride walked down the aisle.

She heard a noise behind her as Sarah and Mr Hewson stepped out from the back of the church. The music played on, filling Ruth's heart so full that she thought it might burst. How happy she was to be there, to be invited to Sarah's special day. She caught sight of Henry in a pew next to a bonny girl in a lemon hat, but gave him no more thought. She dared herself to look sideways, and found her gaze met by Sarah's wide smile. Sarah held a bouquet of pink roses tied with white ribbons. Her head was covered with a white beaded shawl that fell all the way to the floor. How beautiful she looked! Ruth squeezed Mick's hand. At his daughter's side, Mr Hewson walked tall and proud.

When they reached the front of the church, Alan turned to smile at his bride. The organ music came to a close.

'Please be seated,' the vicar said.

The ceremony was as joyous as Ruth could have hoped. Hymns were sung, prayers offered, and when the vicar pronounced Alan and Sarah husband and wife, the church bells pealed long and loud.

'Must have cost Hewson a fortune to get the bells rung today,' Mick whispered. 'It's not cheap, you know.' Ruth wondered how he knew.

Outside the church, a photographer was waiting to capture pictures of the bride and groom.

'Will she throw her bouquet?' Mick asked. 'You never know, you might catch it. It could be your turn next.'

Ruth turned to him. It had been such a wonderful morning, watching Sarah and Alan pledge their love for each other.

'*Will* it be my turn next?' she teased. 'You've still never proposed. You should know by now I'm not a girl to be taken for granted, Mick Carson.'

Mick shuffled uncomfortably and stared at his feet.

Ruth looked at the beautiful roses in Sarah's hands. 'The bouquet's too big, too expensive to throw,' she decided. 'Besides, those roses are special to Sarah and her dad. She'll be wanting to keep it.'

'Alan's got the same rose in his jacket lapel, look,' Mick said.

'Come on, let's get in position to wave them off. There's a chara to take them,' Ruth said.

They made their way hand in hand to the road, where the charabanc waited. A cheer went up as Alan held the door open.

'After you, Mrs Murphy,' he said.

Ruth clapped her hands and Mick whistled, joining in the fun. As the charabanc made its way from the kerb, everyone waved.

Mick took hold of Ruth's hand. 'Listen, we've got the rest of the day off work. Mam's happy to have Maude for a few more hours. What about heading for a walk in Backhouse Park before we catch the tram back to Ryhope?'

Ruth looked up at the cloudless sky. The air was warm, a perfect day for a walk.

'I'd like that,' she said.

They walked slowly, holding hands, talking about the wedding.

'Did you see how proud Mr Hewson looked? How smart he was?'

'He looked a right bobby-dazzler,' Mick agreed.

When they reached Backhouse Park, Ruth suggested they meander along the footpaths, but Mick had another plan. He steered her to a wooden bench under a willow tree. Ruth gazed out at the sloping lawns of the park.

'It's beautiful here,' she said. 'We've nothing like it in Ryhope, no big open space.'

'There's the beach,' Mick reminded her.

'I think I take our beach for granted sometimes.'

'Ruth . . .'

'Yes?'

'You've said . . .' Mick gave a nervous cough. 'You've said that I often take you for granted.'

'It's true,' she laughed.

He shook his head. 'No,' he said. 'It's because I wanted to wait until the time was right. I couldn't talk to you about sharing my future with a debt to Dicky hanging over my head.'

'But it's paid now, it's done,' Ruth said.

Mick reached inside his jacket. It was too large for him; Ruth had already noticed but hadn't said a word. The sleeves reached to the backs of his hands and the shoulders were too broad.

He caught her appraising him. 'It's Dad's old one, the smartest jacket we had in the house and the only one smart enough to wear today.' He pulled something from his inside pocket.

'Our piece of paper!' Ruth cried when she saw what it was. 'But I thought it was stolen from the loft?'

'I took it, Ruth. I couldn't bear to think that someone might destroy it or steal it. I took it home and followed Grandad's advice to dry it slowly.'

'But why have you brought it today?'

He handed her the flimsy sheet. It was delicate and lacy, a fragile wisp that she feared might tear. The tiny rose petals seemed to bind it together.

'It's beautiful,' she whispered.

'Turn it over,' Mick said.

She looked at him, confused, but did as he asked. There was a handwritten message.

Darling Ruth, will you marry me?

Ruth couldn't speak. She daren't. She feared that if she said just one word, she'd burst into tears. She ran her fingers across the rose petals, tracing the outline of Mick's words.

'Well?' he said, desperate for an answer. 'I've asked your dad, did it all properly.'

Ruth threw her arms around him.

'Oh, I will,' she said. 'I will.'

The rose petal paper fluttered in her hand. She held it tight to stop it blowing away on the breeze. It was far too precious to lose.

On Saturday night, Ruth and Mick celebrated their engagement at the Guide Post Inn. Button lay on the floor under Mick's stool. Harry sat at the bar, where he helped Mrs Pike. Maude was fast asleep, safe and sound in the back room. Edie was there with Ted Lumley by her side, and Jane had come too, sitting next to Ted's younger, nervous-looking brother Pete.

The Saturday-night singer was a man singing music-hall songs that everyone knew. The mood was raucous and fun, the air thick with smoke and beer. Ruth and Mick sang along, Gloria and Bob were up dancing, and even Harry joined in loudly from the bar. And then the mood changed, and the singer launched into a soft, mournful tune. Couples snuggled close. Strong men bit their lips and said they weren't crying, no, they just had grit in their eye.

Ruth knew the song only too well. It had been one of her mam's favourites, a song she had sung to Ruth and Bea when they were children. It was the song Harry had serenaded her with on their wedding day. Ruth glanced at her dad and saw him talking to Mrs Pike. All at once, Mrs Pike bustled from behind the bar and headed towards the piano, her fur-trimmed ankle boots scuffing the floor. The singer happily gave up his seat when she explained what she wanted to do, and a cheer went up as she began playing. Then silence fell as the notes from the piano reached out to each corner of the room.

Mrs Pike played the introduction to the song that had just been sung. But this time the melody came from the heart. Ruth felt a lump in her throat as she saw her dad limp towards the piano and with no small amount of effort step up on to the makeshift stage. And then he began to sing.

The following week, Ruth, Edie and Jane were sitting on the sands at Hendon eating cold potatoes and bread for their dinner.

'What'll we do without you when you get married and leave the mill?' Edie asked.

'It won't be for a while yet,' Ruth reassured her friend. 'Mick and I have got to save for a wedding.' She looked shyly at Edie. 'Speaking of which, I'm hoping you might like to be my maid of honour.' She turned to Jane. 'And would you be my bridesmaid?'

The two girls threw their arms around Ruth, almost knocking her over. They were laughing, tumbling on the sand like children, and it took a while for them to compose themselves again. When they did, it was Jane who spoke first.

'Will Mick move into the Guide Post Inn with you?'

It was something that Ruth had talked over with Mick. He was keen to move in once they were wed, but Ruth kept her dad's words at the back of her mind. Bea had died in that room, and it was where her mam had passed too.

'Perhaps it's time to move on somewhere else, with Dad,' she said.

'And who'll be our supervisor once you've gone?' Edie wondered.

'What about one of you two?' Ruth said. 'You both know the rag room like the back of your hand. It's extra money if you do it.'

Jane shook her head. 'I don't think I could.'

Ruth looked at Edie. 'What about you?'

Edie shrugged. 'I'll think about it,' she said. 'I promise.'

As they talked, Ruth noticed Claire and Margaret walking on to the beach. With them was Florence, the new girl who'd started in the rag room that morning. She looked like a startled rabbit. Ruth understood how terrified girls were when they started at the mill, and she'd gone out of her way to make Florence feel at ease. It made her happy to see the younger girls taking her under their wing. She watched as the three of them sat down, spread out their skirts and delved into their pockets to bring out sandwiches and pies their mams had made.

'I don't like pie much,' Claire said. 'Anyone want to swap for a bite of potato?'

Snippets of their conversation carried across the beach. They talked about boys they fancied at the mill. Claire was telling the others about a lad called Tommy she'd met. He was the younger brother of Meg, the rag and bone girl who called at the mill. Ruth remembered seeing Claire and Tommy chatting one day when she'd done a bit of business with Meg.

She laid an arm around Edie's shoulders and another around Jane's. 'They're just like we were five years ago,' she said, nodding towards the three girls. 'Remember when we were young, with no idea of the world? Five years on and here I am about to be wed, Edie's courting Ted Lumley, and Jane . . . well, you'll find someone too, you'll see.'

Jane picked at the shell of her hard-boiled egg.

'I wonder where we'll be five years from now?' Edie said.

Ruth hugged her friends tight. 'Ah, now that's another story.'

The Paper Mill Girl

Bonus Material

Researching *The Paper Mill Girl*

One of my favourite things about writing a novel is the three or four weeks I set aside right at the start. Before I start planning or writing, before creating characters, there is a lot of research to do.

The research for *The Paper Mill Girl* has been a special and different kind of joy because it meant I spoke to people whose lives still revolved around paper mills and paper production. As the saying goes, every day was a school day! I learned an enormous amount about the papermaking process, lots of technical details that I didn't include in the book. If I had, you'd have been bored stiff, I assure you! What was important to include was the story of women working at the paper mills, and I hope I've done this justice in the characters of Ruth, Edie, Jane, Margaret, Claire and all the other girls.

Although my home city of Sunderland once had many paper mills, none of them exist any longer. So while I could read about the history of mills that had once been local to where I lived, and could see pictures of mill workers in archives, libraries and museums, I wondered if there was a paper mill I could visit. Better still, was there a mill still running that had its own archive and might welcome me in to view it and learn more?

As luck would have it, such a mill does exist. It's the Frogmore Mill in Apsley, just a short train ride from London. Frogmore is the world's oldest mechanised paper mill and has a papermaking machine from a hundred years ago that is still making paper. It's a joy to watch it perform. I spent two happy days there, talking to staff and to the mill's very helpful archivist. I went on a guided tour, saw machines working, and tried to imagine how my heroine Ruth would have felt in such a place. I even made my own sheet of paper by hand, and it is this that inspired Mick's proposal to Ruth in the book. My own piece of hand-made paper remains special to me.

My friend Jo Blakeley is an illustrator. She created the map of Ryhope that is included in my novels. Jo very kindly transferred the cover of *The Paper Mill Girl* book on to my hand-made sheet of paper, and I will cherish this for ever.

While at Frogmore Mill I also took in the sights, sounds and smells of the mill, and I hope I have done it justice in bringing it back to life in the pages of this book as the fictional Grange Paper Works. If you're in the area, do visit Frogmore; their website is https://www.frogmorepapermill.org.uk.

If you're interested in finding out more about the history of paper mills, I highly recommend the following, which I used in my research for writing this book.

Grangetown History, Vols. 1–3 (Dr Robert Barry Shepherd)

The Lost Mills: A History of Papermaking in County Durham (Jean Stirk)

'The Role of Women in Papermaking: An Introduction' (Jean Stirk, *The Quarterly* 24, November 1977)

'Memories of Barrow Paper Mills. Salthouse 1928–1936. A conversation with my mother-in-law' (Sylvia Bainbridge, *The Quarterly* 112, October 2019)

Three Hundred Years in Paper (G. T. Mandl)

The Manufacture of Paper (R. W. Sindall)

Papermaking in the British Isles (Alfred H. Shorter)

Also, the British Association of Paper Historians has a very useful and helpful website: http://www.baph.org.uk/

All About Ryhope

Ryhope is a village on the northeastern coast, south of the city of Sunderland in Tyne and Wear. The first mention of Ryhope was in 930AD when the Saxon King Athelstan gave the parish of South Wearmouth to the See of Durham. King Athelstan's name lives on in Ryhope with a street named after him – Athelstan Rigg.

The name Ryhope is an Old English name which means 'rugged valley'. Originally Ryhope is recorded as being called *Rive hope* and has also been recorded as *Refhoppa*, *Reshop* and *Riopp*.

Ryhope developed as a farming community and was popular as a sea bathing resort. However, in 1856 sinking operations reached coal seams deep beneath the magnesian limestone and Ryhope grew as a coal mining village. Ryhope had two separate railways with their own train stations, putting Ryhope within easy commuting distance of Sunderland. By 1905 electric trams also reached Ryhope from Sunderland. The coal mine closed in 1966, marking the end of an era for Ryhope.

For more on Ryhope's past, present and future, Sunderland City Council have a very interesting planning document showing historic pictures. You can find it at http://bit.ly/RyhopeHistory

And if you'd like to know more about the village of Ryhope, here are some good websites you might like to explore for historic maps, guided walks and a visit to the ever-popular Pumping Station at Ryhope Engines Museum.

Glenda Young

A guided walk around Ryhope – From agriculture to coal
http://bit.ly/RyhopeWalks

Historic map of Ryhope
http://bit.ly/RyhopeMap

Ryhope Engines Museum
http://www.ryhopeengines.org.uk/

Historic Pictures of Ryhope
http://east-durham.co.uk/wp/ryhope/

Keep reading for an early preview of
Glenda's next compelling saga,

The
$\mathcal{M}$iner's
$\mathcal{L}$ass

Coming soon from Headline.

Chapter One

July 1919

Ruby ran her finger down the Jobs Vacant column in the *Sunderland Echo*. 'What about this one, Mam? It says "Girl wanted for housework. Must have good character."'

'Where's it at?' Mary replied.

'One of the big houses in the village,' Ruby said excitedly. Her voice sank as she read on. 'But I'm not old enough. It says girls who apply should be aged at least eighteen.'

'You will be in three months,' Mary said.

'But you haven't got a good character,' Michael piped up.

Ruby ignored her brother's taunt and carried on with her search. Michael returned to the adventure comic he was reading, and it caught Mary's eye.

'Where did you get the money to buy that?' she asked.

Michael pulled the comic up to shield himself from his mam's question.

'Michael?' Mary demanded. 'If I find out you've been wasting money when we barely have enough to buy food, I'll give you what for.'

'I got it off Bobby at work. He gives it to me once he's read it.'

Mary knew she shouldn't deny her bairns pleasure, even if it was just a comic, but the truth was that her family needed every penny they could get.

'Here's a good one, Mam,' Ruby said. '"General serving girl wanted. Cleaning and cooking for small family. Wages eight pounds per week."'

'Eight pounds a week?' Mary cried. 'Why, that's a small fortune!'

Ruby held the paper up and Mary peered at the ad.

'The job's at Ryhope Hall,' she read. 'But there's a problem, as you know only too well. Cooking, Ruby? The amount of times I've tried to teach you to cook and bake, you should be able to do it by now.'

Nothing Ruby cooked came out right, no matter how hard she tried. She might have inherited her mam's fair skin and bright eyes, but she'd missed out on her ability in the kitchen. Even under Mary's expert guidance, when Ruby baked bread it came out of the oven unrisen. Her pastry was too hard and she didn't think her mam would ever forgive her when she boiled a pan of potatoes dry.

'She's bloody useless, our Ruby,' Michael quipped.

'We'll have less of your swearing, thank you very much,' Mary said. She whipped a cloth from the kitchen table and flicked it towards Michael's head.

'Ow!' he yelled.

'What are you shouting for? It never touched you.'

Michael put his hand to his brow and swooned in an overly theatrical fashion. 'I'm dying, Mam. You've killed me!'

'You daft lump. I will flamin' kill you if you don't get

off your backside and go and fetch water for your dad's bath. He'll be home from the pit soon. And bring the bath in from the yard.'

Michael's bottom lip shot out. 'It's not my turn to fetch the water, it's our Ruby's. I did it at dinner time. Ah, Mam, it's my day off today. I shouldn't have to do her work for her on my day off. It's not fair.'

'Our Ruby's busy looking for a job.'

'She shouldn't have got herself sacked from the Albion Inn.'

'It wasn't my fault,' Ruby said defensively.

'You gave the customer the wrong change, Ruby. Whose fault was it?'

'For a little lad, you've got a big mouth.'

Michael puffed out his chest. 'I might be little, but at least I've got a job, working on the pit top. And when I turn fourteen in October, I'll be earning even more underground.'

'Michael, there's no need for that kind of talk yet,' Mary said sternly. She dreaded the day when her son would join her husband hewing coal. It was dangerous, heavy work.

'At least me and Dad are bringing money in,' Michael said. 'We're not skiving like our Ruby.'

'She's never skived in her life, Michael. Don't say that about your sister. None of us Dinsdales could ever be accused of skiving. And she didn't give the customer the wrong change, so don't go blaming her, you hear?'

'It was the barmaid's dilemma,' Ruby said.

'Which barmaid?' Michael asked.

She shook her head. 'It's not a person. It's what they call the old four-shilling coin. A fella in the Albion Inn passed it off as five shillings. It's hard to tell the difference between the two coins, and because I was new in the job, I didn't know. So I gave him change from five shillings instead of four, and Jack Burdon sacked me when he found the coin in the till at the end of the day.'

'He's a hard fella, that Jack,' Mary tutted.

'Hetty, his wife, defended me. Said she'd fallen for the trick herself years ago. But Jack wouldn't budge and I was out on my ear.'

'And now you have to find yourself another job. Get your nose stuck back in those ads, Ruby. Michael? What you waiting for, son? The bath's not going to bring itself in.'

Michael did as he was told while Ruby returned her attention to the paper. Surely there must be a suitable job? As she read the ads, her bobbed brown hair fell over her face and she pushed it back behind her ears.

'"House parlourmaid wanted, second week of July only",' she read.

Mary raised her eyebrows. 'Just one week's work? Keep on looking and we'll come back to that one if you can't find anything else.'

'"Nursemaid wanted immediately to care for two children. Must have experience."'

Mary shook her head. 'No, lass. There are some things we know you've got experience in, like cleaning and washing and sewing. But looking after bairns? No. I can't let you pretend you know how to do that, it'd be wrong. You've never done that sort of work. What else is there?'

© Les Mann

Glenda Young credits her local library in the village of Ryhope, where she grew up, for giving her a love of books. She still lives close by in Sunderland and often gets her ideas for her stories on long bike rides along the coast. A life-long fan of *Coronation Street*, she runs two hugely popular fan websites.

For updates on what Glenda is working on, visit her website **glendayoungbooks.com** and to find out more find her on Facebook/**GlendaYoungAuthor** and Twitter **@flaming_nora**.

Don't miss the other enthralling sagas from Glenda Young!

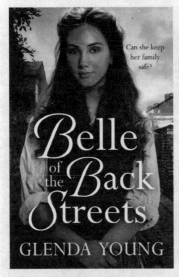

Can she keep her family safe?

Belle of the Back Streets

GLENDA YOUNG

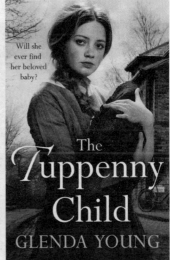

Will she ever find her beloved baby?

The Tuppenny Child

GLENDA YOUNG

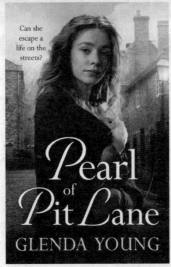

Can she escape a life on the streets?

Pearl of Pit Lane

GLENDA YOUNG

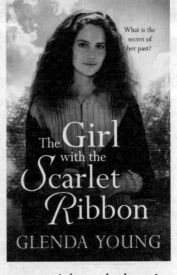

What is the secret of her past?

The Girl with the Scarlet Ribbon

GLENDA YOUNG

'Real sagas with female characters right at the heart'
Jane Garvey, *Woman's Hour*

HEADLINE